THE ODYSSEY
—HOMER—

TO MOM & DAD, WHO NEVER
TOLD ME TO STOP BEING WEIRD.
- TIM

TO MY MOM, WHO LET ME
READ THE WEIRDEST
BOOKS AS A KID.
- BEN

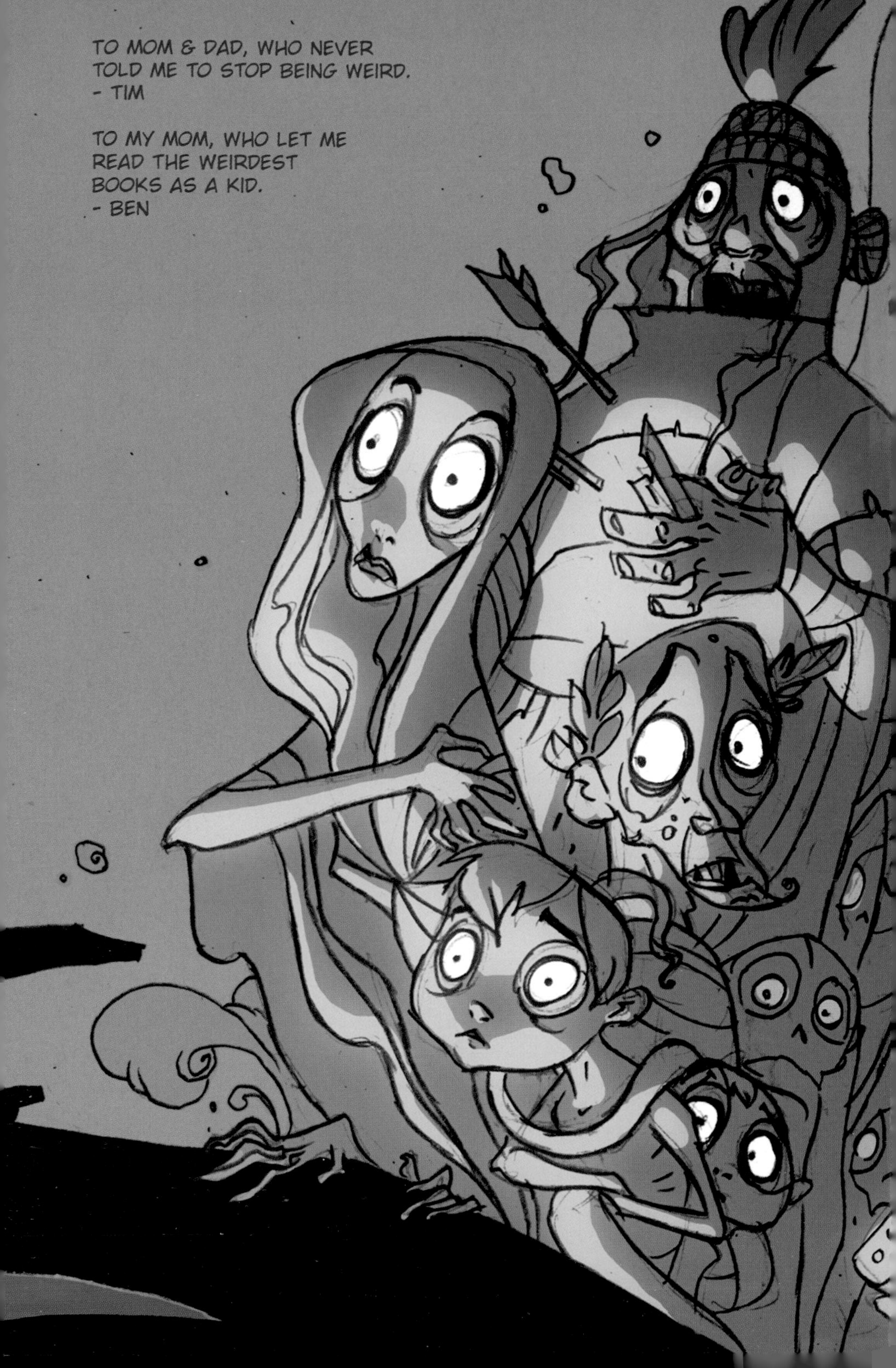

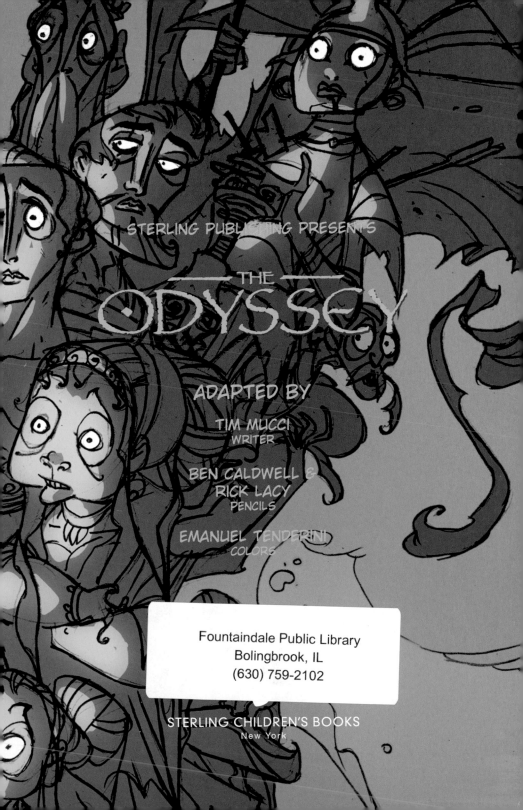

STERLING PUBLISHING PRESENTS

THE ODYSSEY

ADAPTED BY

TIM MUCCI
WRITER

**BEN CALDWELL &
RICK LACY**
PENCILS

EMANUEL TENDERINI
COLORS

STERLING CHILDREN'S BOOKS
New York

STERLING CHILDREN'S BOOKS
New York

An Imprint of Sterling Publishing Co., Inc.
1166 Avenue of the Americas
New York, NY 10036

ISBN 978-1-4549-3815-6

DISTRIBUTED IN CANADA BY STERLING PUBLISHING CO., INC.
C/O CANADIAN MANDA GROUP, 664 ANNETTE STREET
TORONTO, ONTARIO M6S 2C8, CANADA
DISTRIBUTED IN THE UNITED KINGDOM BY GMC DISTRIBUTION SERVICES
CASTLE PLACE, 166 HIGH STREET, LEWES, EAST SUSSEX BN7 1XU, ENGLAND
DISTRIBUTED IN AUSTRALIA BY NEWSOUTH BOOKS, UNIVERSITY OF NEW SOUTH WALES
SYDNEY, NSW 2052, AUSTRALIA

FOR INFORMATION ABOUT CUSTOM EDITIONS, SPECIAL SALES, AND PREMIUM
AND CORPORATE PURCHASES, PLEASE CONTACT STERLING SPECIAL SALES AT 800-805-5489
OR SPECIALSALES@STERLINGPUBLISHING.COM.

MANUFACTURED IN SINGAPORE
LOT #:
2 4 6 8 10 9 7 5 3 1
12/19

STERLINGPUBLISHING.COM

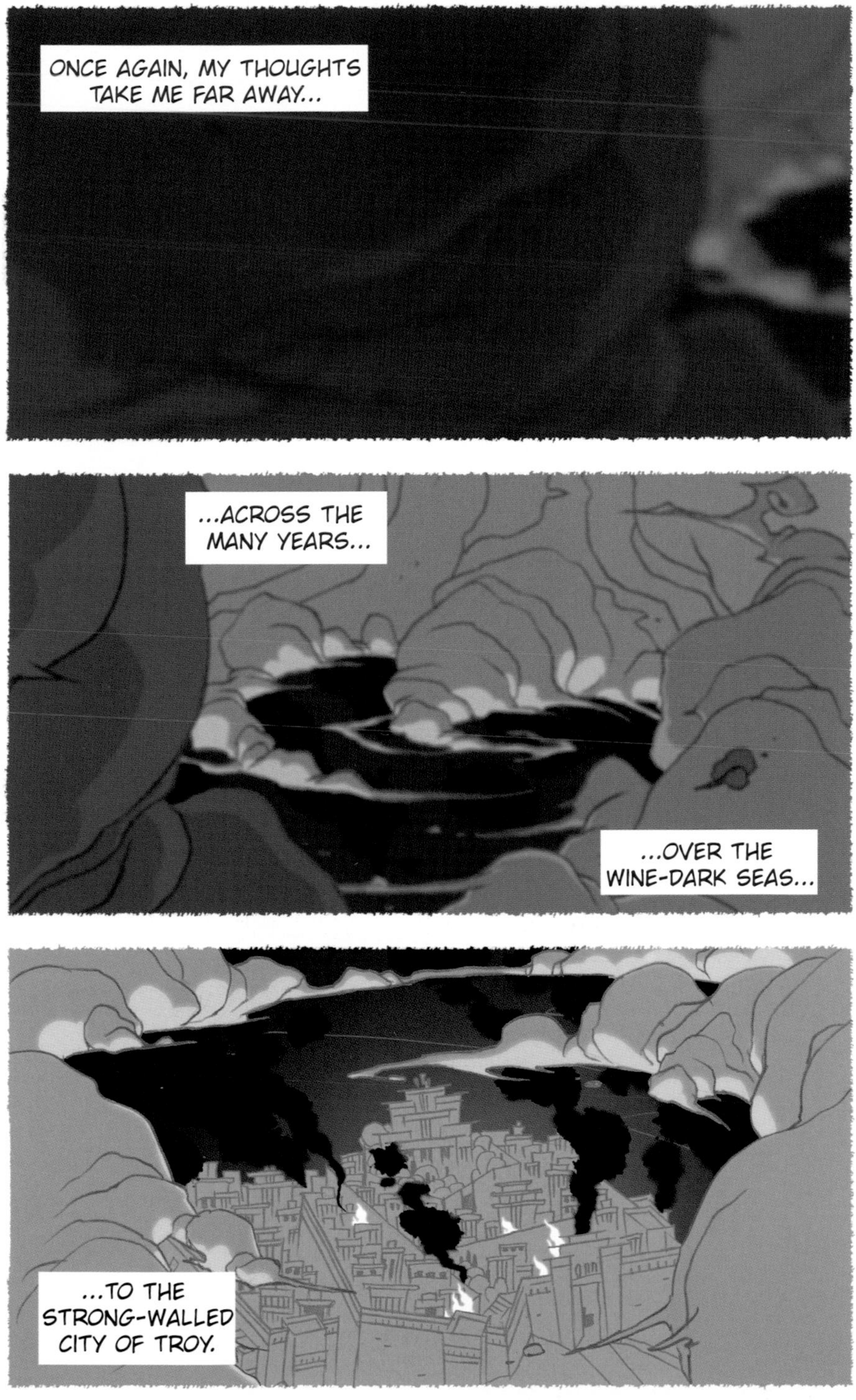
ONCE AGAIN, MY THOUGHTS TAKE ME FAR AWAY...
...ACROSS THE MANY YEARS...
...OVER THE WINE-DARK SEAS...
...TO THE STRONG-WALLED CITY OF TROY.

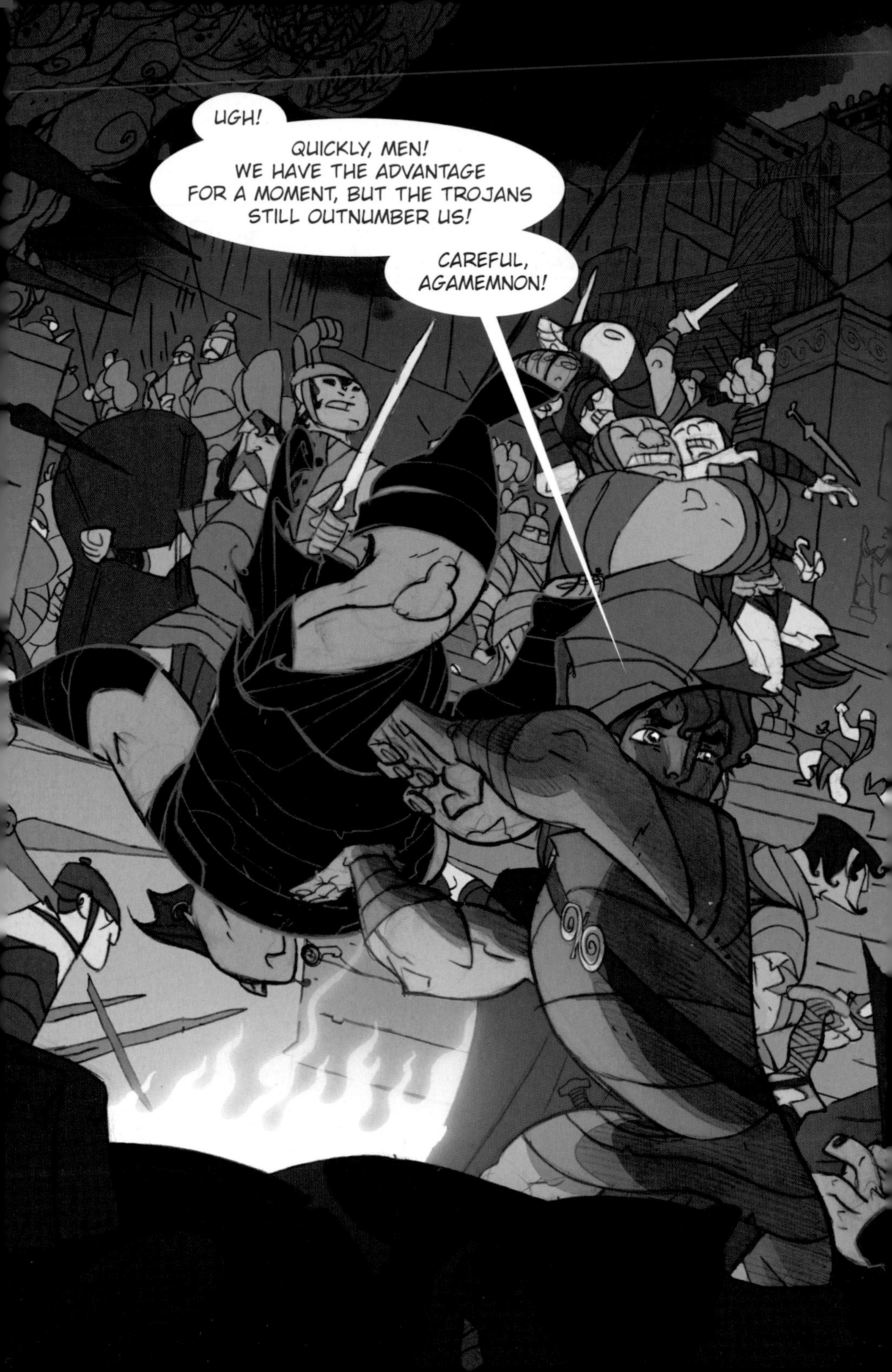
UGH!
QUICKLY, MEN! WE HAVE THE ADVANTAGE FOR A MOMENT, BUT THE TROJANS STILL OUTNUMBER US!
CAREFUL, AGAMEMNON!

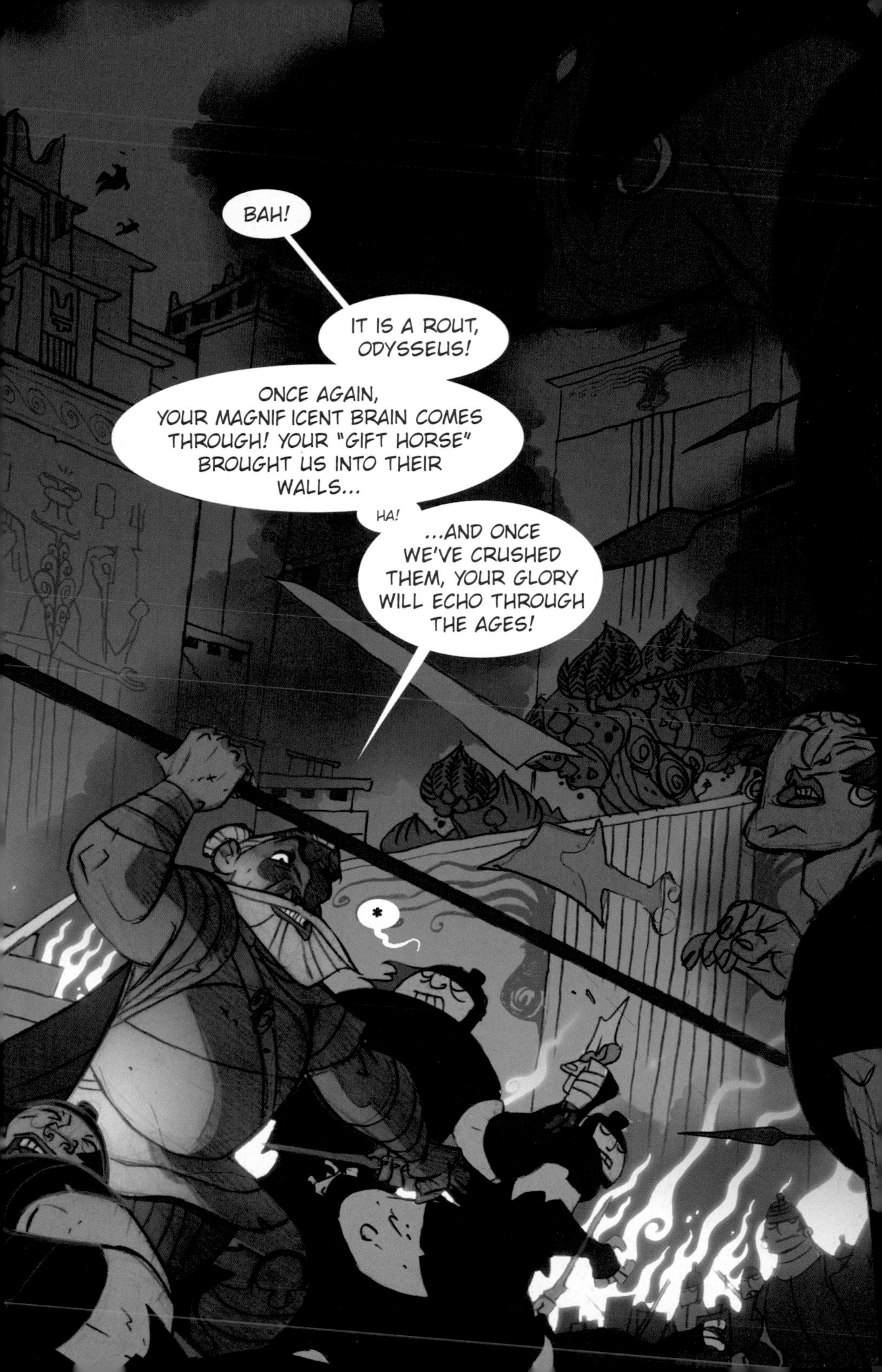
BAH!
IT IS A ROUT, ODYSSEUS!
ONCE AGAIN, YOUR MAGNIFICENT BRAIN COMES THROUGH! YOUR "GIFT HORSE" BROUGHT US INTO THEIR WALLS...
HA!
...AND ONCE WE'VE CRUSHED THEM, YOUR GLORY WILL ECHO THROUGH THE AGES!

I GIVE GLORY TO THE GODS, AGAMEMNON! WHATEVER SKILL I HAVE, THEY GAVE ME...

BAH!

ALWAYS WATCHING MY BACK, EH EURYLO-CHUS?

ALWAYS, MY PRINCE

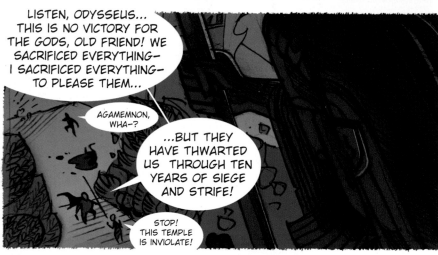

LISTEN, ODYSSEUS... THIS IS NO VICTORY FOR THE GODS, OLD FRIEND! WE SACRIFICED EVERYTHING— I SACRIFICED EVERYTHING— TO PLEASE THEM...

AGAMEMNON, WHA—?

...BUT THEY HAVE THWARTED US THROUGH TEN YEARS OF SIEGE AND STRIFE!

STOP! THIS TEMPLE IS INVIOLATE!

NO, ODYSSEUS...I THANK NO GODS FOR MY VICTORIES...

*

AGAMEMNON! WHERE ARE YOU GOING?

AGAMEMNON?

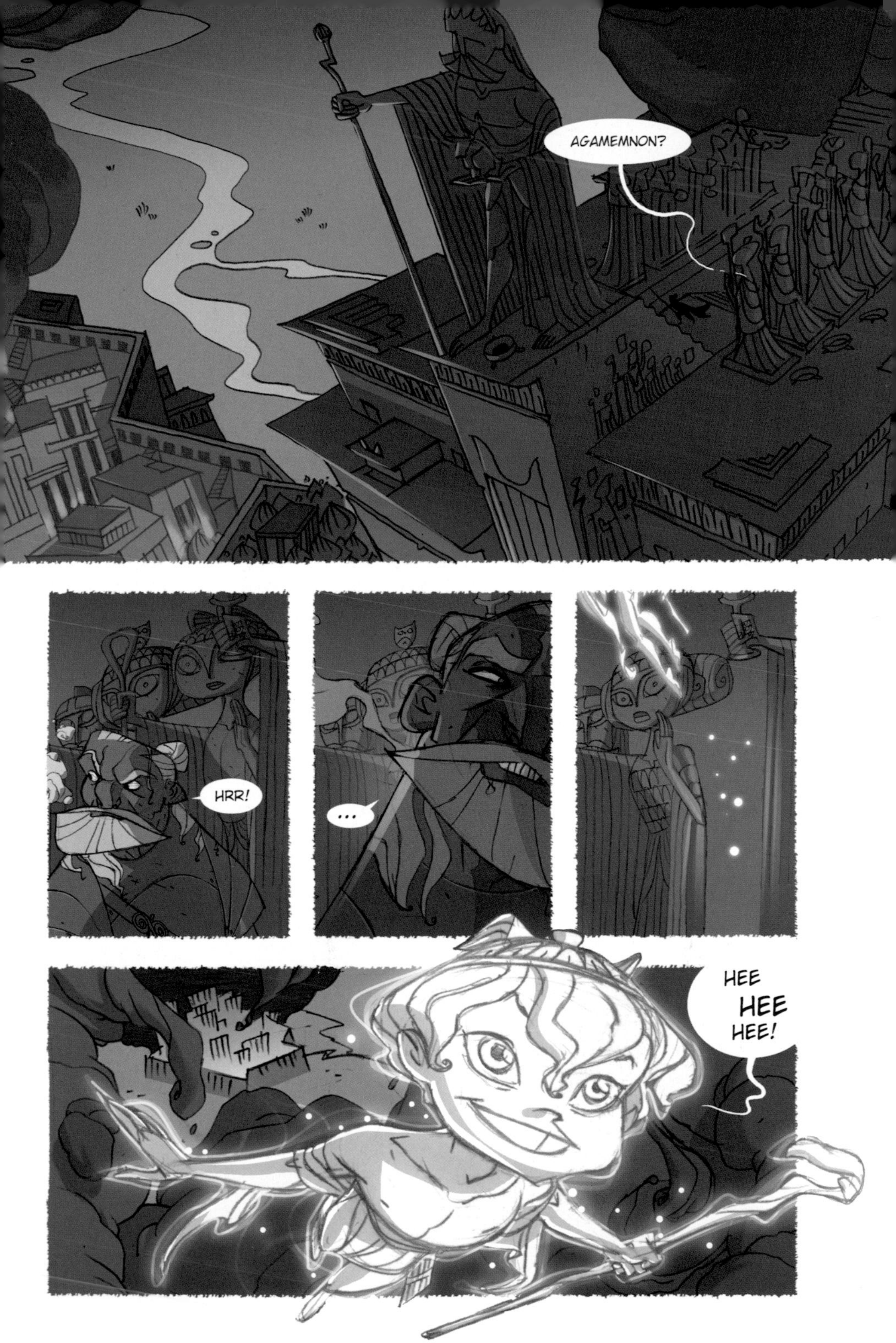
AGAMEMNON?
HRR!
...
HEE HEE HEE!

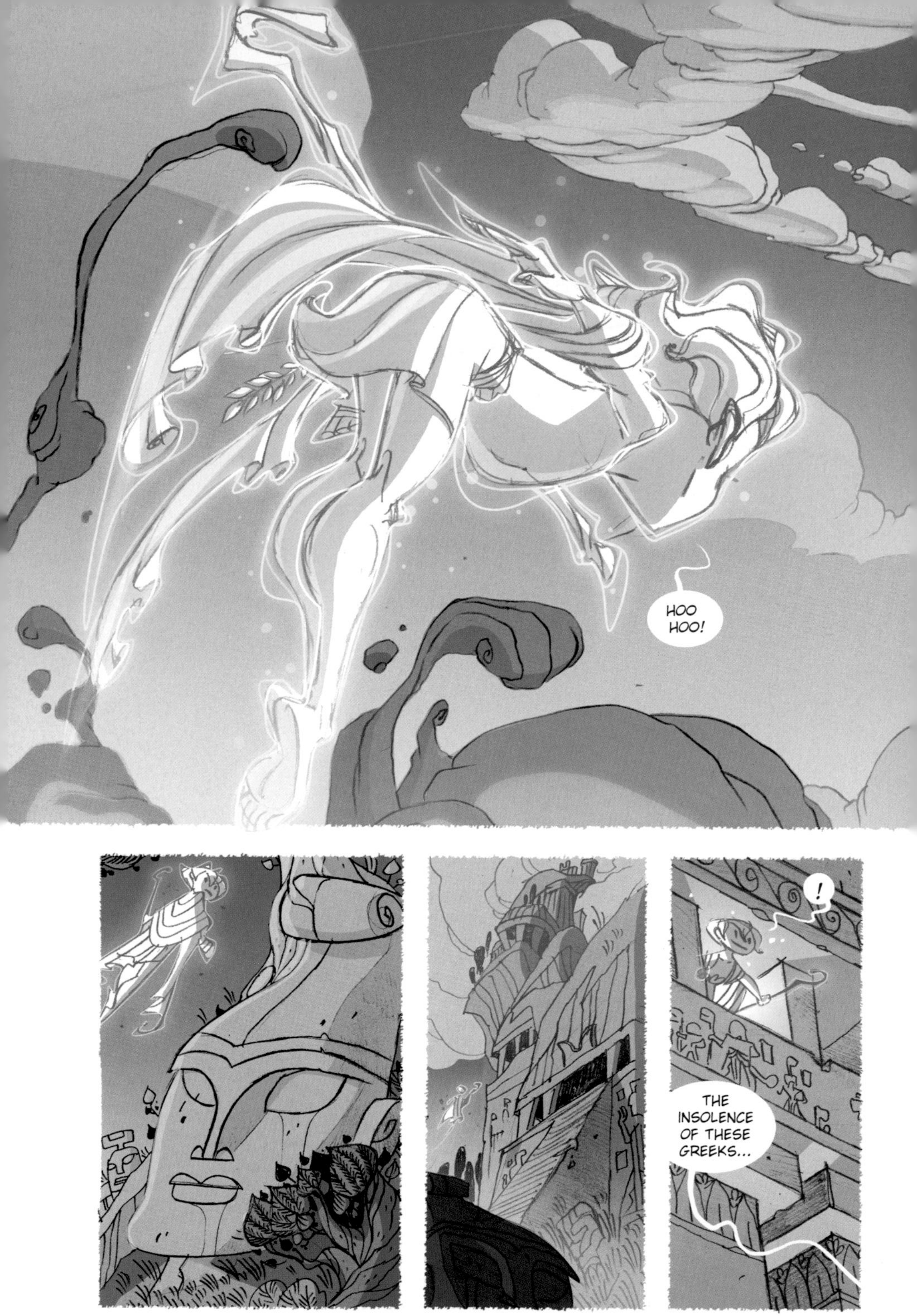
HOO HOO!
!
THE INSOLENCE OF THESE GREEKS...

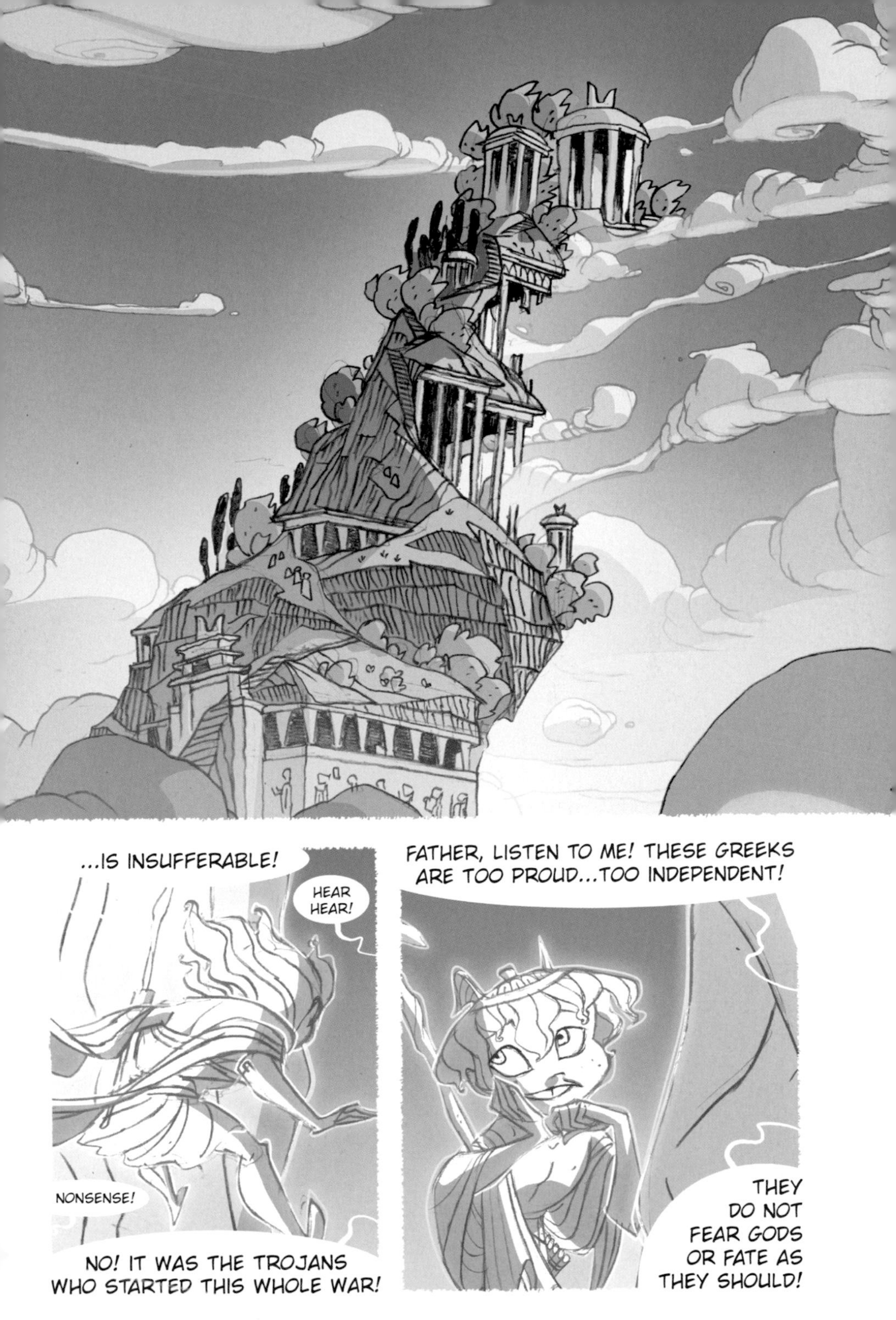

...IS INSUFFERABLE!
HEAR HEAR!
NONSENSE!
NO! IT WAS THE TROJANS WHO STARTED THIS WHOLE WAR!
FATHER, LISTEN TO ME! THESE GREEKS ARE TOO PROUD...TOO INDEPENDENT!
THEY DO NOT FEAR GODS OR FATE AS THEY SHOULD!

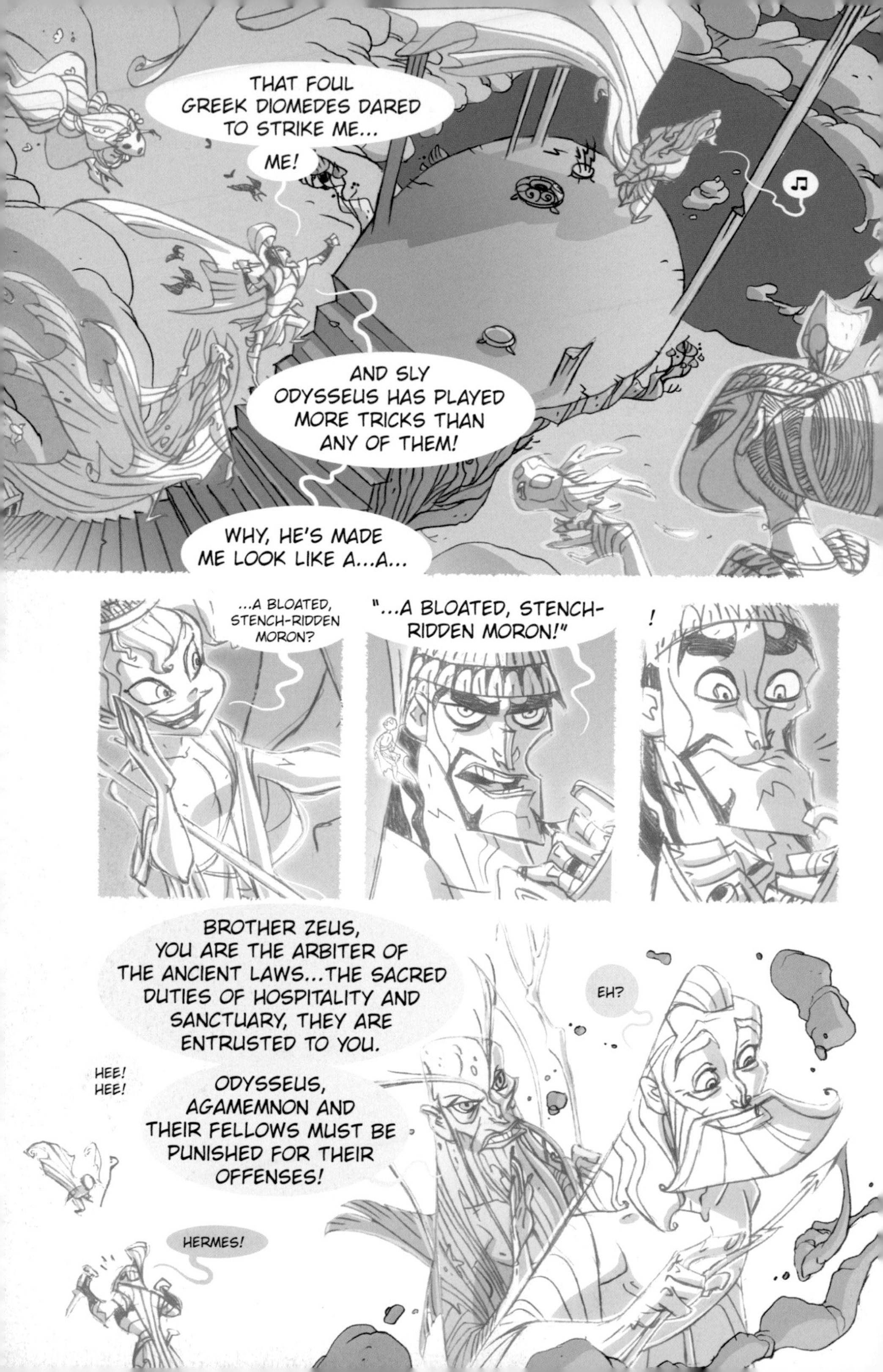
THAT FOUL GREEK DIOMEDES DARED TO STRIKE ME...
ME!
AND SLY ODYSSEUS HAS PLAYED MORE TRICKS THAN ANY OF THEM!
WHY, HE'S MADE ME LOOK LIKE A...A...
...A BLOATED, STENCH-RIDDEN MORON?
"...A BLOATED, STENCH-RIDDEN MORON!"
!
BROTHER ZEUS, YOU ARE THE ARBITER OF THE ANCIENT LAWS...THE SACRED DUTIES OF HOSPITALITY AND SANCTUARY, THEY ARE ENTRUSTED TO YOU.
EH?
HEE! HEE!
ODYSSEUS, AGAMEMNON AND THEIR FELLOWS MUST BE PUNISHED FOR THEIR OFFENSES!
HERMES!

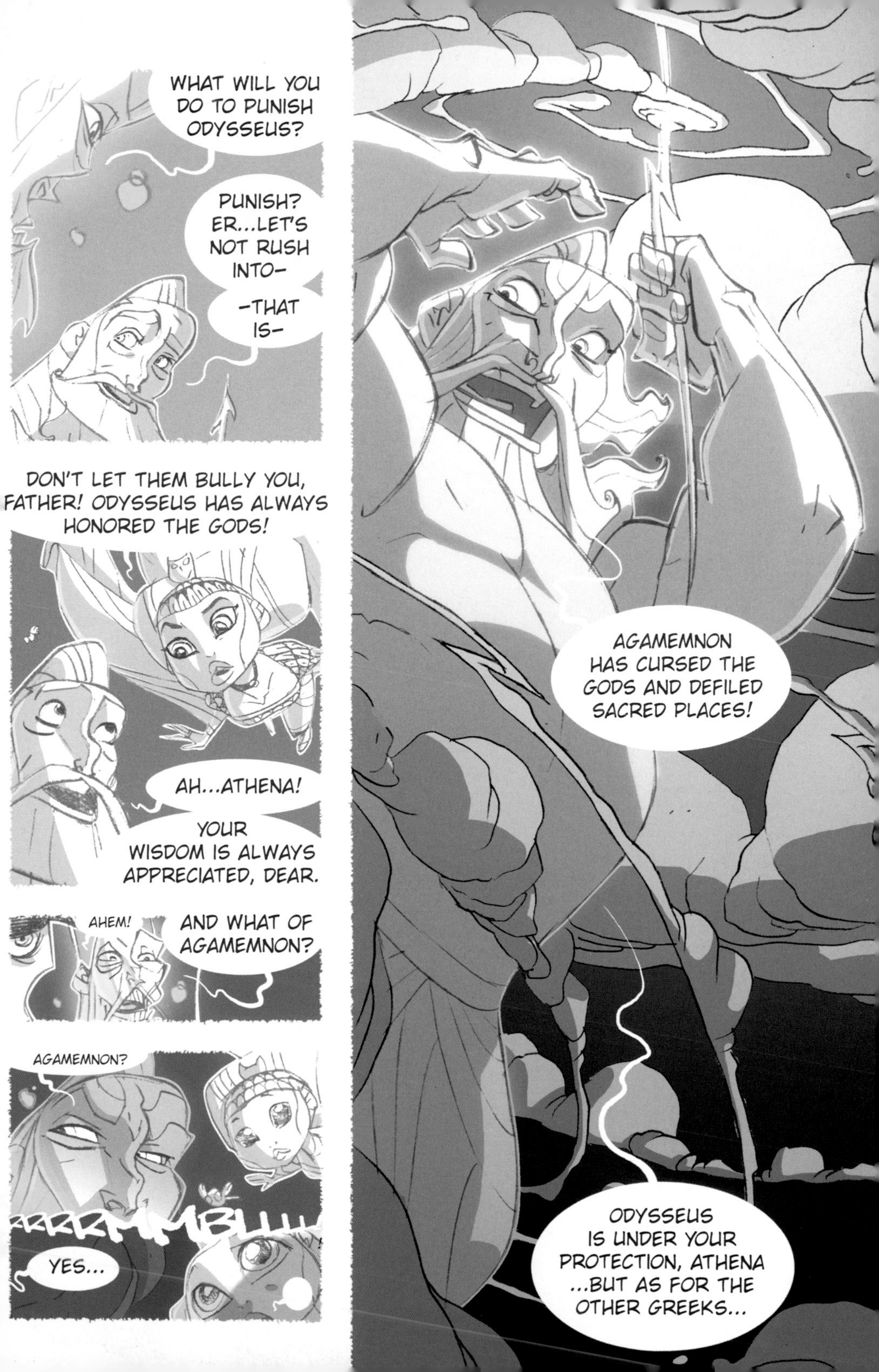
WHAT WILL YOU DO TO PUNISH ODYSSEUS?
PUNISH? ER...LET'S NOT RUSH INTO–
–THAT IS–
DON'T LET THEM BULLY YOU, FATHER! ODYSSEUS HAS ALWAYS HONORED THE GODS!
AH...ATHENA!
YOUR WISDOM IS ALWAYS APPRECIATED, DEAR.
AHEM!
AND WHAT OF AGAMEMNON?
AGAMEMNON?
RRRRMMBLLL
YES...
AGAMEMNON HAS CURSED THE GODS AND DEFILED SACRED PLACES!
ODYSSEUS IS UNDER YOUR PROTECTION, ATHENA ...BUT AS FOR THE OTHER GREEKS...

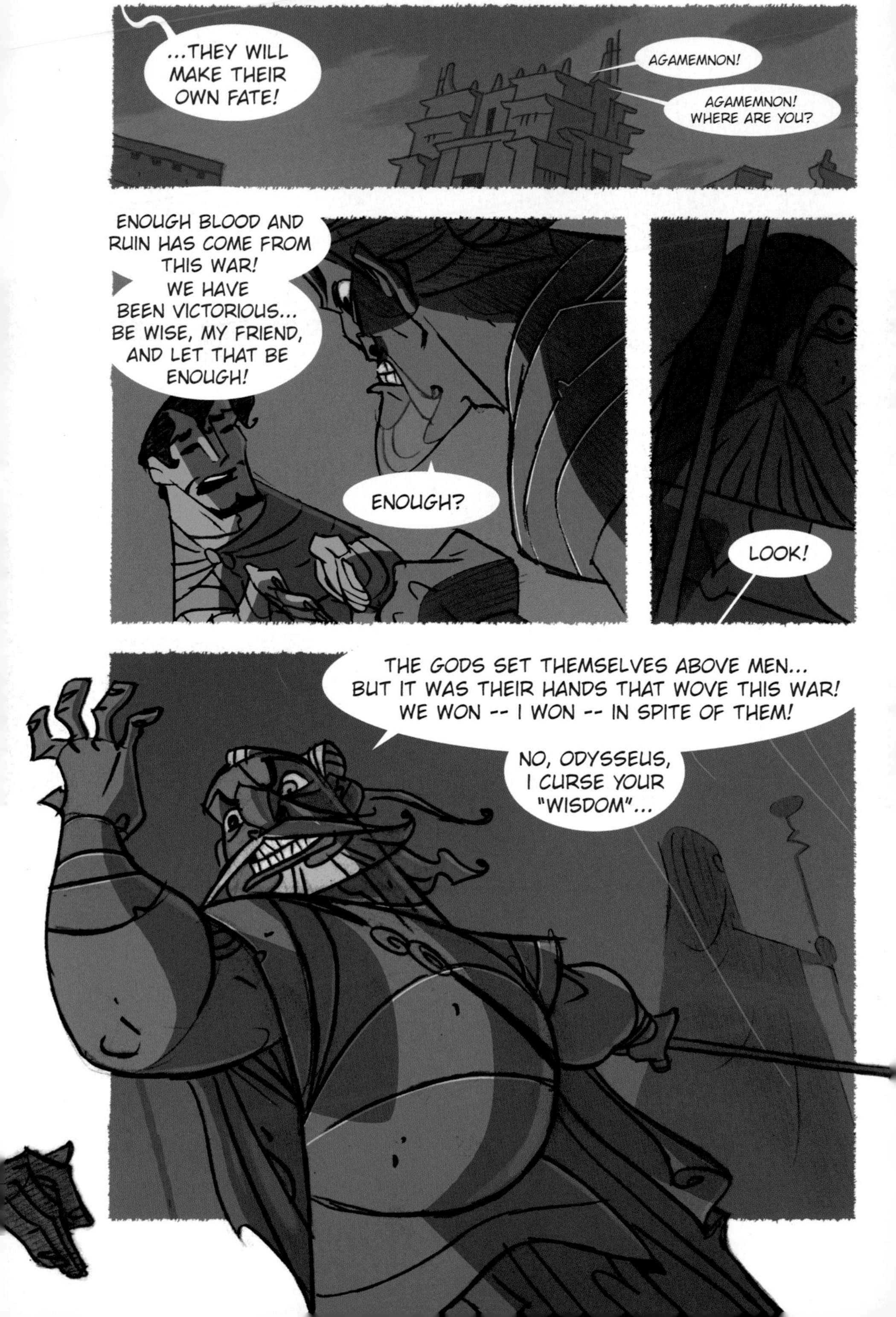

...THEY WILL MAKE THEIR OWN FATE!
AGAMEMNON!
AGAMEMNON! WHERE ARE YOU?
ENOUGH BLOOD AND RUIN HAS COME FROM THIS WAR!
WE HAVE BEEN VICTORIOUS... BE WISE, MY FRIEND, AND LET THAT BE ENOUGH!
ENOUGH?
LOOK!
THE GODS SET THEMSELVES ABOVE MEN... BUT IT WAS THEIR HANDS THAT WOVE THIS WAR! WE WON -- I WON -- IN SPITE OF THEM!
NO, ODYSSEUS, I CURSE YOUR "WISDOM"...

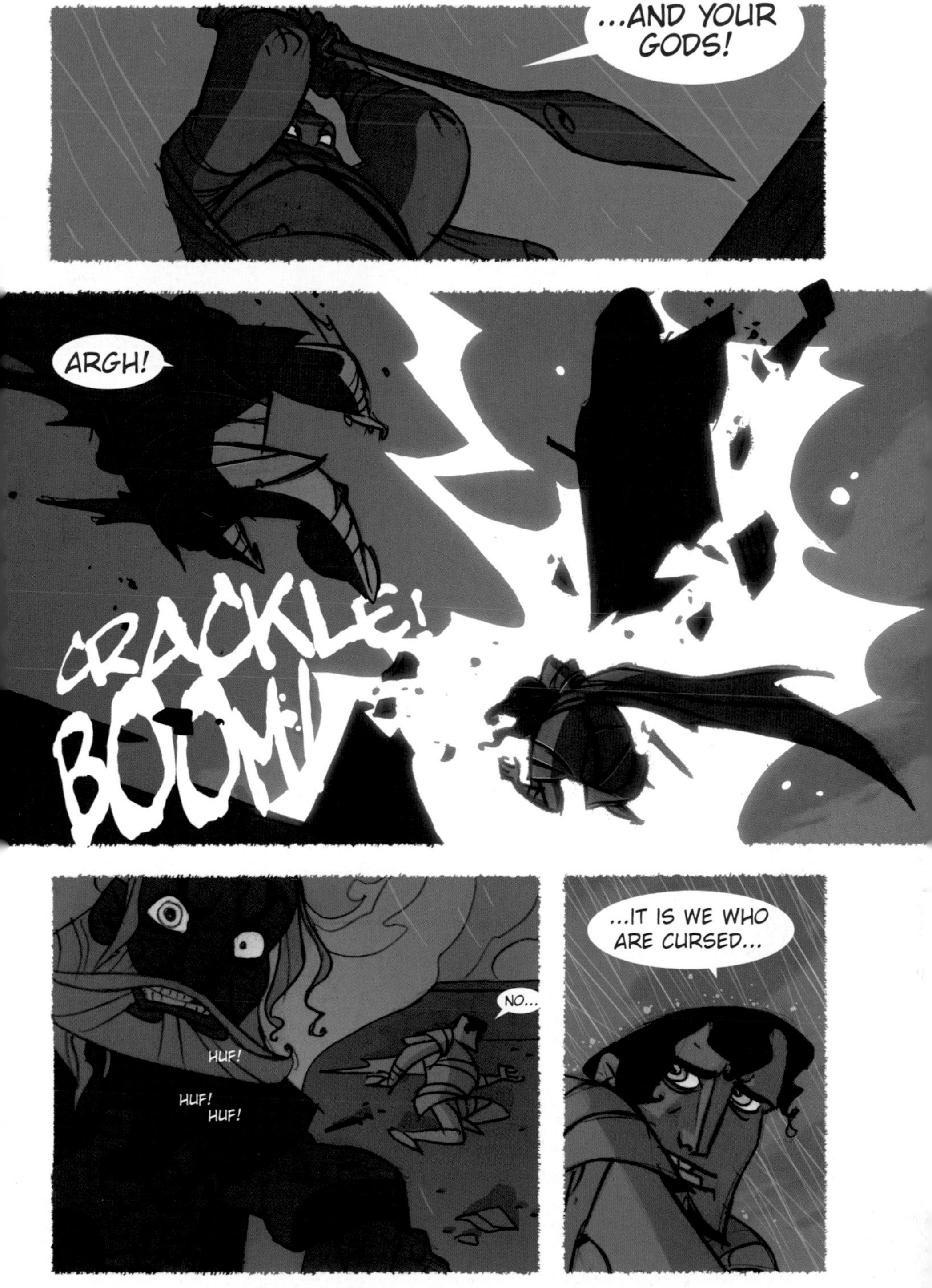
...AND YOUR GODS!
ARGH!
CRACKLE!
BOOM!
NO...
HUF!
HUF!
HUF!
...IT IS WE WHO ARE CURSED...

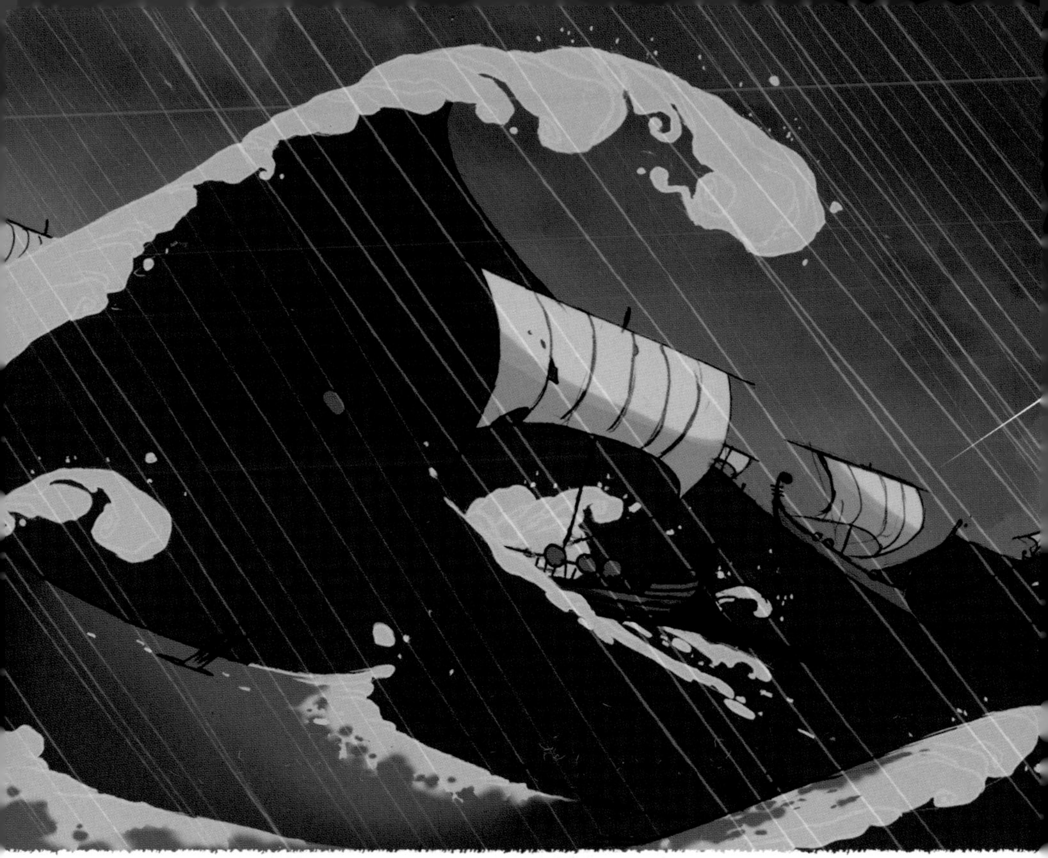

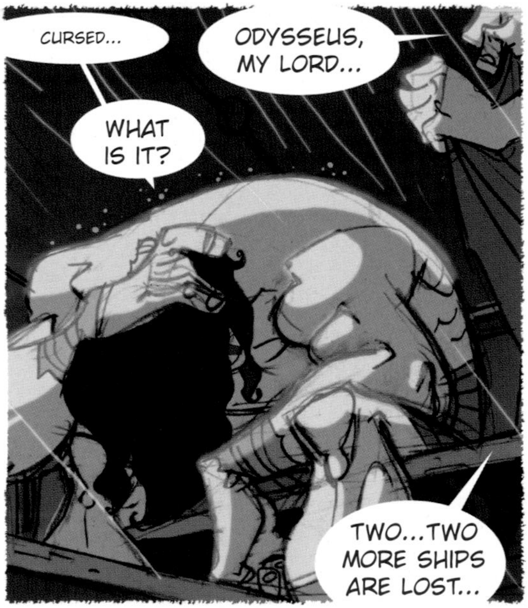
CURSED...
WHAT IS IT?
ODYSSEUS, MY LORD...
TWO...TWO MORE SHIPS ARE LOST...

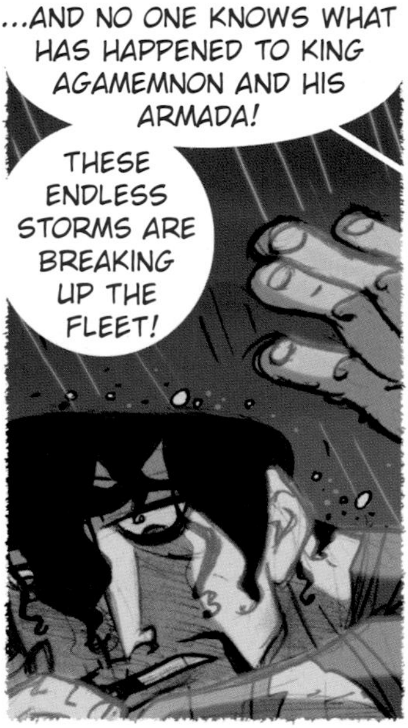
...AND NO ONE KNOWS WHAT HAS HAPPENED TO KING AGAMEMNON AND HIS ARMADA!
THESE ENDLESS STORMS ARE BREAKING UP THE FLEET!

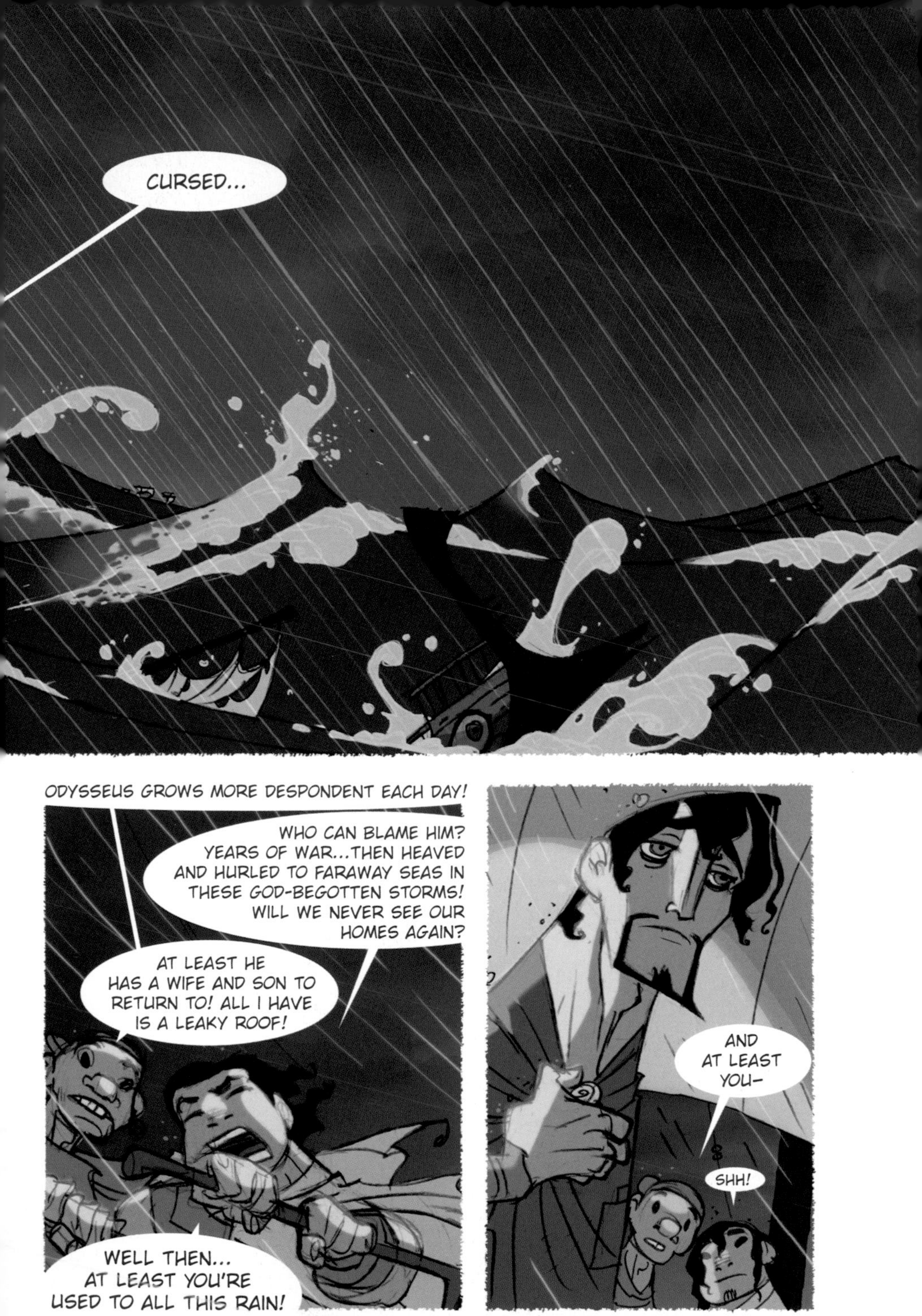
CURSED...
ODYSSEUS GROWS MORE DESPONDENT EACH DAY!
WHO CAN BLAME HIM? YEARS OF WAR...THEN HEAVED AND HURLED TO FARAWAY SEAS IN THESE GOD-BEGOTTEN STORMS! WILL WE NEVER SEE OUR HOMES AGAIN?
AT LEAST HE HAS A WIFE AND SON TO RETURN TO! ALL I HAVE IS A LEAKY ROOF!
WELL THEN... AT LEAST YOU'RE USED TO ALL THIS RAIN!
AND AT LEAST YOU–
SHH!

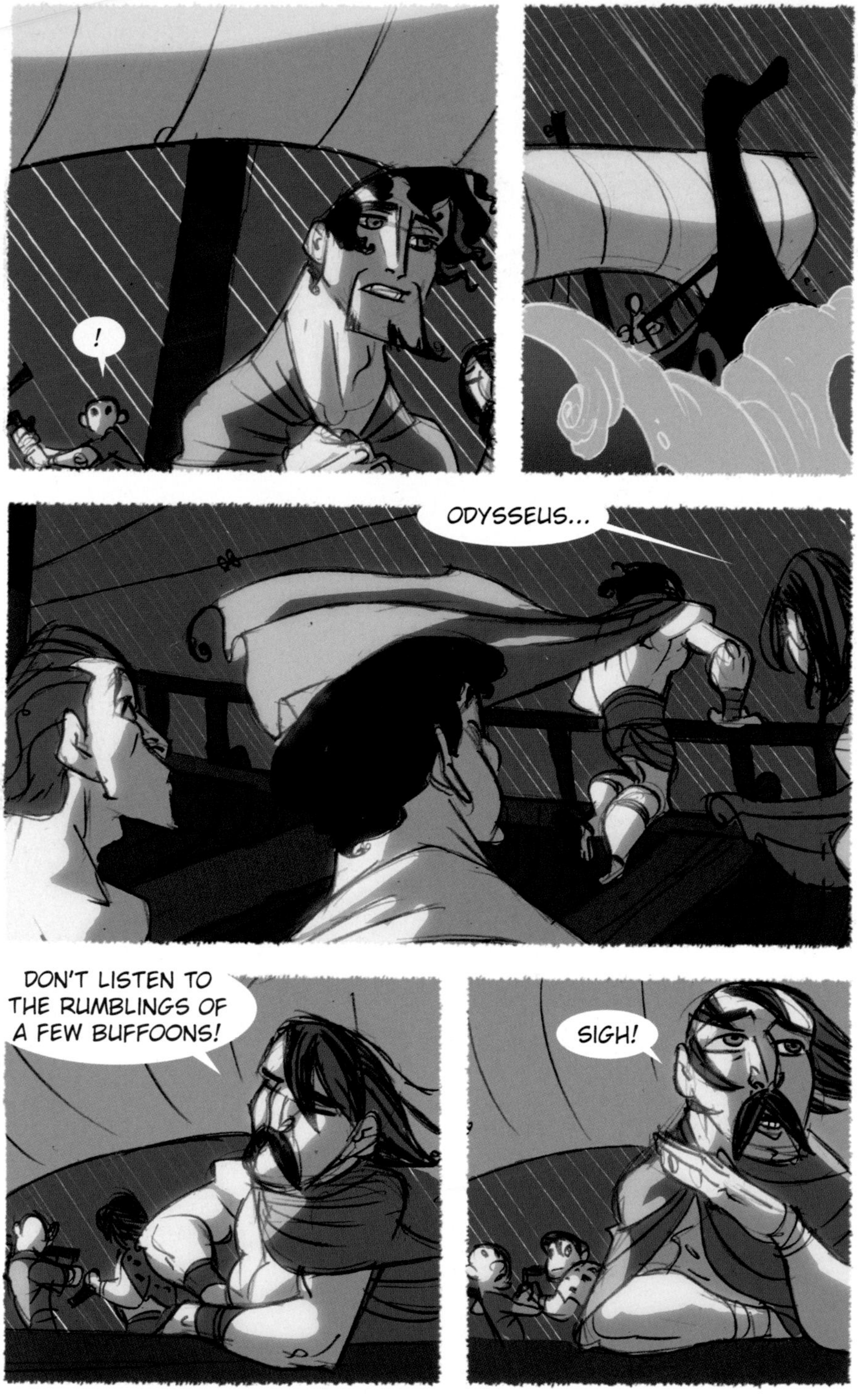
!
ODYSSEUS...
DON'T LISTEN TO
THE RUMBLINGS OF
A FEW BUFFOONS!
SIGH!

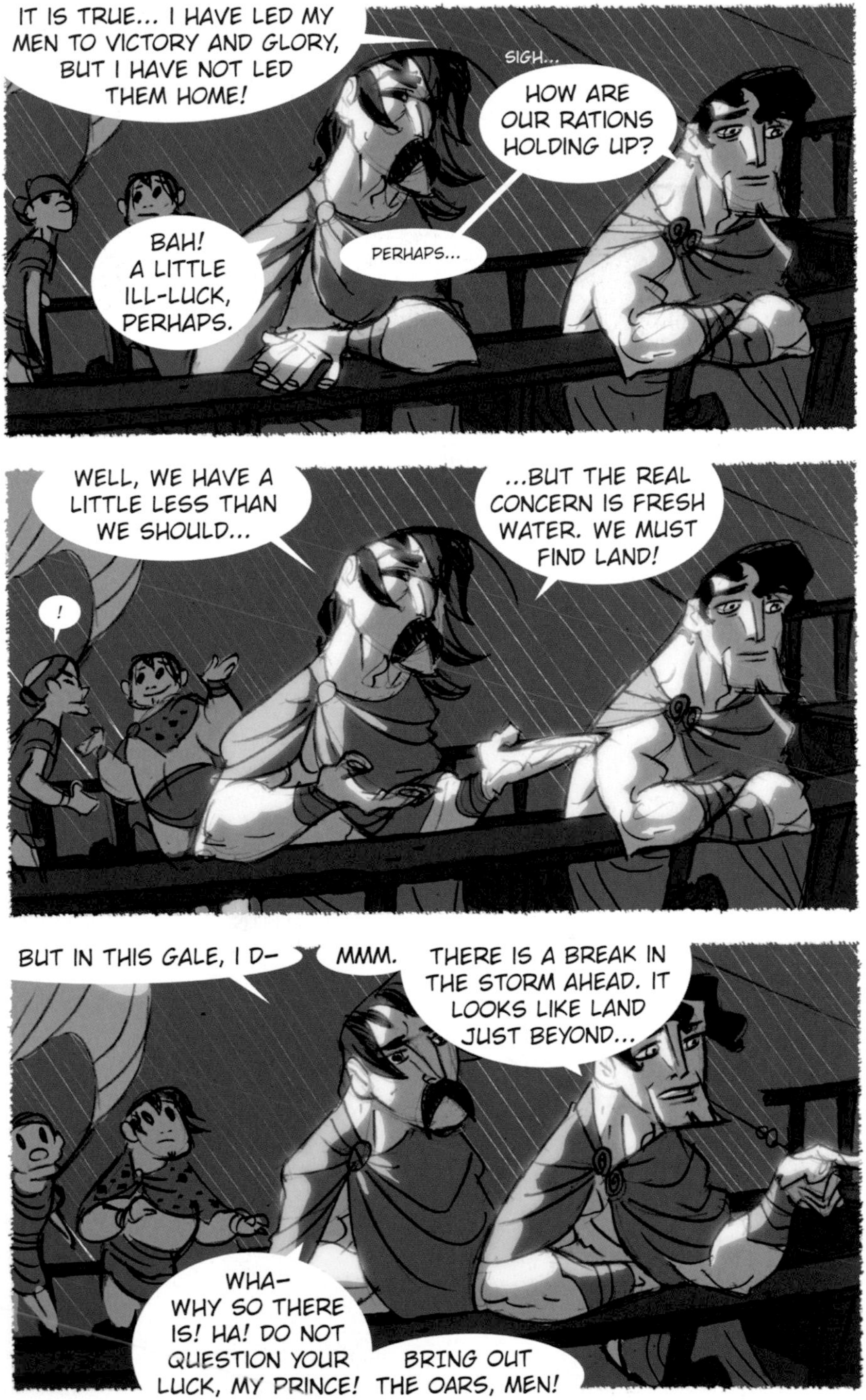
IT IS TRUE... I HAVE LED MY MEN TO VICTORY AND GLORY, BUT I HAVE NOT LED THEM HOME!
SIGH...
HOW ARE OUR RATIONS HOLDING UP?
BAH! A LITTLE ILL-LUCK, PERHAPS.
PERHAPS...
WELL, WE HAVE A LITTLE LESS THAN WE SHOULD...
...BUT THE REAL CONCERN IS FRESH WATER. WE MUST FIND LAND!
!
BUT IN THIS GALE, I D–
MMM.
THERE IS A BREAK IN THE STORM AHEAD. IT LOOKS LIKE LAND JUST BEYOND...
WHA– WHY SO THERE IS! HA! DO NOT QUESTION YOUR LUCK, MY PRINCE!
BRING OUT THE OARS, MEN!

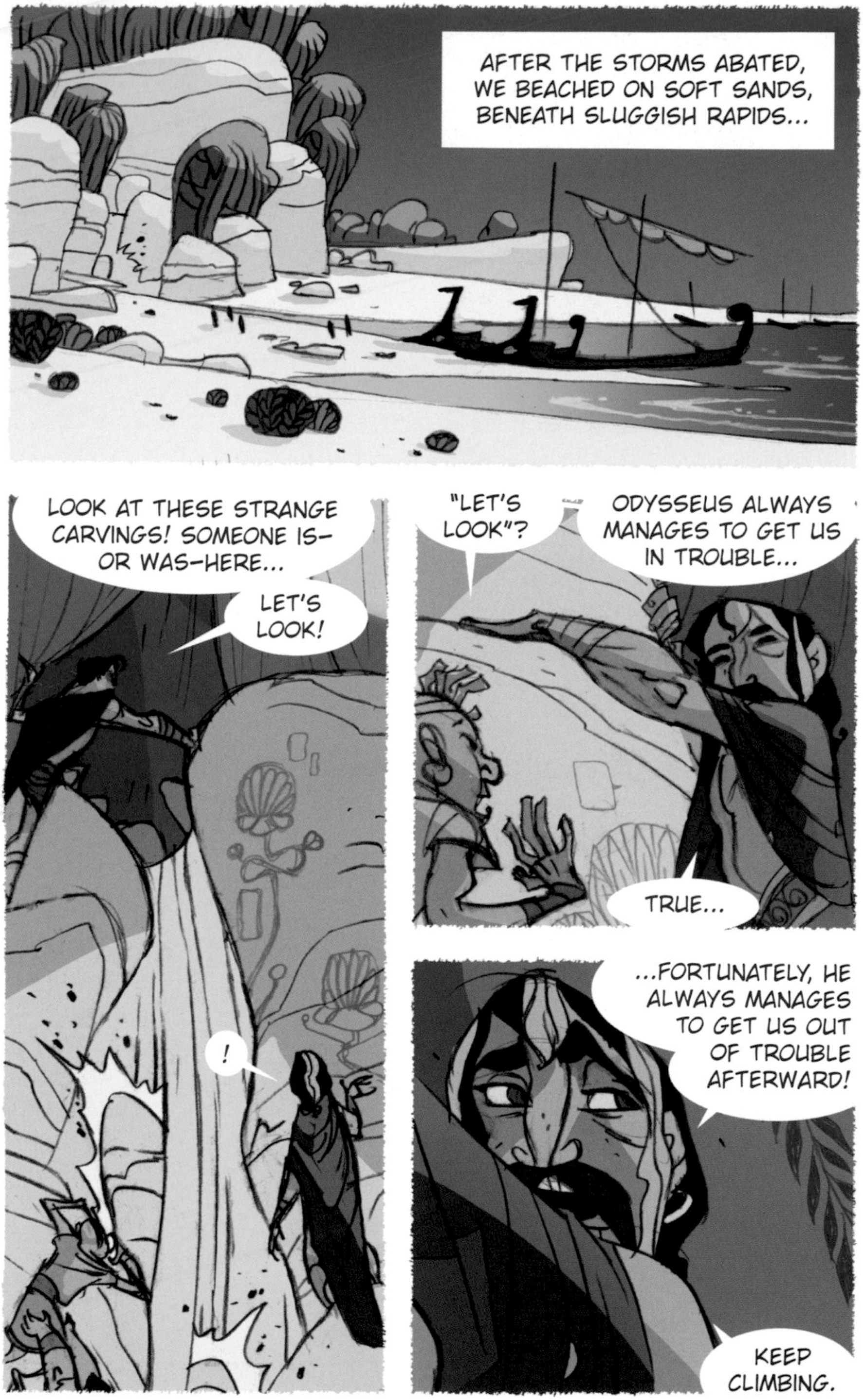
AFTER THE STORMS ABATED, WE BEACHED ON SOFT SANDS, BENEATH SLUGGISH RAPIDS...
LOOK AT THESE STRANGE CARVINGS! SOMEONE IS—OR WAS—HERE...
LET'S LOOK!
!
"LET'S LOOK"?
ODYSSEUS ALWAYS MANAGES TO GET US IN TROUBLE...
TRUE...
...FORTUNATELY, HE ALWAYS MANAGES TO GET US OUT OF TROUBLE AFTERWARD!
KEEP CLIMBING.

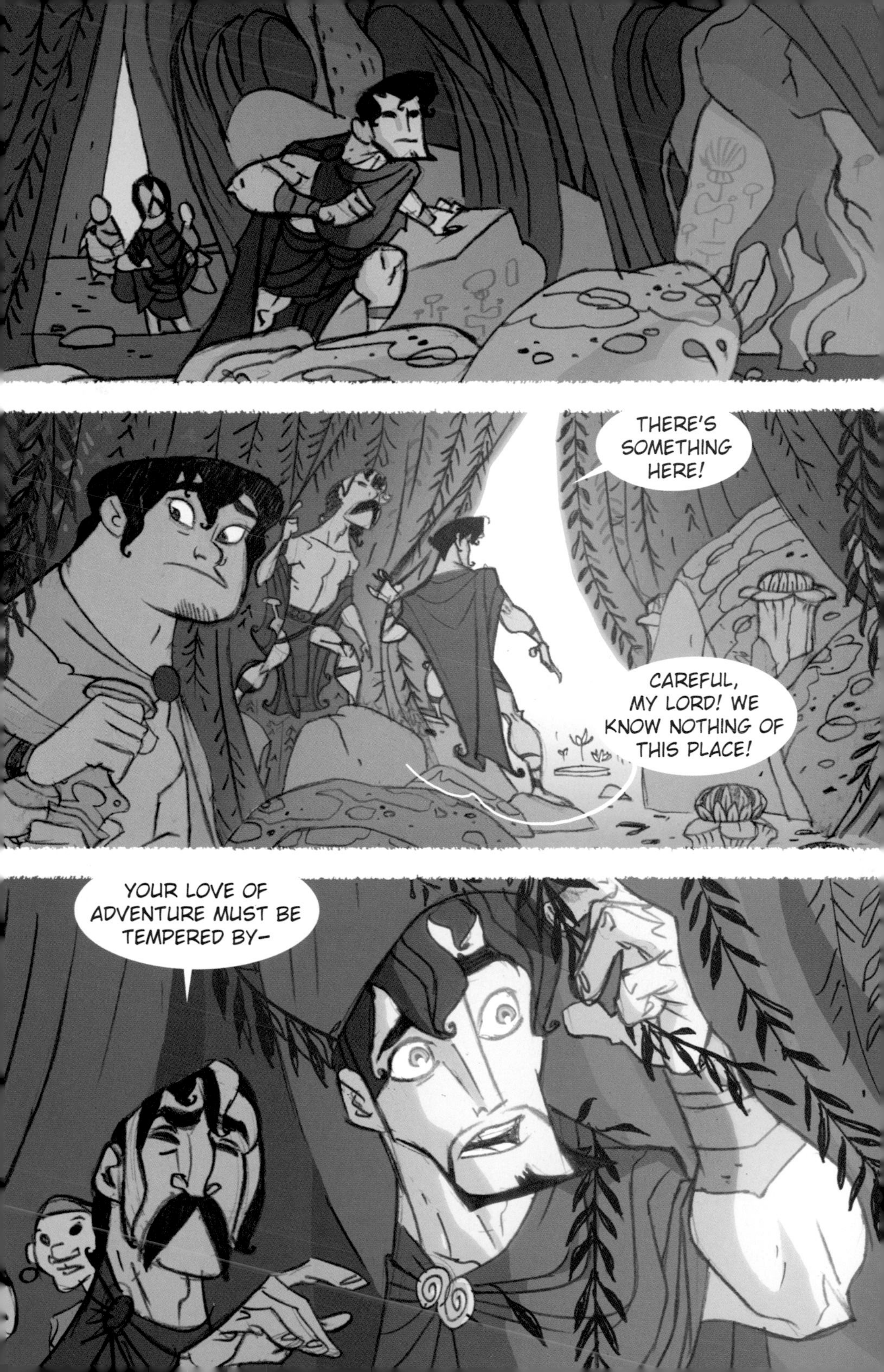
THERE'S SOMETHING HERE!
CAREFUL, MY LORD! WE KNOW NOTHING OF THIS PLACE!
YOUR LOVE OF ADVENTURE MUST BE TEMPERED BY–

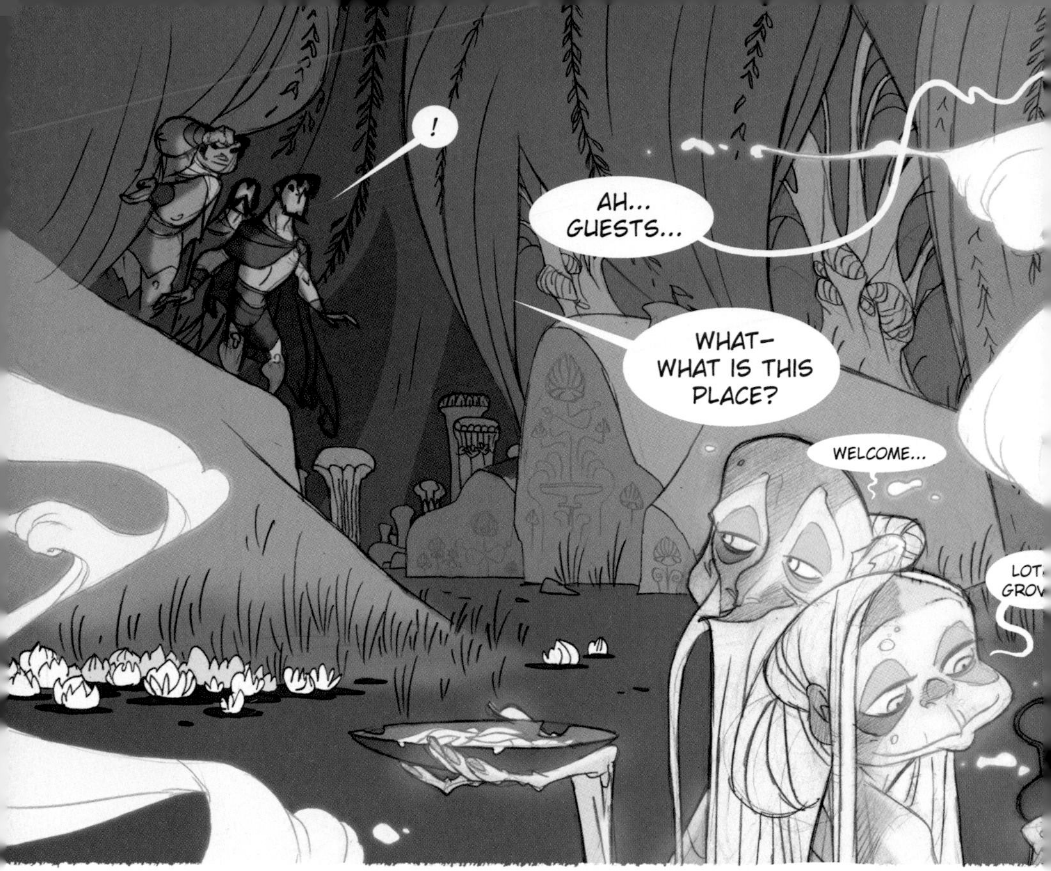
!
AH... GUESTS...
WHAT- WHAT IS THIS PLACE?
WELCOME...

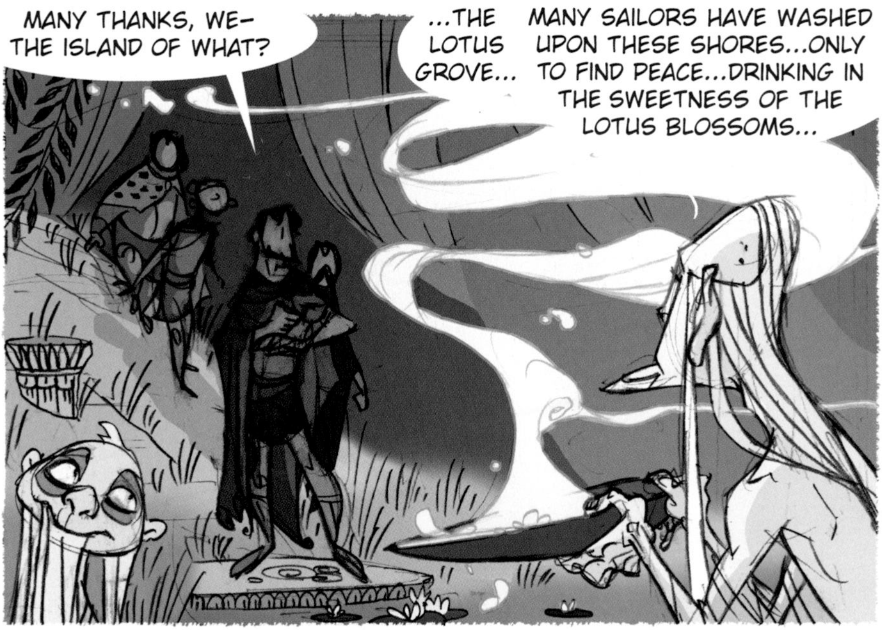
MANY THANKS, WE- THE ISLAND OF WHAT?
...THE LOTUS GROVE...
MANY SAILORS HAVE WASHED UPON THESE SHORES...ONLY TO FIND PEACE...DRINKING IN THE SWEETNESS OF THE LOTUS BLOSSOMS...

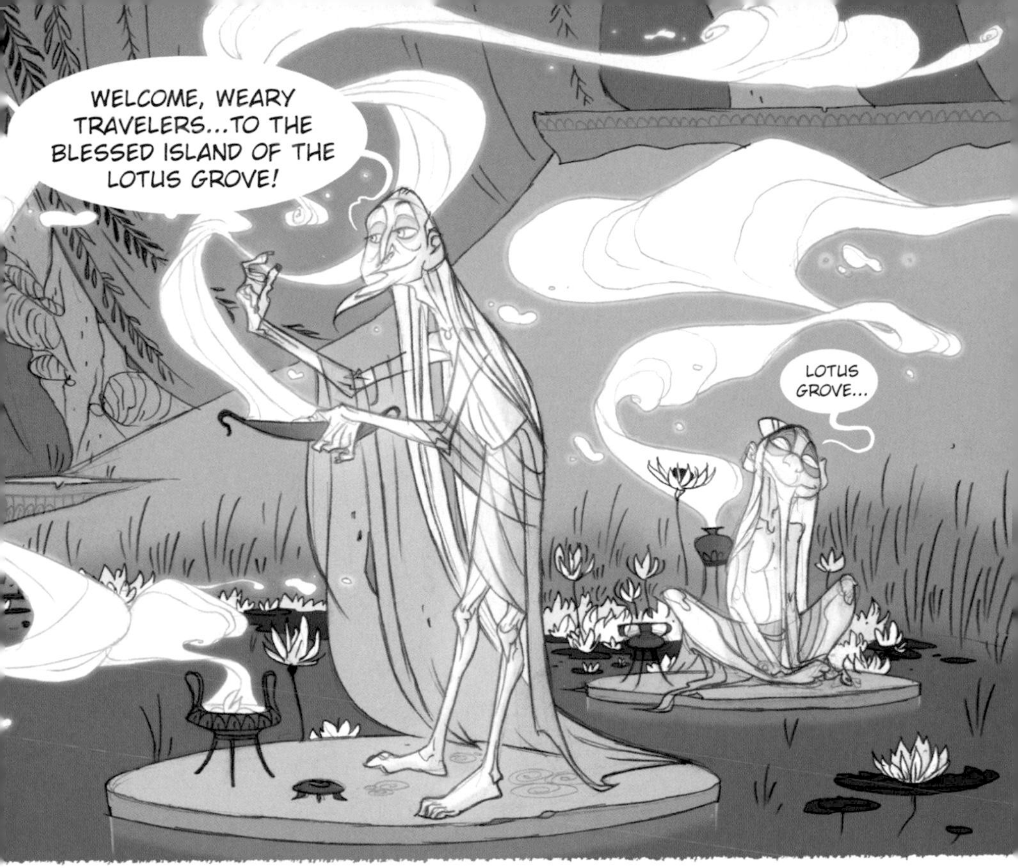
WELCOME, WEARY TRAVELERS...TO THE BLESSED ISLAND OF THE LOTUS GROVE!
LOTUS GROVE...

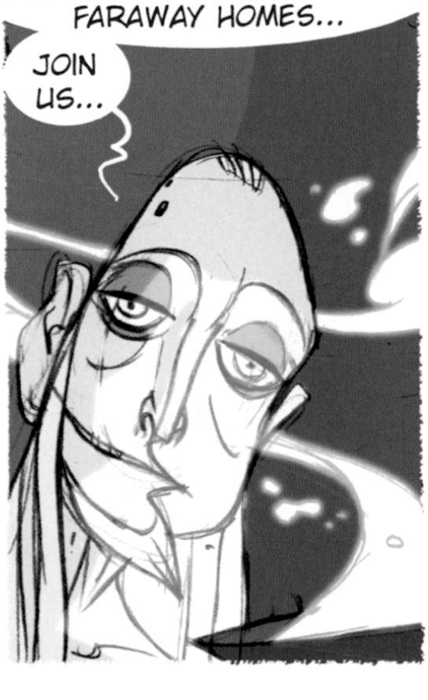
...ONE TASTE OF THE LOTUS, AND YOU WILL FORGET YOUR TROUBLES.. YOUR PAIN... YOUR FARAWAY HOMES...
JOIN US...

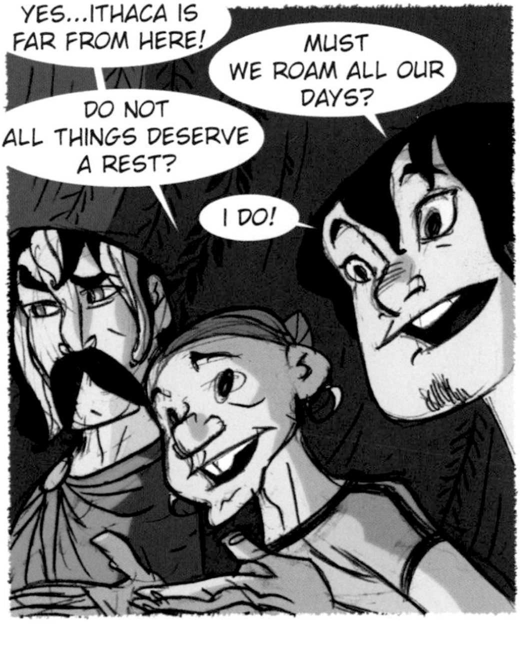
YES...ITHACA IS FAR FROM HERE!
MUST WE ROAM ALL OUR DAYS?
DO NOT ALL THINGS DESERVE A REST?
I DO!

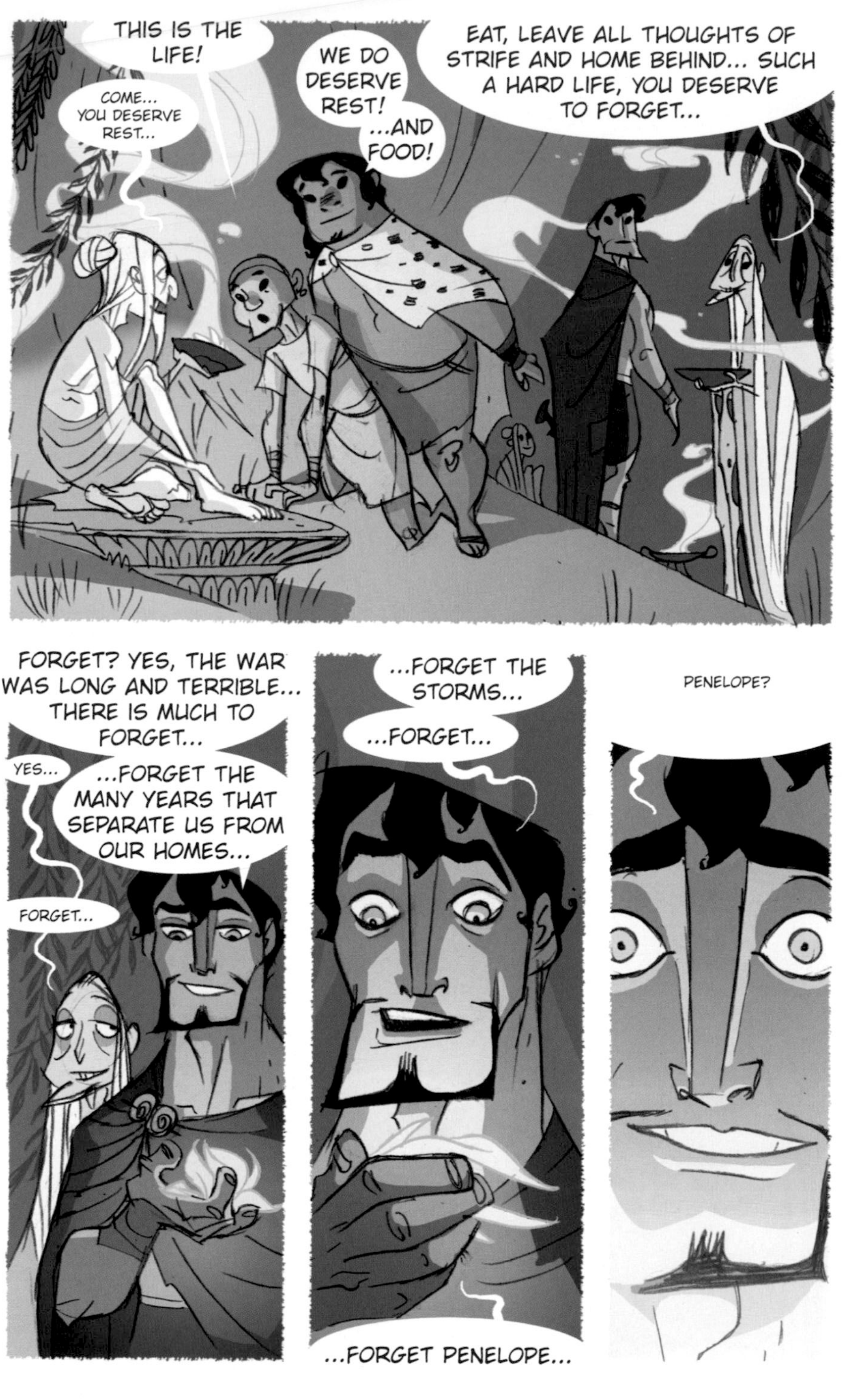
THIS IS THE LIFE!
COME... YOU DESERVE REST...
WE DO DESERVE REST!
...AND FOOD!
EAT, LEAVE ALL THOUGHTS OF STRIFE AND HOME BEHIND... SUCH A HARD LIFE, YOU DESERVE TO FORGET...
FORGET? YES, THE WAR WAS LONG AND TERRIBLE... THERE IS MUCH TO FORGET...
YES...
...FORGET THE MANY YEARS THAT SEPARATE US FROM OUR HOMES...
FORGET...
...FORGET THE STORMS...
...FORGET...
...FORGET PENELOPE...
PENELOPE?

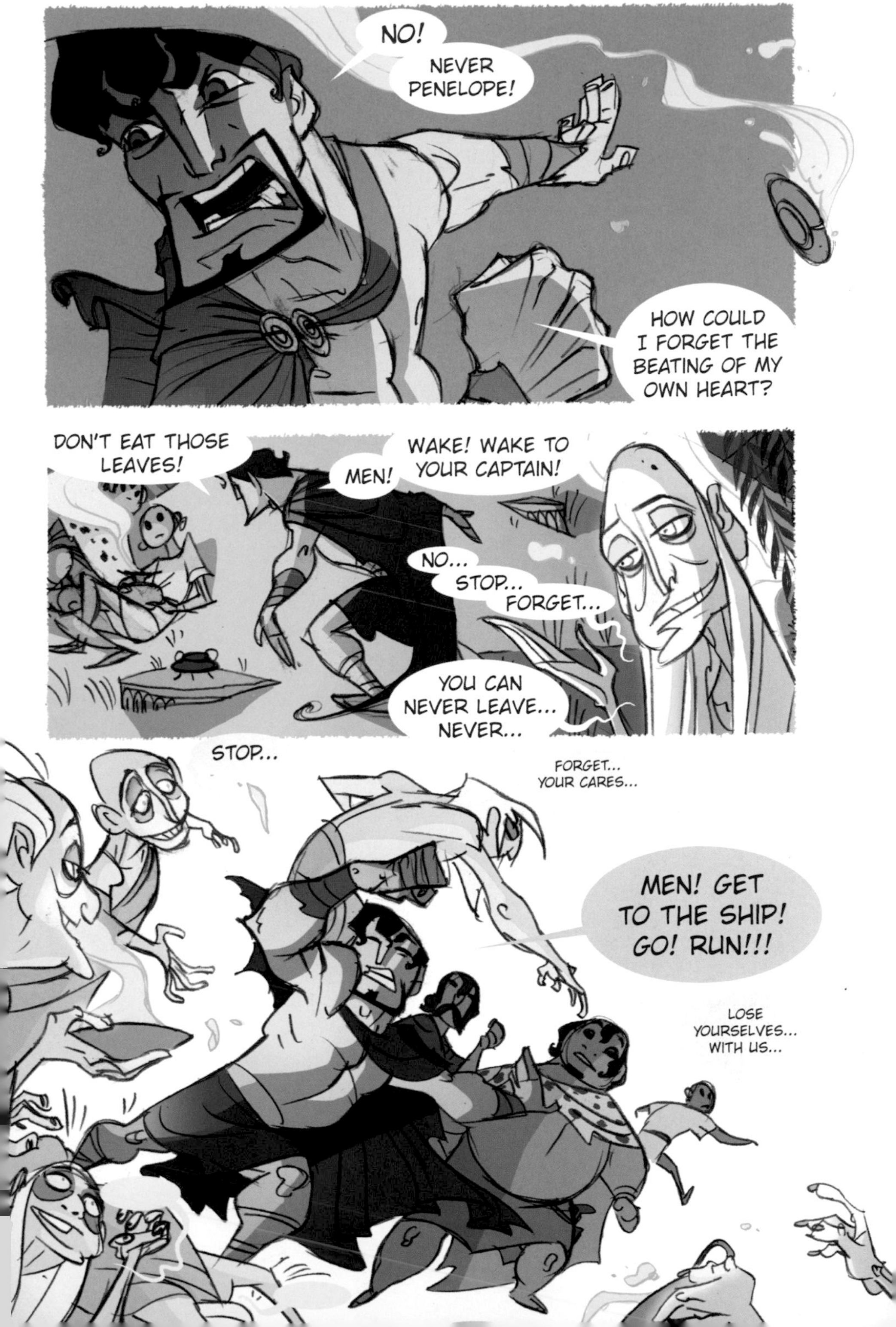
NO!
NEVER PENELOPE!
HOW COULD I FORGET THE BEATING OF MY OWN HEART?
DON'T EAT THOSE LEAVES!
MEN!
WAKE! WAKE TO YOUR CAPTAIN!
NO... STOP... FORGET...
YOU CAN NEVER LEAVE... NEVER...
STOP...
FORGET... YOUR CARES...
MEN! GET TO THE SHIP! GO! RUN!!!
LOSE YOURSELVES... WITH US...

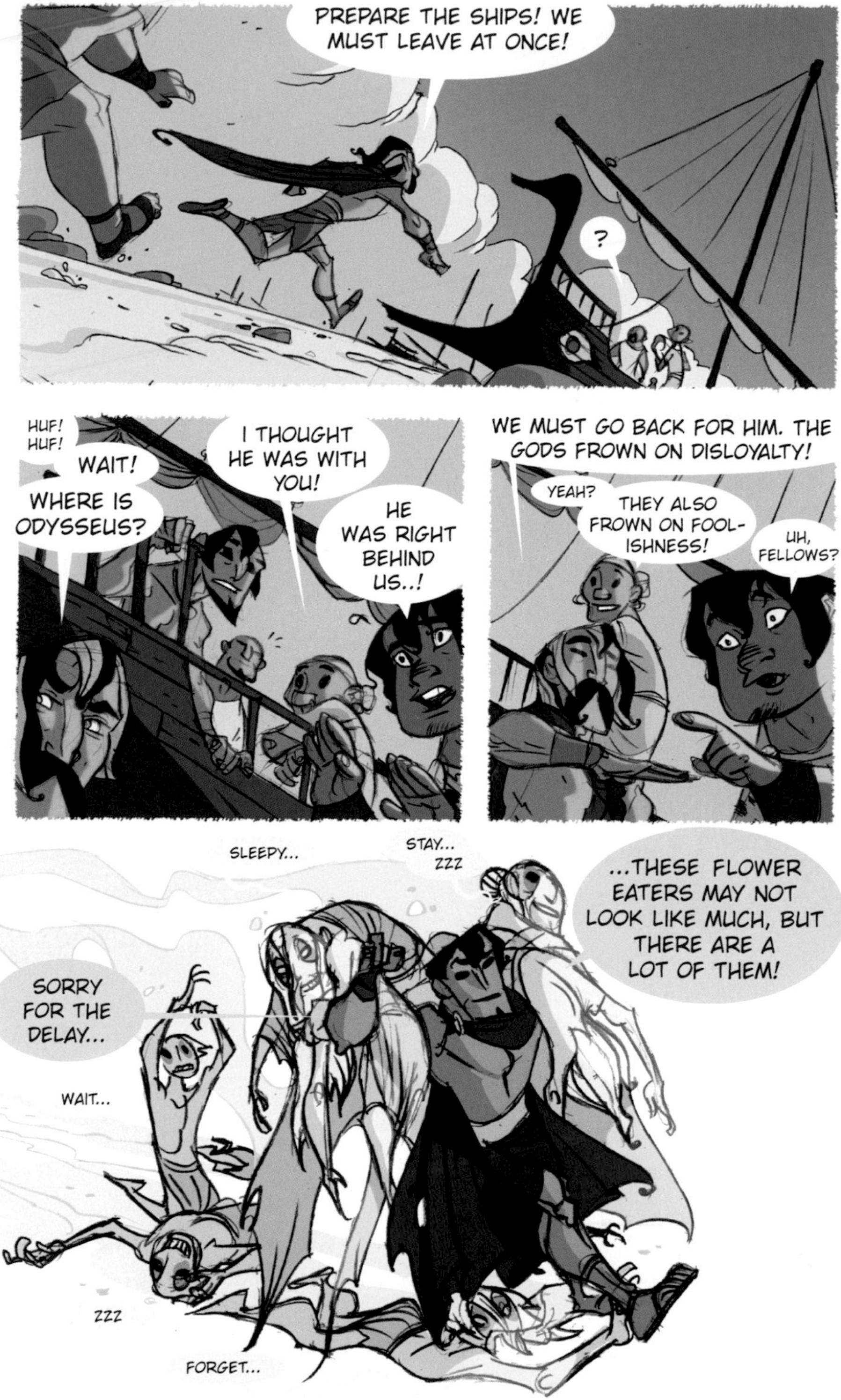
PREPARE THE SHIPS! WE MUST LEAVE AT ONCE!
?
HUF! HUF!
WAIT!
WHERE IS ODYSSEUS?
I THOUGHT HE WAS WITH YOU!
HE WAS RIGHT BEHIND US..!
WE MUST GO BACK FOR HIM. THE GODS FROWN ON DISLOYALTY!
YEAH?
THEY ALSO FROWN ON FOOL-ISHNESS!
UH, FELLOWS?
SLEEPY...
STAY... ZZZ
...THESE FLOWER EATERS MAY NOT LOOK LIKE MUCH, BUT THERE ARE A LOT OF THEM!
SORRY FOR THE DELAY...
WAIT...
ZZZ
FORGET...

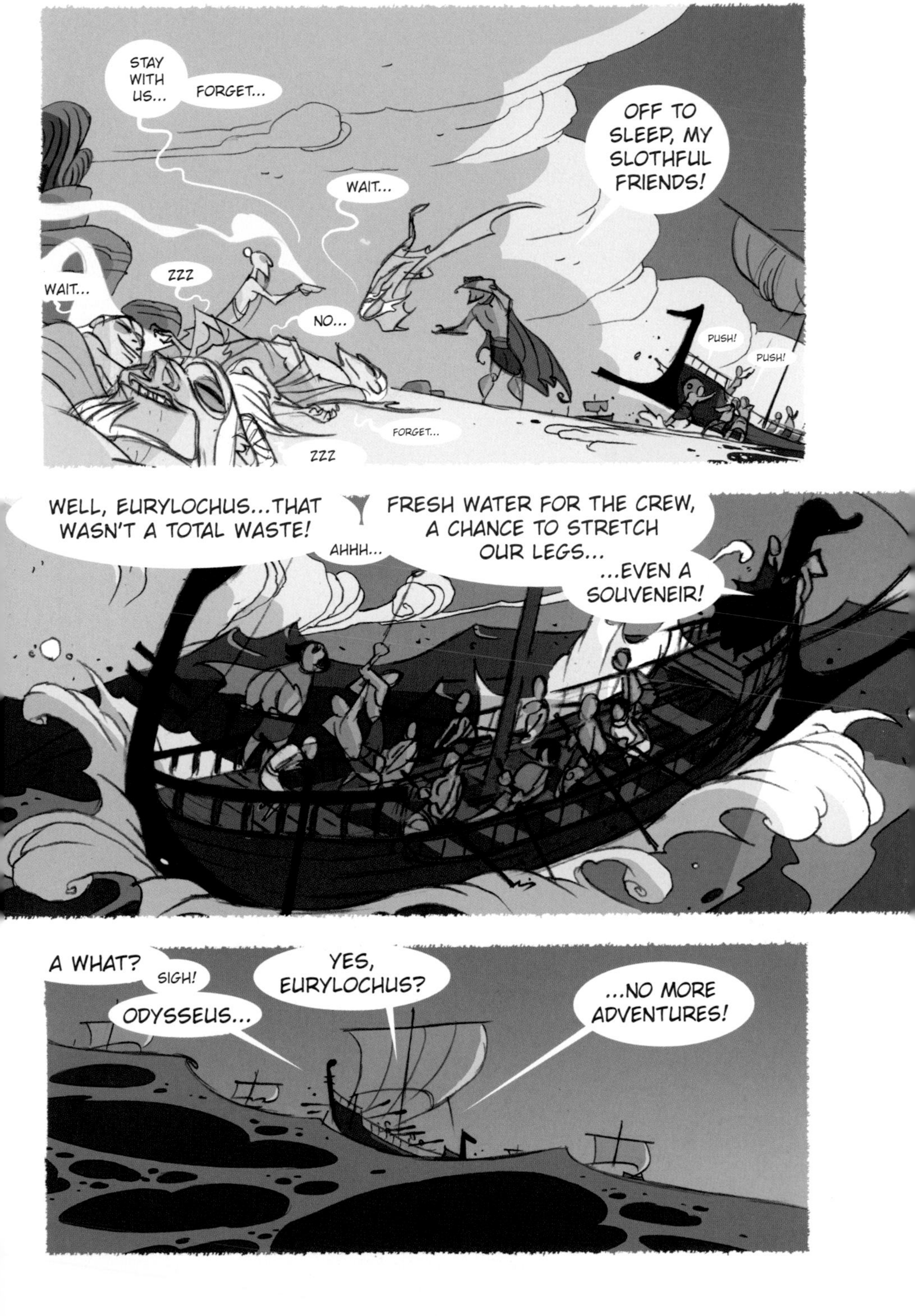
STAY WITH US...
FORGET...
OFF TO SLEEP, MY SLOTHFUL FRIENDS!
WAIT...
WAIT...
ZZZ
NO...
PUSH!
PUSH!
FORGET...
ZZZ
WELL, EURYLOCHUS...THAT WASN'T A TOTAL WASTE!
FRESH WATER FOR THE CREW, A CHANCE TO STRETCH OUR LEGS...
AHHH...
...EVEN A SOUVENEIR!
A WHAT?
SIGH!
ODYSSEUS...
YES, EURYLOCHUS?
...NO MORE ADVENTURES!

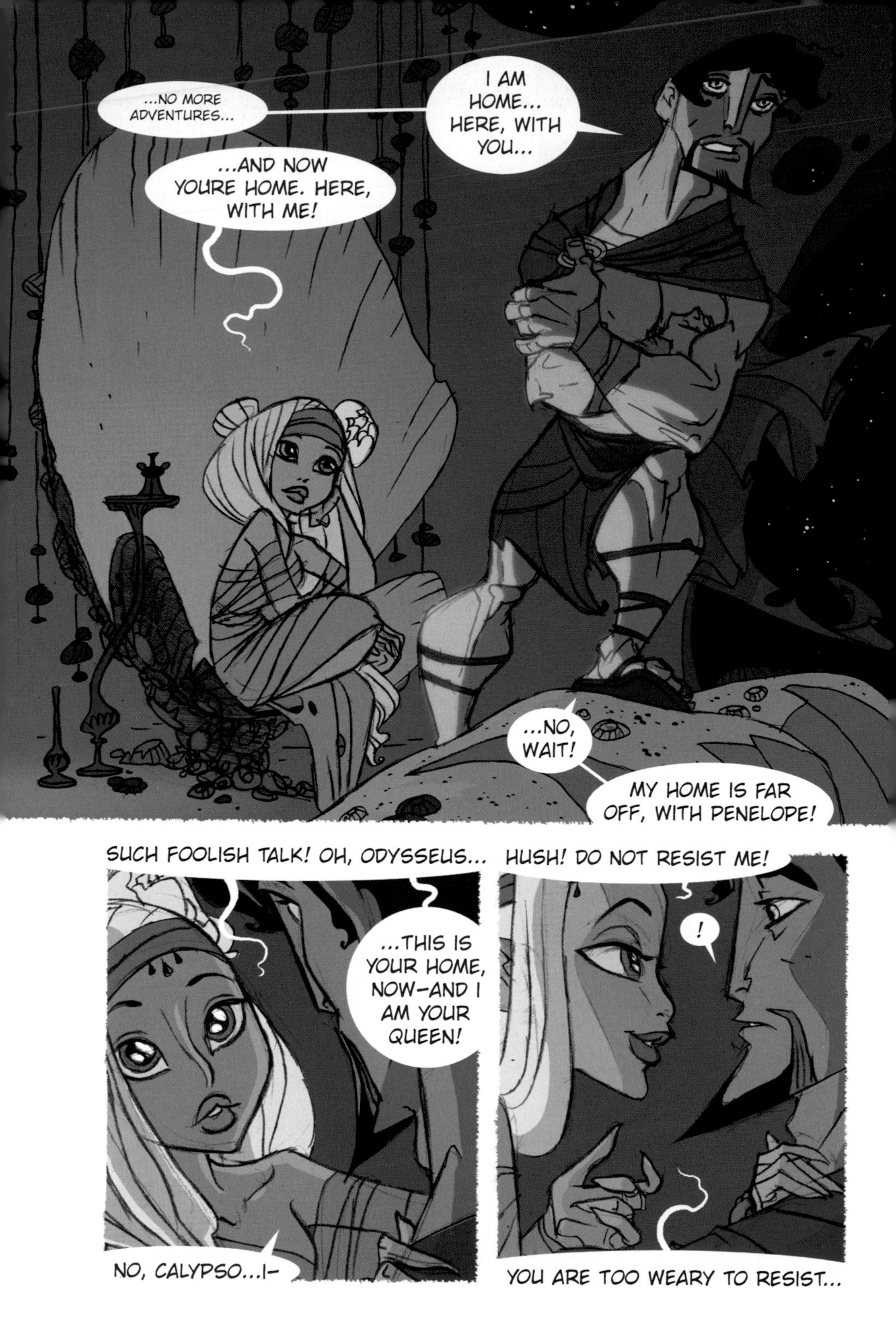
...NO MORE ADVENTURES...
I AM HOME... HERE, WITH YOU...
...AND NOW YOURE HOME. HERE, WITH ME!
...NO, WAIT!
MY HOME IS FAR OFF, WITH PENELOPE!
SUCH FOOLISH TALK! OH, ODYSSEUS...
...THIS IS YOUR HOME, NOW—AND I AM YOUR QUEEN!
NO, CALYPSO...I—
HUSH! DO NOT RESIST ME!
!
YOU ARE TOO WEARY TO RESIST...

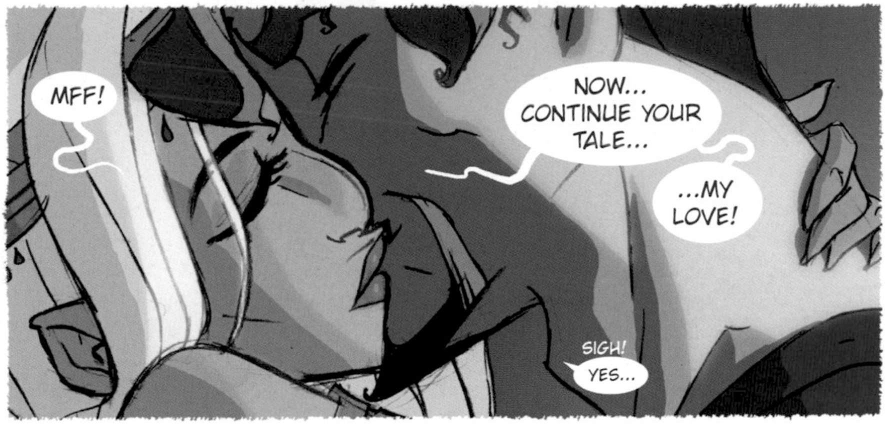
MFF!
NOW... CONTINUE YOUR TALE...
...MY LOVE!
SIGH! YES...

WE ESCAPED THE LOTUS-EATERS, AND SAILED ON FOR DAYS. OUR SPIRITS BEGAN TO EBB...UNTIL FINALLY WE CAME TO A WILD, JAGGED LAND.

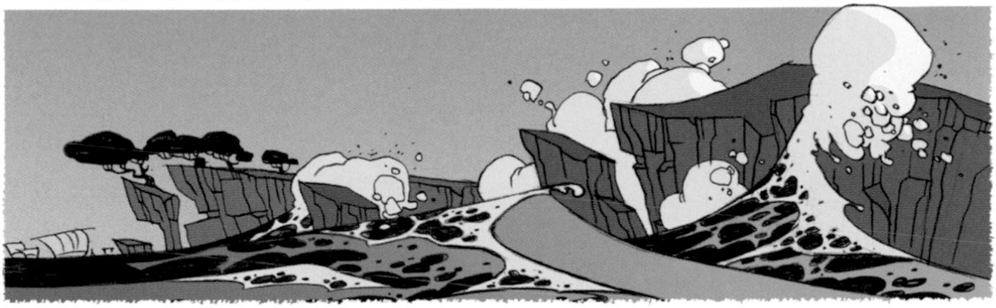

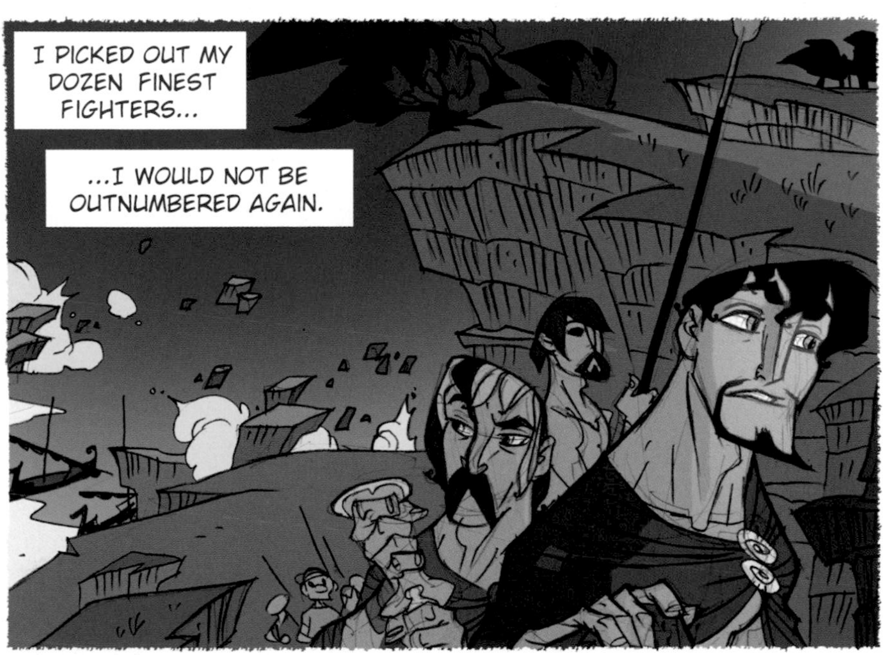
I PICKED OUT MY DOZEN FINEST FIGHTERS...
...I WOULD NOT BE OUTNUMBERED AGAIN.

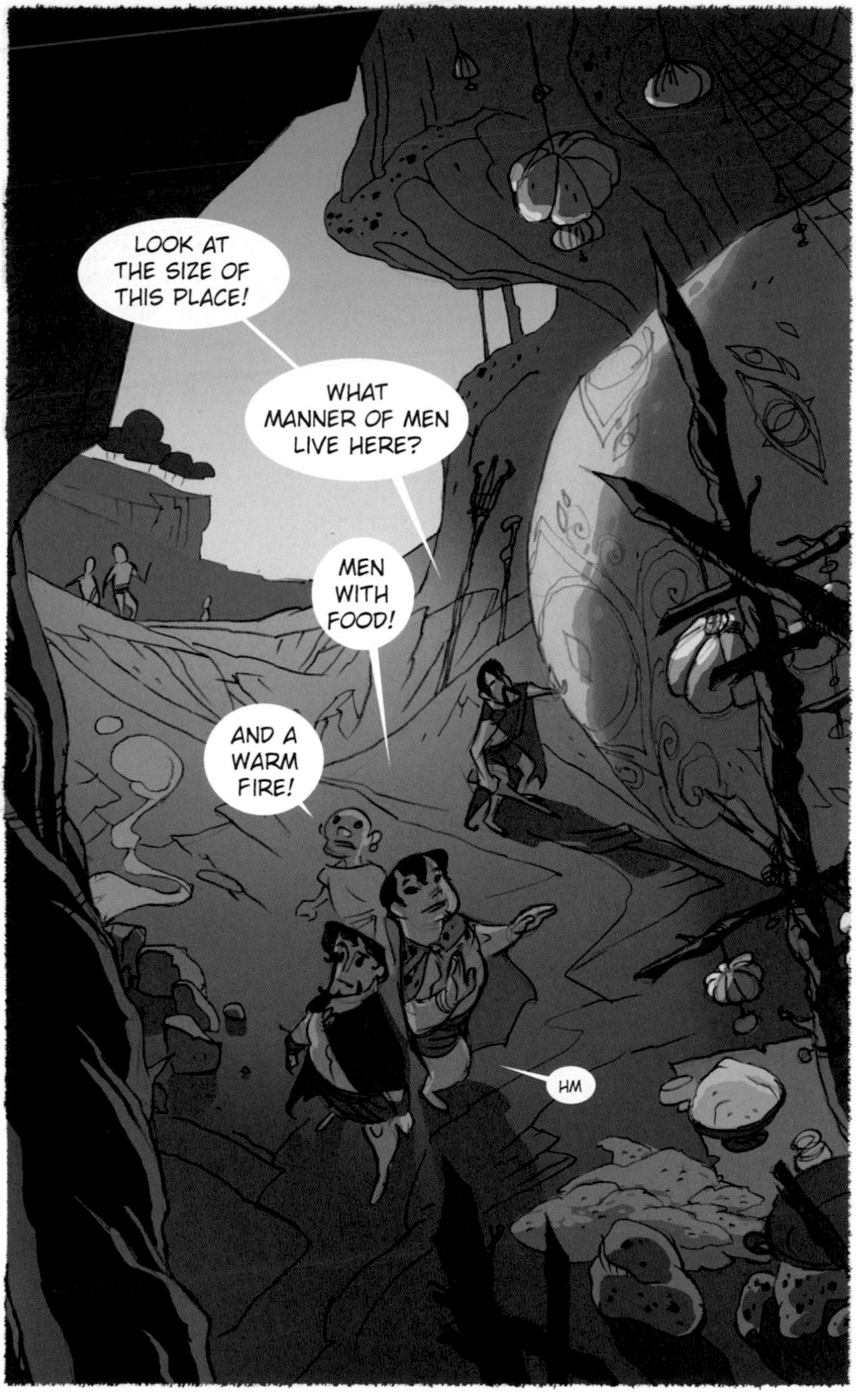
LOOK AT THE SIZE OF THIS PLACE!
WHAT MANNER OF MEN LIVE HERE?
MEN WITH FOOD!
AND A WARM FIRE!
HM

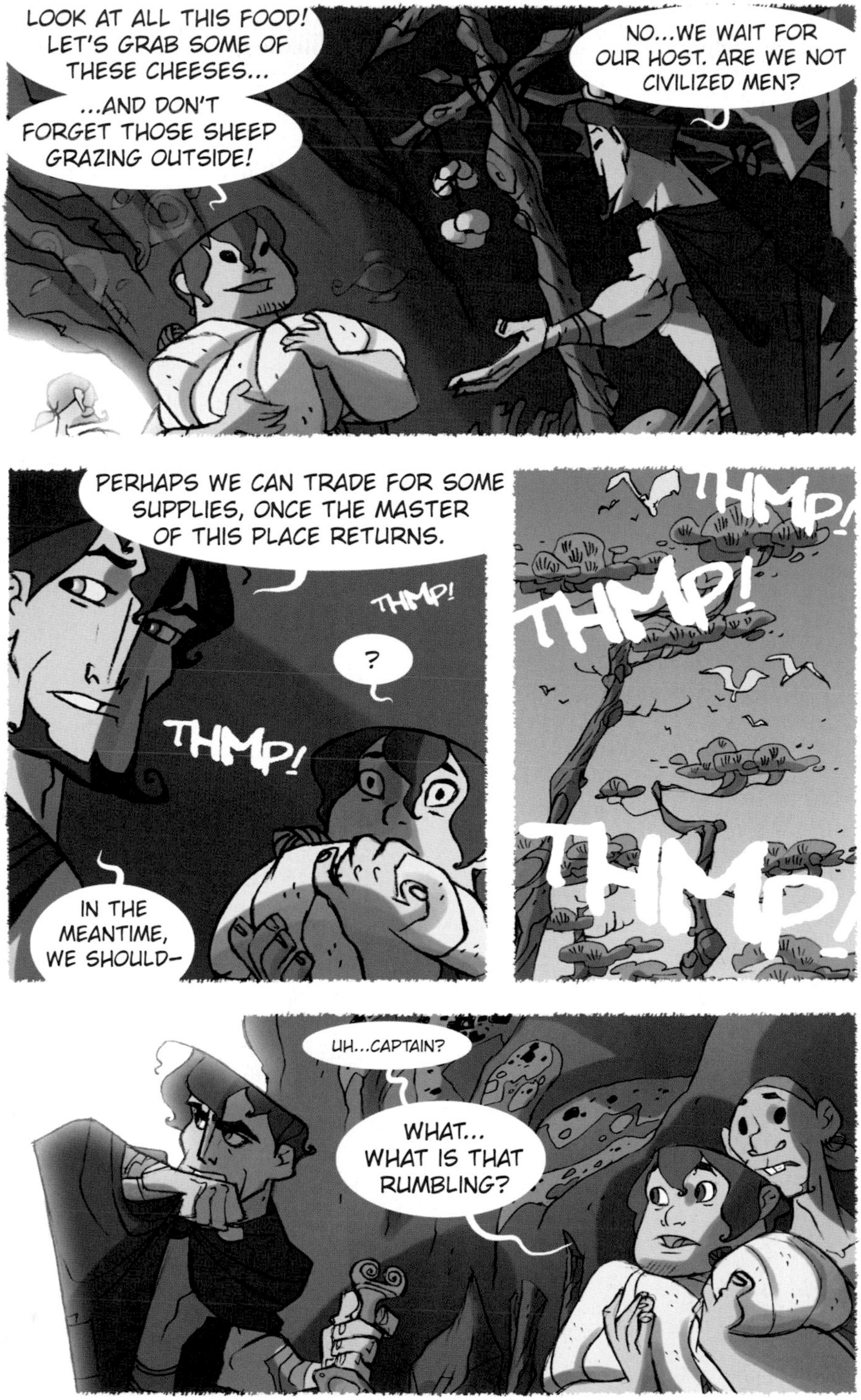
LOOK AT ALL THIS FOOD! LET'S GRAB SOME OF THESE CHEESES...
...AND DON'T FORGET THOSE SHEEP GRAZING OUTSIDE!
NO...WE WAIT FOR OUR HOST. ARE WE NOT CIVILIZED MEN?
PERHAPS WE CAN TRADE FOR SOME SUPPLIES, ONCE THE MASTER OF THIS PLACE RETURNS.
THMP!
?
THMP!
IN THE MEANTIME, WE SHOULD–
THMP!
THMP!
THMP!
UH...CAPTAIN?
WHAT... WHAT IS THAT RUMBLING?

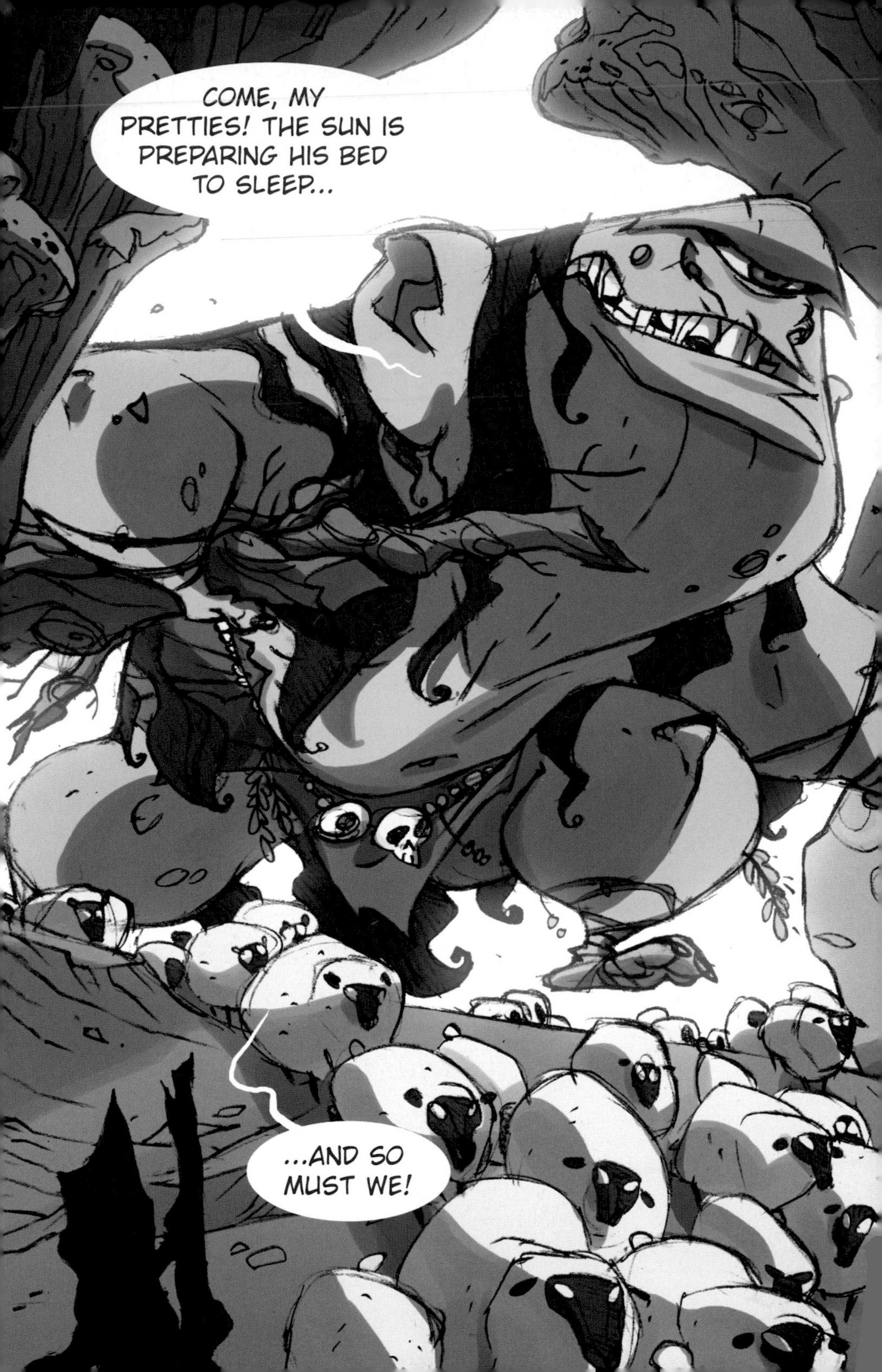
COME, MY PRETTIES! THE SUN IS PREPARING HIS BED TO SLEEP...
...AND SO MUST WE!

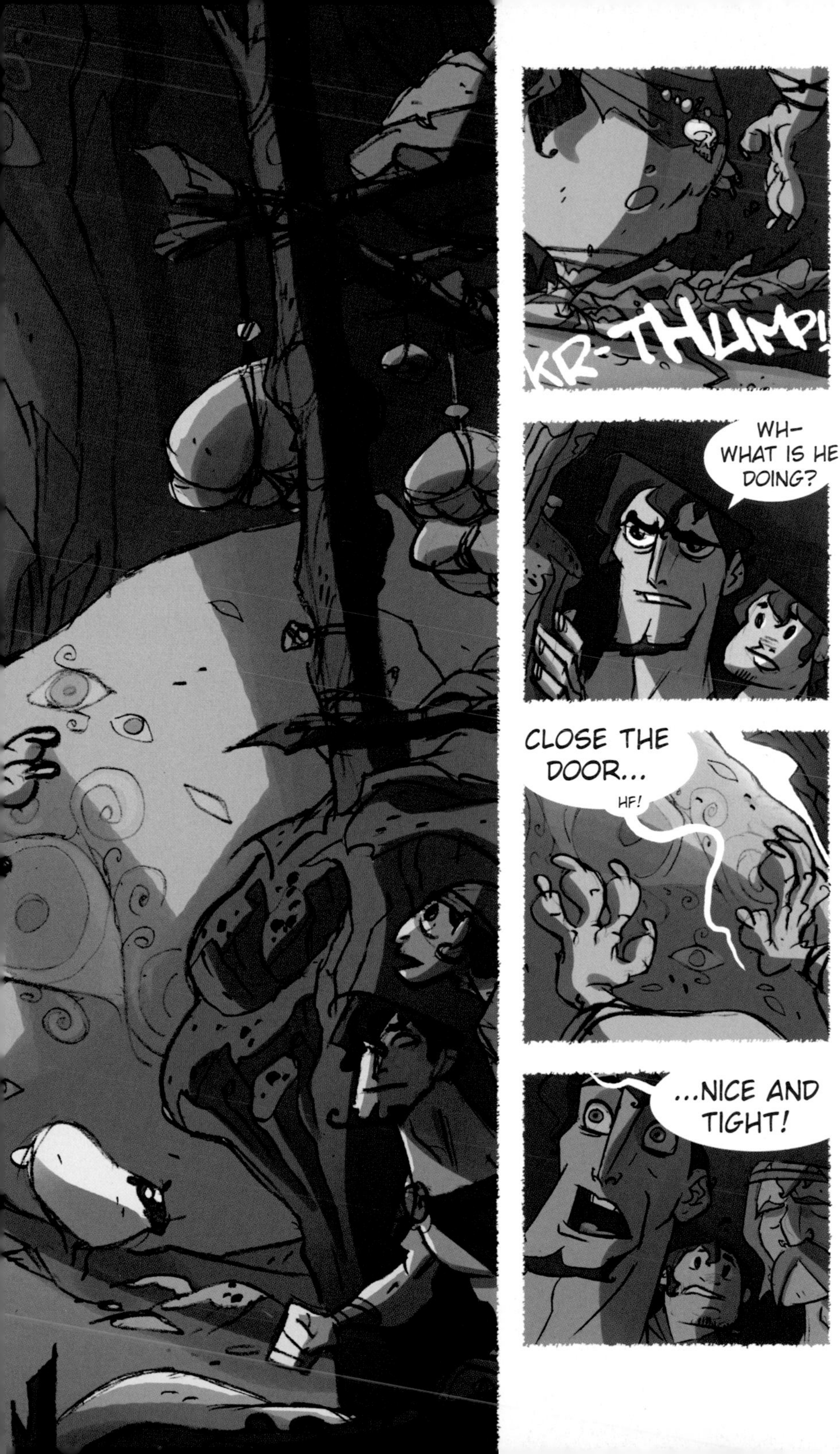
KR-THUMP!
WH- WHAT IS HE DOING?
CLOSE THE DOOR...
HF!
...NICE AND TIGHT!

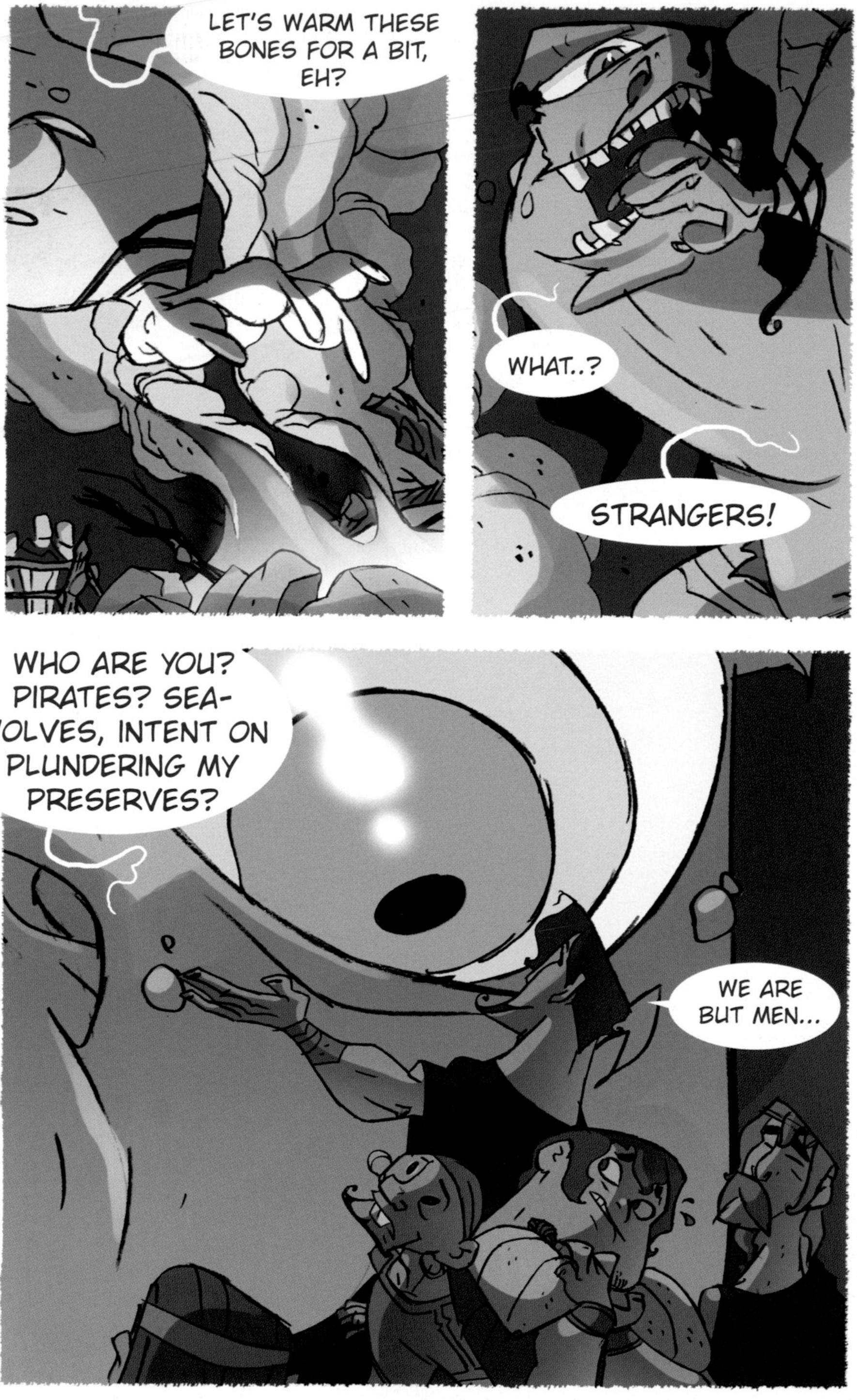
LET'S WARM THESE BONES FOR A BIT, EH?
WHAT..?
STRANGERS!
WHO ARE YOU? PIRATES? SEA-WOLVES, INTENT ON PLUNDERING MY PRESERVES?
WE ARE BUT MEN...

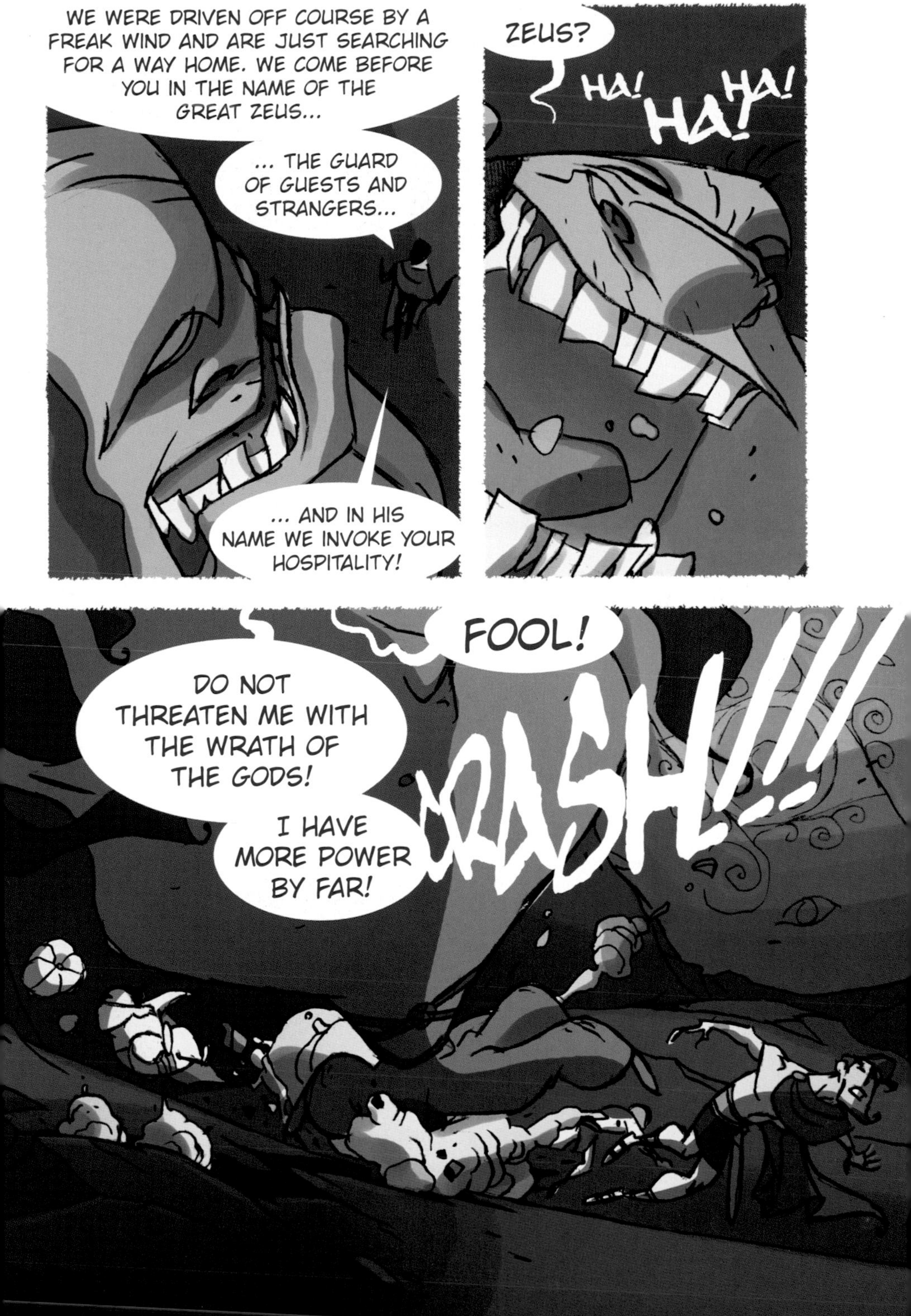
WE WERE DRIVEN OFF COURSE BY A FREAK WIND AND ARE JUST SEARCHING FOR A WAY HOME. WE COME BEFORE YOU IN THE NAME OF THE GREAT ZEUS...
... THE GUARD OF GUESTS AND STRANGERS...
... AND IN HIS NAME WE INVOKE YOUR HOSPITALITY!
ZEUS?
HA! HA! HA!
FOOL!
DO NOT THREATEN ME WITH THE WRATH OF THE GODS!
I HAVE MORE POWER BY FAR!
CRASH!!!

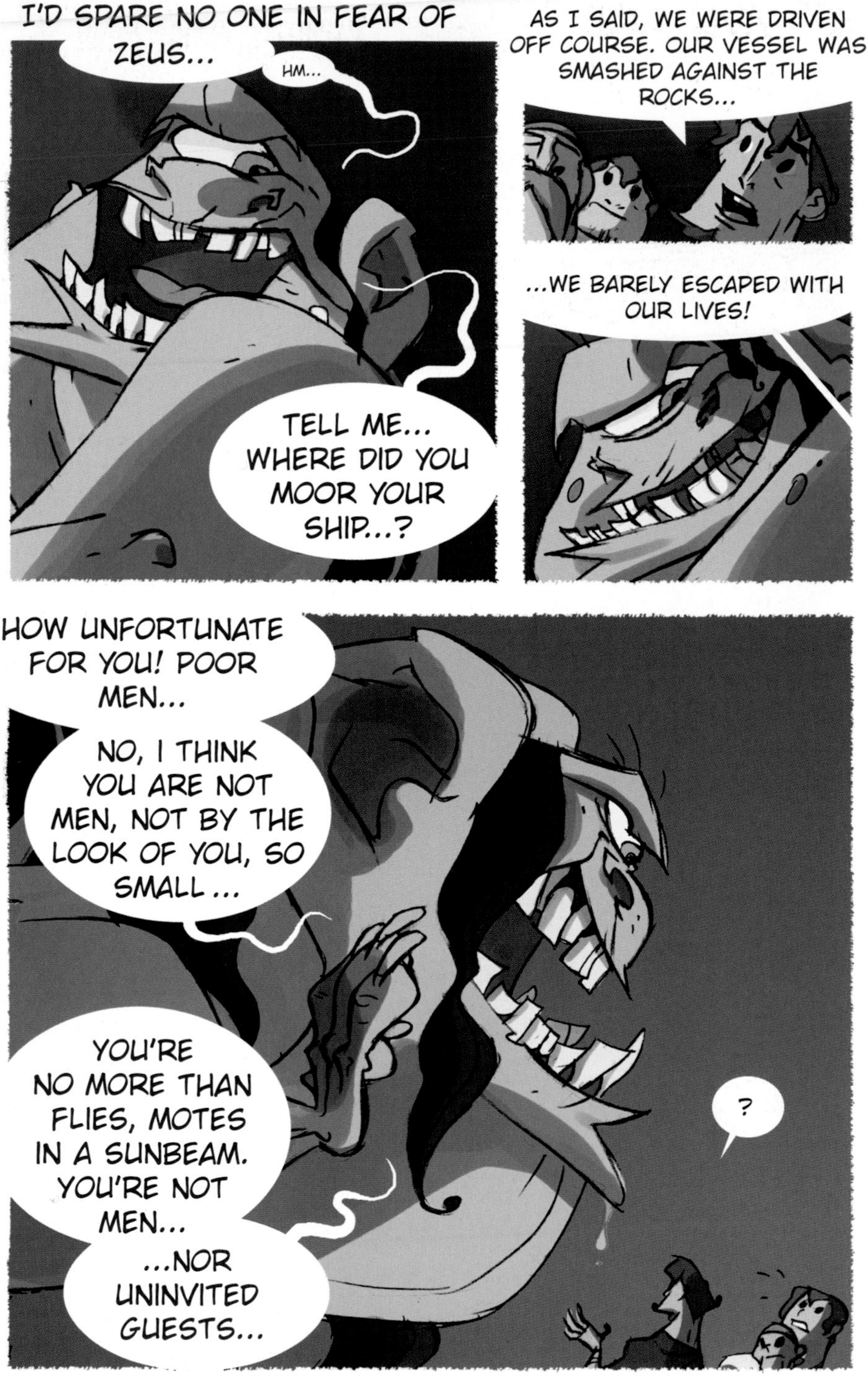

I'D SPARE NO ONE IN FEAR OF ZEUS...
HM...
TELL ME... WHERE DID YOU MOOR YOUR SHIP...?
AS I SAID, WE WERE DRIVEN OFF COURSE. OUR VESSEL WAS SMASHED AGAINST THE ROCKS...
...WE BARELY ESCAPED WITH OUR LIVES!
HOW UNFORTUNATE FOR YOU! POOR MEN...
NO, I THINK YOU ARE NOT MEN, NOT BY THE LOOK OF YOU, SO SMALL ...
YOU'RE NO MORE THAN FLIES, MOTES IN A SUNBEAM. YOU'RE NOT MEN...
...NOR UNINVITED GUESTS...
?

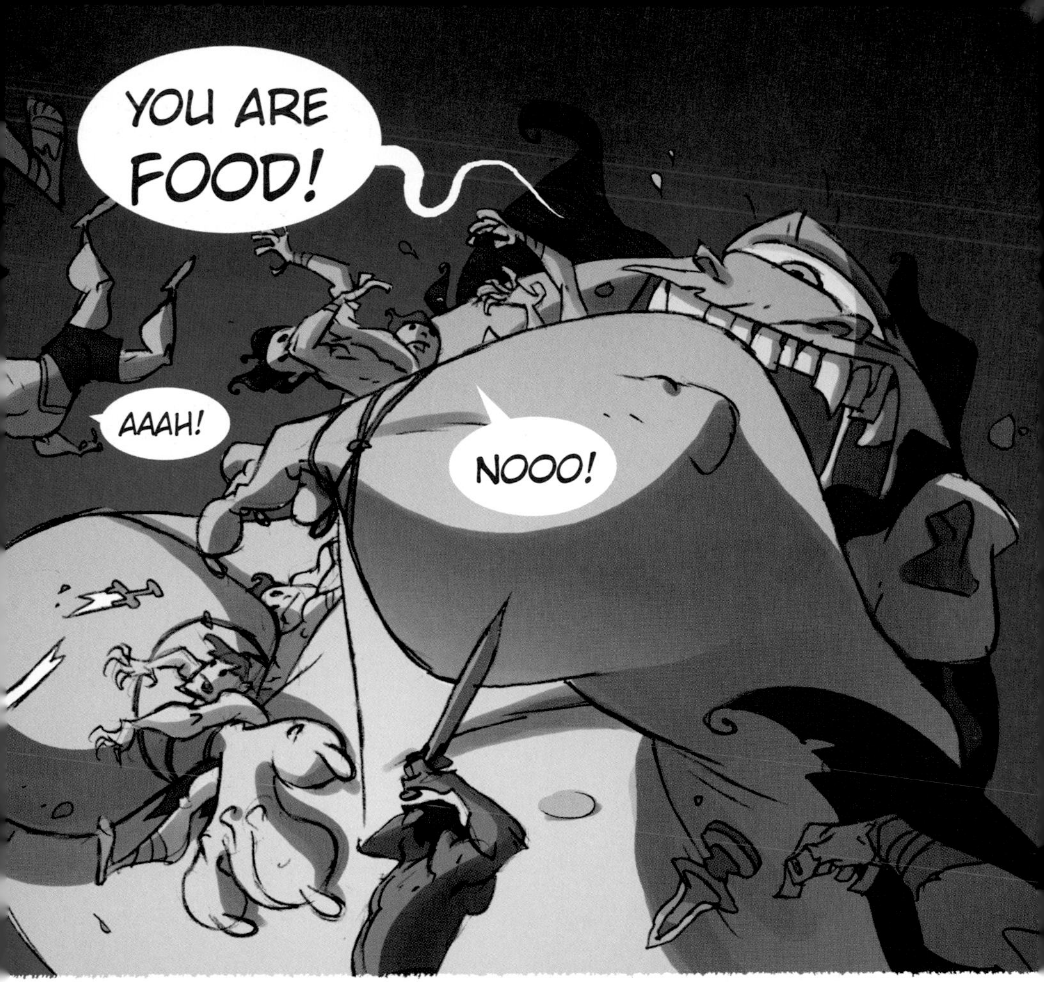
YOU ARE FOOD!
AAAH!
NOOO!

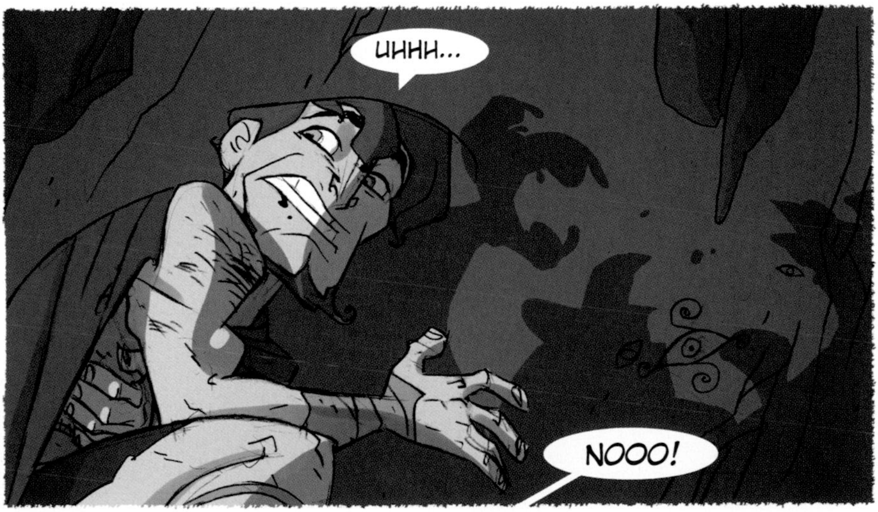
UHHH...
NOOO!

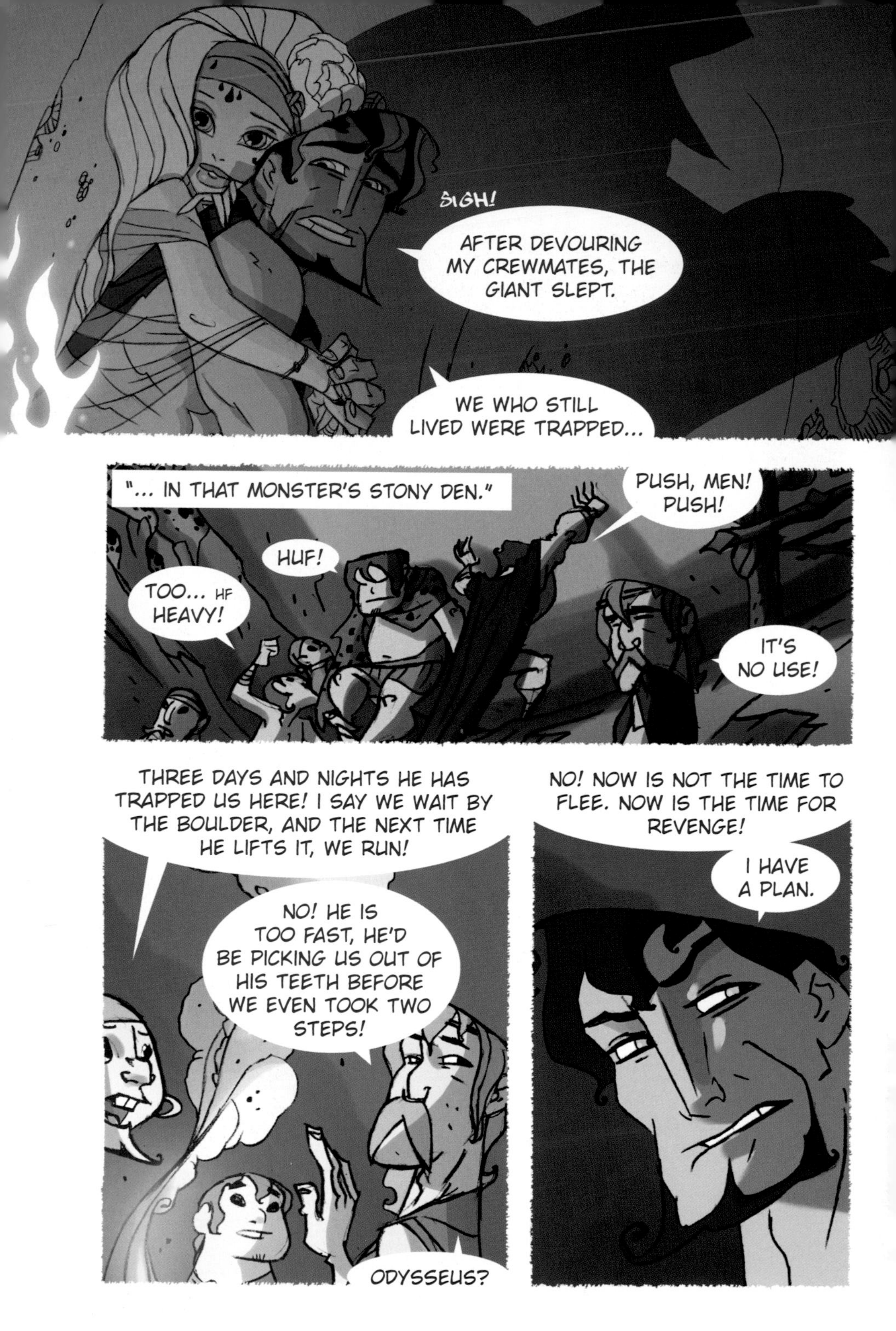
SIGH!
AFTER DEVOURING MY CREWMATES, THE GIANT SLEPT.
WE WHO STILL LIVED WERE TRAPPED...
"... IN THAT MONSTER'S STONY DEN."
PUSH, MEN! PUSH!
HUF!
TOO... HF HEAVY!
IT'S NO USE!
THREE DAYS AND NIGHTS HE HAS TRAPPED US HERE! I SAY WE WAIT BY THE BOULDER, AND THE NEXT TIME HE LIFTS IT, WE RUN!
NO! HE IS TOO FAST, HE'D BE PICKING US OUT OF HIS TEETH BEFORE WE EVEN TOOK TWO STEPS!
ODYSSEUS?
NO! NOW IS NOT THE TIME TO FLEE. NOW IS THE TIME FOR REVENGE!
I HAVE A PLAN.

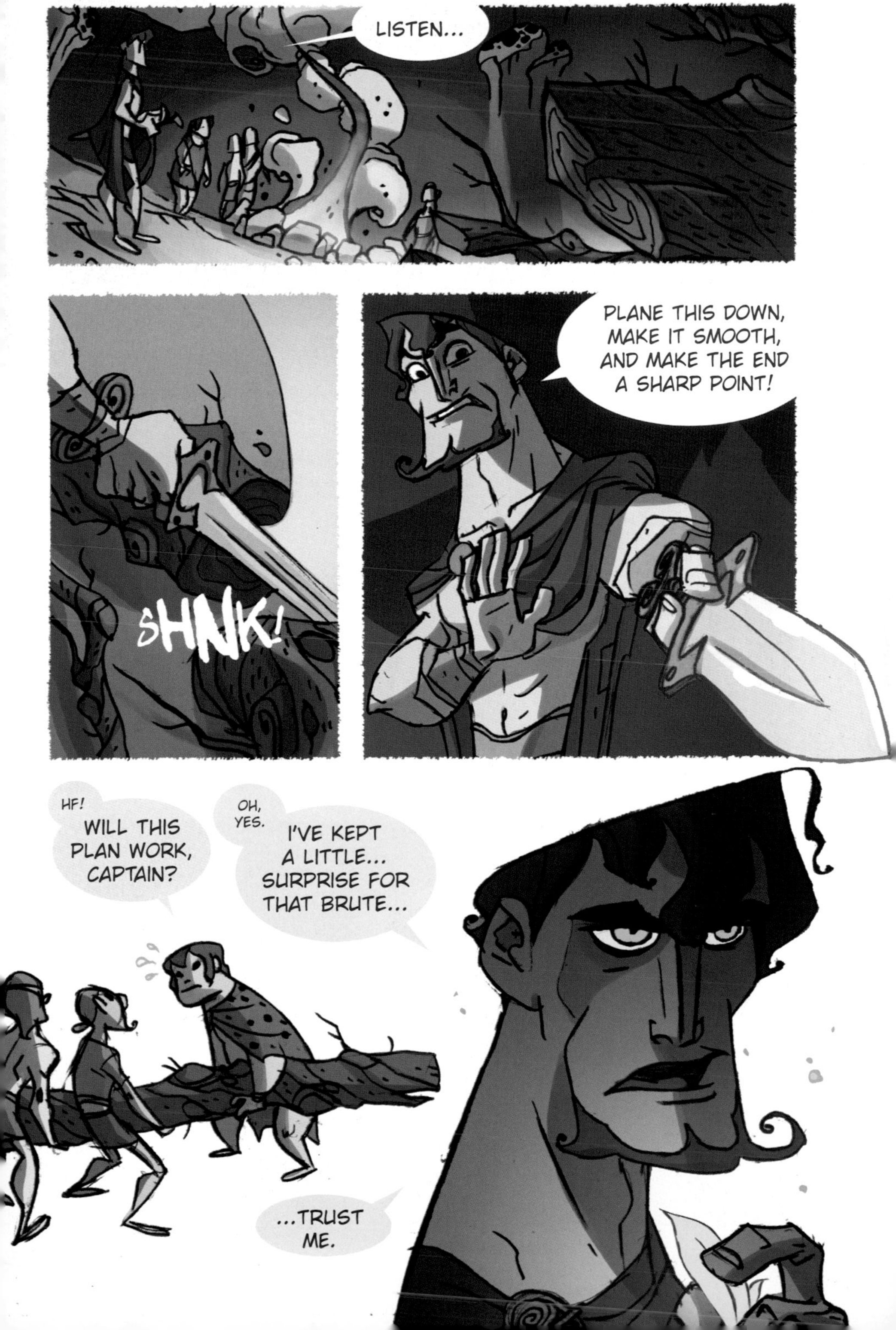
LISTEN...
SHNK!
PLANE THIS DOWN, MAKE IT SMOOTH, AND MAKE THE END A SHARP POINT!
HF!
WILL THIS PLAN WORK, CAPTAIN?
OH, YES.
I'VE KEPT A LITTLE... SURPRISE FOR THAT BRUTE...
...TRUST ME.

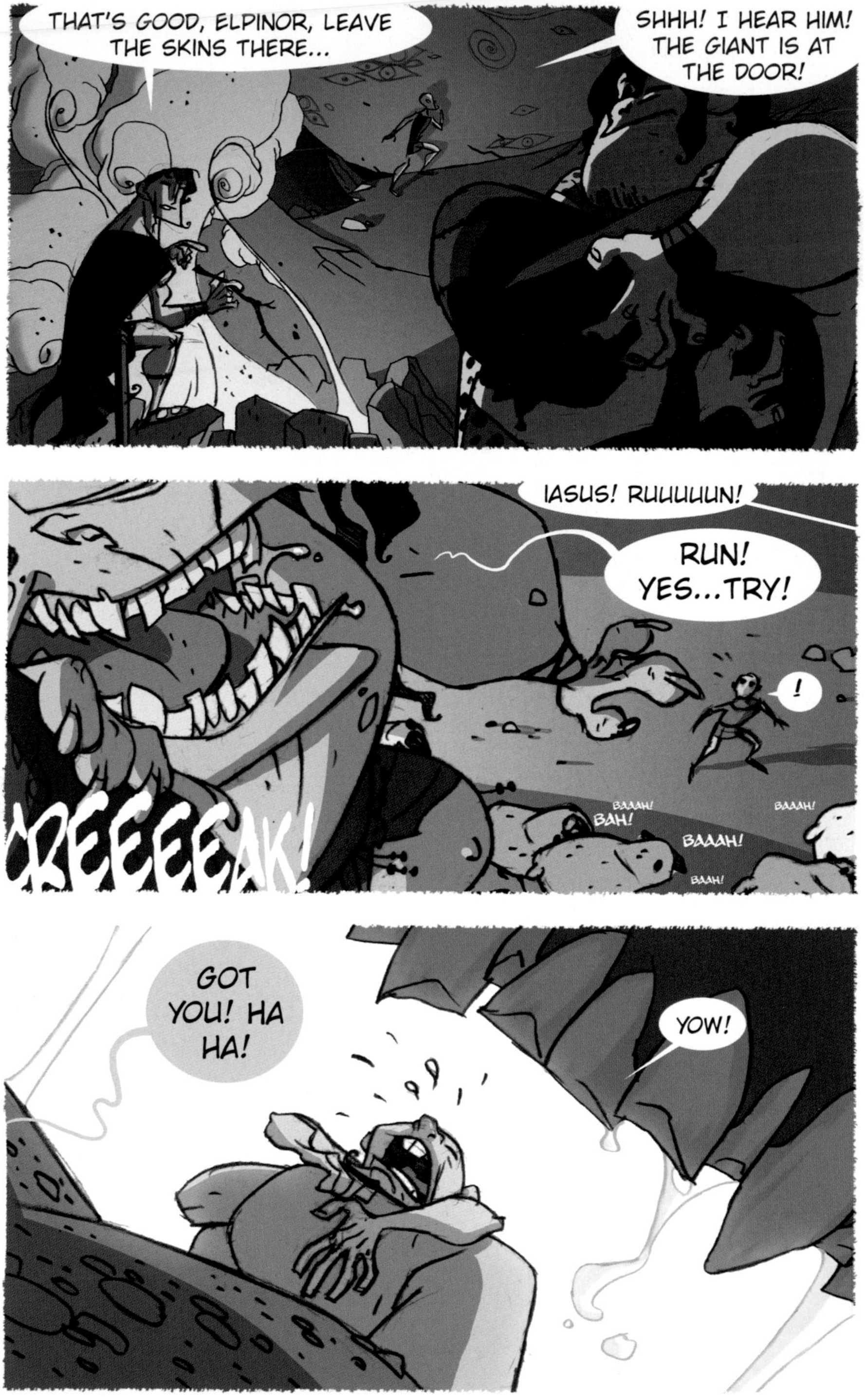
THAT'S GOOD, ELPINOR, LEAVE THE SKINS THERE...
SHHH! I HEAR HIM! THE GIANT IS AT THE DOOR!
IASUS! RUUUUUN!
RUN! YES...TRY!
!
CREEEEAK!
BAAAH!
BAH!
BAAAH!
BAAAH!
BAAH!
GOT YOU! HA HA!
YOW!

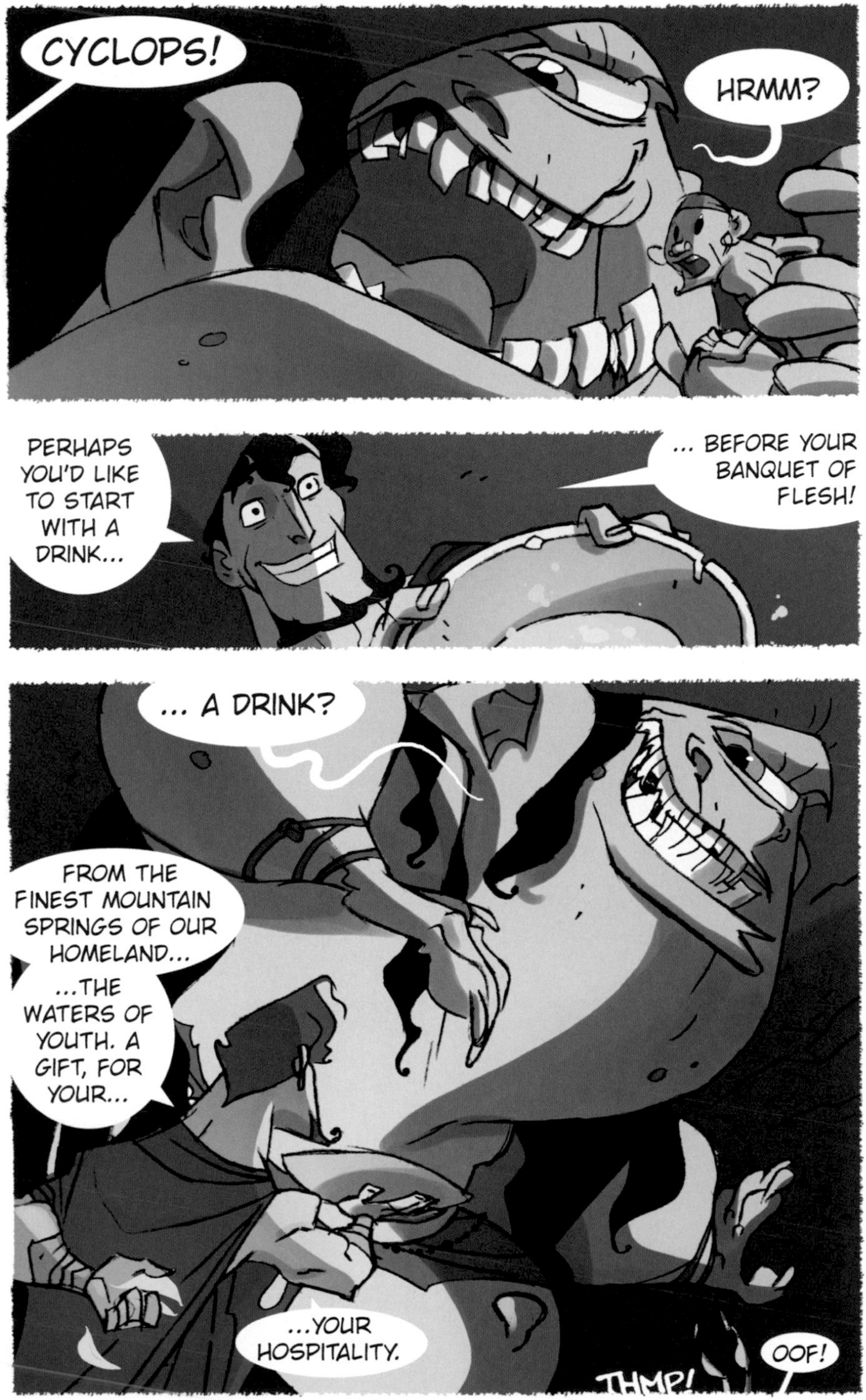
CYCLOPS!
HRMM?
PERHAPS YOU'D LIKE TO START WITH A DRINK...
... BEFORE YOUR BANQUET OF FLESH!
... A DRINK?
FROM THE FINEST MOUNTAIN SPRINGS OF OUR HOMELAND...
...THE WATERS OF YOUTH. A GIFT, FOR YOUR...
...YOUR HOSPITALITY.
THMP!
OOF!

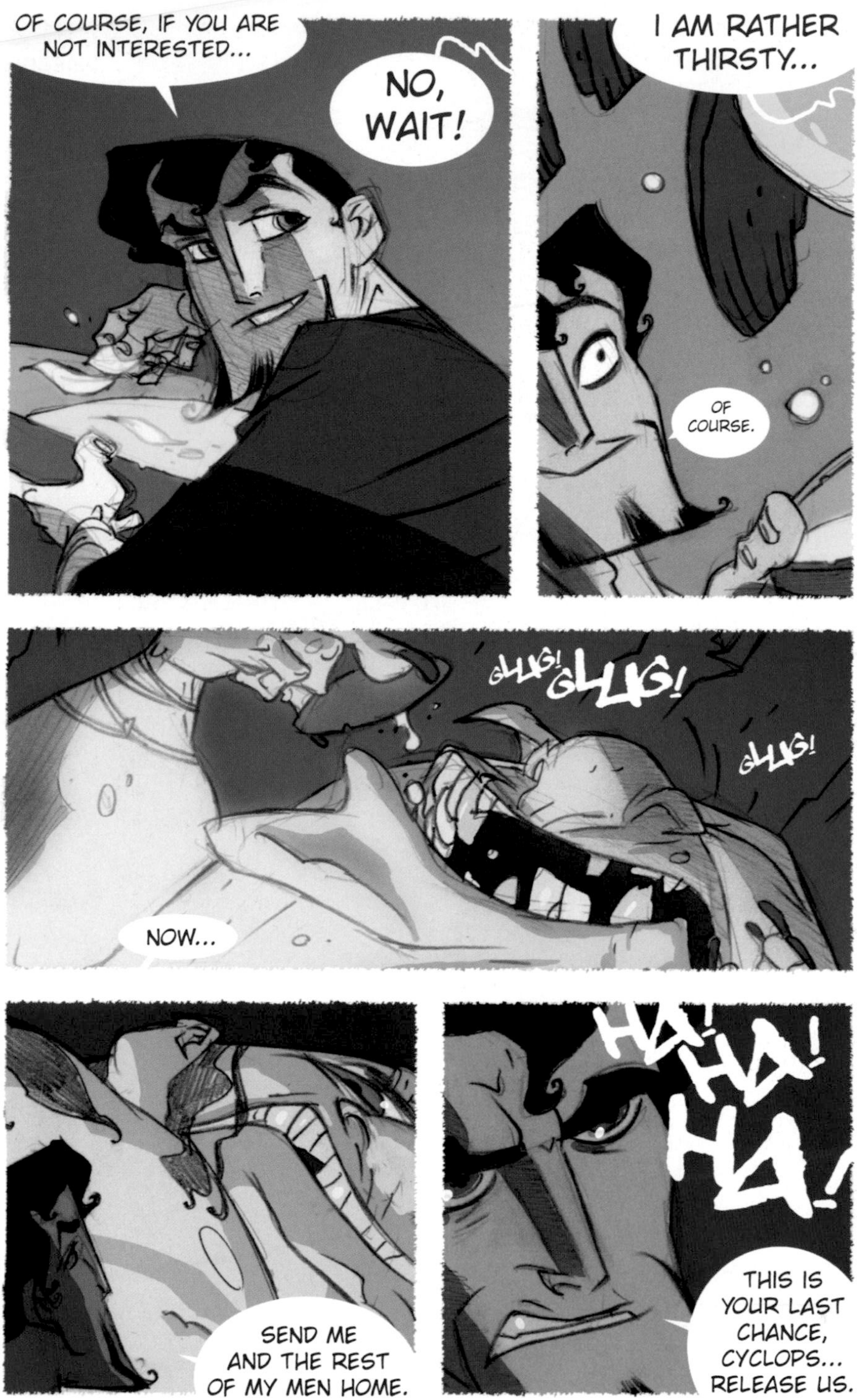

OF COURSE, IF YOU ARE NOT INTERESTED...
NO, WAIT!
I AM RATHER THIRSTY...
OF COURSE.
GLUG! GLUG!
GLUG!
NOW...
SEND ME AND THE REST OF MY MEN HOME.
HA! HA! HA!
THIS IS YOUR LAST CHANCE, CYCLOPS... RELEASE US.

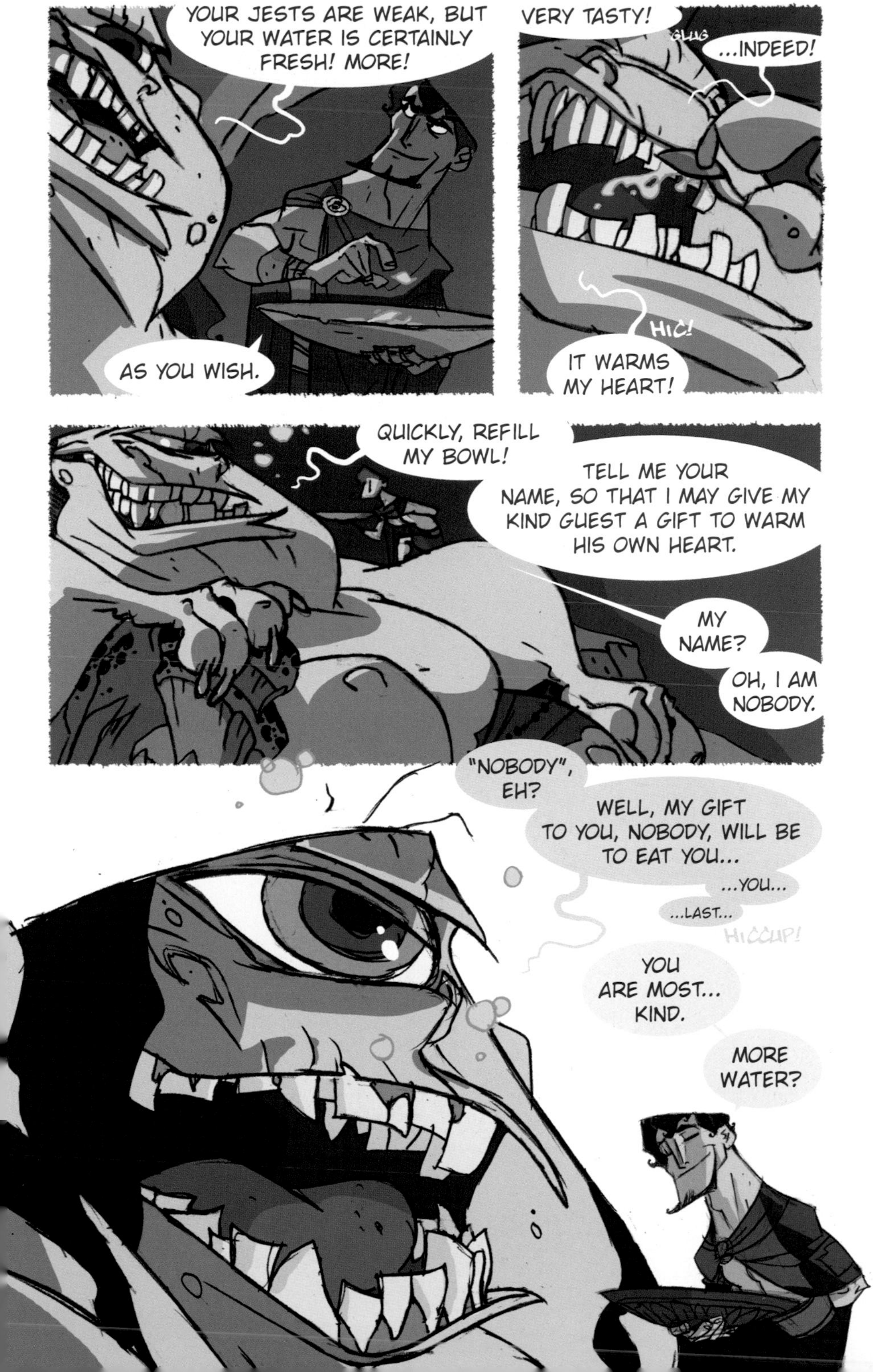
YOUR JESTS ARE WEAK, BUT YOUR WATER IS CERTAINLY FRESH! MORE!
AS YOU WISH.
VERY TASTY!
GLUG
...INDEED!
HIC!
IT WARMS MY HEART!
QUICKLY, REFILL MY BOWL!
TELL ME YOUR NAME, SO THAT I MAY GIVE MY KIND GUEST A GIFT TO WARM HIS OWN HEART.
MY NAME?
OH, I AM NOBODY.
"NOBODY", EH?
WELL, MY GIFT TO YOU, NOBODY, WILL BE TO EAT YOU...
...YOU...
...LAST...
HICCUP!
YOU ARE MOST... KIND.
MORE WATER?

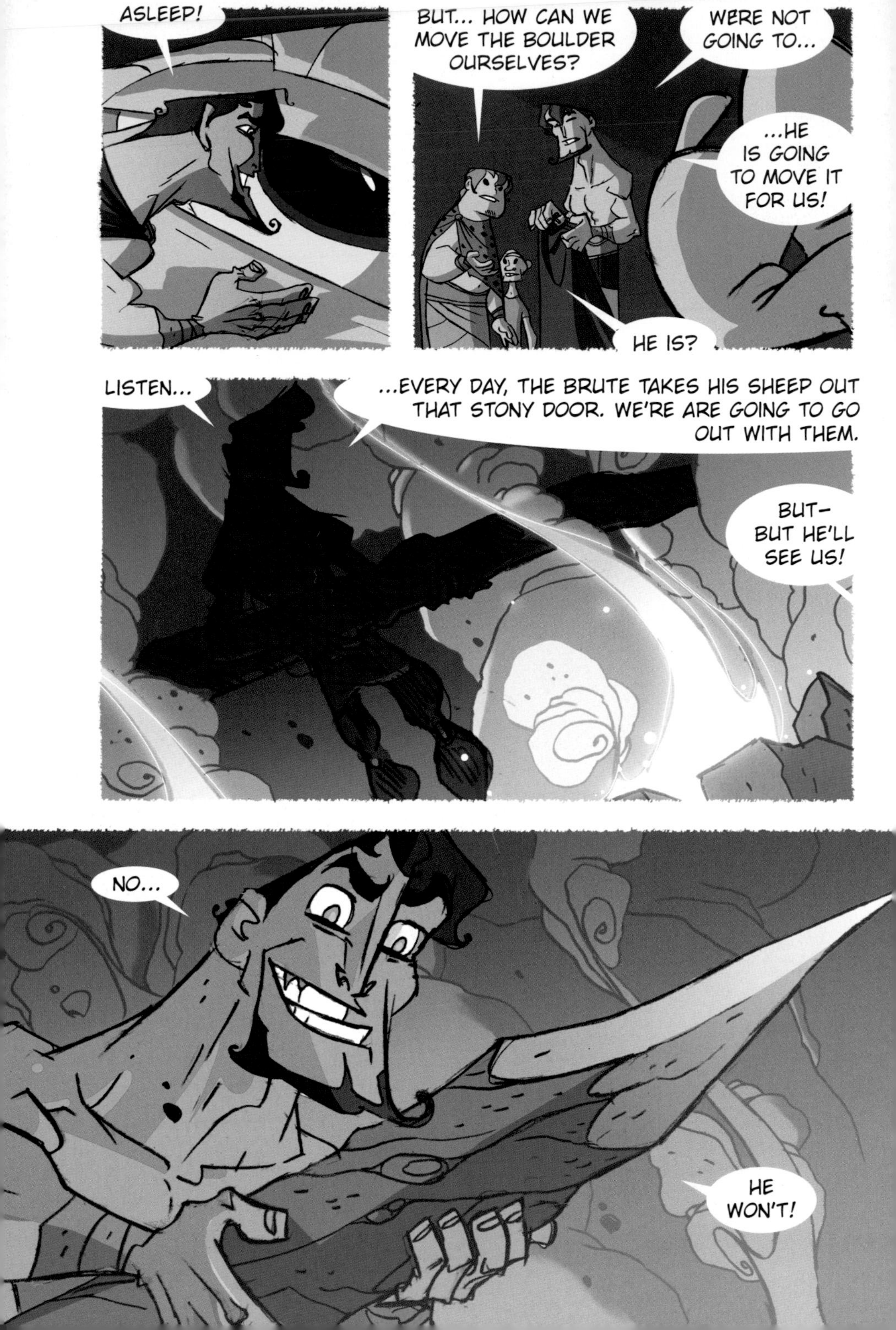
ASLEEP!
BUT... HOW CAN WE MOVE THE BOULDER OURSELVES?
WERE NOT GOING TO...
...HE IS GOING TO MOVE IT FOR US!
HE IS?
LISTEN...
...EVERY DAY, THE BRUTE TAKES HIS SHEEP OUT THAT STONY DOOR. WE'RE ARE GOING TO GO OUT WITH THEM.
BUT-BUT HE'LL SEE US!
NO...
HE WON'T!

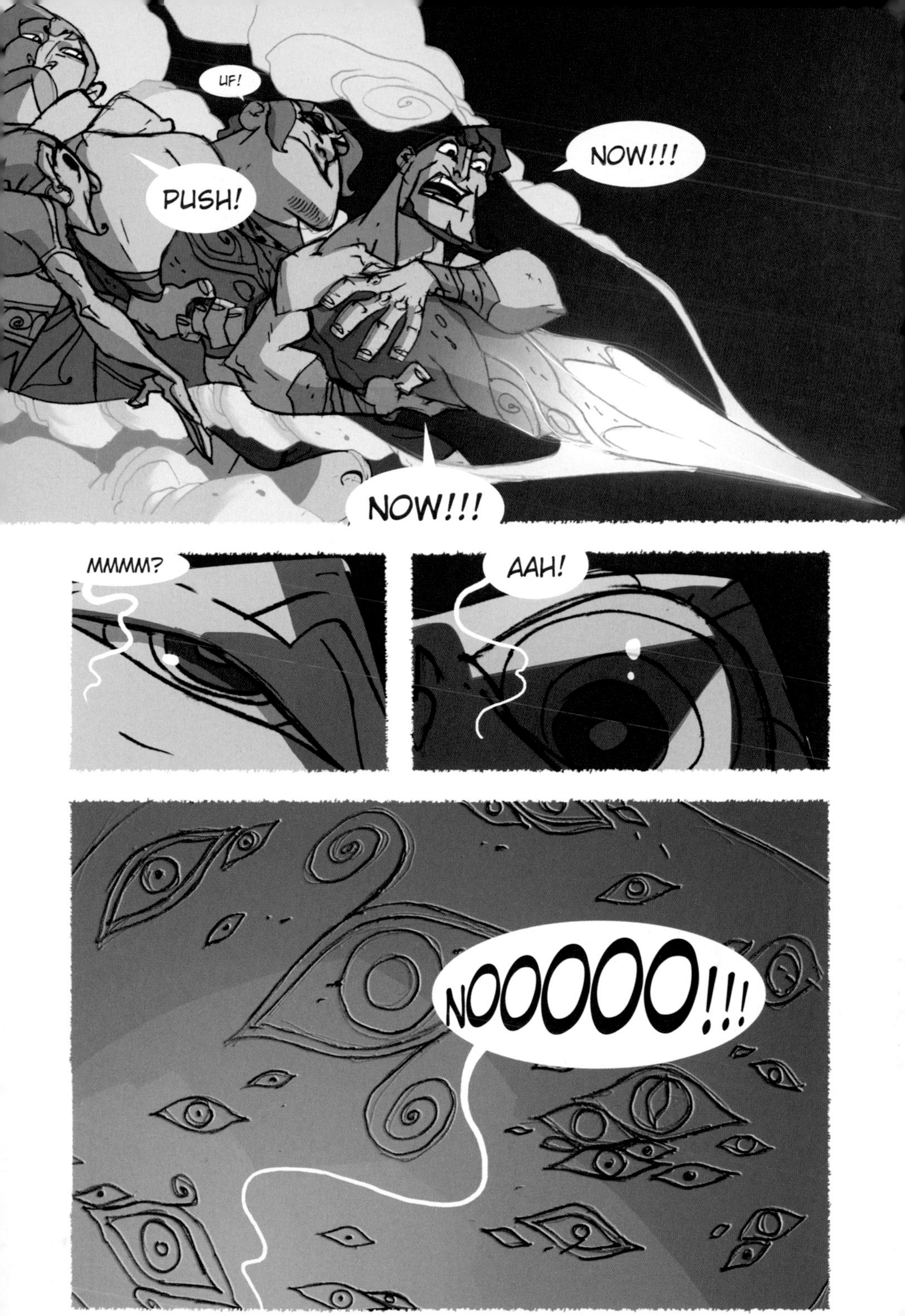

UF!
PUSH!
NOW!!!
NOW!!!
MMMM?
AAH!
NOOOOO!!!

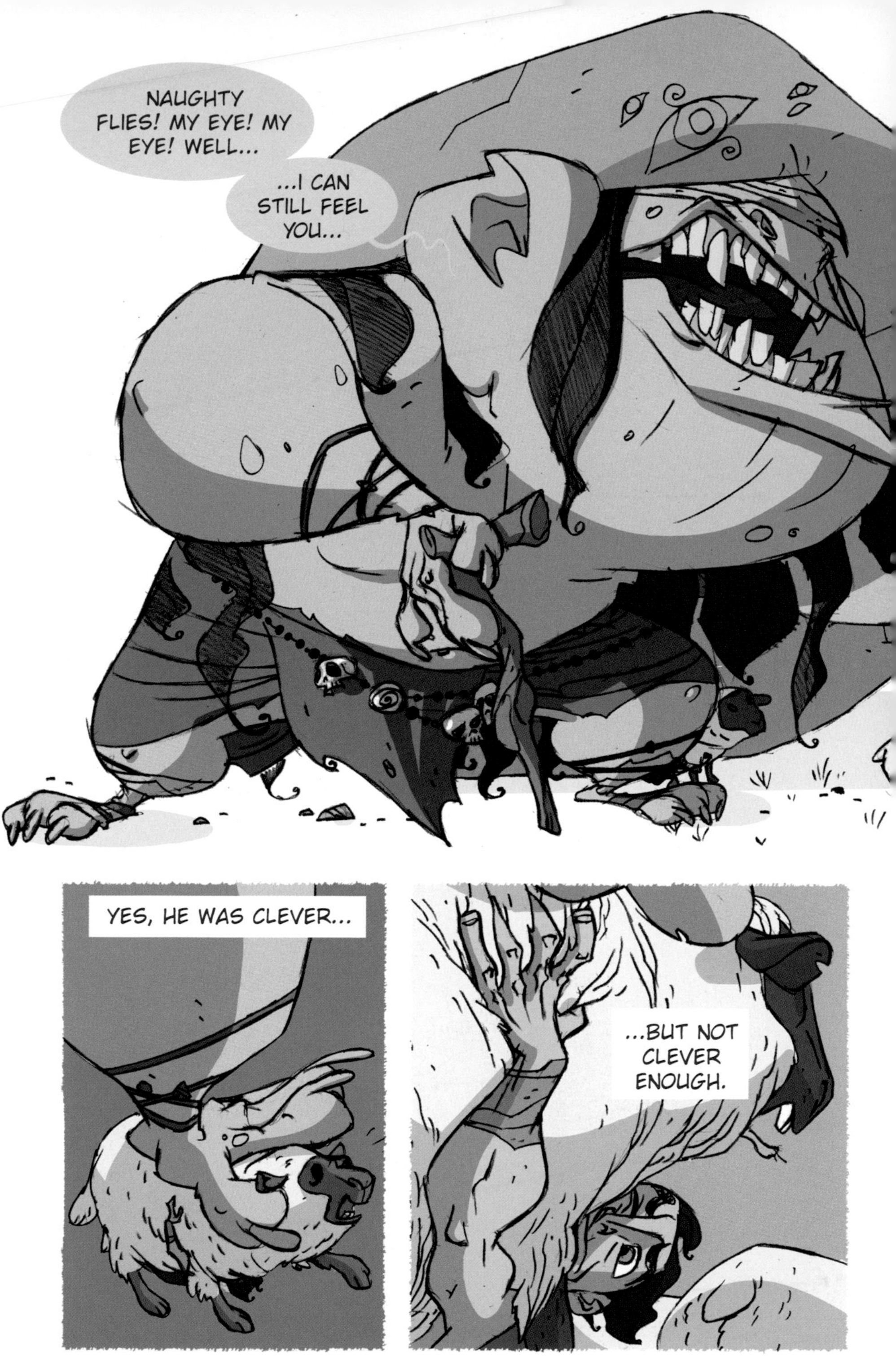
NAUGHTY FLIES! MY EYE! MY EYE! WELL...
...I CAN STILL FEEL YOU...
YES, HE WAS CLEVER...
...BUT NOT CLEVER ENOUGH.

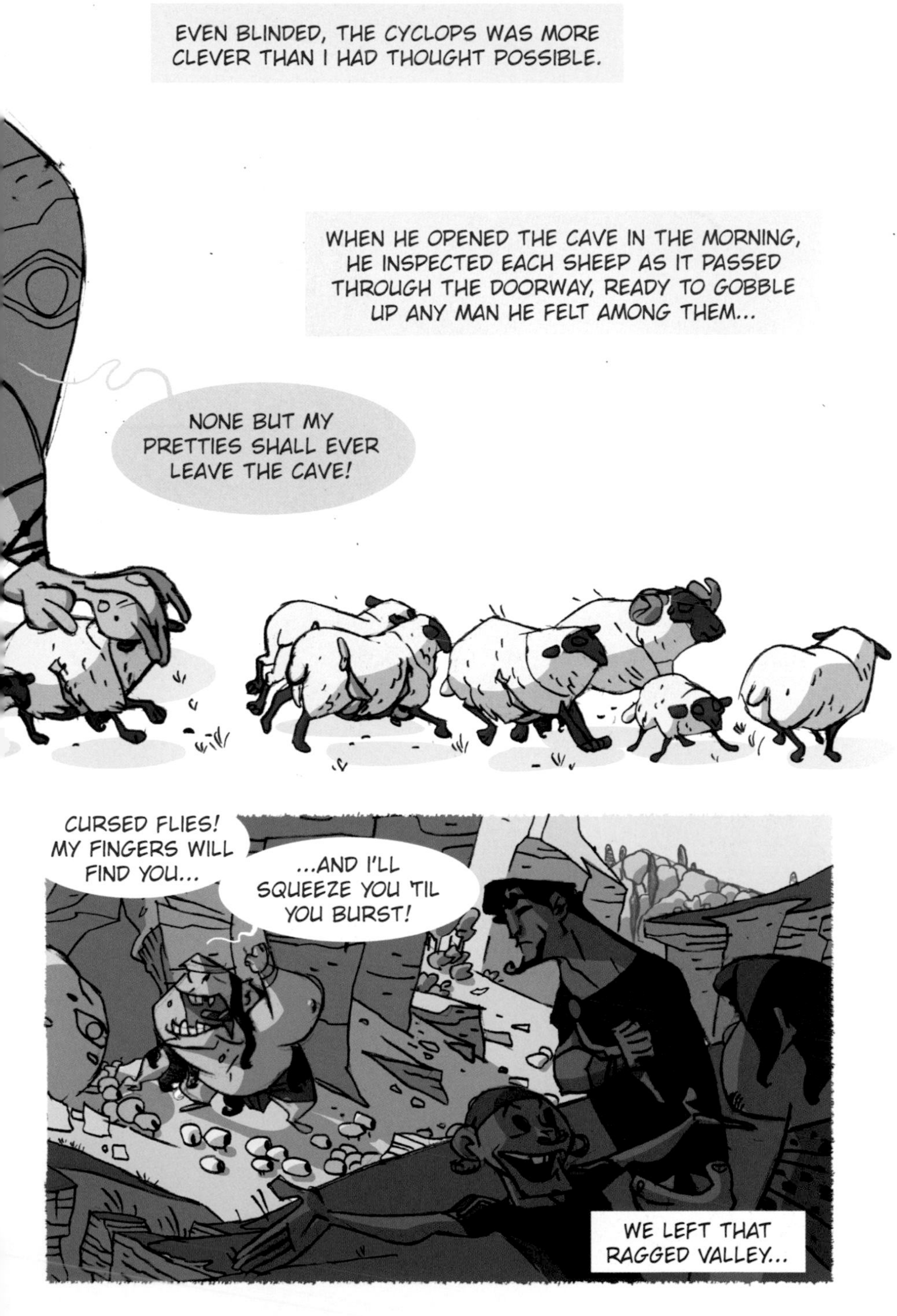
EVEN BLINDED, THE CYCLOPS WAS MORE CLEVER THAN I HAD THOUGHT POSSIBLE.
WHEN HE OPENED THE CAVE IN THE MORNING, HE INSPECTED EACH SHEEP AS IT PASSED THROUGH THE DOORWAY, READY TO GOBBLE UP ANY MAN HE FELT AMONG THEM...
NONE BUT MY PRETTIES SHALL EVER LEAVE THE CAVE!
CURSED FLIES! MY FINGERS WILL FIND YOU...
...AND I'LL SQUEEZE YOU 'TIL YOU BURST!
WE LEFT THAT RAGGED VALLEY...

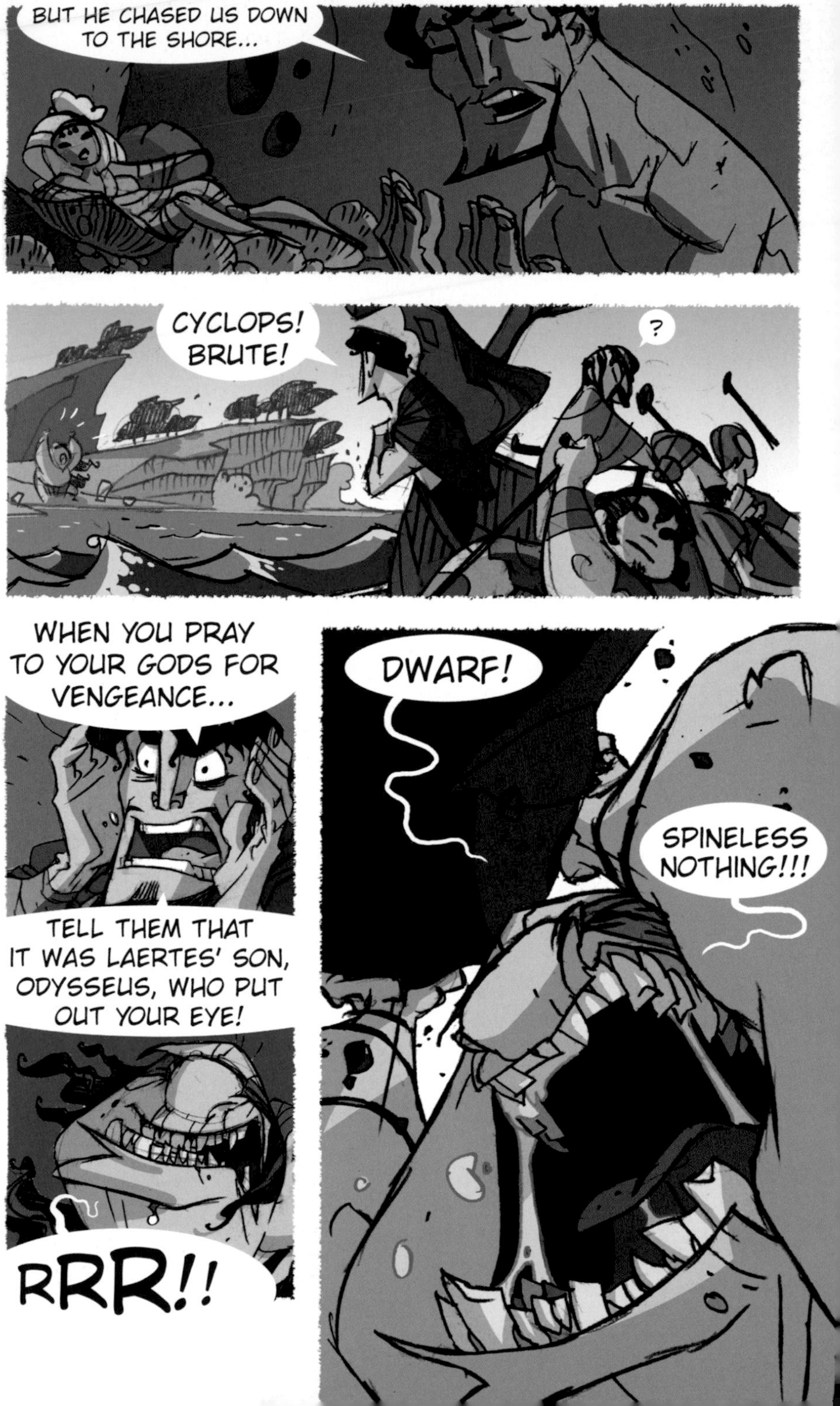
BUT HE CHASED US DOWN TO THE SHORE...
CYCLOPS! BRUTE!
?
WHEN YOU PRAY TO YOUR GODS FOR VENGEANCE...
TELL THEM THAT IT WAS LAERTES' SON, ODYSSEUS, WHO PUT OUT YOUR EYE!
RRR!!
DWARF!
SPINELESS NOTHING!!!

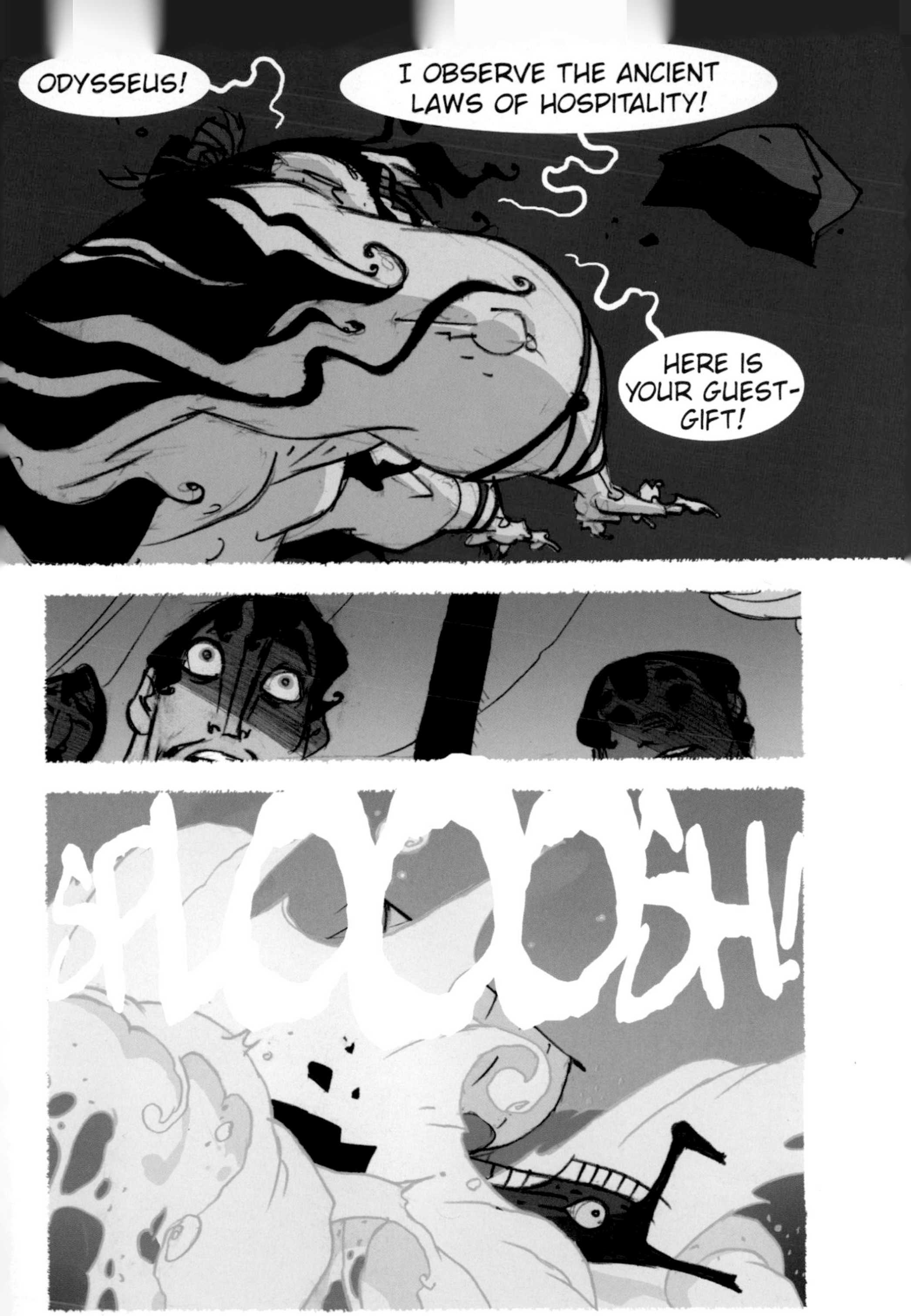
ODYSSEUS!
I OBSERVE THE ANCIENT LAWS OF HOSPITALITY!
HERE IS YOUR GUEST-GIFT!
SPLOOOOSH!

HFF!

PLEASE, OLD FRIEND, BE CALM! YOUR TRICKS HAVE SAVED US ONCE AGAIN...DO NOT TEMPT FATE WITH YOUR RECKLESS INSULTS!

WOO!

FIVE OF MY MEN WILL NEVER SEE THEIR WIVES AND CHILDREN AGAIN...NOT UNTIL THEY ARE REUNITED IN THE SHADE OF HADES. THAT THING IS LUCKY I ONLY TOOK HIS EYE...

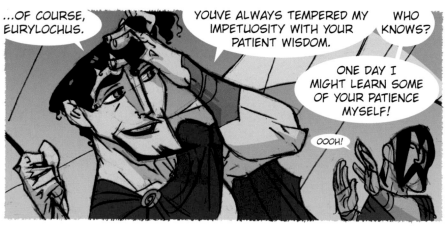

...OF COURSE, EURYLOCHUS.

YOU'VE ALWAYS TEMPERED MY IMPETUOSITY WITH YOUR PATIENT WISDOM.

WHO KNOWS?

ONE DAY I MIGHT LEARN SOME OF YOUR PATIENCE MYSELF!

OOOH!

HA HA! I'VE KNOWN YOU SINCE YOU WERE A WET YOUTH, MY PRINCE...

...YOU'LL NEVER LEARN PATIENCE!

HA HA!

NO... PERHAPS NOT!

COWARD! FILTH! YOU MAY HAVE ESCAPED MY VENGEANCE...

...BUT YOU CAN'T ESCAPE MY FATHER!

HEAR ME, FATHER! HEAR ME, O POSEIDON, GOD OF THE SEA-BLUE MANE, WHO ROCKS THE EARTH!

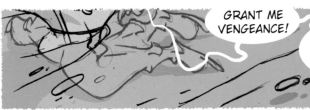

GRANT ME VENGEANCE!

GRANT ME THAT ODYSSEUS, RAIDER AND COWARD, FINDS NO PEACE...

...NO REST...

...THAT ALL HE LOVES IS DESTROYED OR LOST...

...UNTIL HE HAS SUFFERED AS I SUFFER!

...

YOUR PLEAS ARE HEARD, MY SON...

HEARD AND ANSWERED...

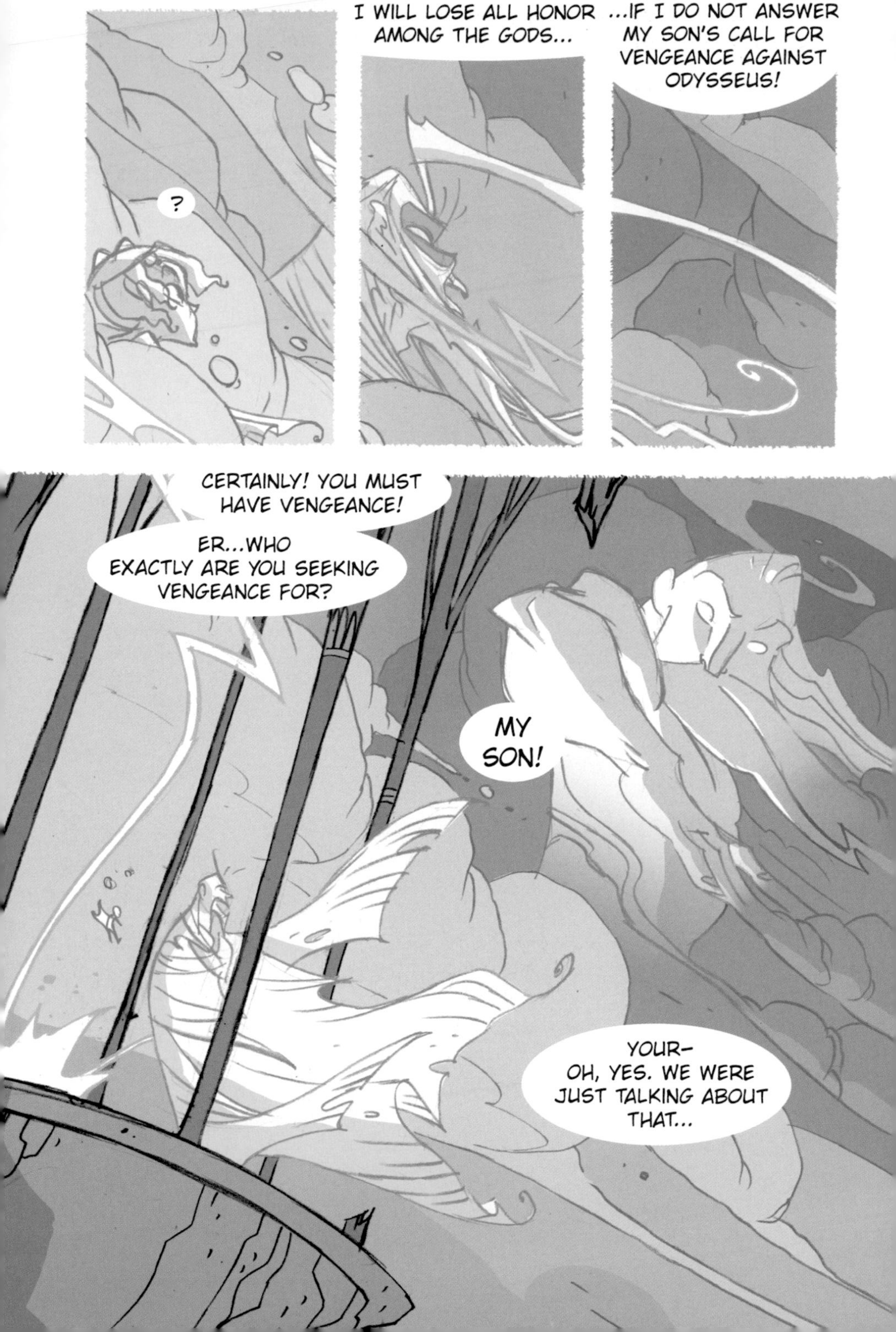
?
I WILL LOSE ALL HONOR AMONG THE GODS...
...IF I DO NOT ANSWER MY SON'S CALL FOR VENGEANCE AGAINST ODYSSEUS!
CERTAINLY! YOU MUST HAVE VENGEANCE!
ER...WHO EXACTLY ARE YOU SEEKING VENGEANCE FOR?
MY SON!
YOUR— OH, YES. WE WERE JUST TALKING ABOUT THAT...

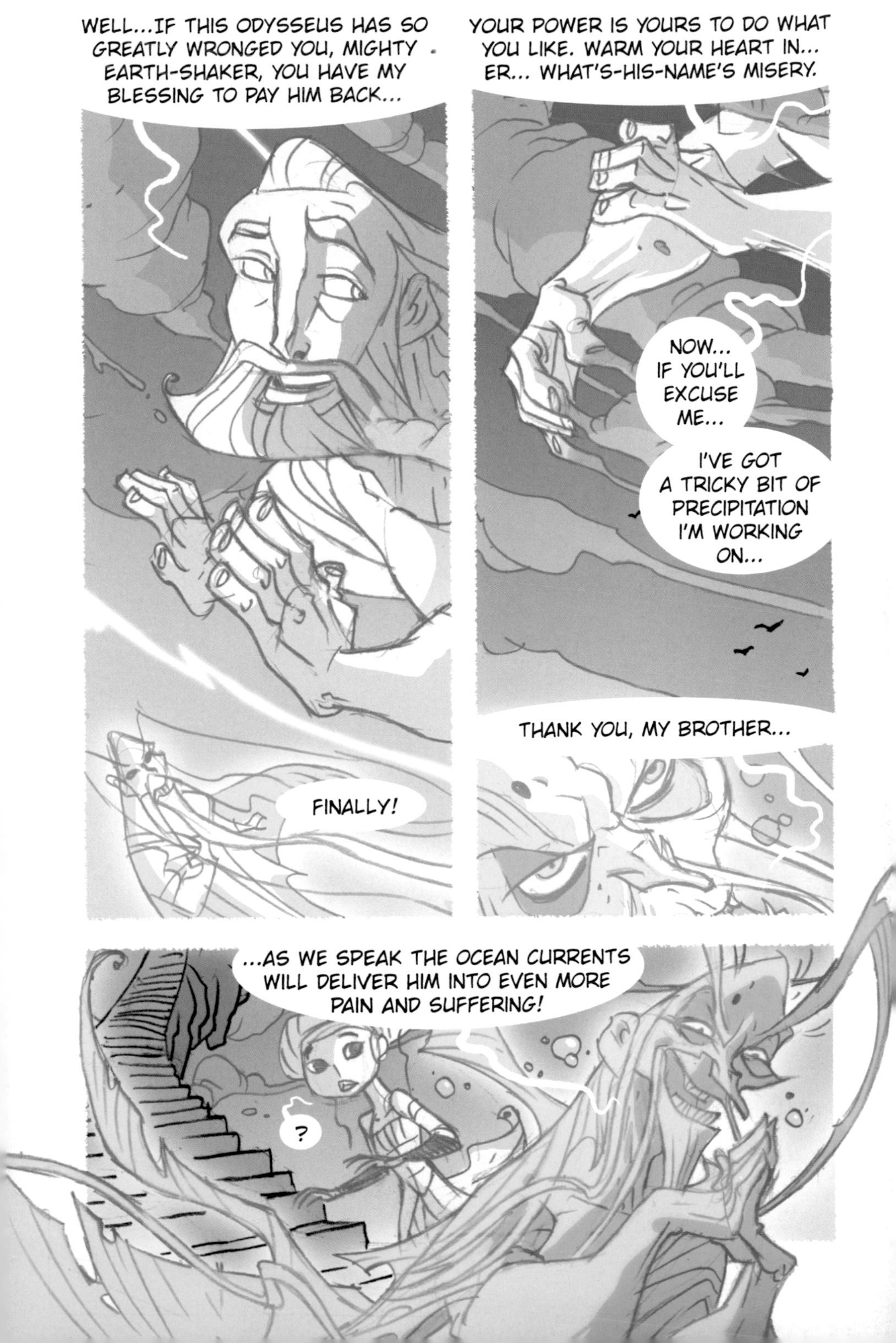
WELL...IF THIS ODYSSEUS HAS SO GREATLY WRONGED YOU, MIGHTY EARTH-SHAKER, YOU HAVE MY BLESSING TO PAY HIM BACK...
YOUR POWER IS YOURS TO DO WHAT YOU LIKE. WARM YOUR HEART IN... ER... WHAT'S-HIS-NAME'S MISERY.
NOW... IF YOU'LL EXCUSE ME...
I'VE GOT A TRICKY BIT OF PRECIPITATION I'M WORKING ON...
FINALLY!
THANK YOU, MY BROTHER...
...AS WE SPEAK THE OCEAN CURRENTS WILL DELIVER HIM INTO EVEN MORE PAIN AND SUFFERING!
?

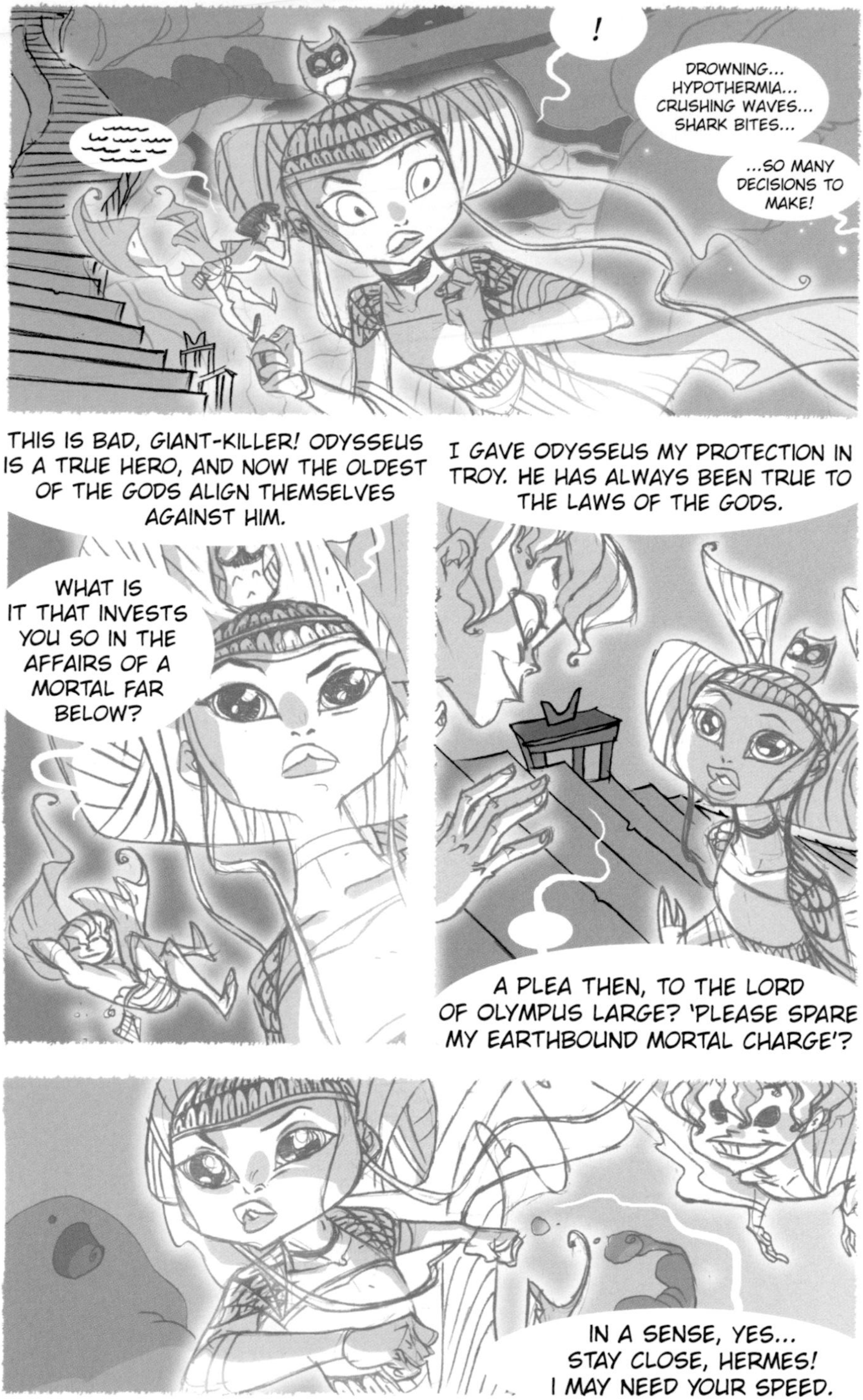
!
DROWNING... HYPOTHERMIA... CRUSHING WAVES... SHARK BITES...
...SO MANY DECISIONS TO MAKE!
THIS IS BAD, GIANT-KILLER! ODYSSEUS IS A TRUE HERO, AND NOW THE OLDEST OF THE GODS ALIGN THEMSELVES AGAINST HIM.
WHAT IS IT THAT INVESTS YOU SO IN THE AFFAIRS OF A MORTAL FAR BELOW?
I GAVE ODYSSEUS MY PROTECTION IN TROY. HE HAS ALWAYS BEEN TRUE TO THE LAWS OF THE GODS.
A PLEA THEN, TO THE LORD OF OLYMPUS LARGE? 'PLEASE SPARE MY EARTHBOUND MORTAL CHARGE'?
IN A SENSE, YES... STAY CLOSE, HERMES! I MAY NEED YOUR SPEED.

FATHER! I SEEK AN AUDIENCE!

FATHER!

EH?

OH...ATHENA!

FATHER! I—

SHH!!! NOT SO LOUD, MY DEAR...YOUR UNCLE IS STORMING AROUND IN A FOUL MOOD, WON'T LET ME WORK ON MY NEW CLOUDS...

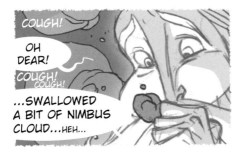

COUGH!

OH DEAR!

COUGH!
COUGH!

...SWALLOWED A BIT OF NIMBUS CLOUD...HEH...

WHY HAVE YOU AGREED TO LAY THESE LOW PLOTS AGAINST ODYSSEUS? HE HAS NEVER NEGLECTED HIS SACRIFICES FOR YOU! WHY SET YOUR POWERS AGAINST HIM?

MY POWERS? CERTAINLY NOT!

ER...

...WHO IS ODYSSEUS?

FATHER! YOU WERE JUST...TALKING...ABOUT...HIM!

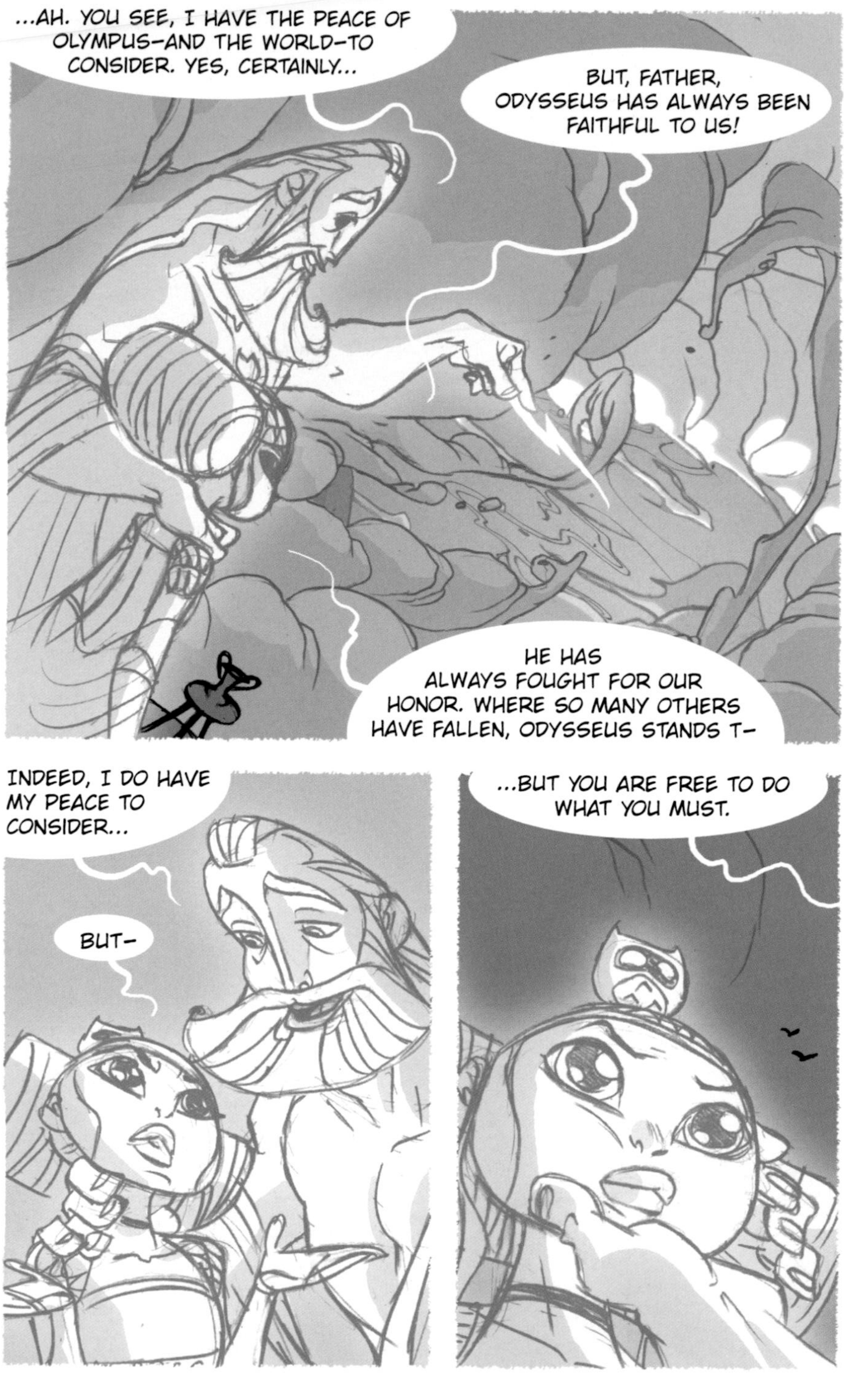
...AH. YOU SEE, I HAVE THE PEACE OF OLYMPUS—AND THE WORLD—TO CONSIDER. YES, CERTAINLY...
BUT, FATHER, ODYSSEUS HAS ALWAYS BEEN FAITHFUL TO US!
HE HAS ALWAYS FOUGHT FOR OUR HONOR. WHERE SO MANY OTHERS HAVE FALLEN, ODYSSEUS STANDS T-
INDEED, I DO HAVE MY PEACE TO CONSIDER...
BUT-
...BUT YOU ARE FREE TO DO WHAT YOU MUST.

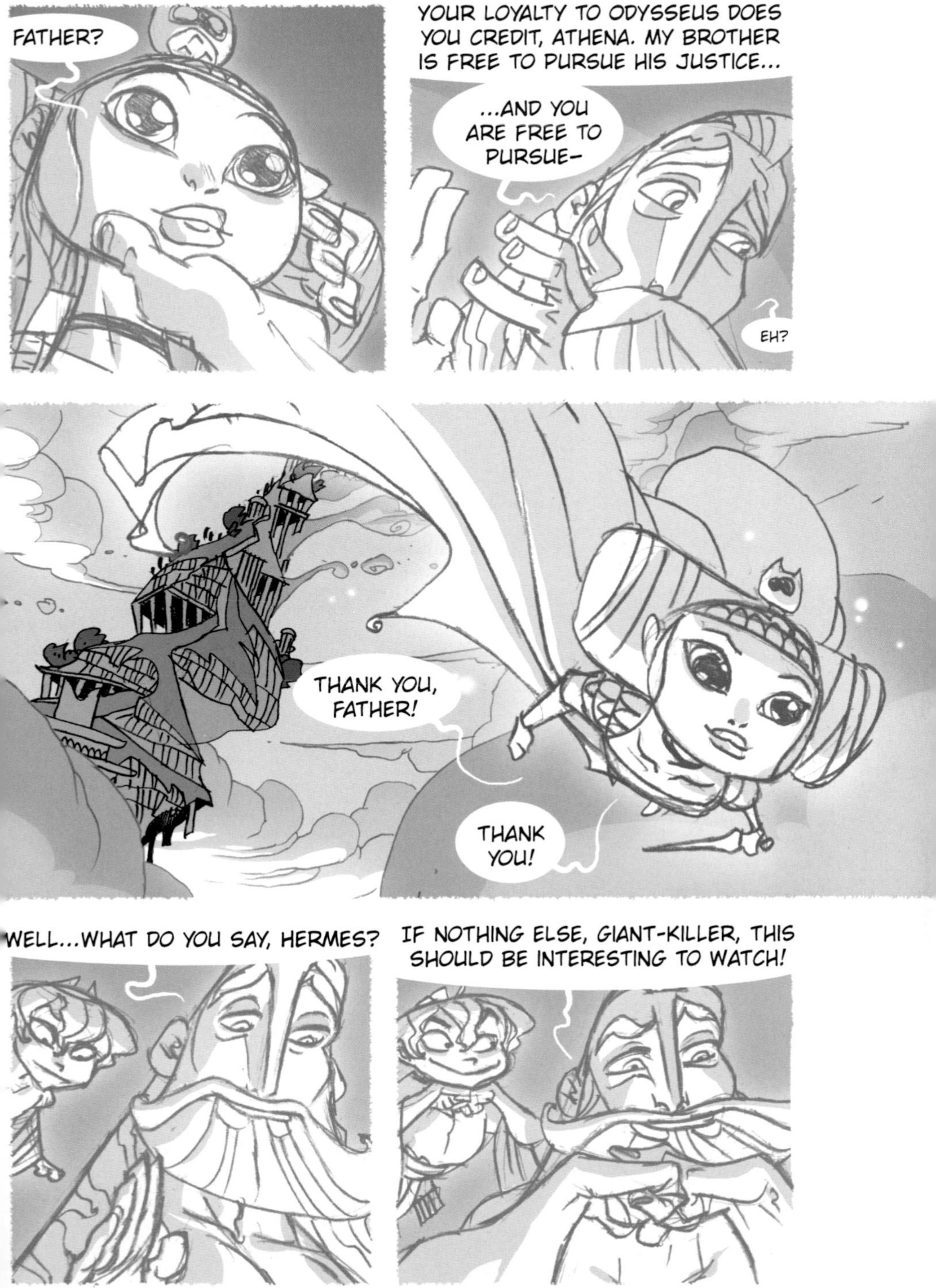
FATHER?
YOUR LOYALTY TO ODYSSEUS DOES YOU CREDIT, ATHENA. MY BROTHER IS FREE TO PURSUE HIS JUSTICE...
...AND YOU ARE FREE TO PURSUE-
EH?
THANK YOU, FATHER!
THANK YOU!
WELL...WHAT DO YOU SAY, HERMES?
IF NOTHING ELSE, GIANT-KILLER, THIS SHOULD BE INTERESTING TO WATCH!

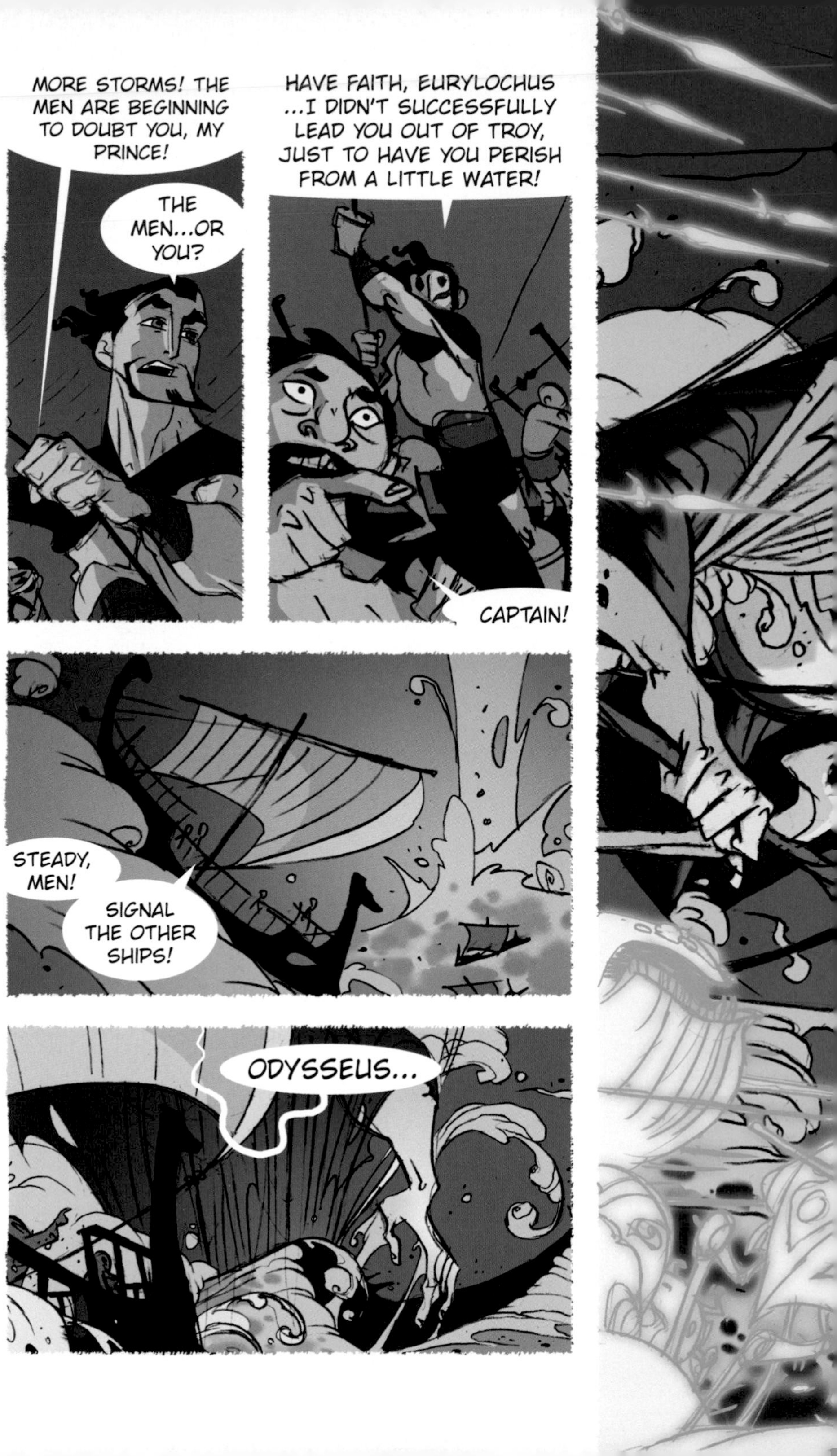
MORE STORMS! THE MEN ARE BEGINNING TO DOUBT YOU, MY PRINCE!
THE MEN...OR YOU?
HAVE FAITH, EURYLOCHUS ...I DIDN'T SUCCESSFULLY LEAD YOU OUT OF TROY, JUST TO HAVE YOU PERISH FROM A LITTLE WATER!
CAPTAIN!
STEADY, MEN!
SIGNAL THE OTHER SHIPS!
ODYSSEUS...

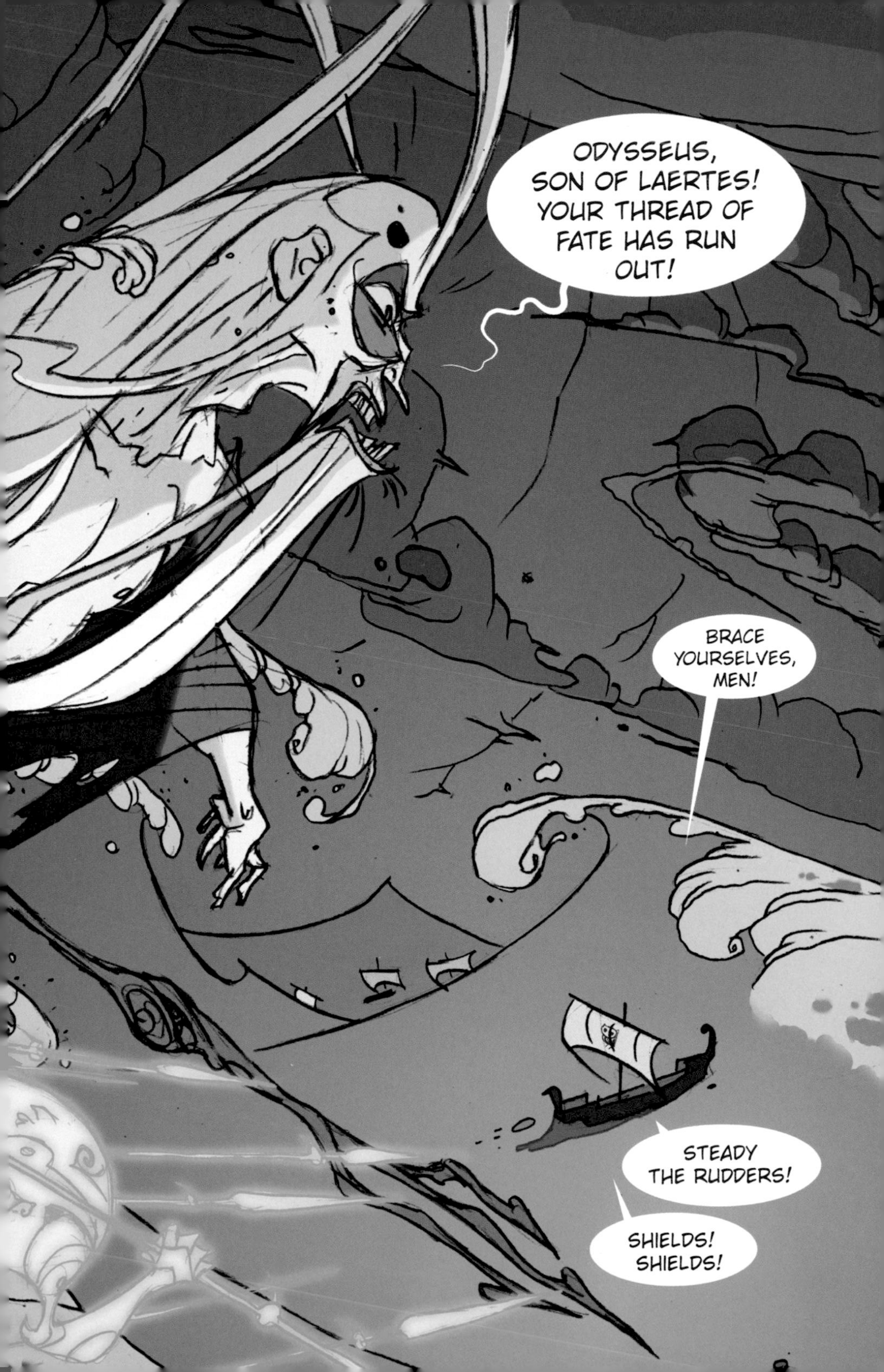

ODYSSEUS, SON OF LAERTES! YOUR THREAD OF FATE HAS RUN OUT!
BRACE YOURSELVES, MEN!
STEADY THE RUDDERS!
SHIELDS! SHIELDS!

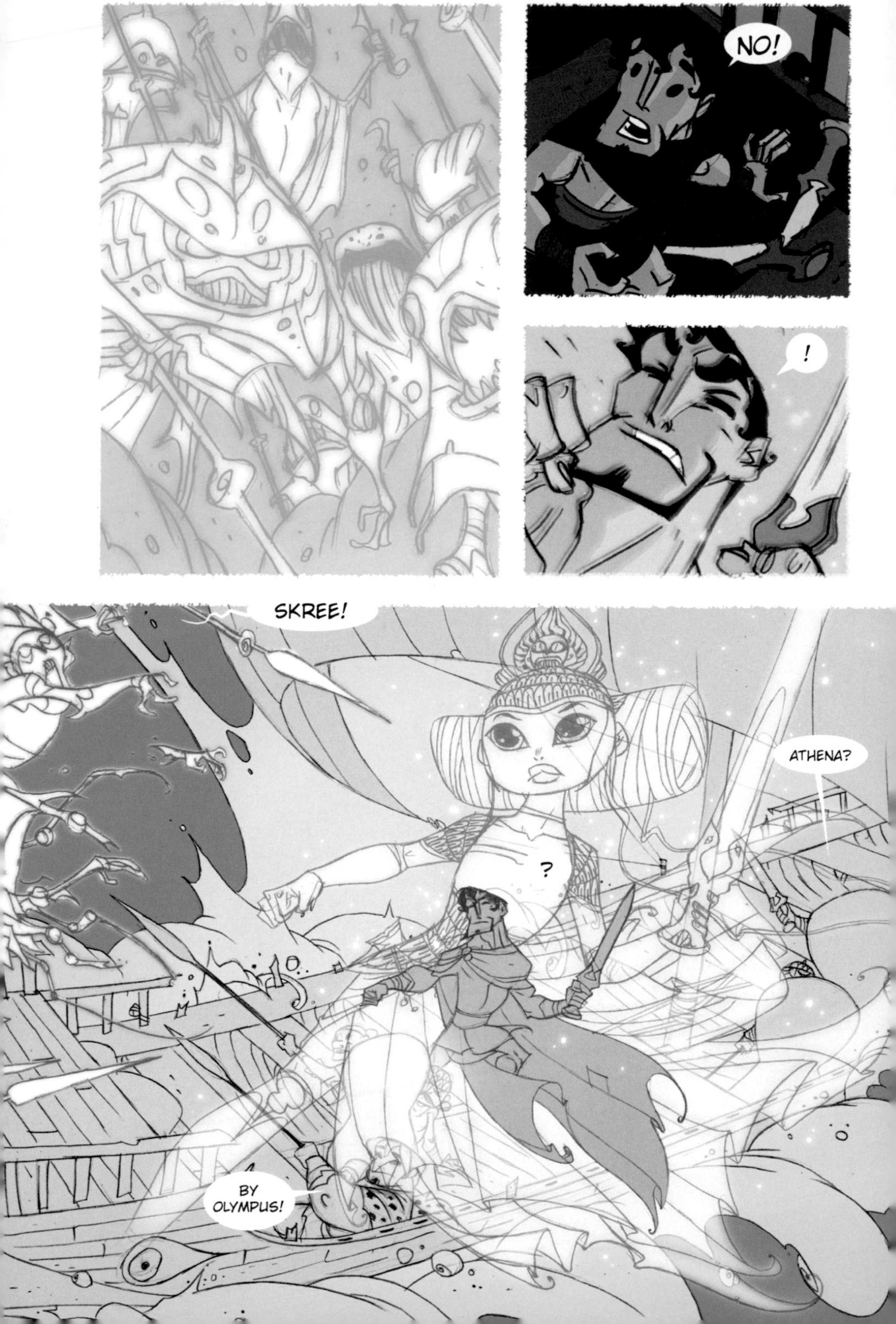
NO!
!
SKREE!
ATHENA?
?
BY OLYMPUS!

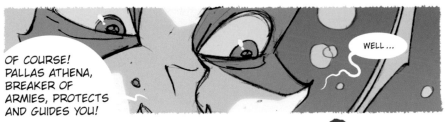

WELL...

OF COURSE! PALLAS ATHENA, BREAKER OF ARMIES, PROTECTS AND GUIDES YOU!

...IF I CANNOT HAVE YOUR LIFE, THEN I WILL TAKE ALL ALL THAT YOU LOVE!

WHOOOSH!

YOUR MEN AND SHIPS ARE FORFEIT, O PRINCE OF ITHACA...

NOOO!

...AND YOU WILL FIND EVEN THE WALLS OF YOUR OWN HOME SHUT UP AGAINST YOU!

HISS!

CRASH!

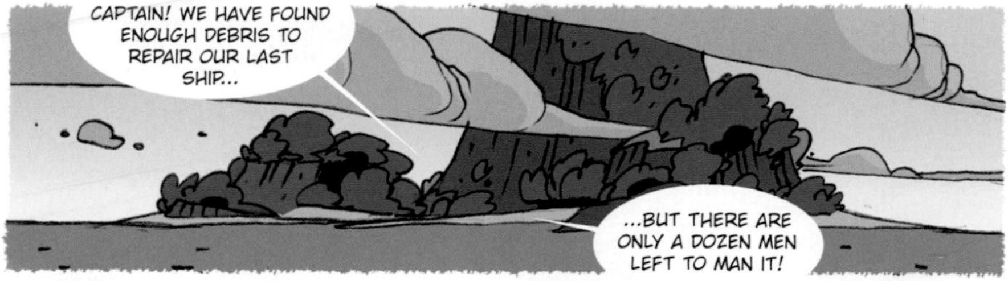
CAPTAIN! WE HAVE FOUND ENOUGH DEBRIS TO REPAIR OUR LAST SHIP...
...BUT THERE ARE ONLY A DOZEN MEN LEFT TO MAN IT!

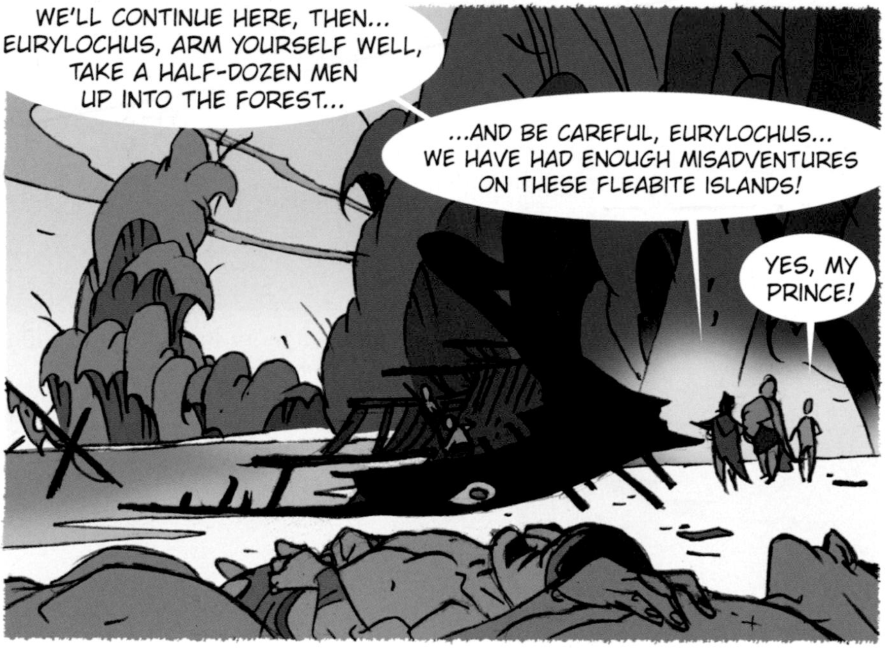
WE'LL CONTINUE HERE, THEN... EURYLOCHUS, ARM YOURSELF WELL, TAKE A HALF-DOZEN MEN UP INTO THE FOREST...
...AND BE CAREFUL, EURYLOCHUS... WE HAVE HAD ENOUGH MISADVENTURES ON THESE FLEABITE ISLANDS!
YES, MY PRINCE!

THERE MAY BE PEOPLE UP THERE, WITH MAPS AND CHARTS WE CAN USE TO FINALLY GET HOME.

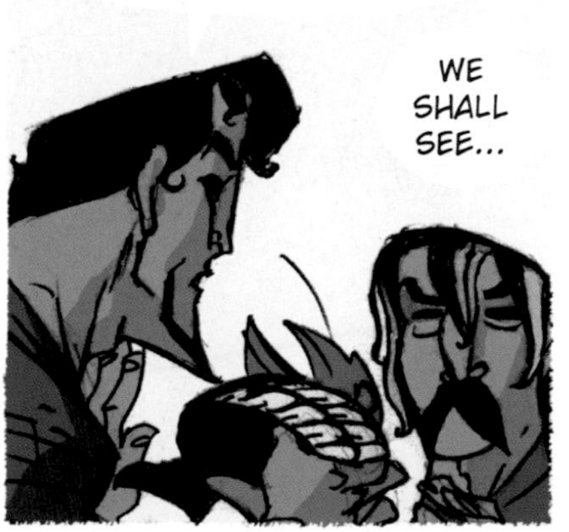
WE SHALL SEE...

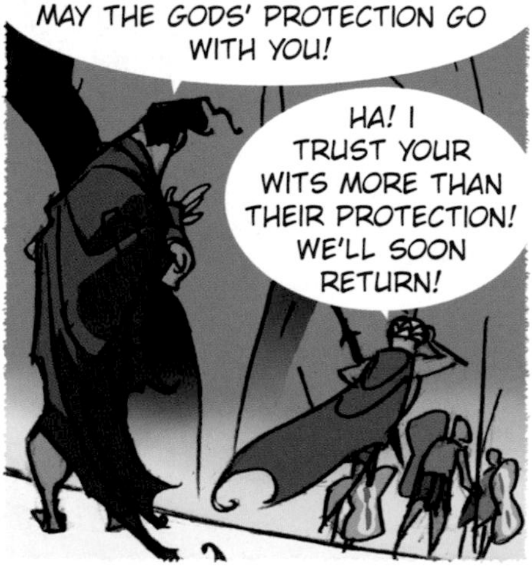
COURAGE, LORD EURYLOCHUS...AND MAY THE GODS' PROTECTION GO WITH YOU!
HA! I TRUST YOUR WITS MORE THAN THEIR PROTECTION! WE'LL SOON RETURN!

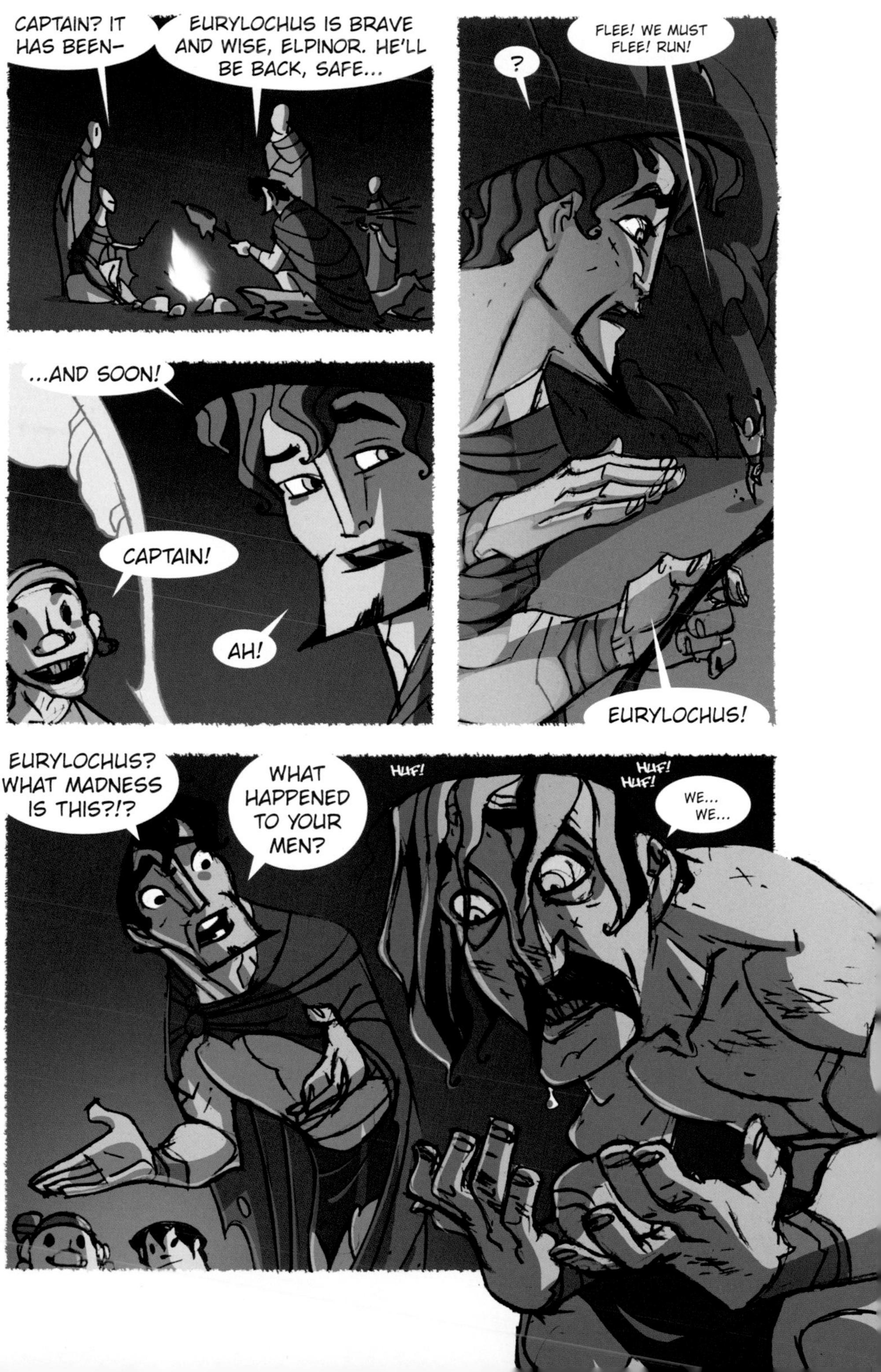
CAPTAIN? IT HAS BEEN–
EURYLOCHUS IS BRAVE AND WISE, ELPINOR. HE'LL BE BACK, SAFE...
...AND SOON!
CAPTAIN!
AH!
?
FLEE! WE MUST FLEE! RUN!
EURYLOCHUS!
EURYLOCHUS? WHAT MADNESS IS THIS?!?
WHAT HAPPENED TO YOUR MEN?
HUF!
HUF! HUF!
WE... WE...

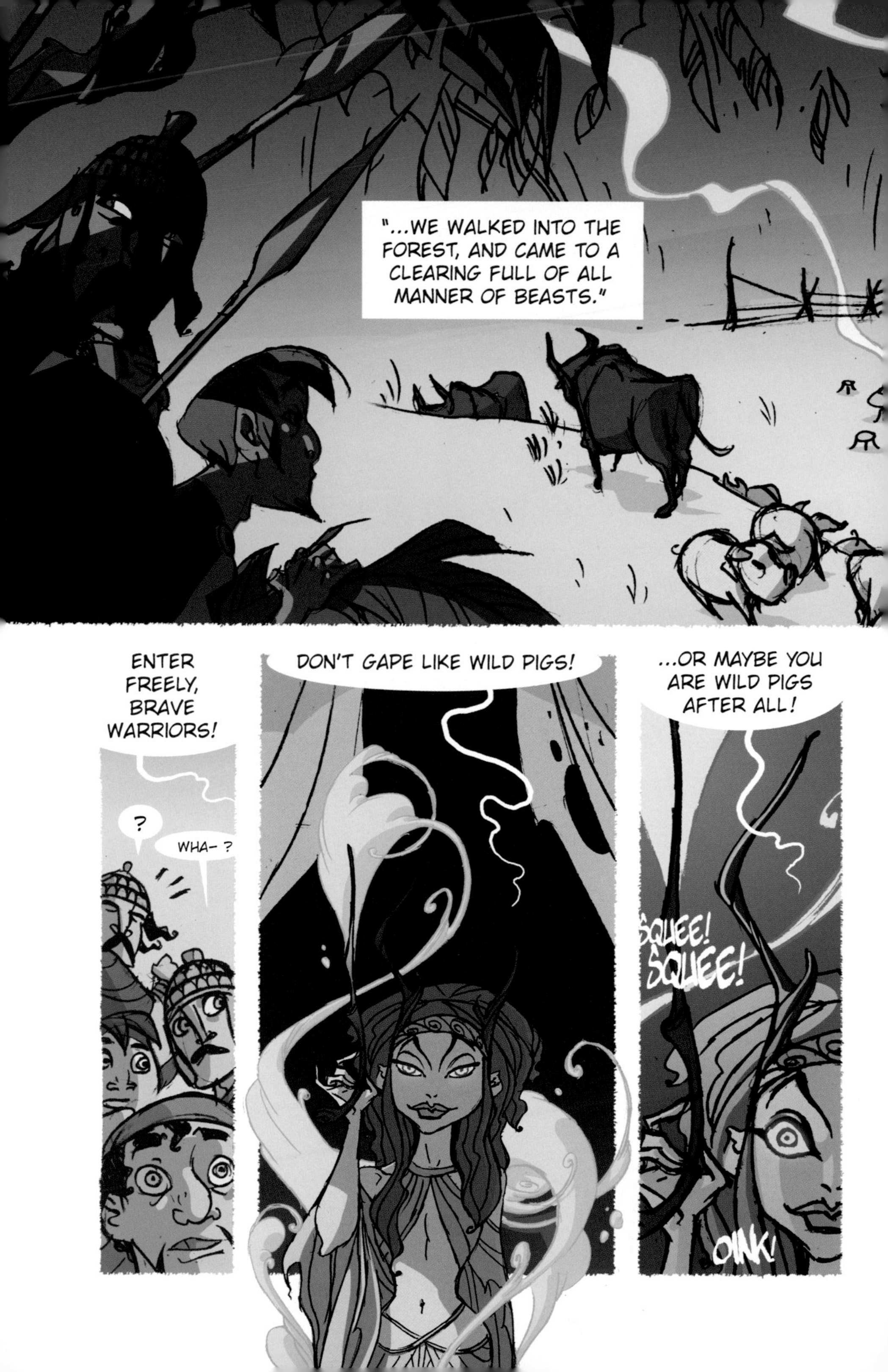
"...WE WALKED INTO THE FOREST, AND CAME TO A CLEARING FULL OF ALL MANNER OF BEASTS."
ENTER FREELY, BRAVE WARRIORS!
?
WHA- ?
DON'T GAPE LIKE WILD PIGS!
...OR MAYBE YOU ARE WILD PIGS AFTER ALL!
SQUEE! SQUEE!
OINK!

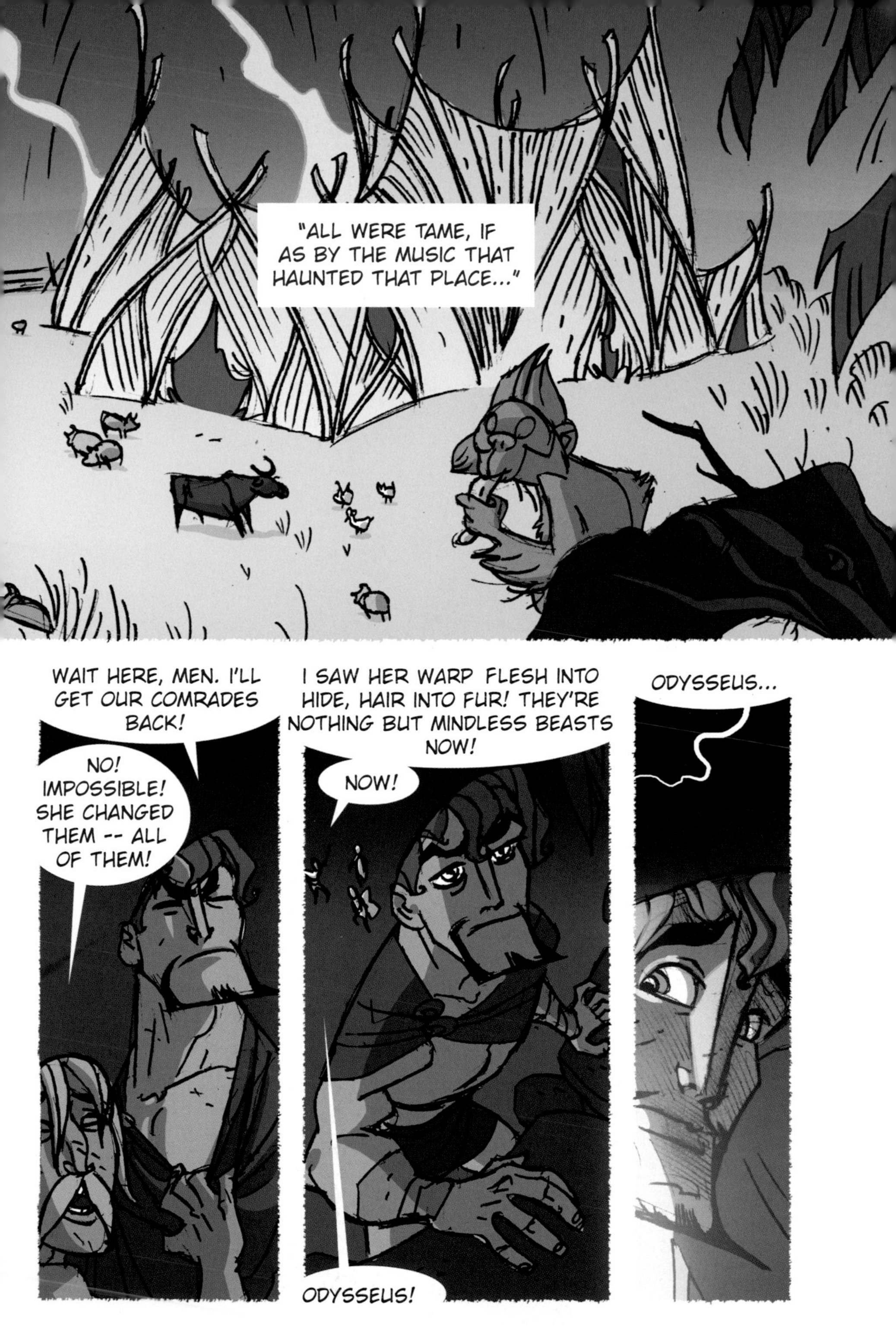
"ALL WERE TAME, IF AS BY THE MUSIC THAT HAUNTED THAT PLACE..."
WAIT HERE, MEN. I'LL GET OUR COMRADES BACK!
NO! IMPOSSIBLE! SHE CHANGED THEM -- ALL OF THEM!
I SAW HER WARP FLESH INTO HIDE, HAIR INTO FUR! THEY'RE NOTHING BUT MINDLESS BEASTS NOW!
NOW!
ODYSSEUS!
ODYSSEUS...

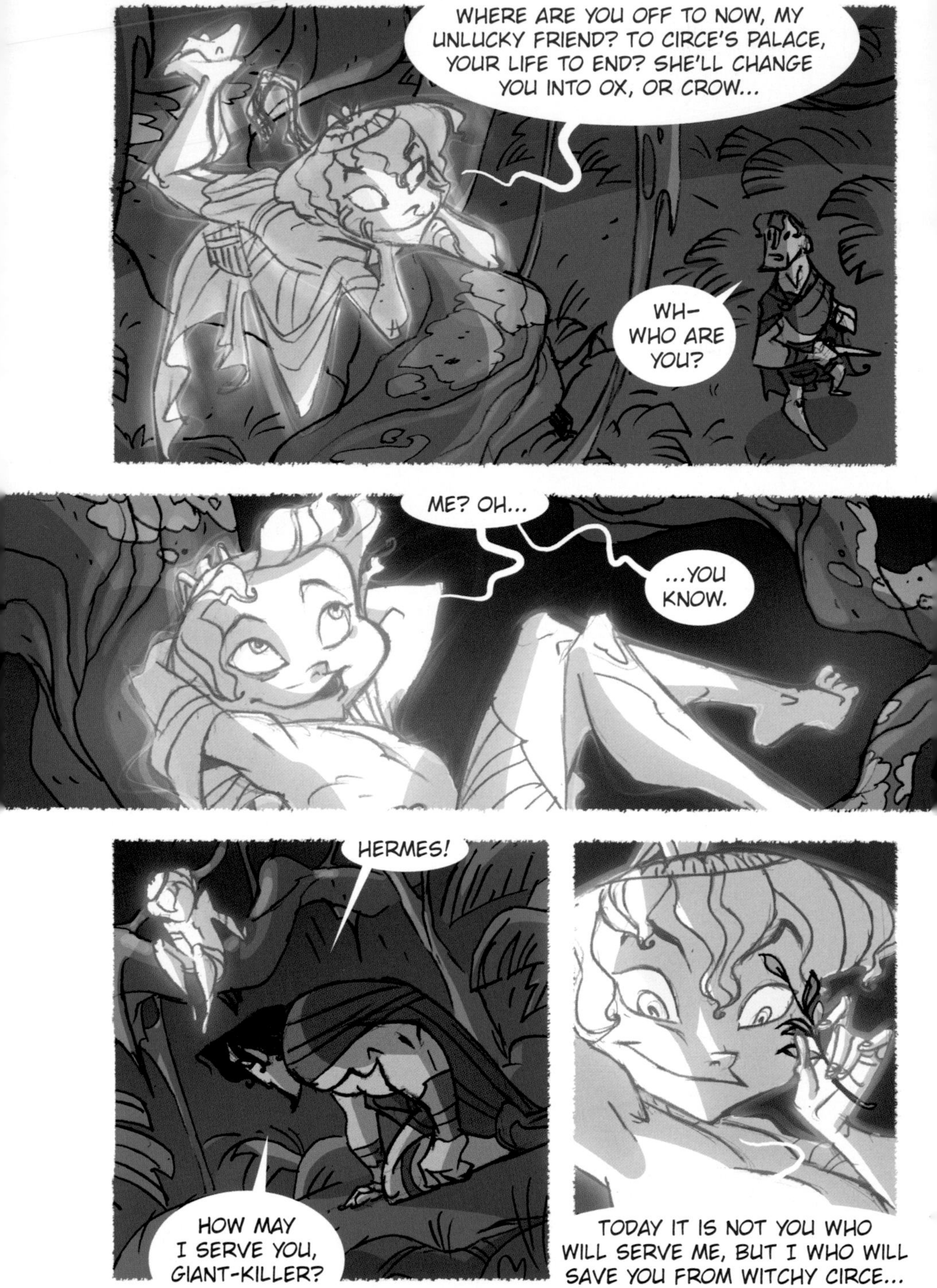
WHERE ARE YOU OFF TO NOW, MY UNLUCKY FRIEND? TO CIRCE'S PALACE, YOUR LIFE TO END? SHE'LL CHANGE YOU INTO OX, OR CROW...
WH- WHO ARE YOU?
ME? OH...
...YOU KNOW.
HERMES!
HOW MAY I SERVE YOU, GIANT-KILLER?
TODAY IT IS NOT YOU WHO WILL SERVE ME, BUT I WHO WILL SAVE YOU FROM WITCHY CIRCE...

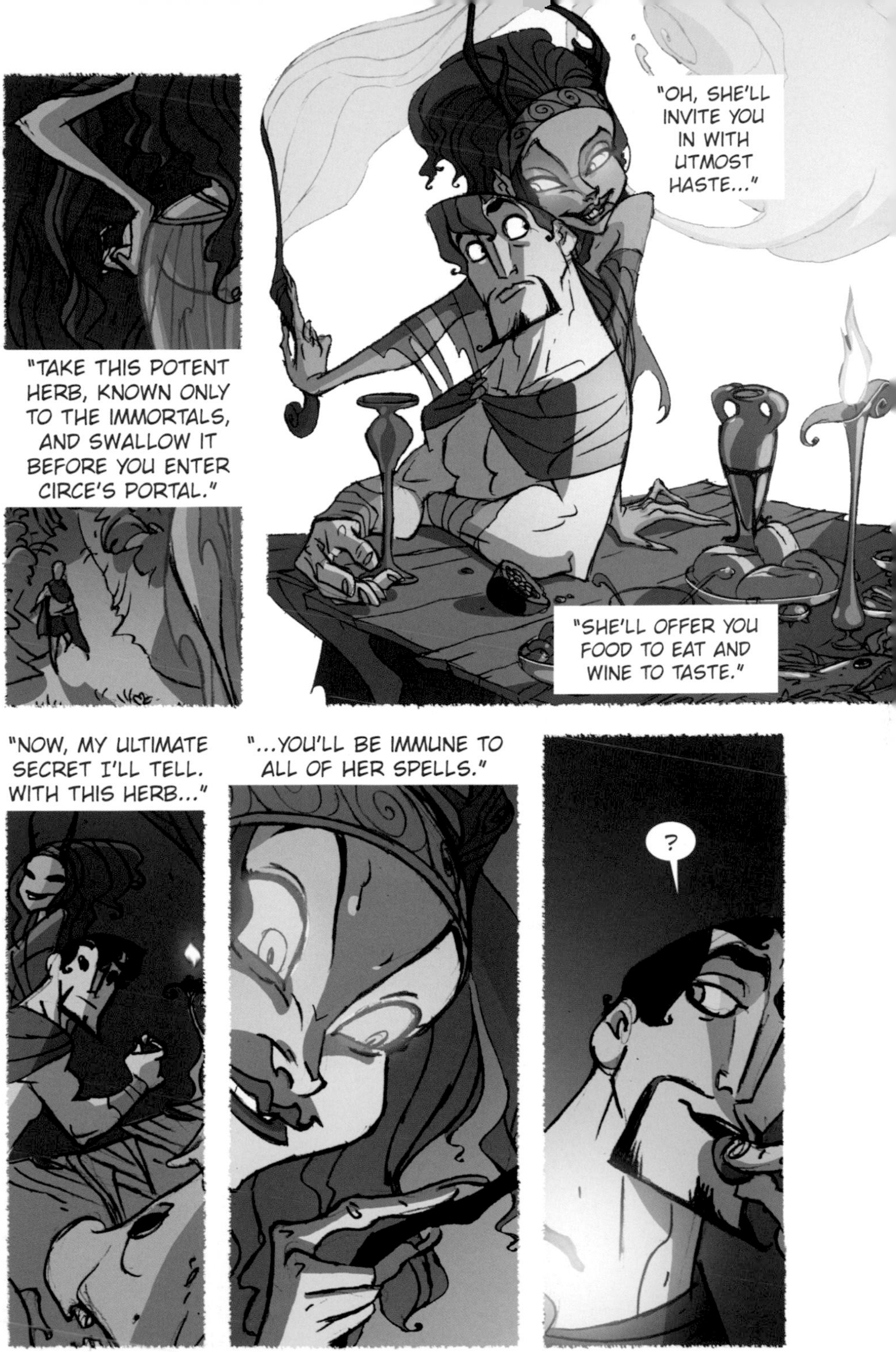
"OH, SHE'LL INVITE YOU IN WITH UTMOST HASTE..."
"TAKE THIS POTENT HERB, KNOWN ONLY TO THE IMMORTALS, AND SWALLOW IT BEFORE YOU ENTER CIRCE'S PORTAL."
"SHE'LL OFFER YOU FOOD TO EAT AND WINE TO TASTE."
"NOW, MY ULTIMATE SECRET I'LL TELL. WITH THIS HERB..."
"...YOU'LL BE IMMUNE TO ALL OF HER SPELLS."
?

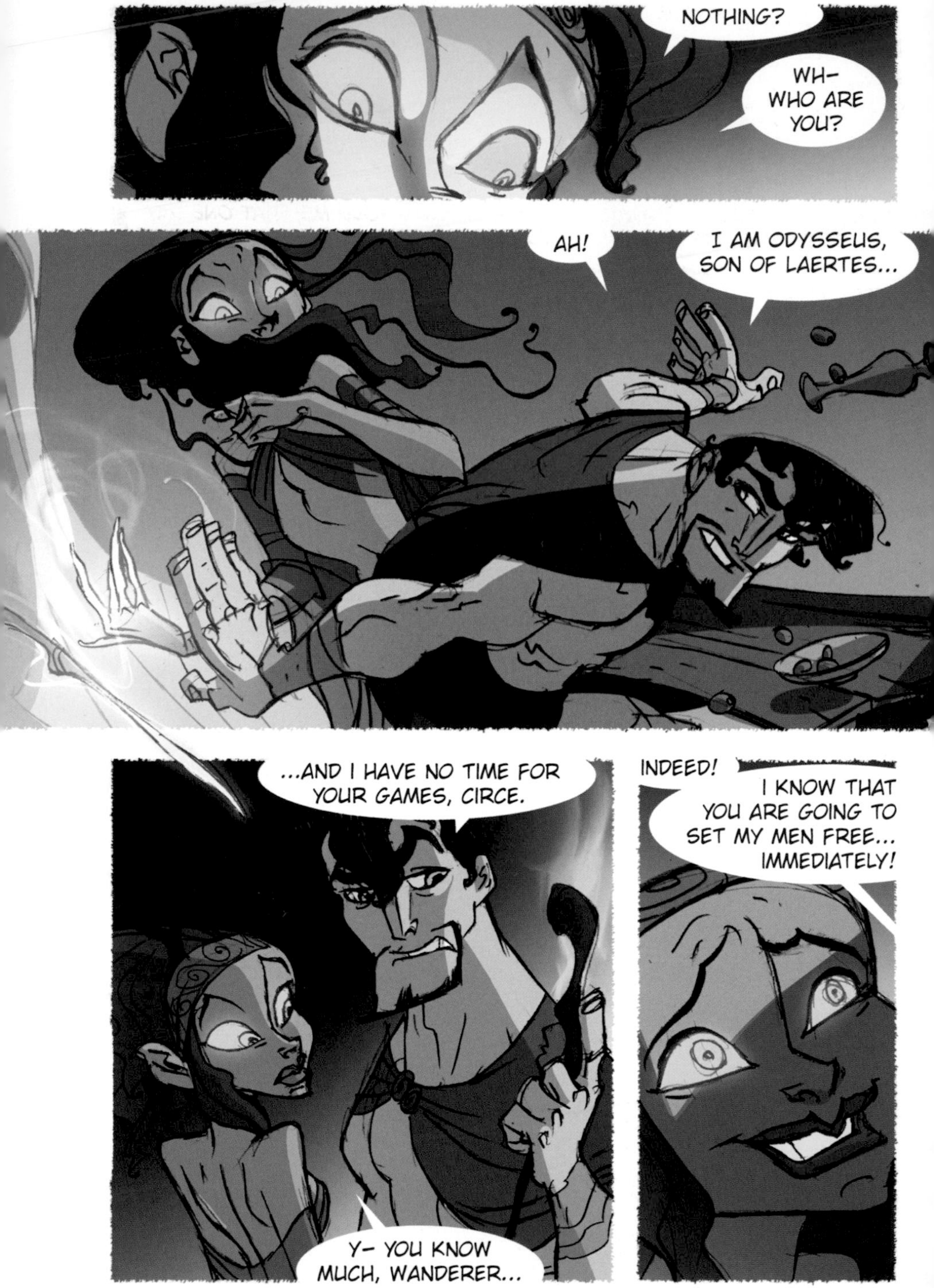
NOTHING?
WH- WHO ARE YOU?
AH!
I AM ODYSSEUS, SON OF LAERTES...
...AND I HAVE NO TIME FOR YOUR GAMES, CIRCE.
Y- YOU KNOW MUCH, WANDERER...
INDEED!
I KNOW THAT YOU ARE GOING TO SET MY MEN FREE... IMMEDIATELY!

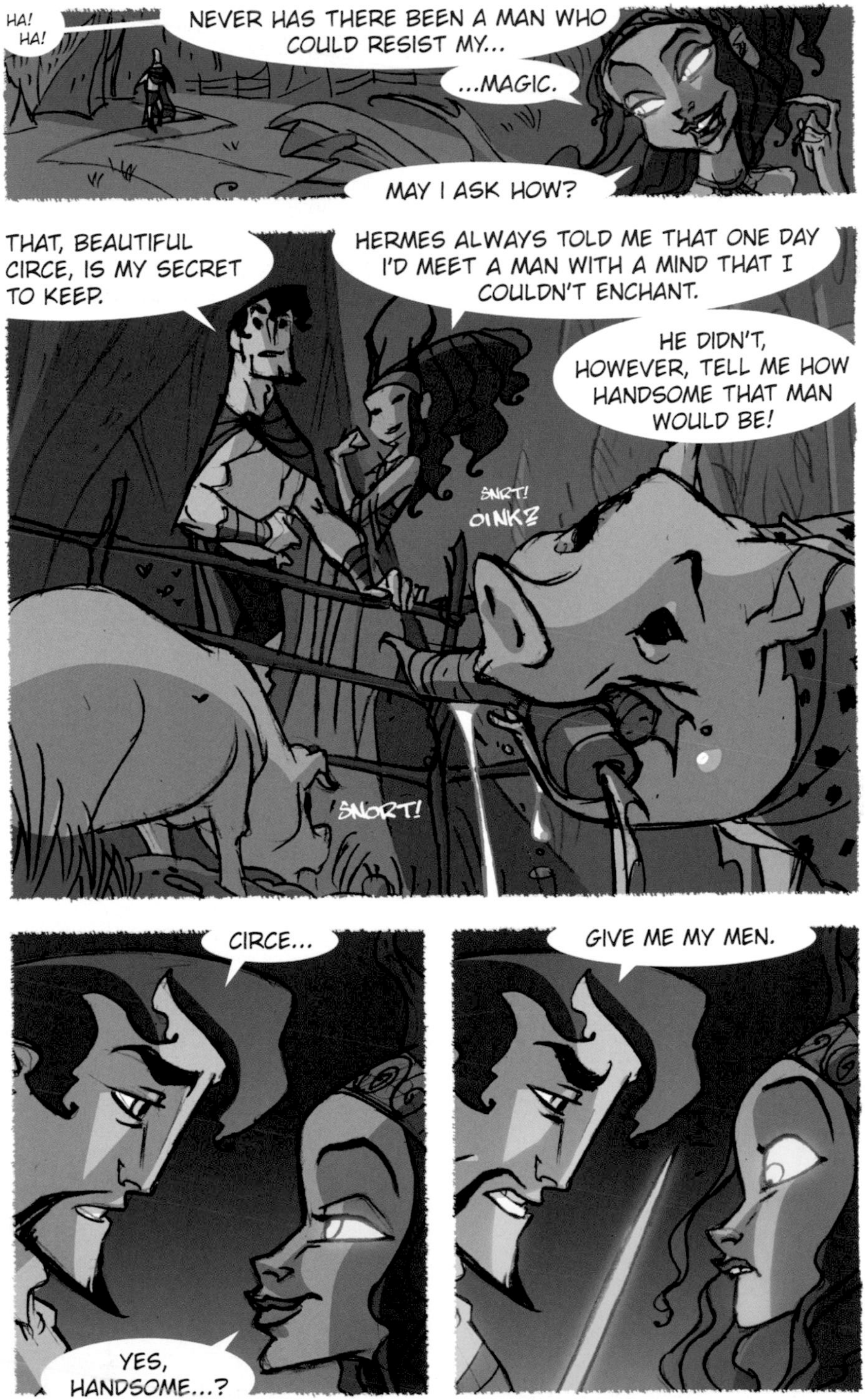
HA! HA!
NEVER HAS THERE BEEN A MAN WHO COULD RESIST MY...
...MAGIC.
MAY I ASK HOW?
THAT, BEAUTIFUL CIRCE, IS MY SECRET TO KEEP.
HERMES ALWAYS TOLD ME THAT ONE DAY I'D MEET A MAN WITH A MIND THAT I COULDN'T ENCHANT.
HE DIDN'T, HOWEVER, TELL ME HOW HANDSOME THAT MAN WOULD BE!
SNRT!
OINK?
SNORT!
CIRCE...
YES, HANDSOME...?
GIVE ME MY MEN.

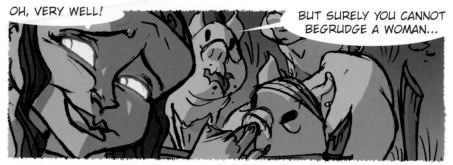

OH, VERY WELL!

BUT SURELY YOU CANNOT BEGRUDGE A WOMAN...

...HER LITTLE FUN?

...

ODYSSEUS, YOU HAVE BESTED MY MAGIC, A FEAT NO OTHER MORTAL CAN CLAIM. I URGE YOU AND YOUR MEN TO JOIN ME HERE.

SNORT?

?

!

REST, RE-SUPPLY... NO TRICKS, NO MAGIC! YOU HAVE MY WORD.

SIGH!

HMM.

THE WORD OF A GODDESS IS NOT TO BE TAKEN LIGHTLY. I ACCEPT YOUR OFFER, AND I THANK YOU.

MEN! FETCH YOUR COMRADES FROM THE BEACH...

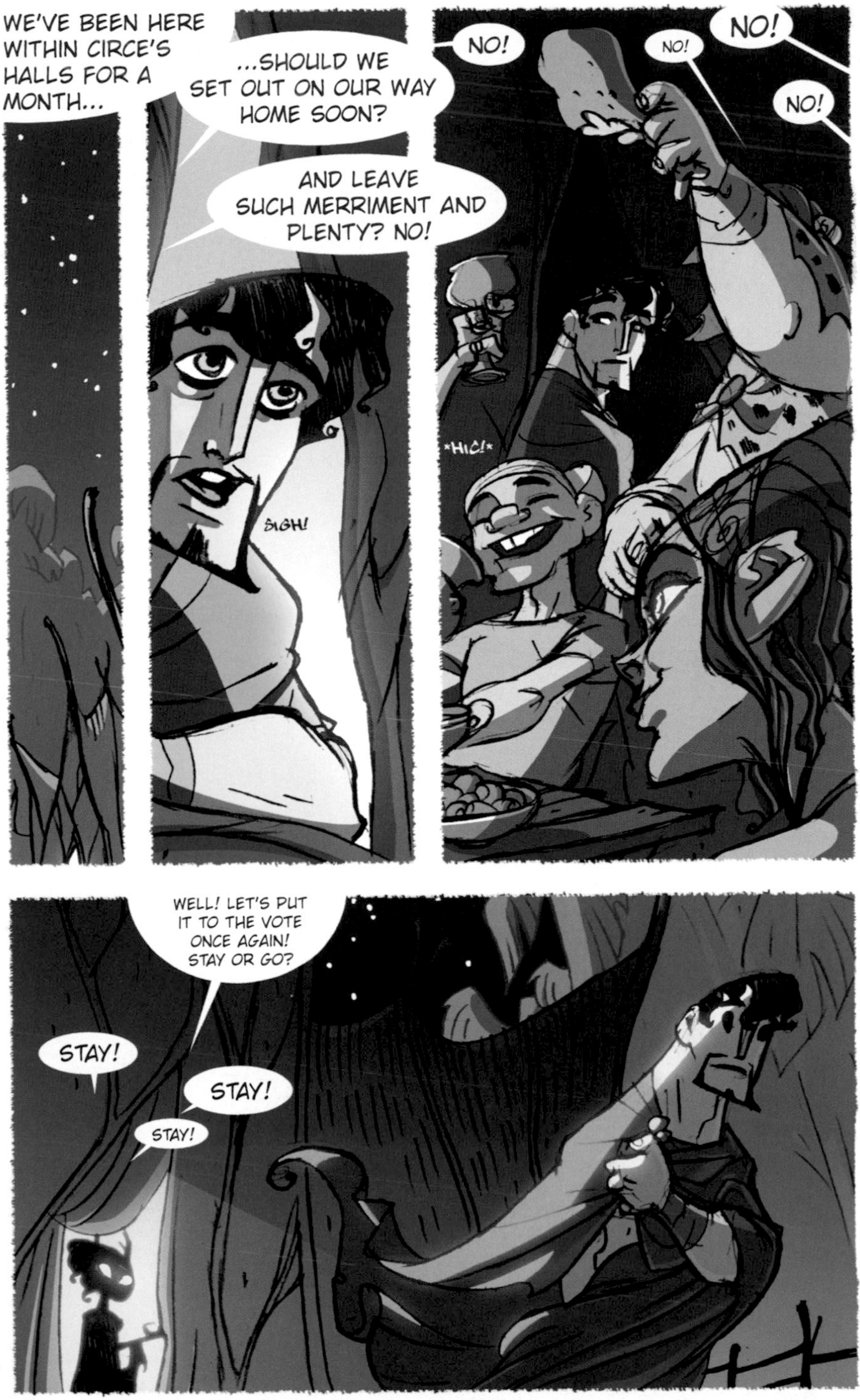
WE'VE BEEN HERE WITHIN CIRCE'S HALLS FOR A MONTH...
...SHOULD WE SET OUT ON OUR WAY HOME SOON?
AND LEAVE SUCH MERRIMENT AND PLENTY? NO!
SIGH!
NO!
NO!
NO!
NO!
HIC!
WELL! LET'S PUT IT TO THE VOTE ONCE AGAIN! STAY OR GO?
STAY!
STAY!
STAY!

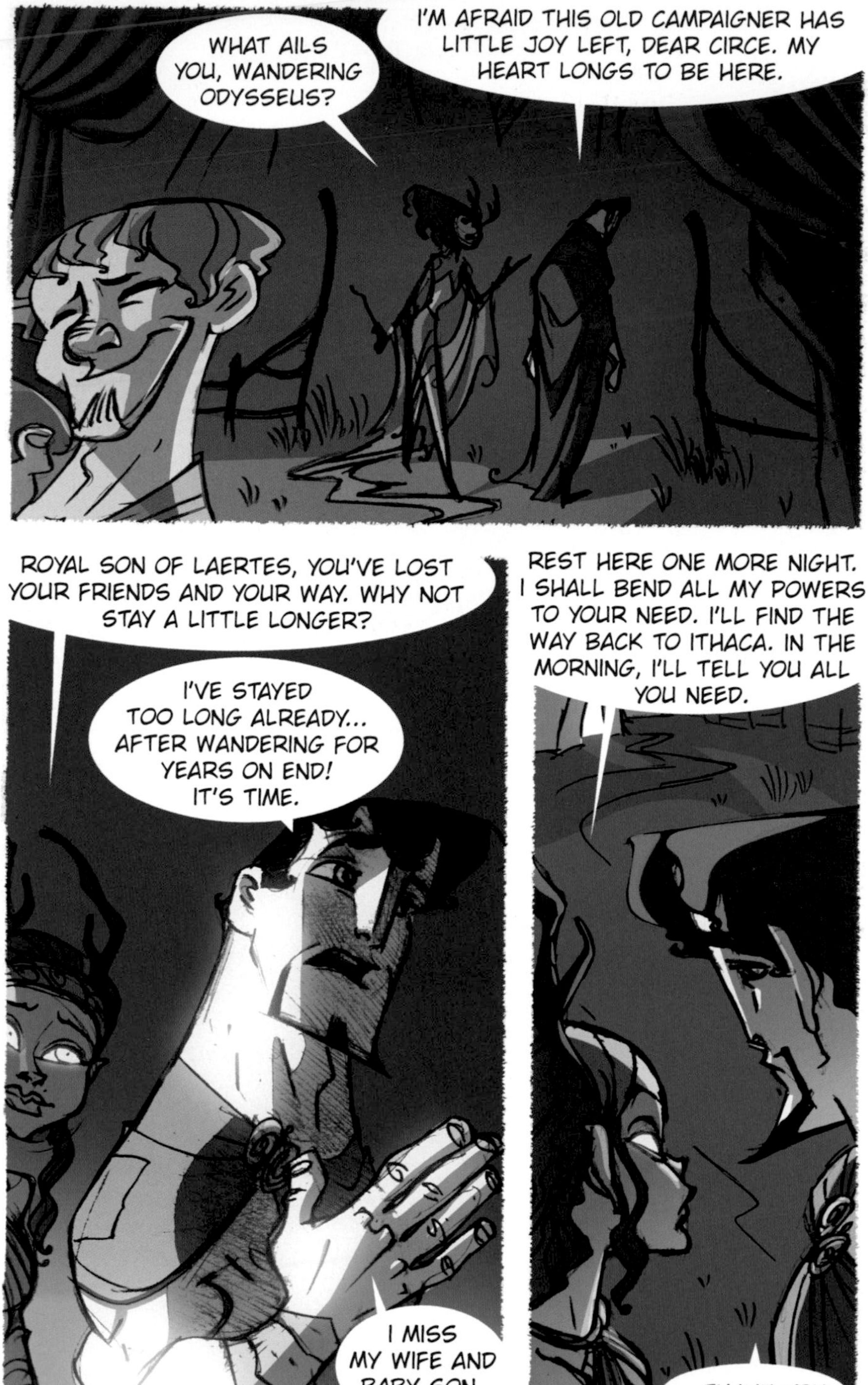
WHAT AILS YOU, WANDERING ODYSSEUS?
I'M AFRAID THIS OLD CAMPAIGNER HAS LITTLE JOY LEFT, DEAR CIRCE. MY HEART LONGS TO BE HERE.
ROYAL SON OF LAERTES, YOU'VE LOST YOUR FRIENDS AND YOUR WAY. WHY NOT STAY A LITTLE LONGER?
I'VE STAYED TOO LONG ALREADY... AFTER WANDERING FOR YEARS ON END! IT'S TIME.
I MISS MY WIFE AND BABY SON.
REST HERE ONE MORE NIGHT. I SHALL BEND ALL MY POWERS TO YOUR NEED. I'LL FIND THE WAY BACK TO ITHACA. IN THE MORNING, I'LL TELL YOU ALL YOU NEED.
...THANK YOU.

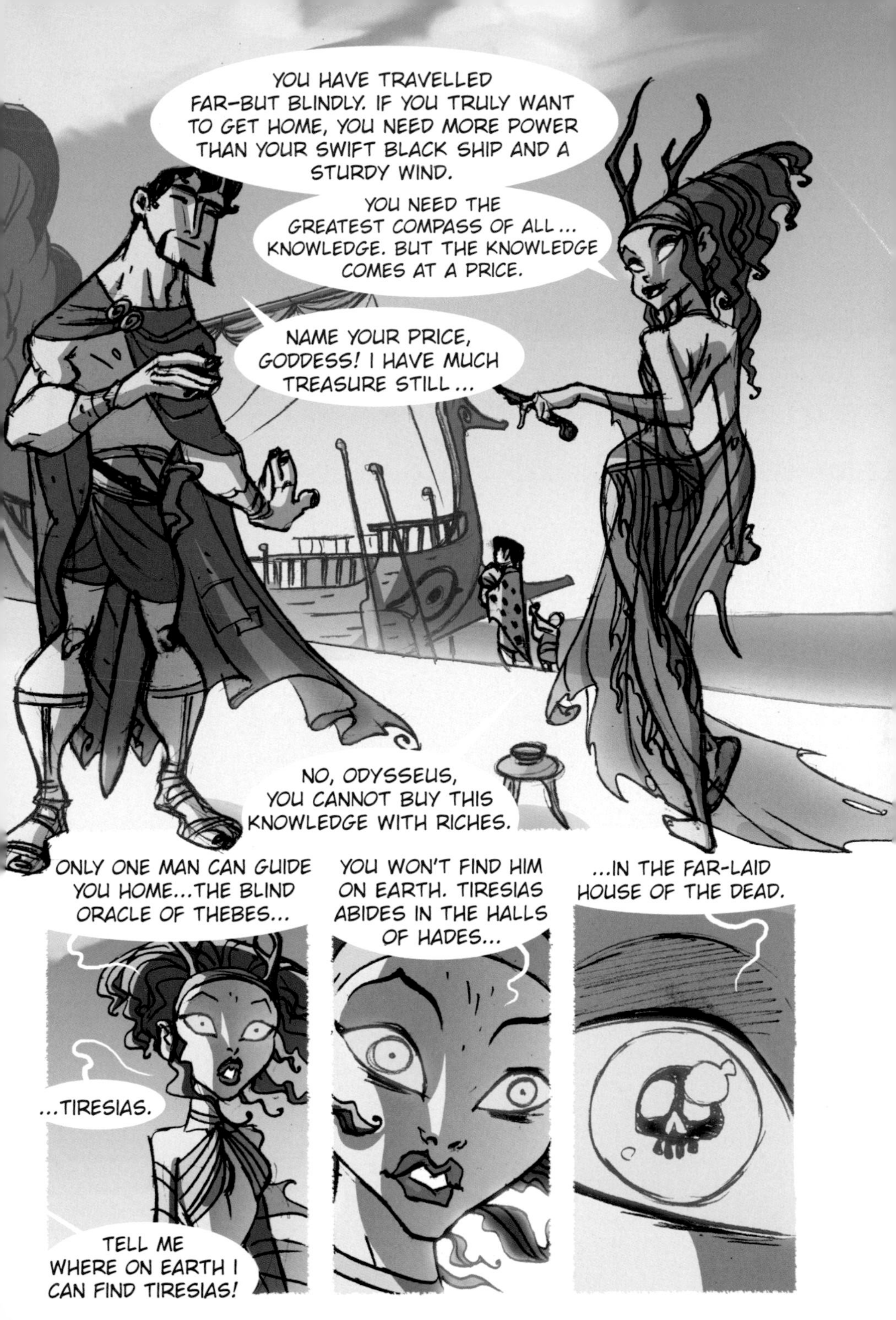
YOU HAVE TRAVELLED FAR–BUT BLINDLY. IF YOU TRULY WANT TO GET HOME, YOU NEED MORE POWER THAN YOUR SWIFT BLACK SHIP AND A STURDY WIND.
YOU NEED THE GREATEST COMPASS OF ALL ... KNOWLEDGE. BUT THE KNOWLEDGE COMES AT A PRICE.
NAME YOUR PRICE, GODDESS! I HAVE MUCH TREASURE STILL ...
NO, ODYSSEUS, YOU CANNOT BUY THIS KNOWLEDGE WITH RICHES.
ONLY ONE MAN CAN GUIDE YOU HOME...THE BLIND ORACLE OF THEBES...
...TIRESIAS.
TELL ME WHERE ON EARTH I CAN FIND TIRESIAS!
YOU WON'T FIND HIM ON EARTH. TIRESIAS ABIDES IN THE HALLS OF HADES...
...IN THE FAR-LAID HOUSE OF THE DEAD.

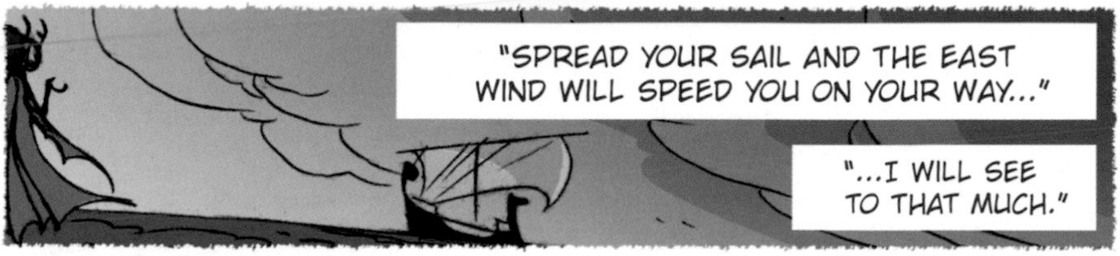
"SPREAD YOUR SAIL AND THE EAST WIND WILL SPEED YOU ON YOUR WAY..."
"...I WILL SEE TO THAT MUCH."

"ACROSS THE OCEAN RIVER, YOU WILL COME UPON THE CHURNING BLACK SHORES OF PERSEPHONE'S GROVE. BEWARE THE SHADES OF LETHE, WHICH ROB YOU OF YOUR EARTHLY MEMORIES..."

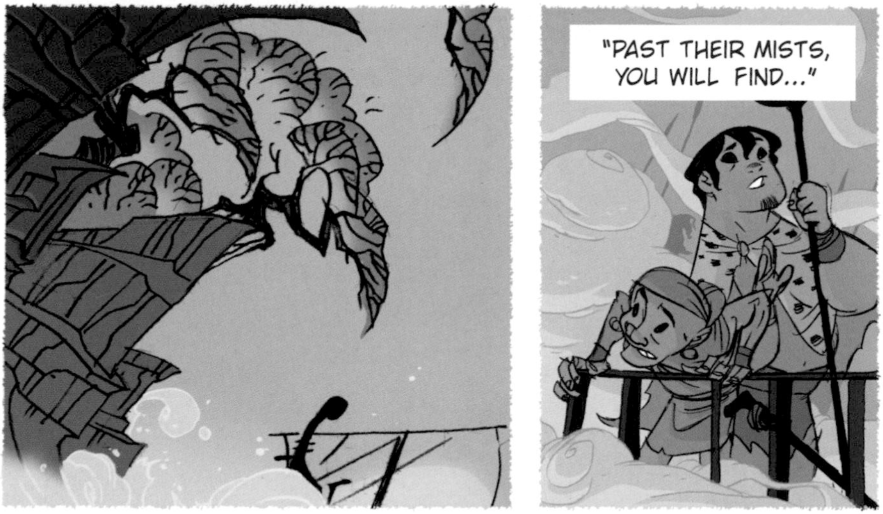
"PAST THEIR MISTS, YOU WILL FIND..."

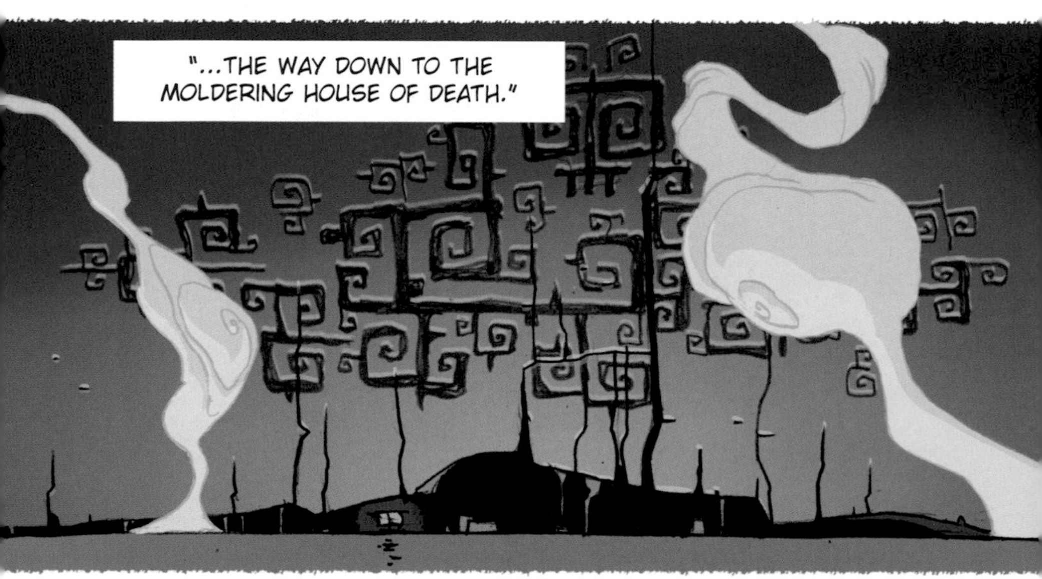
"...THE WAY DOWN TO THE MOLDERING HOUSE OF DEATH."

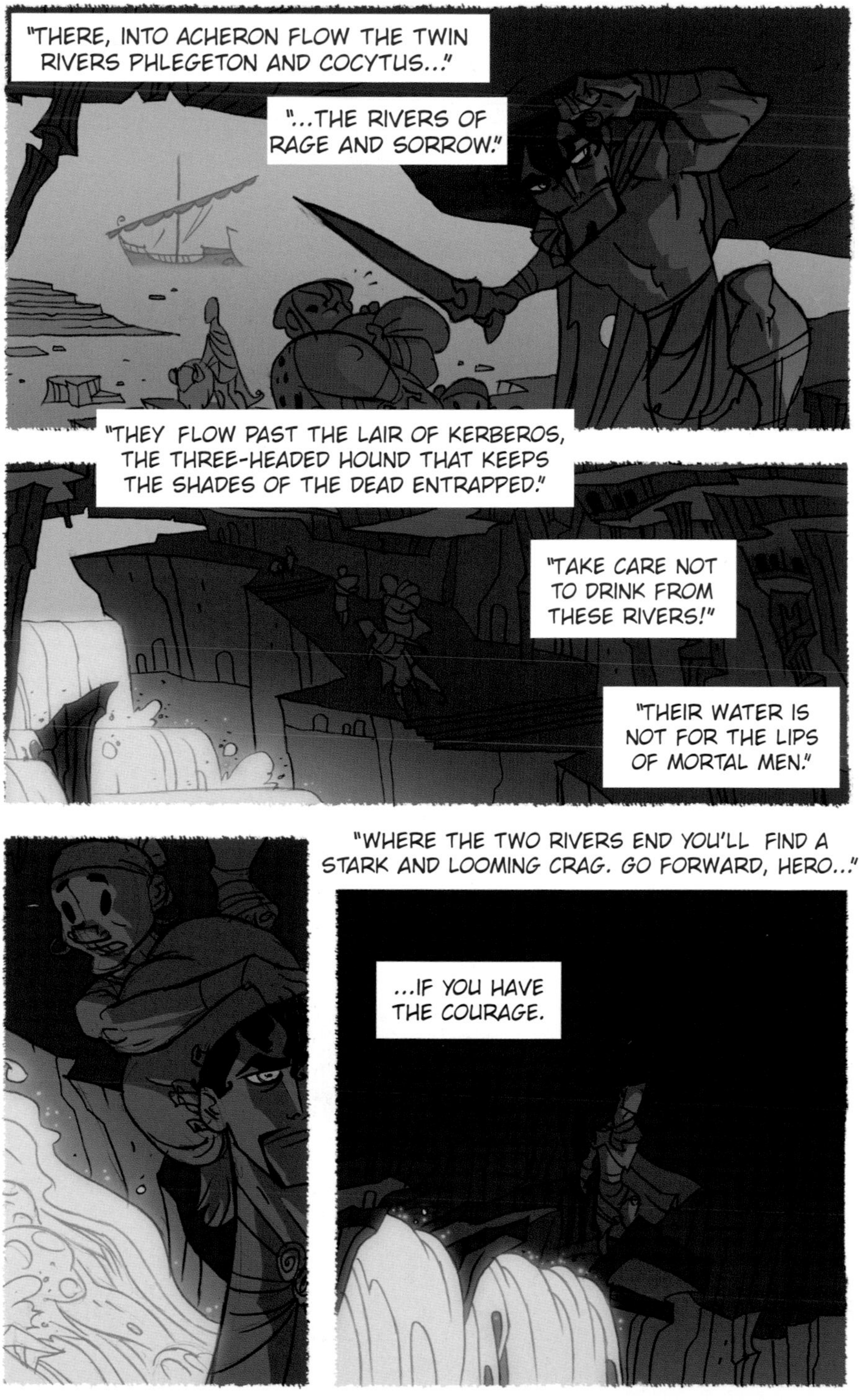
"THERE, INTO ACHERON FLOW THE TWIN RIVERS PHLEGETON AND COCYTUS..."
"...THE RIVERS OF RAGE AND SORROW."
"THEY FLOW PAST THE LAIR OF KERBEROS, THE THREE-HEADED HOUND THAT KEEPS THE SHADES OF THE DEAD ENTRAPPED."
"TAKE CARE NOT TO DRINK FROM THESE RIVERS!"
"THEIR WATER IS NOT FOR THE LIPS OF MORTAL MEN."
"WHERE THE TWO RIVERS END YOU'LL FIND A STARK AND LOOMING CRAG. GO FORWARD, HERO..."
...IF YOU HAVE THE COURAGE.

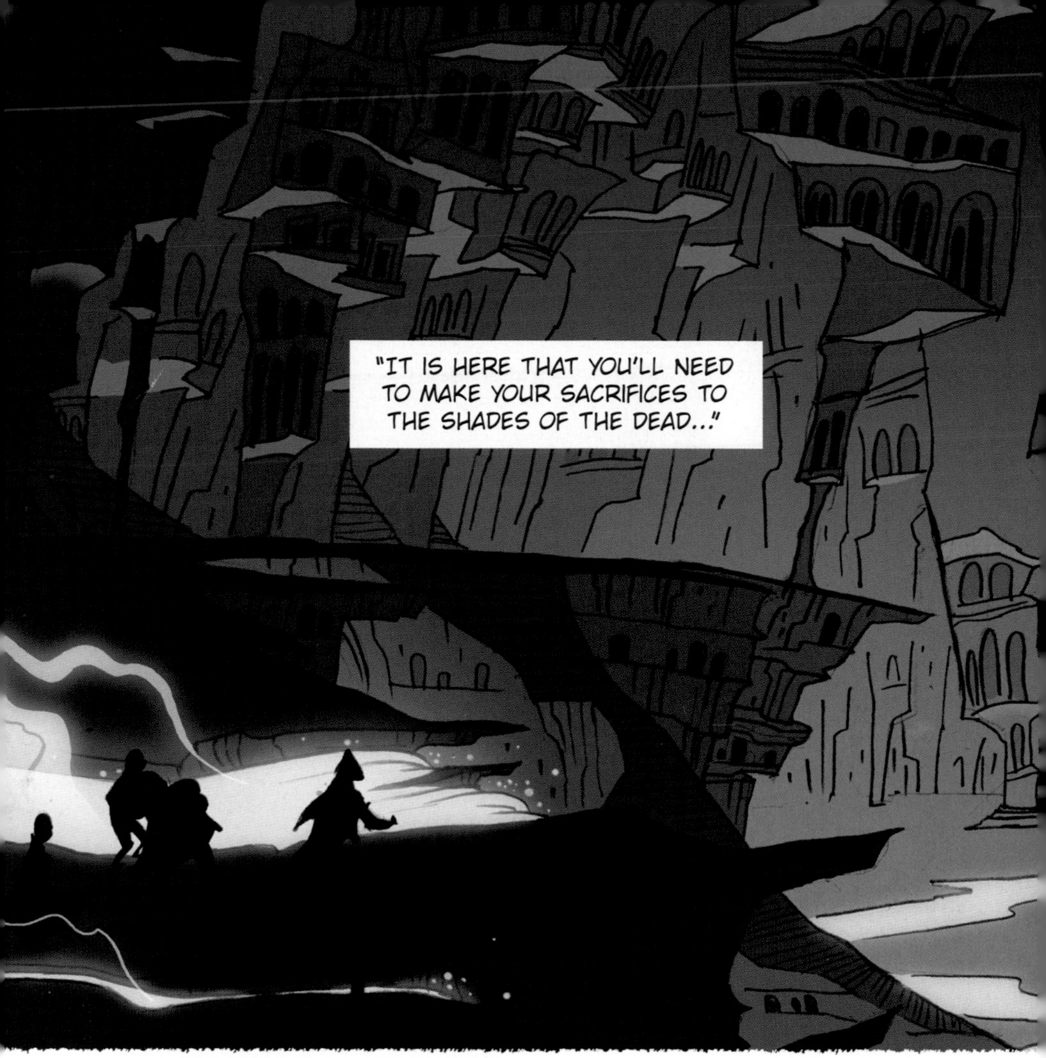
"IT IS HERE THAT YOU'LL NEED TO MAKE YOUR SACRIFICES TO THE SHADES OF THE DEAD..."

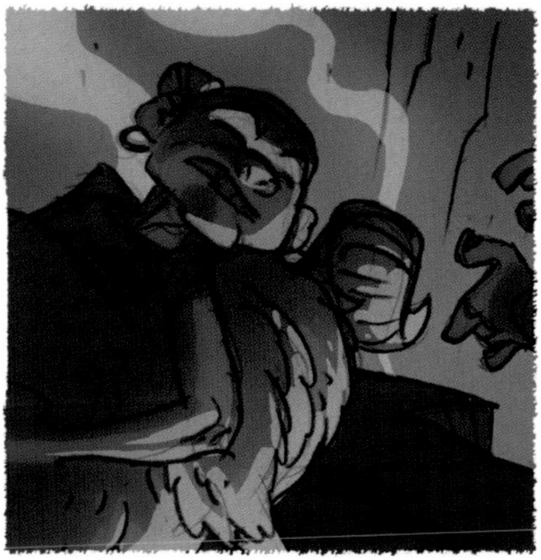

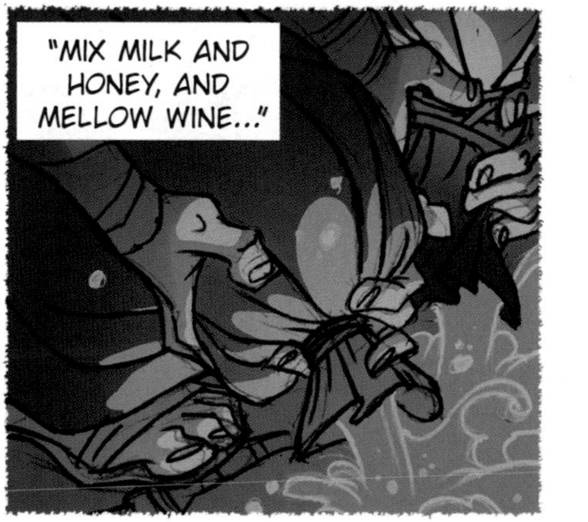
"MIX MILK AND HONEY, AND MELLOW WINE..."

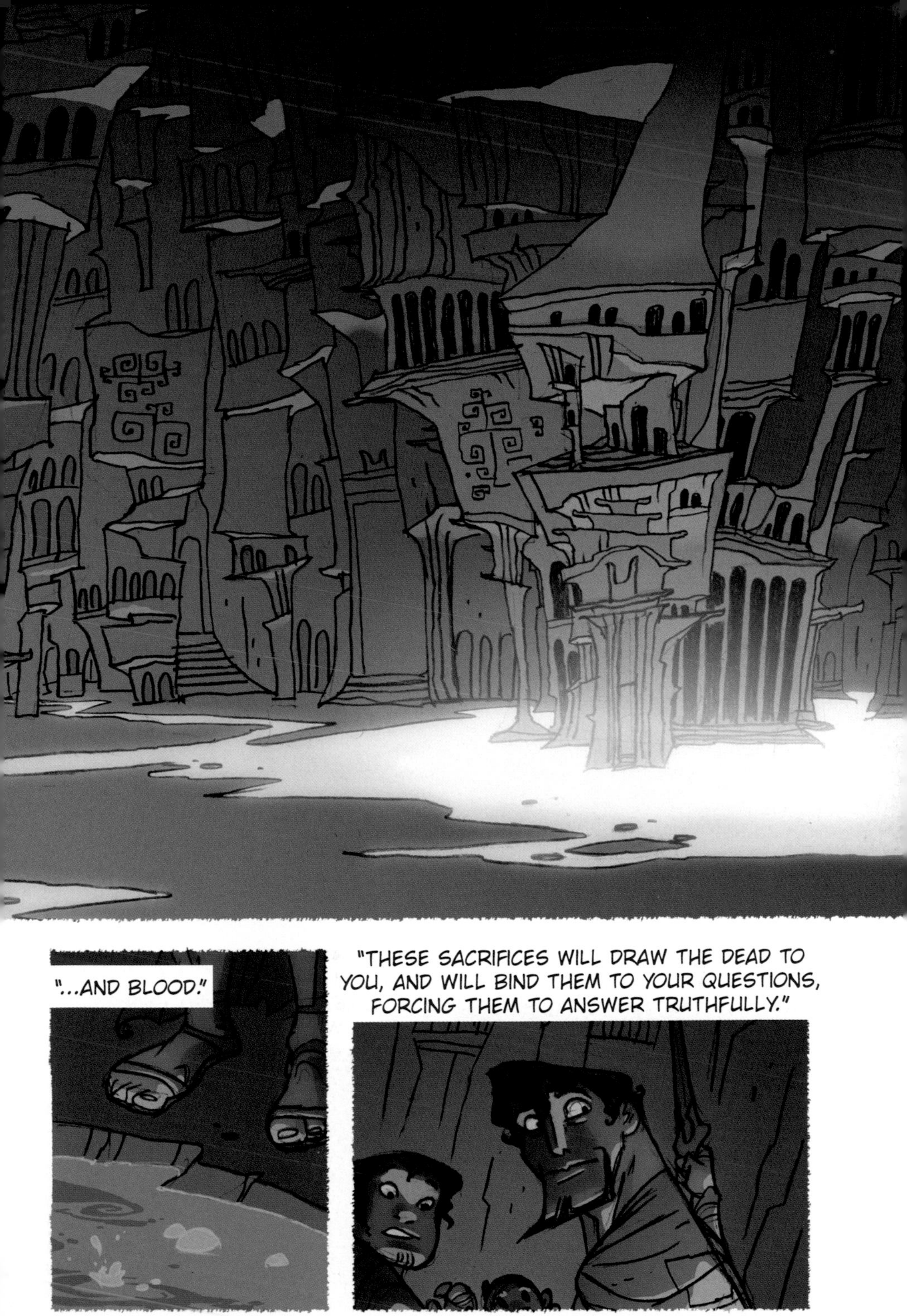
"...AND BLOOD."
"THESE SACRIFICES WILL DRAW THE DEAD TO YOU, AND WILL BIND THEM TO YOUR QUESTIONS, FORCING THEM TO ANSWER TRUTHFULLY."

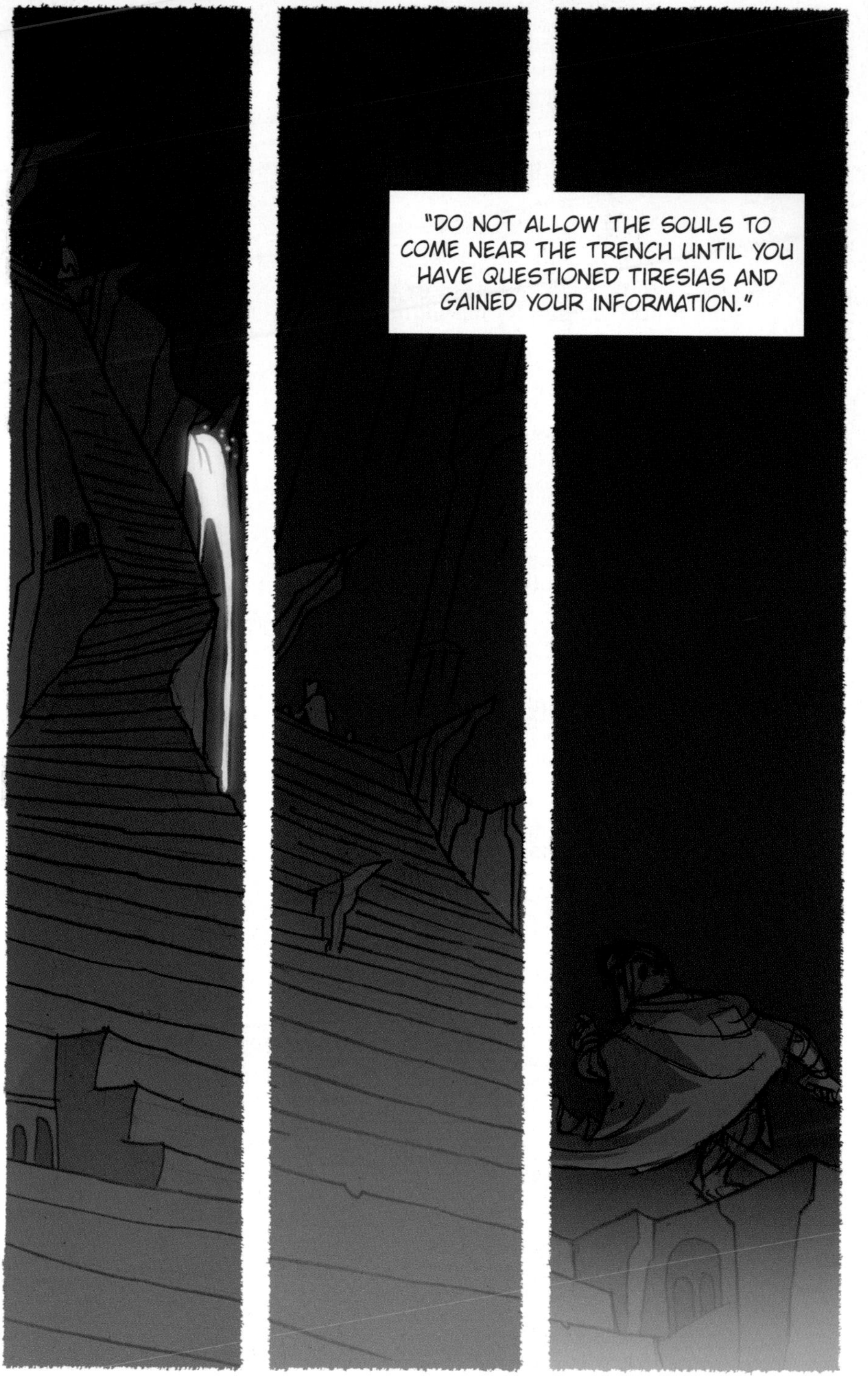
"DO NOT ALLOW THE SOULS TO COME NEAR THE TRENCH UNTIL YOU HAVE QUESTIONED TIRESIAS AND GAINED YOUR INFORMATION."

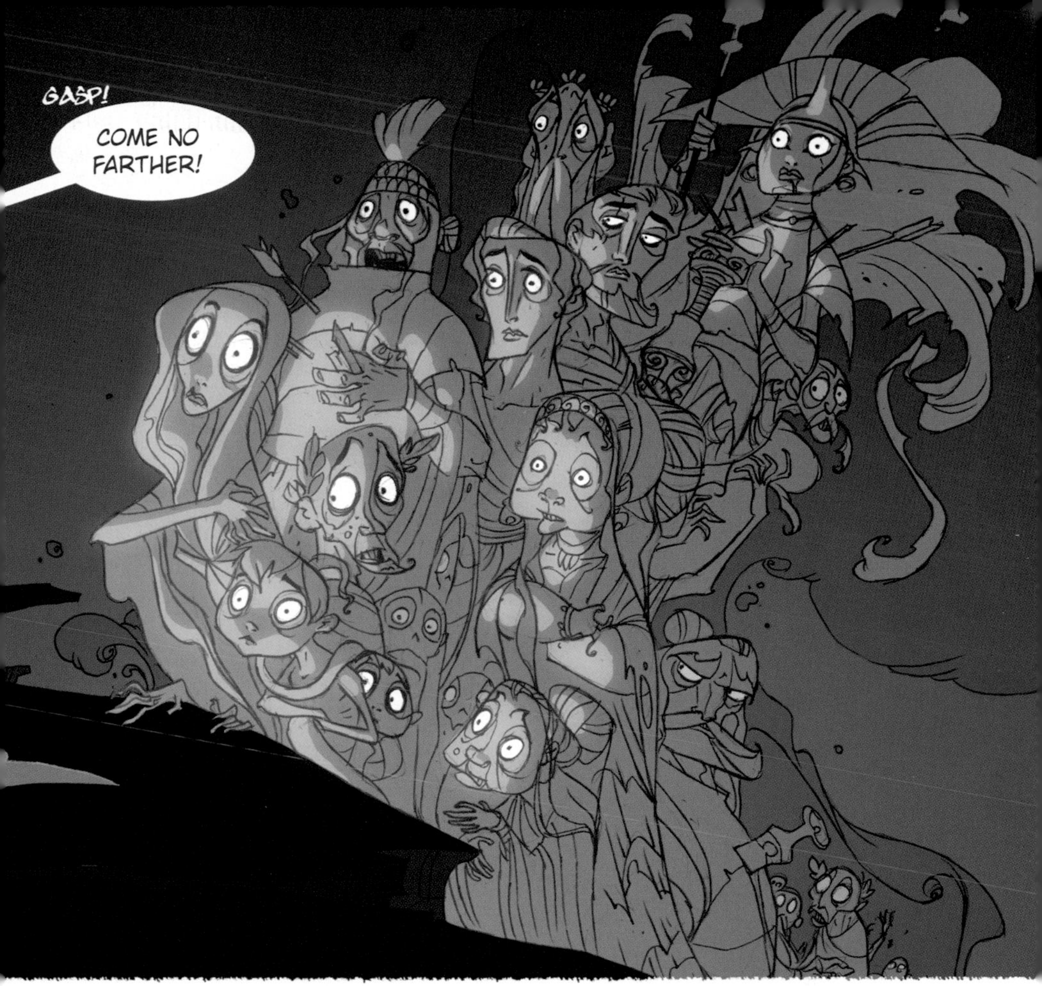
GASP!
COME NO FARTHER!
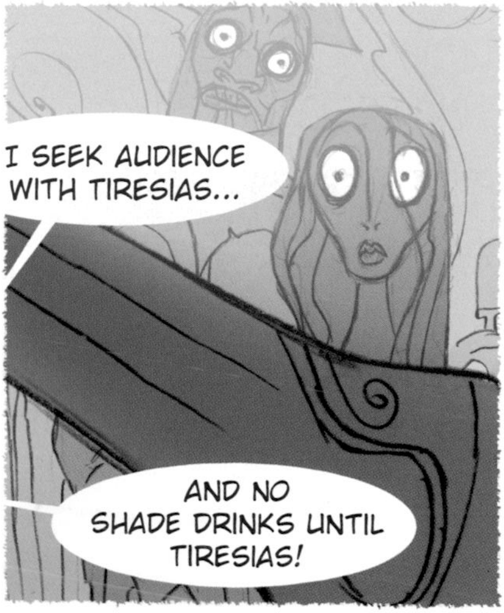
I SEEK AUDIENCE WITH TIRESIAS...
AND NO SHADE DRINKS UNTIL TIRESIAS!
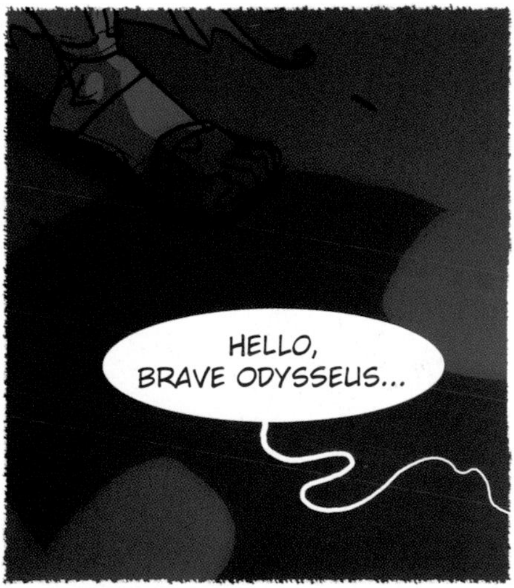
HELLO, BRAVE ODYSSEUS...

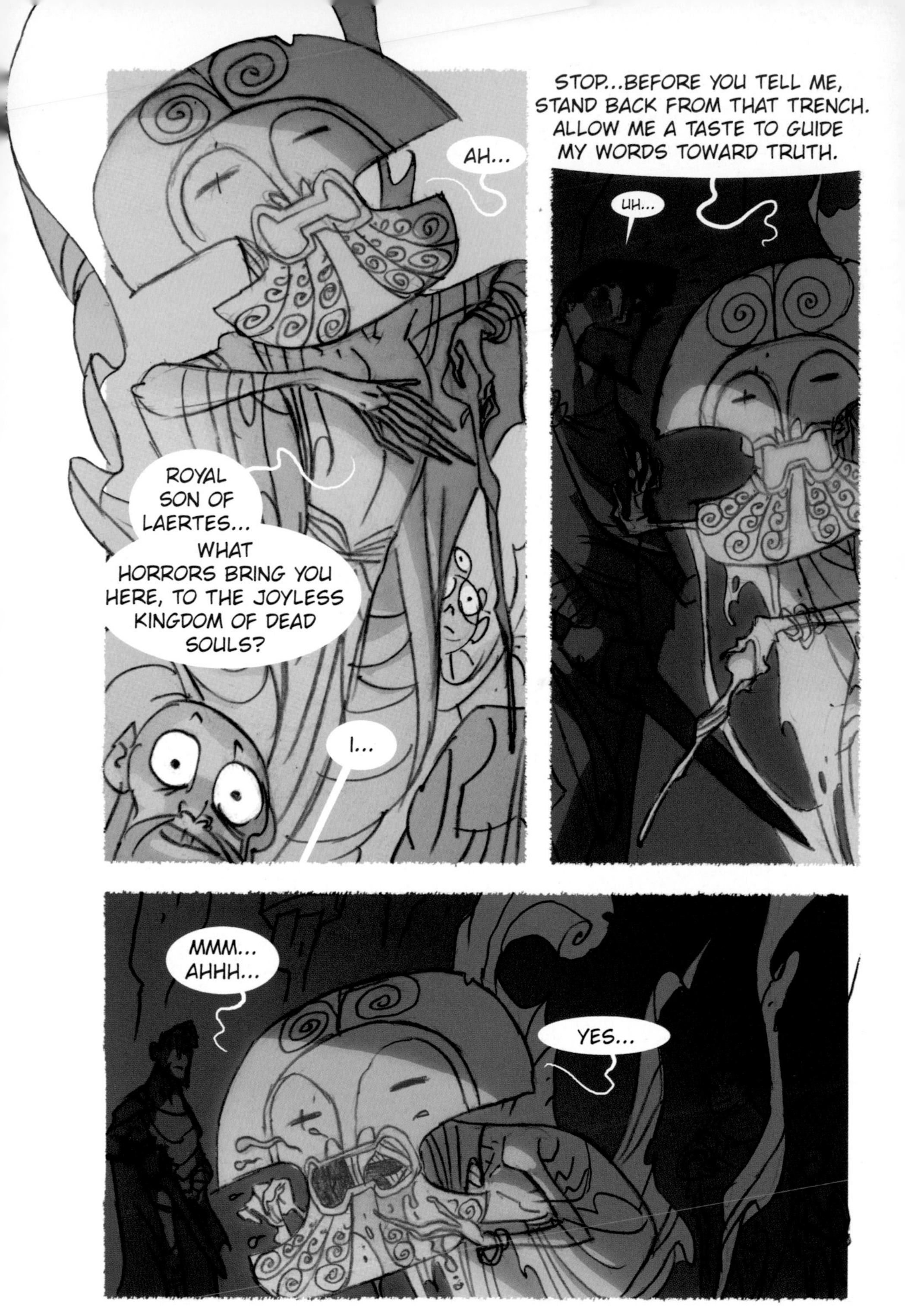
AH...
ROYAL SON OF LAERTES...
WHAT HORRORS BRING YOU HERE, TO THE JOYLESS KINGDOM OF DEAD SOULS?
I...
STOP...BEFORE YOU TELL ME, STAND BACK FROM THAT TRENCH. ALLOW ME A TASTE TO GUIDE MY WORDS TOWARD TRUTH.
UH...
MMM... AHHH...
YES...

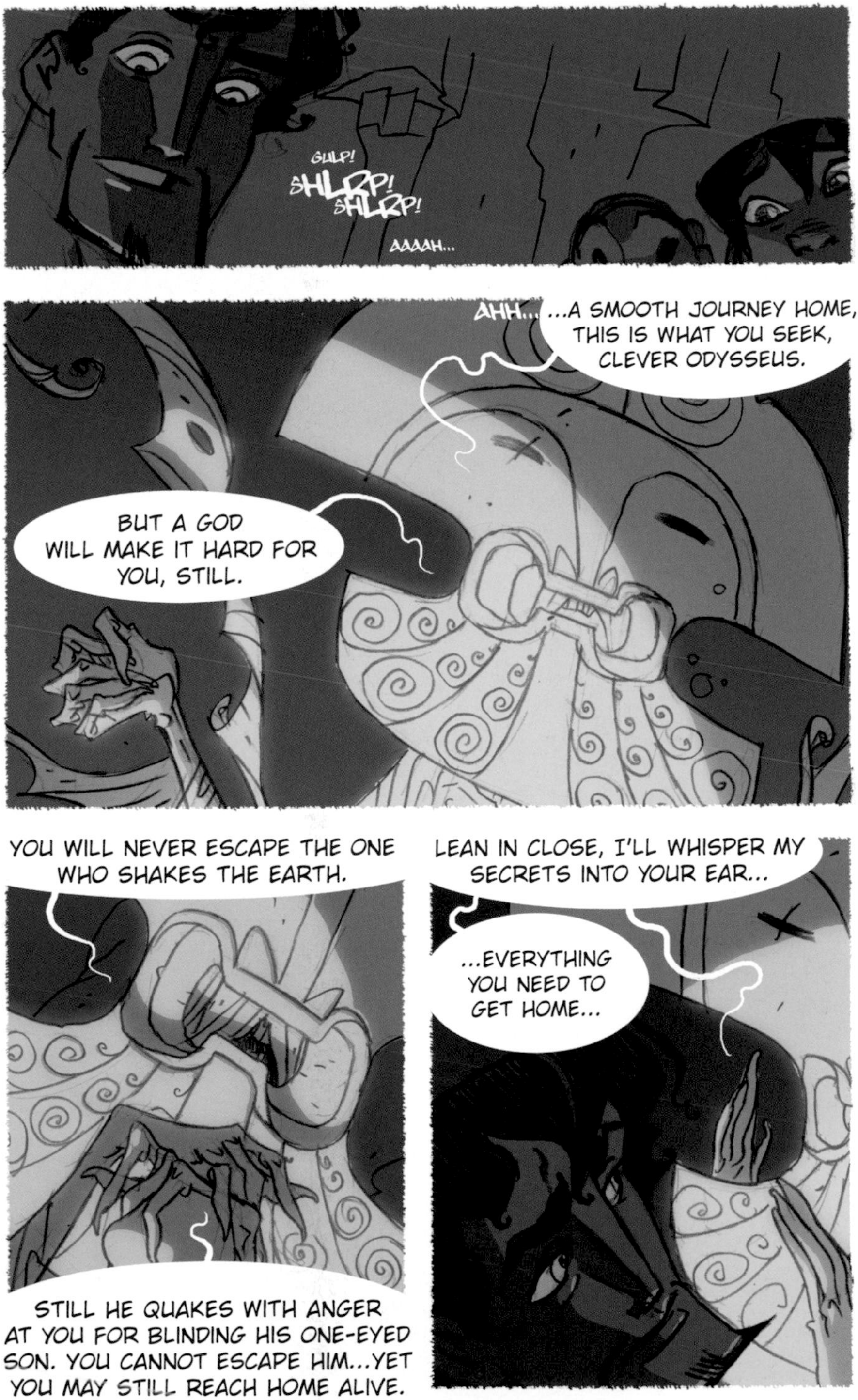
GULP!
SHLRP!
SHLRP!
AAAAH...
AHH...
...A SMOOTH JOURNEY HOME, THIS IS WHAT YOU SEEK, CLEVER ODYSSEUS.
BUT A GOD WILL MAKE IT HARD FOR YOU, STILL.
YOU WILL NEVER ESCAPE THE ONE WHO SHAKES THE EARTH.
STILL HE QUAKES WITH ANGER AT YOU FOR BLINDING HIS ONE-EYED SON. YOU CANNOT ESCAPE HIM...YET YOU MAY STILL REACH HOME ALIVE.
LEAN IN CLOSE, I'LL WHISPER MY SECRETS INTO YOUR EAR...
...EVERYTHING YOU NEED TO GET HOME...

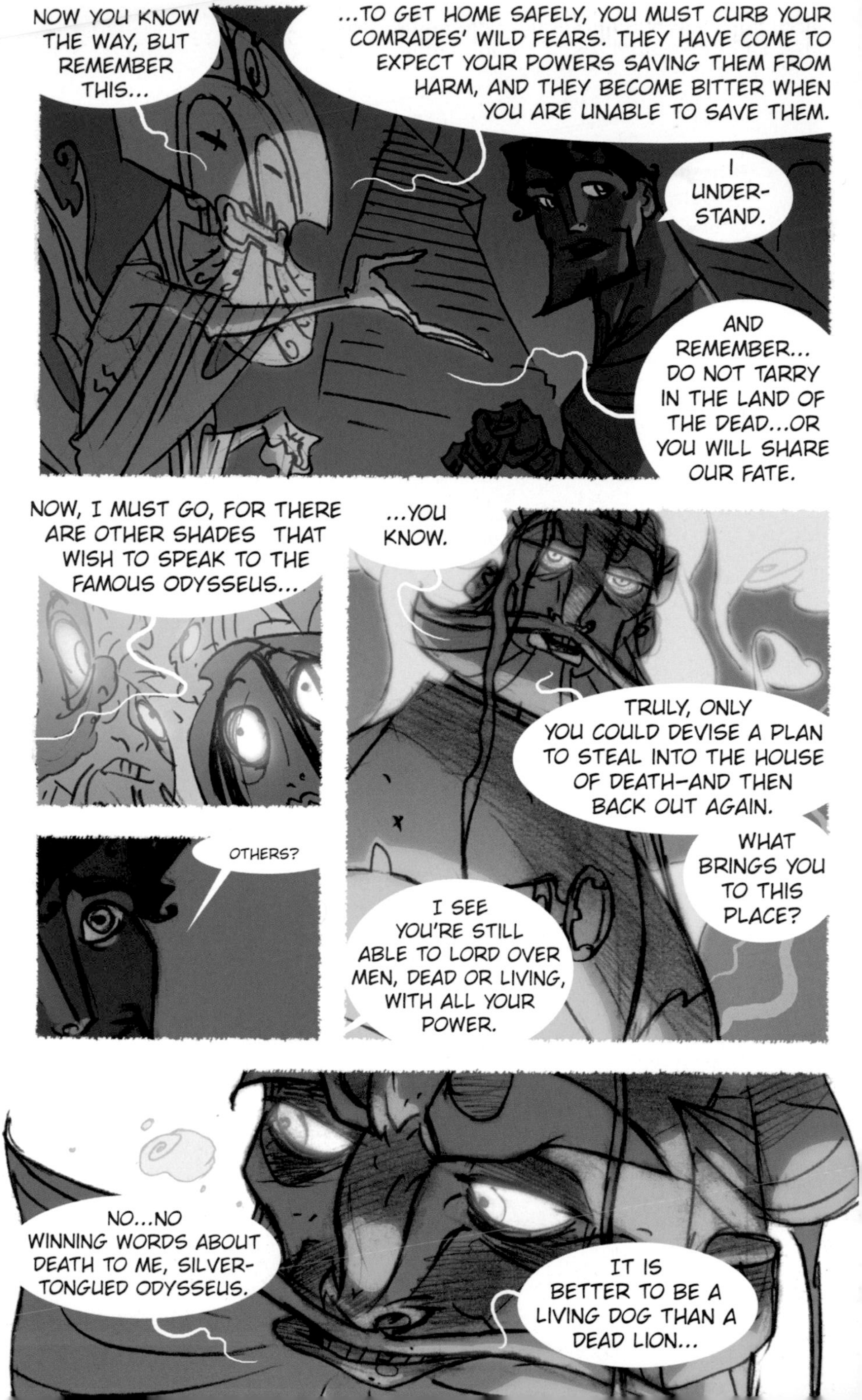
NOW YOU KNOW THE WAY, BUT REMEMBER THIS...
...TO GET HOME SAFELY, YOU MUST CURB YOUR COMRADES' WILD FEARS. THEY HAVE COME TO EXPECT YOUR POWERS SAVING THEM FROM HARM, AND THEY BECOME BITTER WHEN YOU ARE UNABLE TO SAVE THEM.
I UNDER-STAND.
AND REMEMBER... DO NOT TARRY IN THE LAND OF THE DEAD...OR YOU WILL SHARE OUR FATE.
NOW, I MUST GO, FOR THERE ARE OTHER SHADES THAT WISH TO SPEAK TO THE FAMOUS ODYSSEUS...
OTHERS?
...YOU KNOW.
TRULY, ONLY YOU COULD DEVISE A PLAN TO STEAL INTO THE HOUSE OF DEATH—AND THEN BACK OUT AGAIN.
WHAT BRINGS YOU TO THIS PLACE?
I SEE YOU'RE STILL ABLE TO LORD OVER MEN, DEAD OR LIVING, WITH ALL YOUR POWER.
NO...NO WINNING WORDS ABOUT DEATH TO ME, SILVER-TONGUED ODYSSEUS.
IT IS BETTER TO BE A LIVING DOG THAN A DEAD LION...

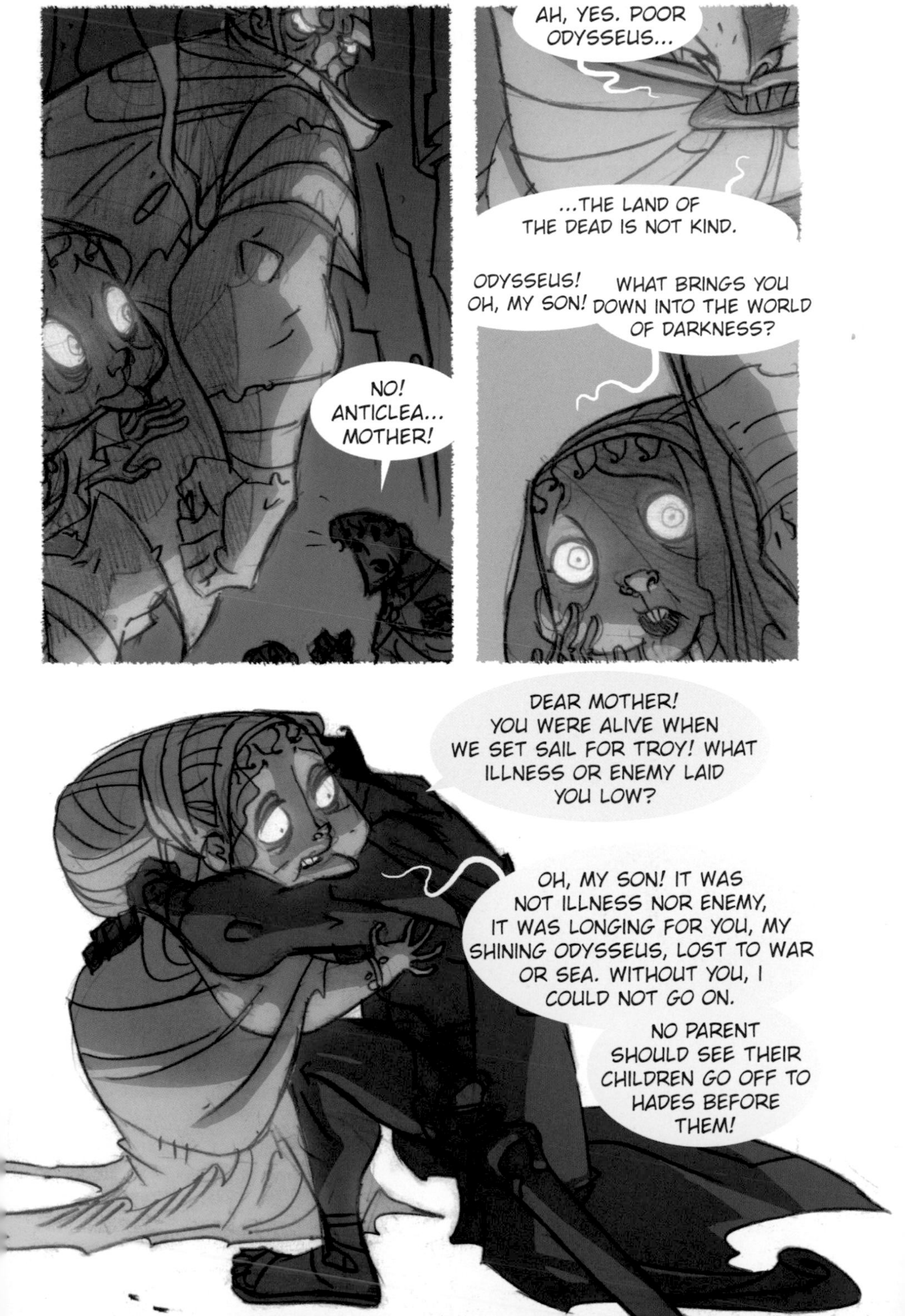
NO!
ANTICLEA...
MOTHER!
AH, YES. POOR
ODYSSEUS...
...THE LAND OF
THE DEAD IS NOT KIND.
ODYSSEUS!
OH, MY SON!
WHAT BRINGS YOU
DOWN INTO THE WORLD
OF DARKNESS?
DEAR MOTHER!
YOU WERE ALIVE WHEN
WE SET SAIL FOR TROY! WHAT
ILLNESS OR ENEMY LAID
YOU LOW?
OH, MY SON! IT WAS
NOT ILLNESS NOR ENEMY,
IT WAS LONGING FOR YOU, MY
SHINING ODYSSEUS, LOST TO WAR
OR SEA. WITHOUT YOU, I
COULD NOT GO ON.
NO PARENT
SHOULD SEE THEIR
CHILDREN GO OFF TO
HADES BEFORE
THEM!

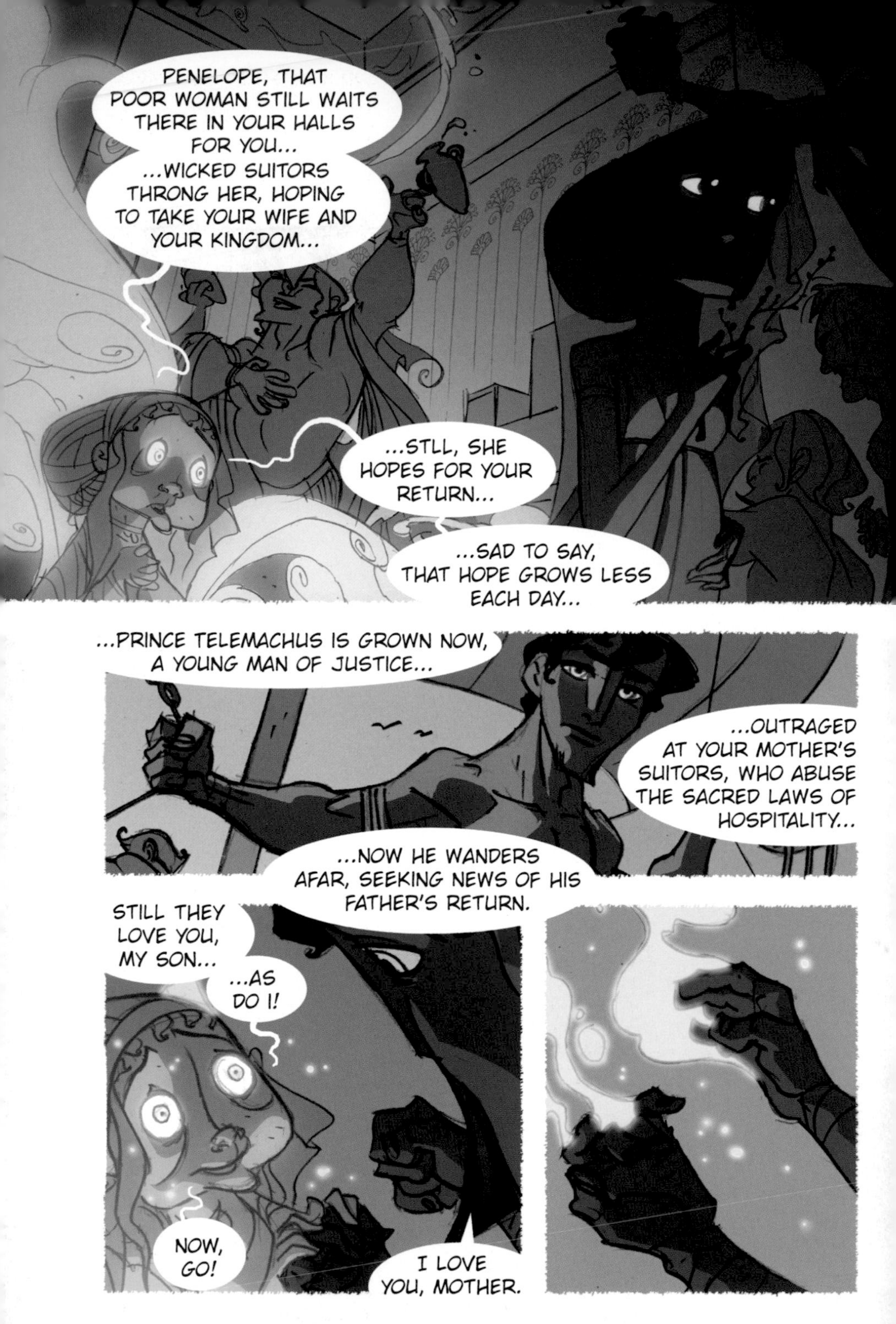
PENELOPE, THAT POOR WOMAN STILL WAITS THERE IN YOUR HALLS FOR YOU...
...WICKED SUITORS THRONG HER, HOPING TO TAKE YOUR WIFE AND YOUR KINGDOM...
...STLL, SHE HOPES FOR YOUR RETURN...
...SAD TO SAY, THAT HOPE GROWS LESS EACH DAY...
...PRINCE TELEMACHUS IS GROWN NOW, A YOUNG MAN OF JUSTICE...
...OUTRAGED AT YOUR MOTHER'S SUITORS, WHO ABUSE THE SACRED LAWS OF HOSPITALITY...
...NOW HE WANDERS AFAR, SEEKING NEWS OF HIS FATHER'S RETURN.
STILL THEY LOVE YOU, MY SON...
...AS DO I!
NOW, GO!
I LOVE YOU, MOTHER.

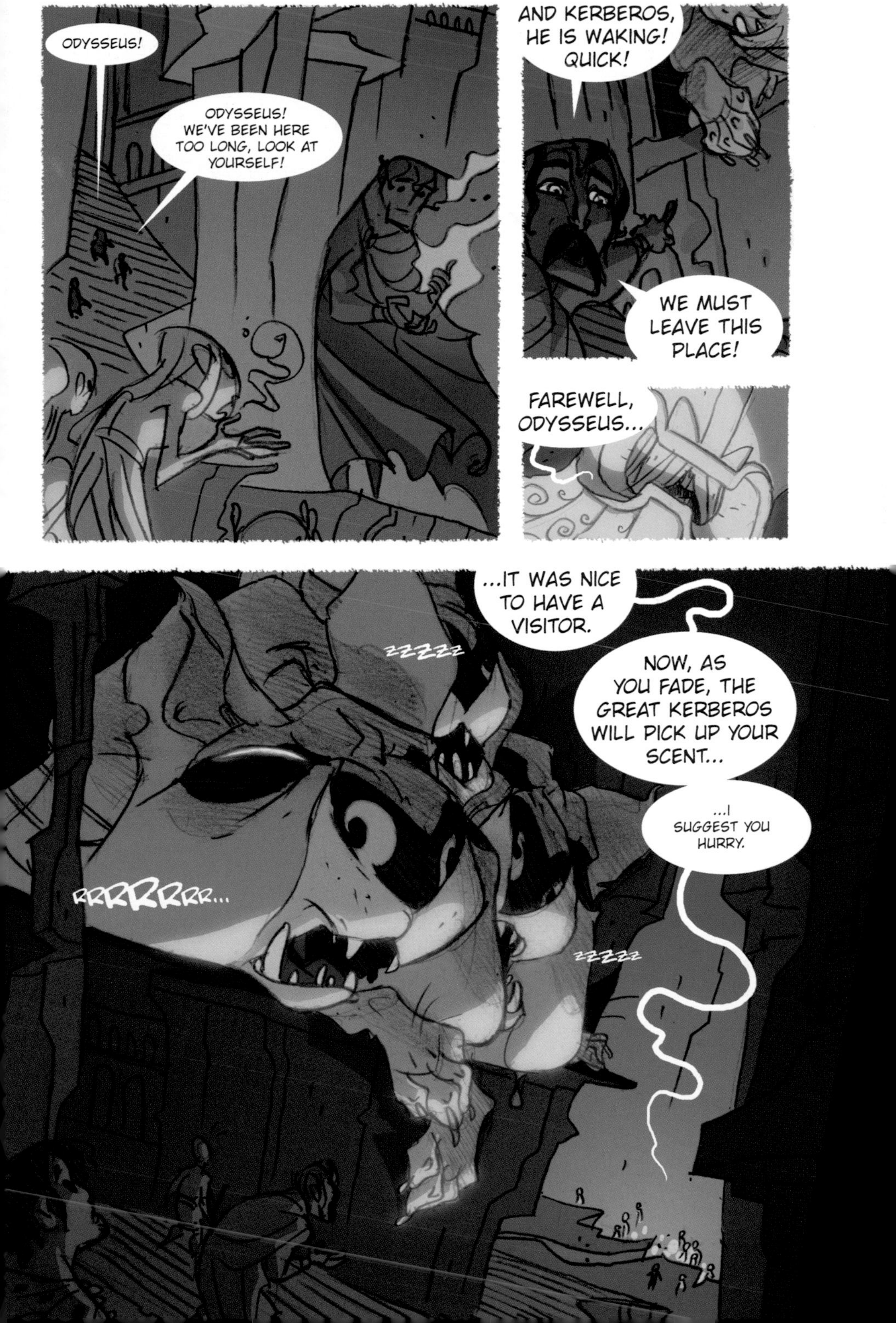
ODYSSEUS!
ODYSSEUS! WE'VE BEEN HERE TOO LONG, LOOK AT YOURSELF!
AND KERBEROS, HE IS WAKING! QUICK!
WE MUST LEAVE THIS PLACE!
FAREWELL, ODYSSEUS...
...IT WAS NICE TO HAVE A VISITOR.
ZZZZZ
NOW, AS YOU FADE, THE GREAT KERBEROS WILL PICK UP YOUR SCENT...
...I SUGGEST YOU HURRY.
RRRRRRRR...
ZZZZZ

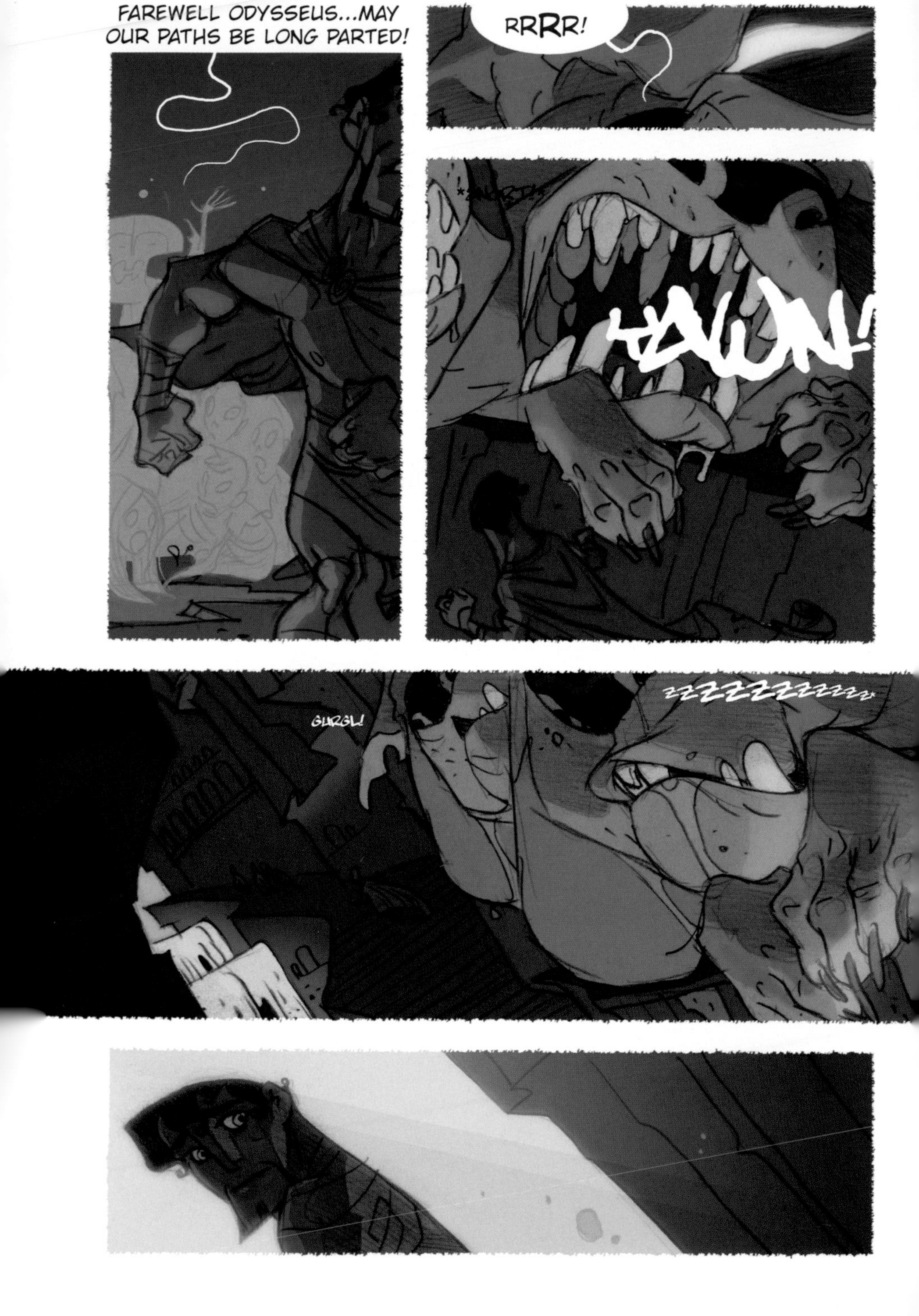
FAREWELL ODYSSEUS...MAY OUR PATHS BE LONG PARTED!
RRRR!
YAWN!
GURGL!
ZZZZZZZZZZZZZ*

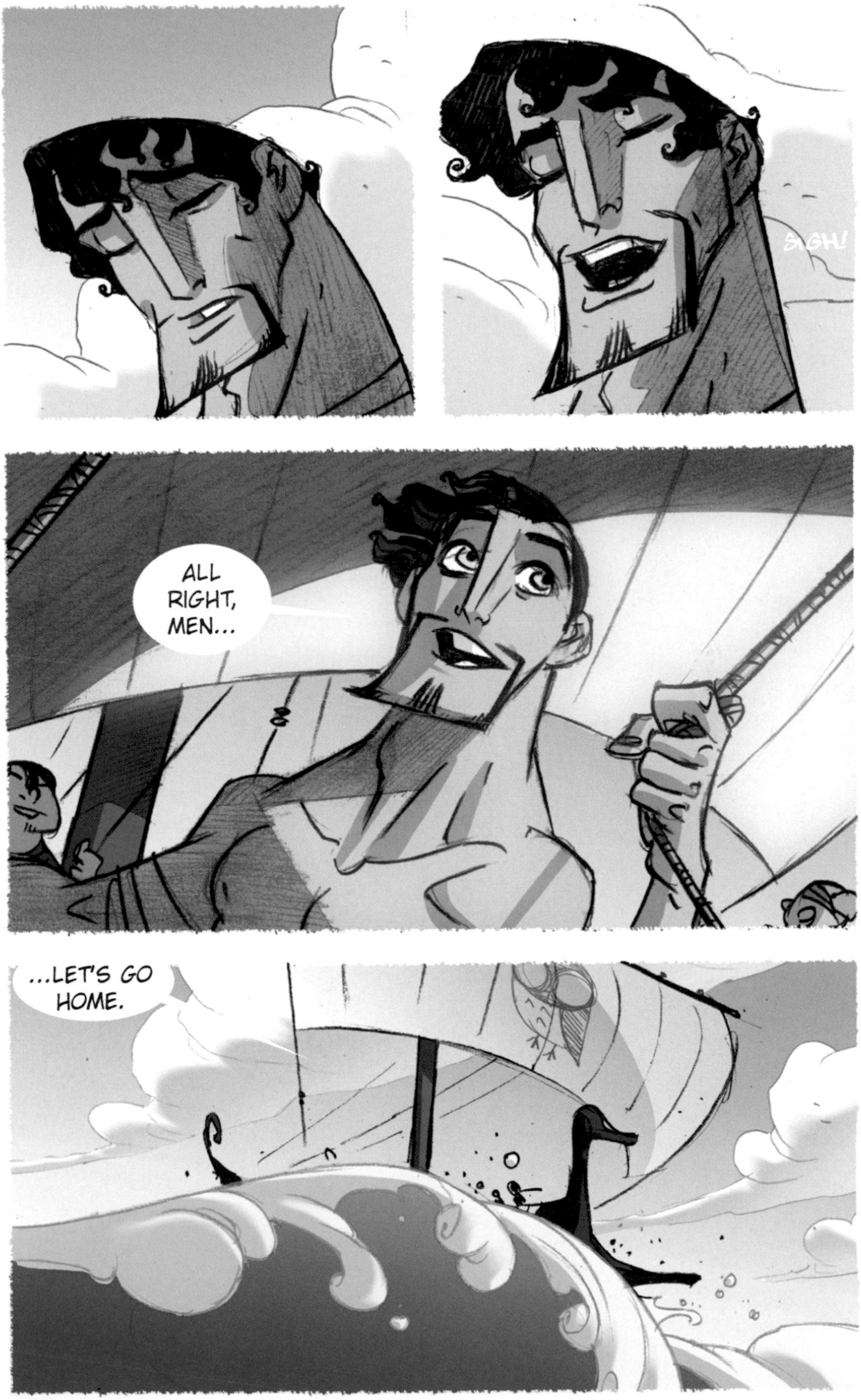
SIGH!
ALL RIGHT, MEN...
...LET'S GO HOME.

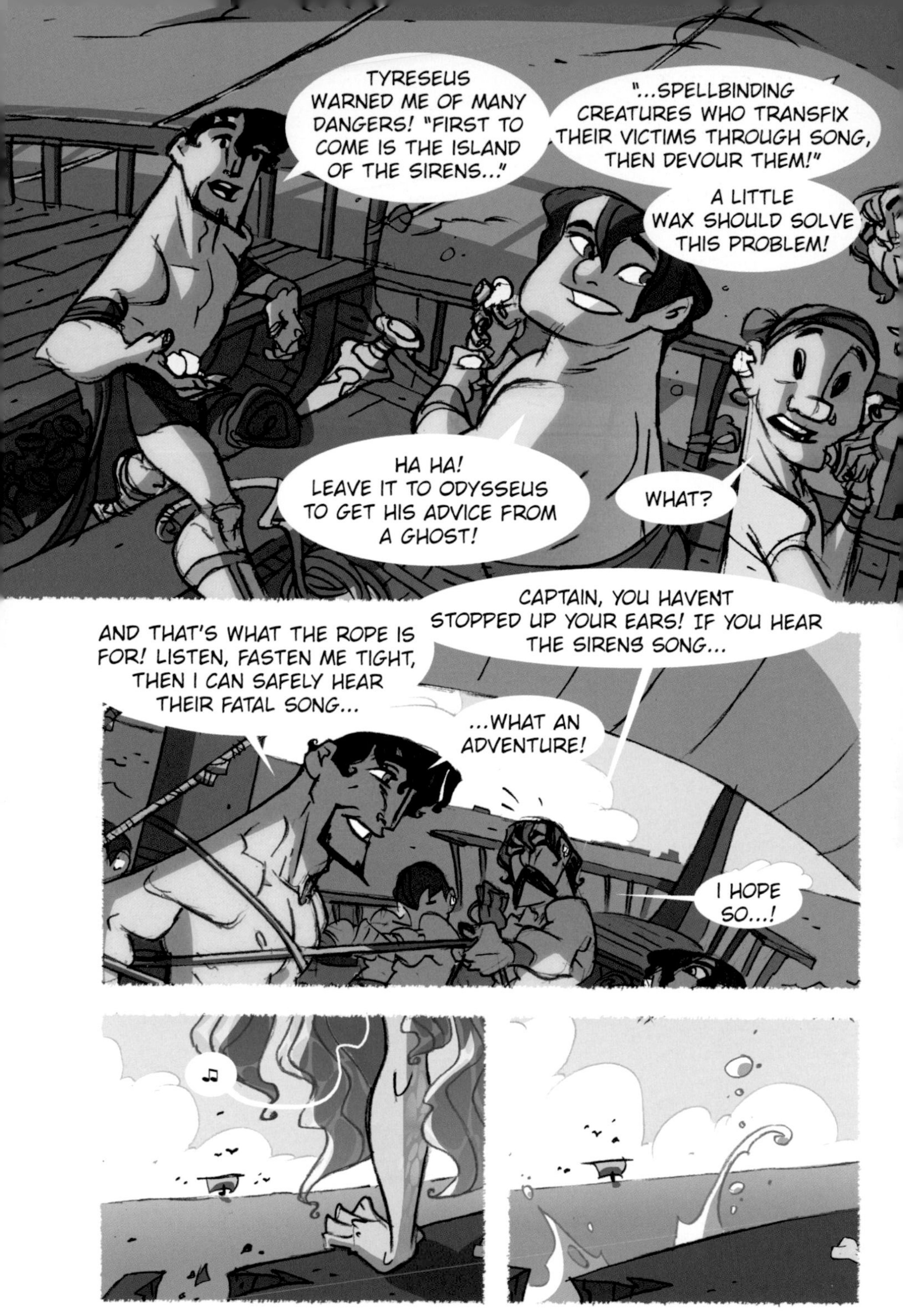
TYRESEUS WARNED ME OF MANY DANGERS! "FIRST TO COME IS THE ISLAND OF THE SIRENS..."
"...SPELLBINDING CREATURES WHO TRANSFIX THEIR VICTIMS THROUGH SONG, THEN DEVOUR THEM!"
A LITTLE WAX SHOULD SOLVE THIS PROBLEM!
HA HA! LEAVE IT TO ODYSSEUS TO GET HIS ADVICE FROM A GHOST!
WHAT?
CAPTAIN, YOU HAVENT STOPPED UP YOUR EARS! IF YOU HEAR THE SIRENS SONG...
AND THAT'S WHAT THE ROPE IS FOR! LISTEN, FASTEN ME TIGHT, THEN I CAN SAFELY HEAR THEIR FATAL SONG...
...WHAT AN ADVENTURE!
I HOPE SO...!
♫

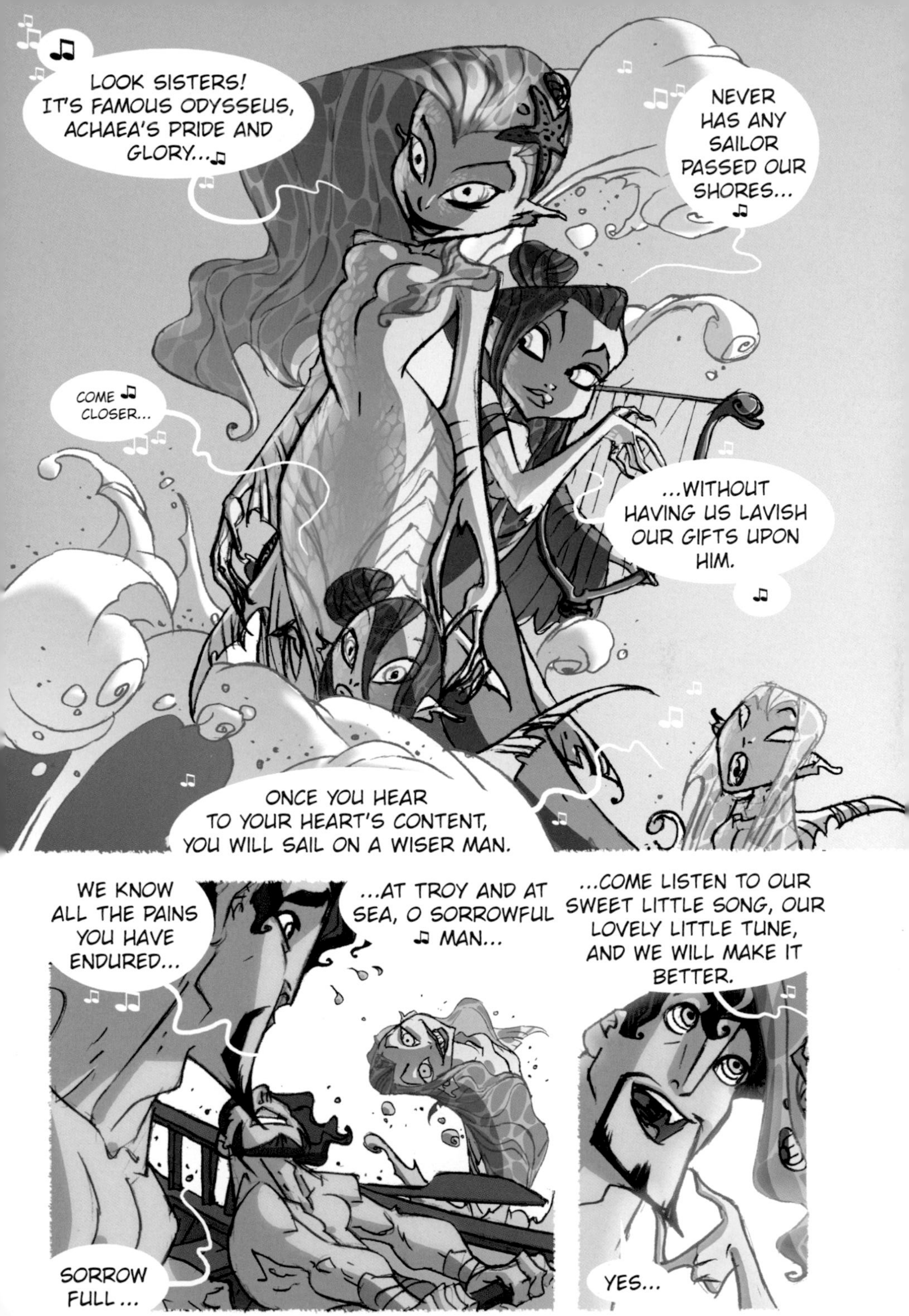
LOOK SISTERS! IT'S FAMOUS ODYSSEUS, ACHAEA'S PRIDE AND GLORY...
NEVER HAS ANY SAILOR PASSED OUR SHORES...
COME CLOSER...
...WITHOUT HAVING US LAVISH OUR GIFTS UPON HIM.
ONCE YOU HEAR TO YOUR HEART'S CONTENT, YOU WILL SAIL ON A WISER MAN.
WE KNOW ALL THE PAINS YOU HAVE ENDURED...
...AT TROY AND AT SEA, O SORROWFUL MAN...
SORROW FULL...
...COME LISTEN TO OUR SWEET LITTLE SONG, OUR LOVELY LITTLE TUNE, AND WE WILL MAKE IT BETTER.
YES...

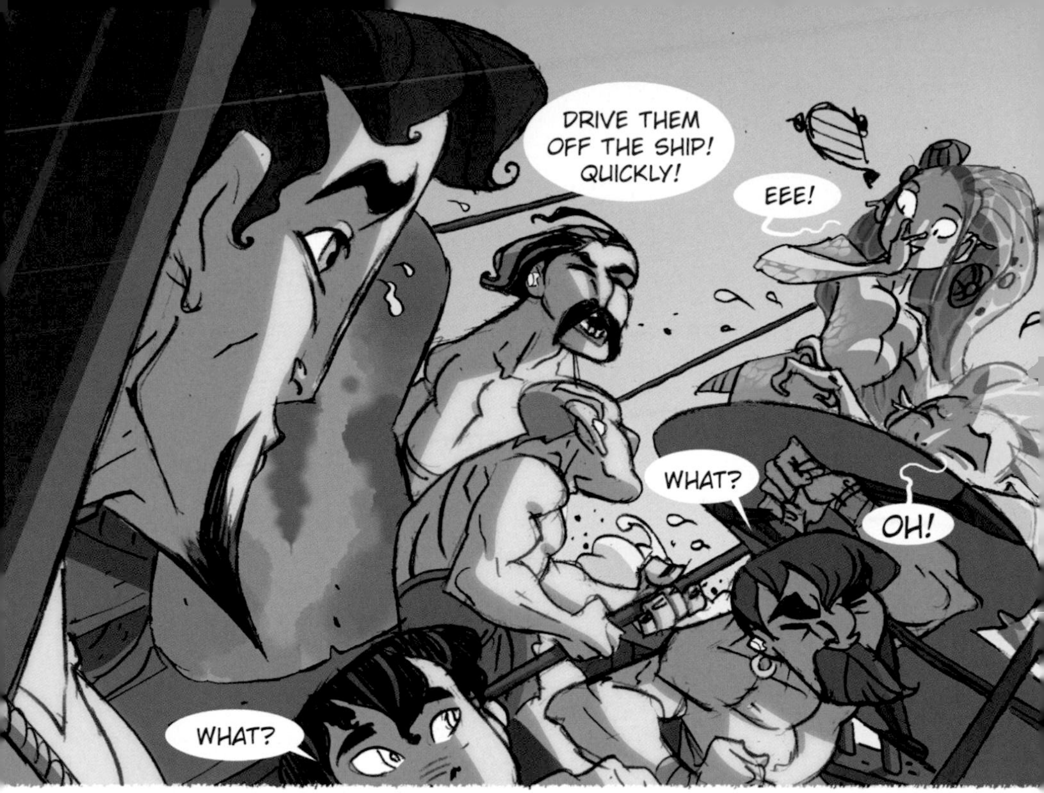
DRIVE THEM OFF THE SHIP! QUICKLY!
EEE!
WHAT?
OH!
WHAT?

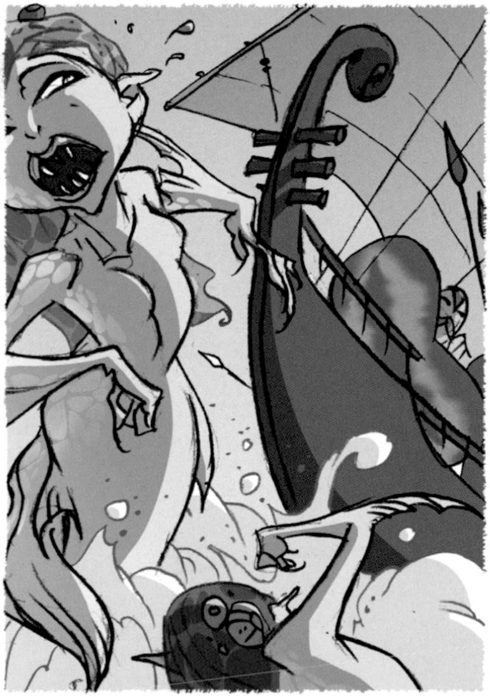

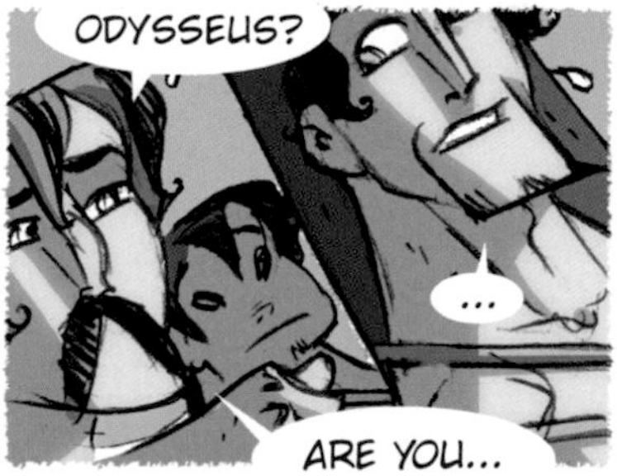
ODYSSEUS?
...
ARE YOU...

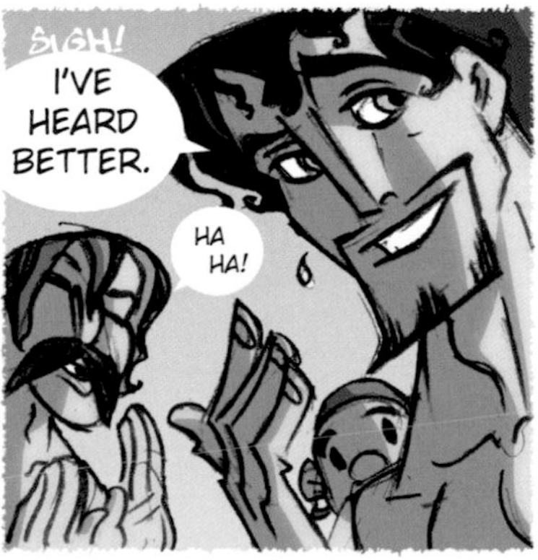
SIGH!
I'VE HEARD BETTER.
HA HA!

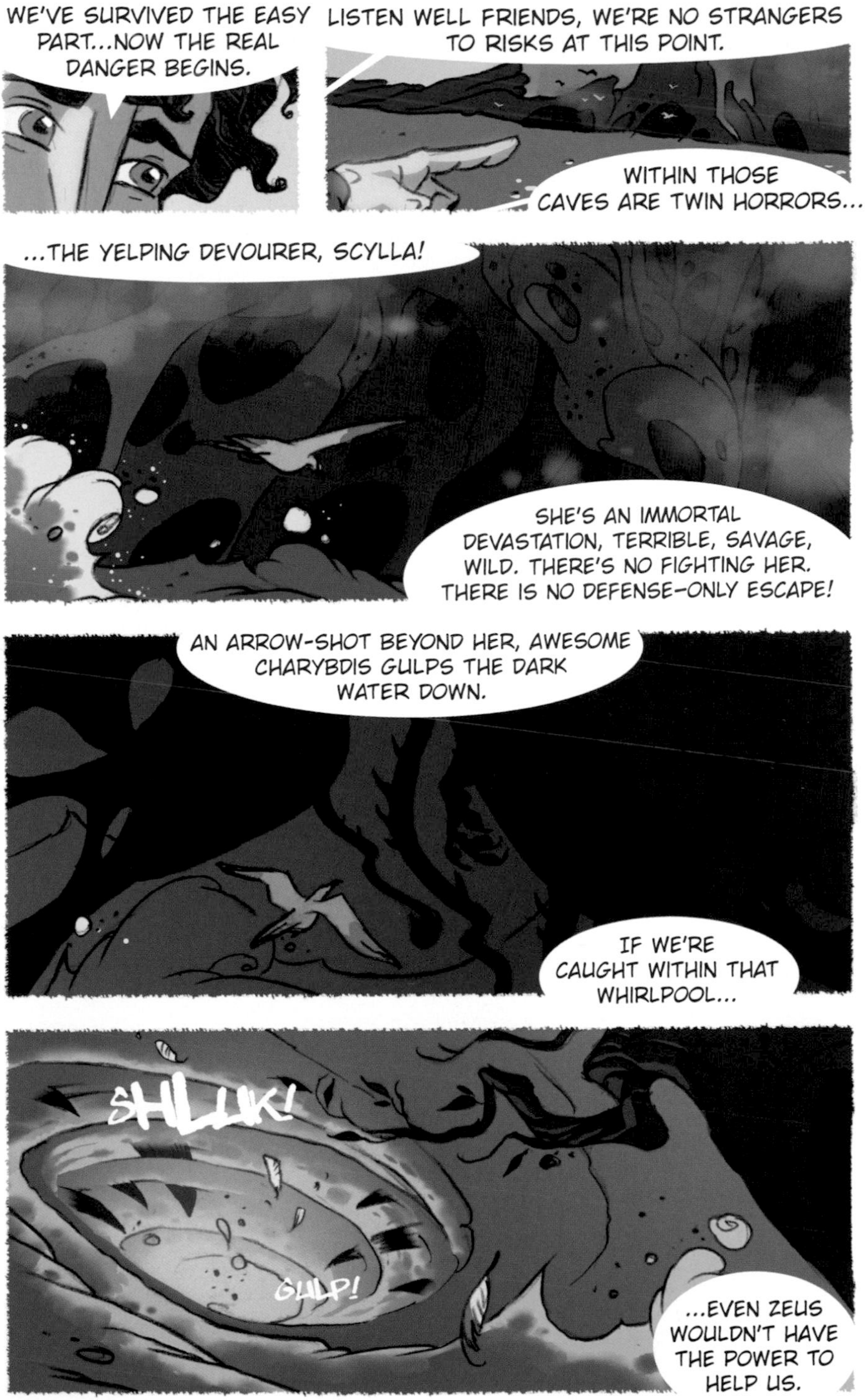
WE'VE SURVIVED THE EASY PART...NOW THE REAL DANGER BEGINS.
LISTEN WELL FRIENDS, WE'RE NO STRANGERS TO RISKS AT THIS POINT.
WITHIN THOSE CAVES ARE TWIN HORRORS...
...THE YELPING DEVOURER, SCYLLA!
SHE'S AN IMMORTAL DEVASTATION, TERRIBLE, SAVAGE, WILD. THERE'S NO FIGHTING HER. THERE IS NO DEFENSE–ONLY ESCAPE!
AN ARROW-SHOT BEYOND HER, AWESOME CHARYBDIS GULPS THE DARK WATER DOWN.
IF WE'RE CAUGHT WITHIN THAT WHIRLPOOL...
SHLLUK!
GULP!
...EVEN ZEUS WOULDN'T HAVE THE POWER TO HELP US.

STOW THE MAST AND SAIL...THEY'D BE CRUSHED IN THE NARROWS AHEAD! LAY ON WITH YOUR OARS, WE'LL DRIVE THROUGH THE STRAIGHTS WITH BRUTE FORCE...

...BUT REMEMBER... KEEP CLEAR OF CHARYBDIS! HUG THE CRAGS AND RISK SCYLLA, BUT KEEP US AWAY FROM THE BREAKERS...

RIG OUT THE OARS!

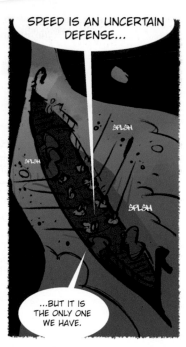

SPEED IS AN UNCERTAIN DEFENSE...

SPLSH

SPLSH

SPLSH

...BUT IT IS THE ONLY ONE WE HAVE.

KLAK!

KRRRRK!

SPLSH!

WHAT WAS THAT?

SPLSH!

SPLSH!

STEADY...

SPLSH!

SPLSH!

SPLSH!

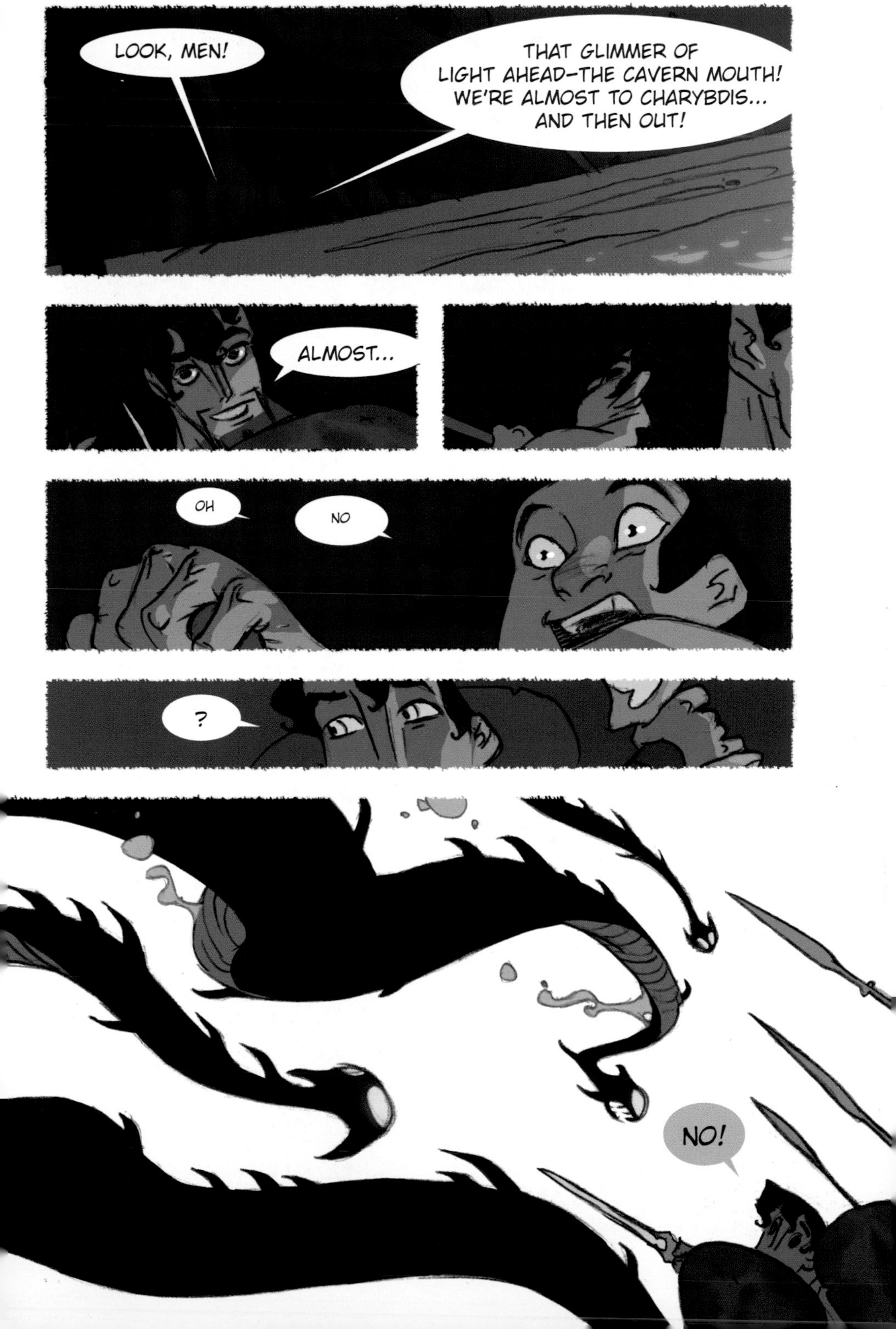
LOOK, MEN!
THAT GLIMMER OF LIGHT AHEAD—THE CAVERN MOUTH! WE'RE ALMOST TO CHARYBDIS... AND THEN OUT!
ALMOST...
OH
NO
?
NO!

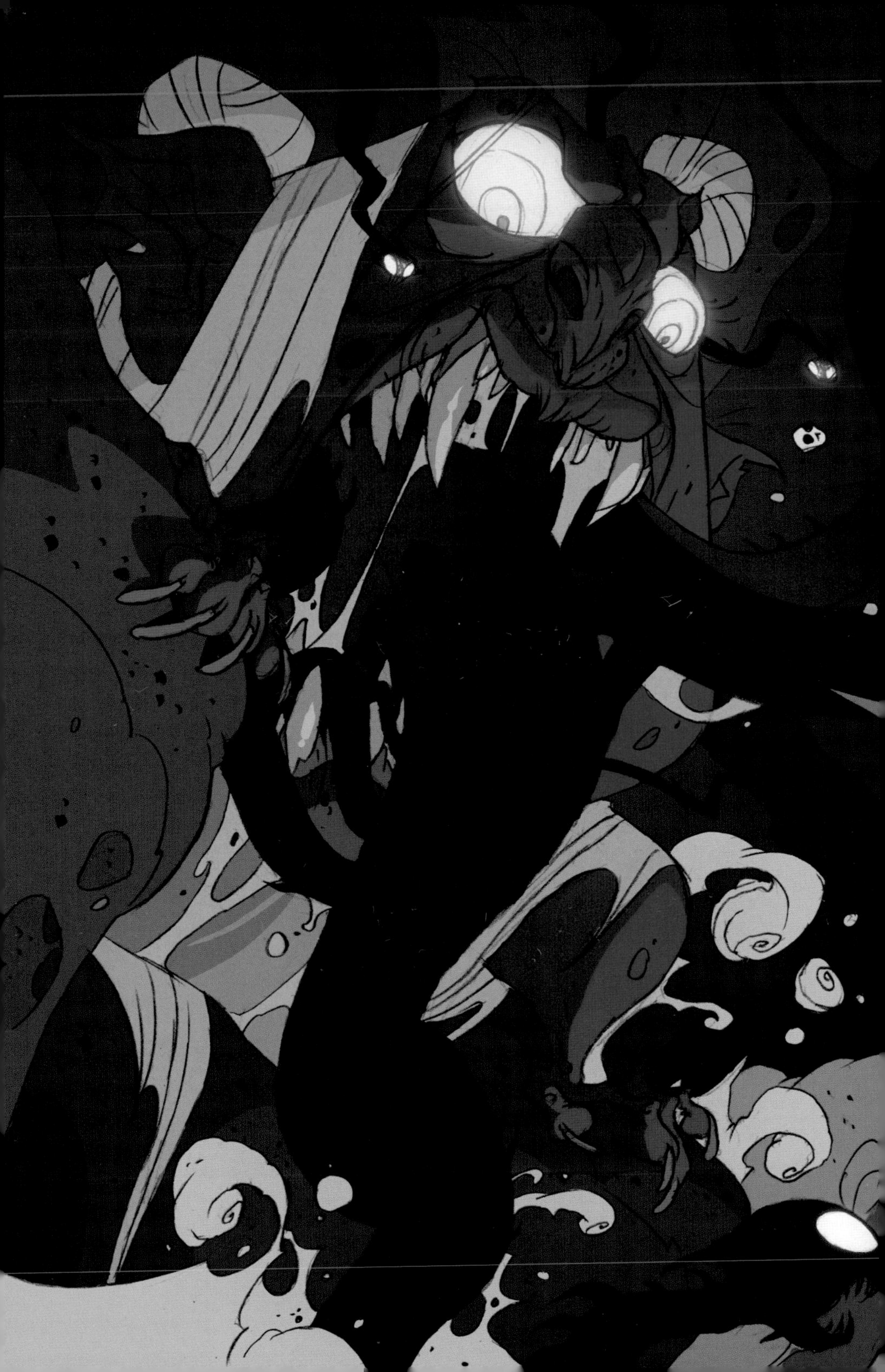

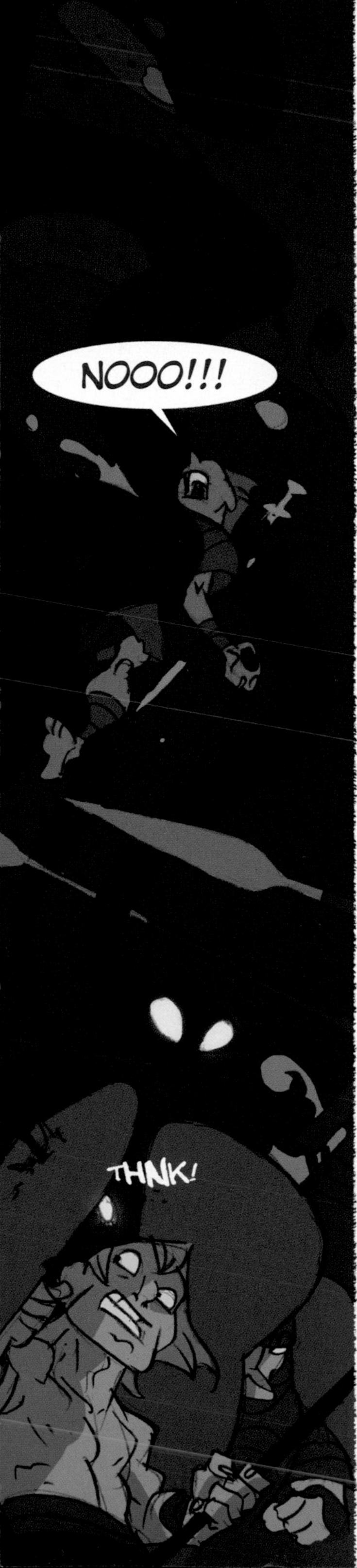
NOOO!!!
THNK!

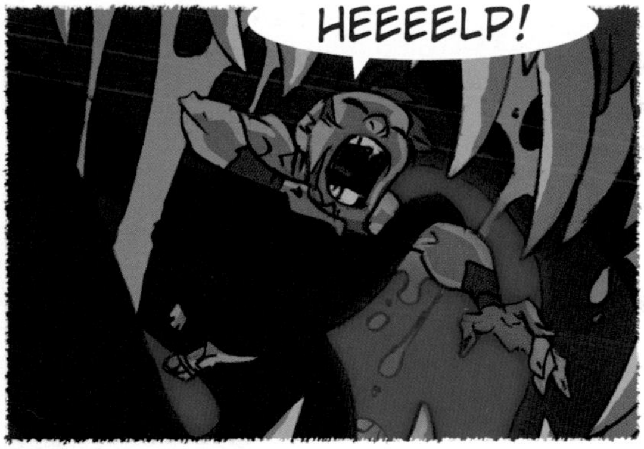
HEEEELP!

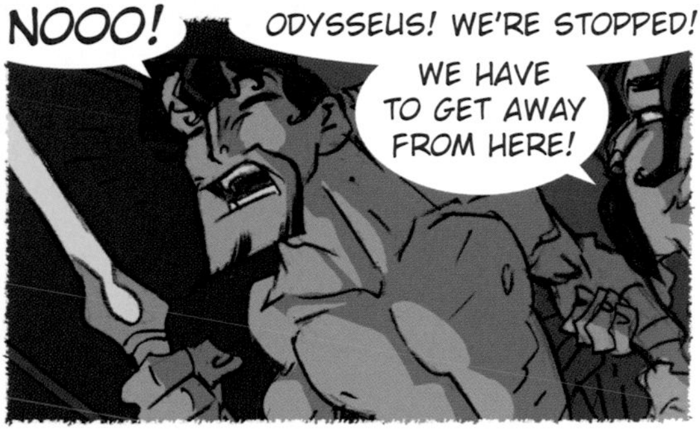
NOOO!
ODYSSEUS! WE'RE STOPPED!
WE HAVE TO GET AWAY FROM HERE!

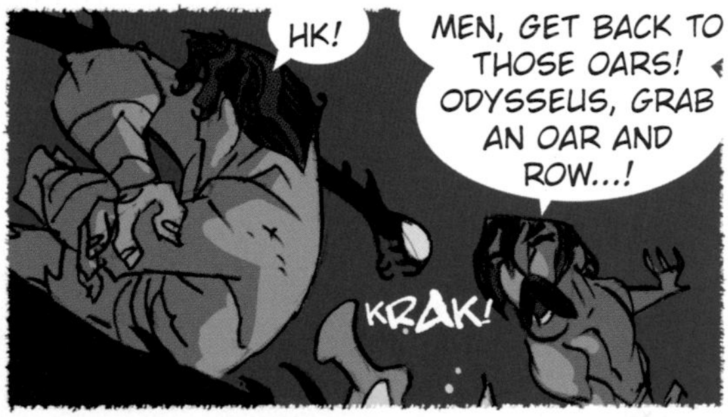
HK!
MEN, GET BACK TO THOSE OARS! ODYSSEUS, GRAB AN OAR AND ROW...!
KRAK!

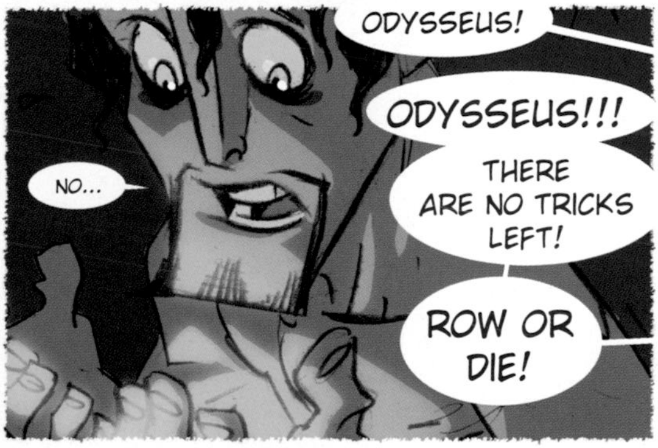
ODYSSEUS!
ODYSSEUS!!!
NO...
THERE ARE NO TRICKS LEFT!
ROW OR DIE!

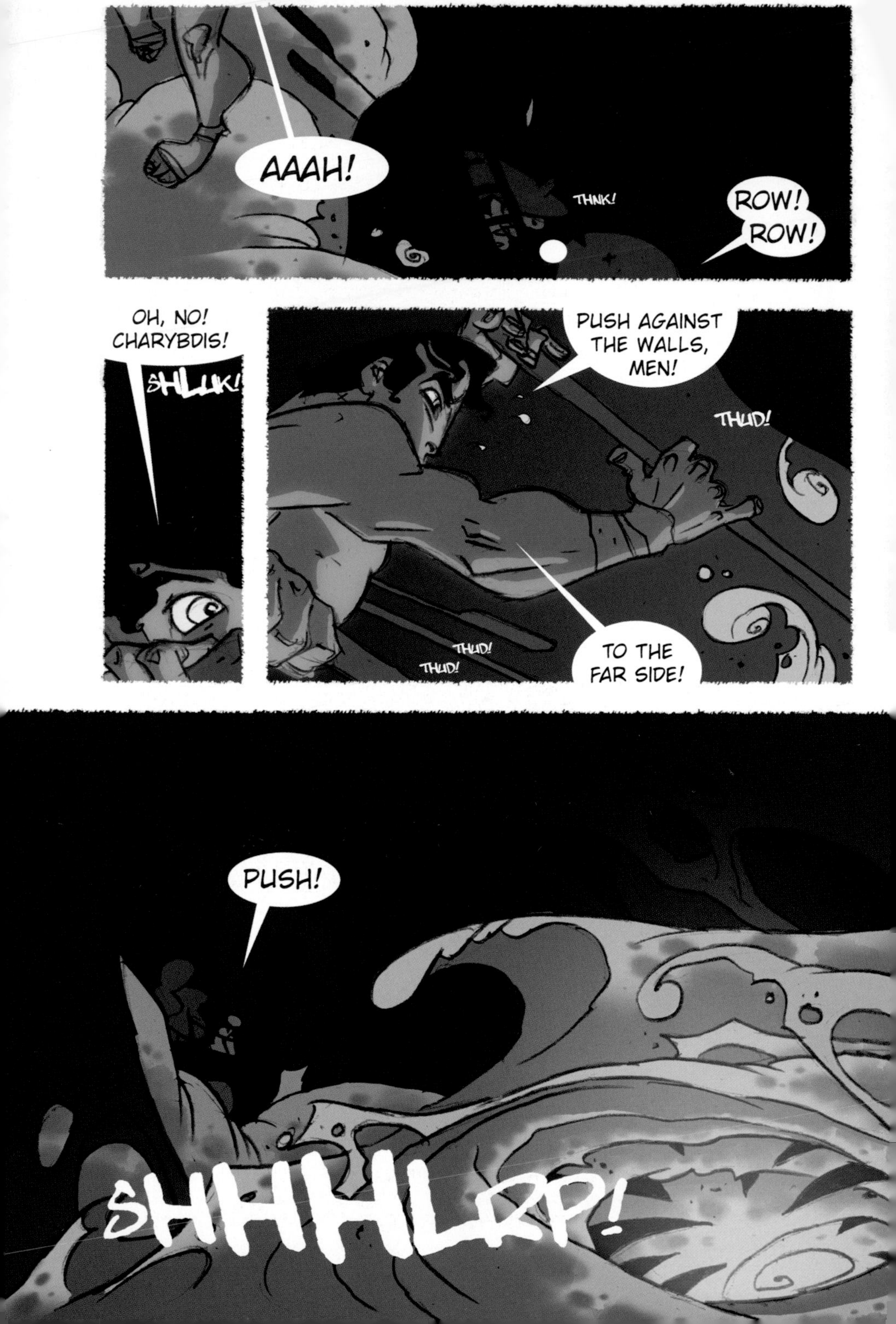
AAAH!
THNK!
ROW! ROW!
OH, NO! CHARYBDIS!
SHLUK!
PUSH AGAINST THE WALLS, MEN!
THUD!
TO THE FAR SIDE!
THUD!
THUD!
PUSH!
SHHHLRP!

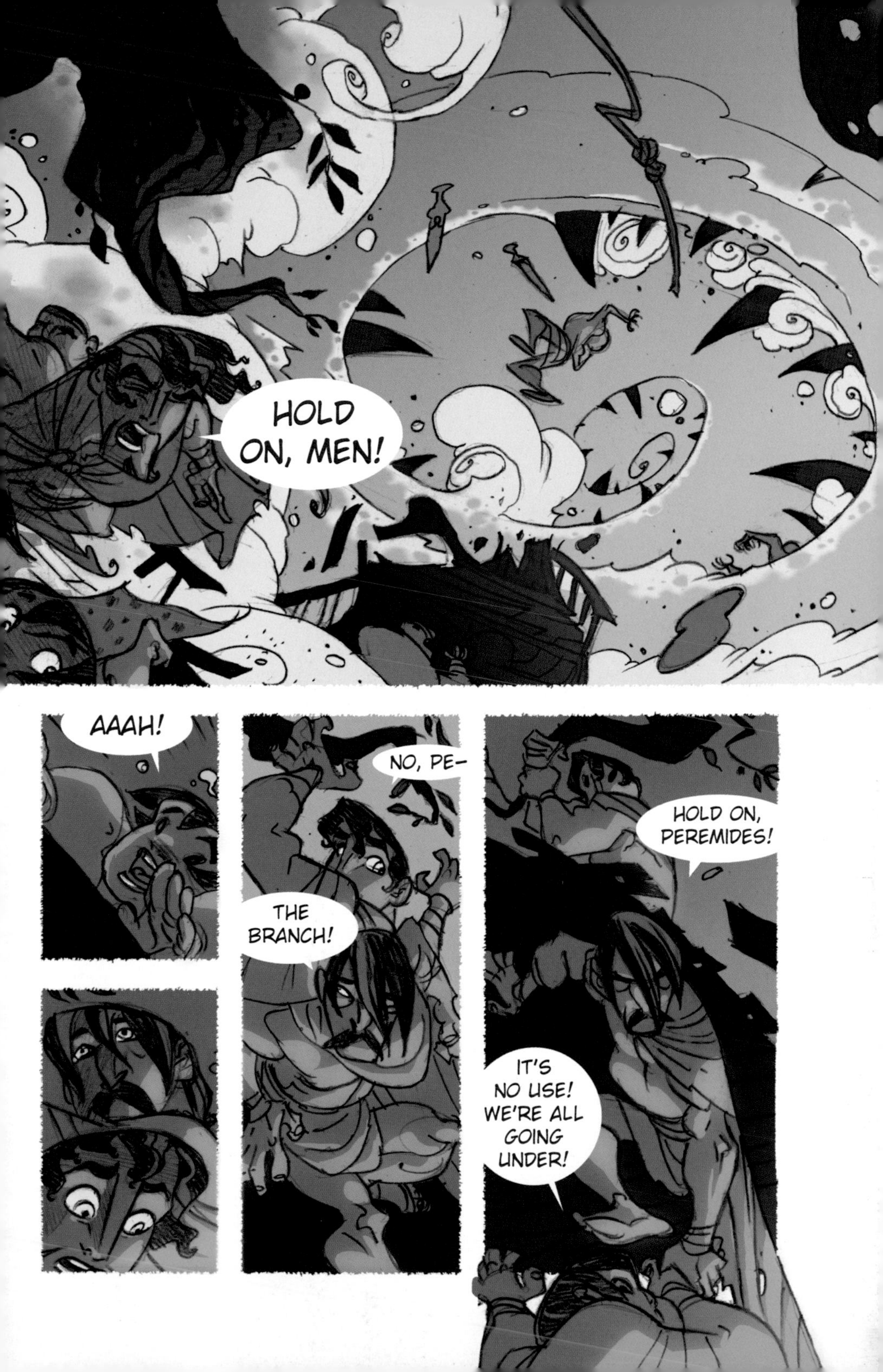
HOLD ON, MEN!
AAAH!
NO, PE-
THE BRANCH!
HOLD ON, PEREMIDES!
IT'S NO USE! WE'RE ALL GOING UNDER!

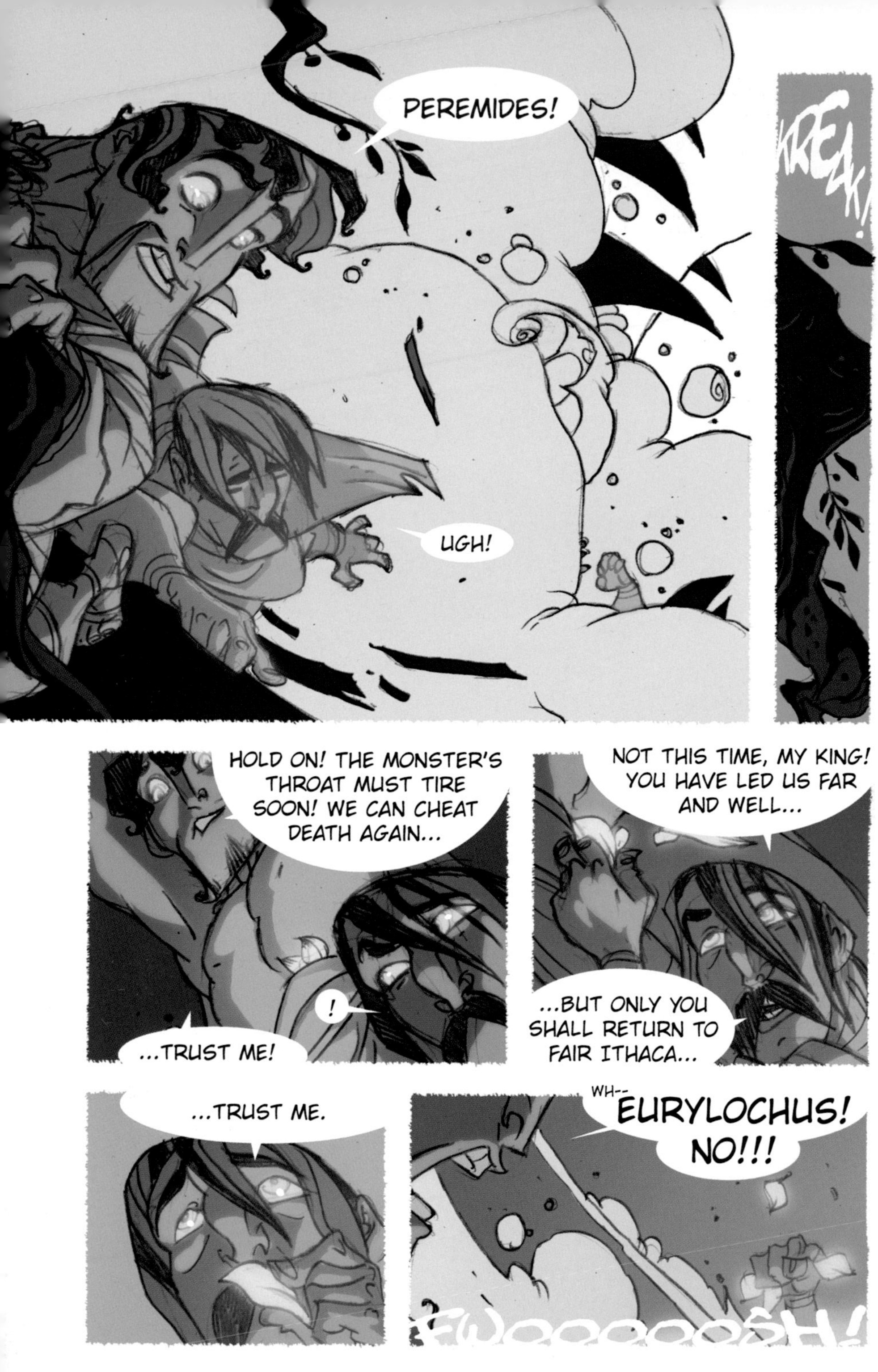
PEREMIDES!
UGH!
KREAK!
HOLD ON! THE MONSTER'S THROAT MUST TIRE SOON! WE CAN CHEAT DEATH AGAIN...
...TRUST ME!
!
NOT THIS TIME, MY KING! YOU HAVE LED US FAR AND WELL...
...BUT ONLY YOU SHALL RETURN TO FAIR ITHACA...
...TRUST ME.
WH--
EURYLOCHUS! NO!!!
FWOOOOOSH!

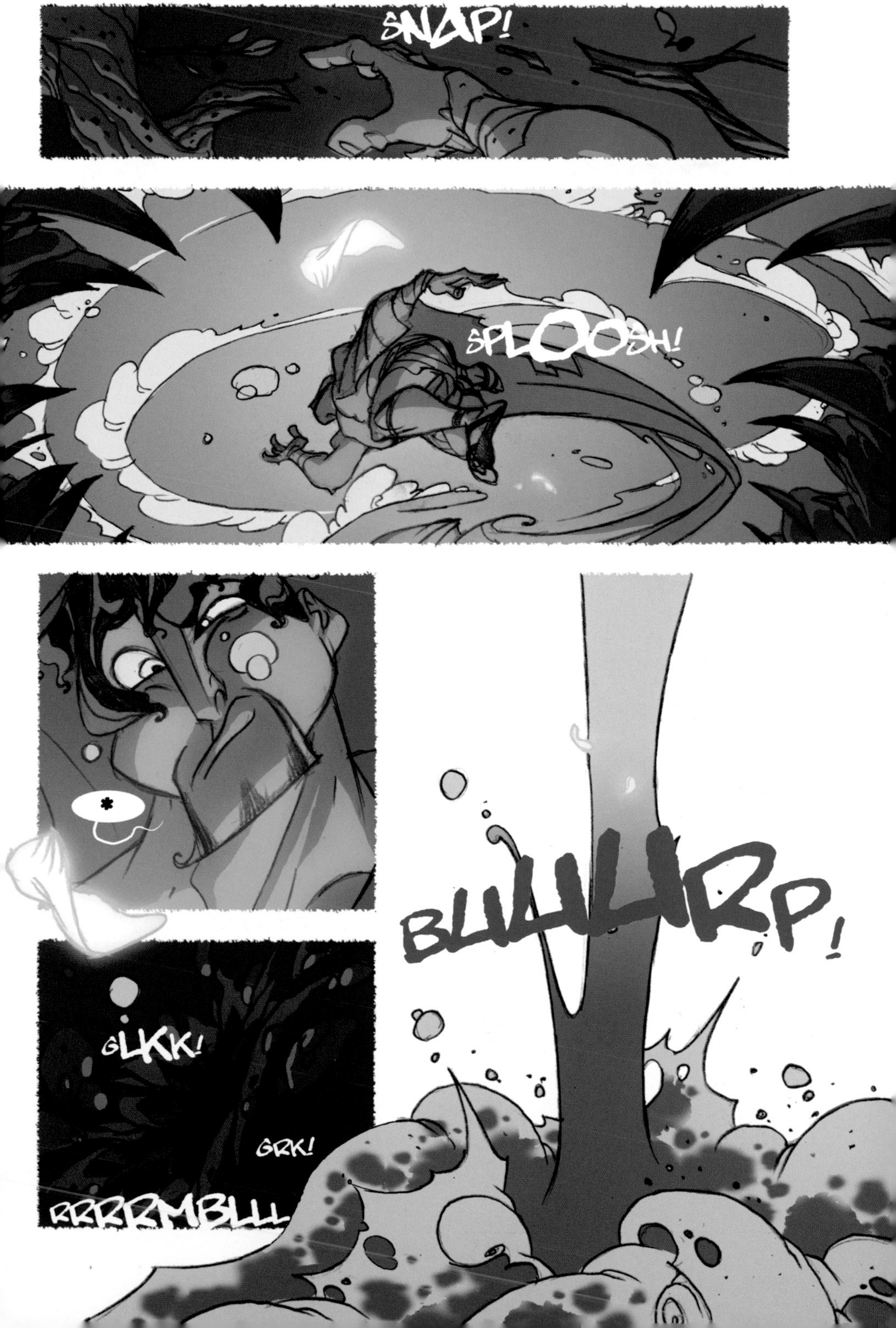
SNAP!
SPLOOOSH!
*
GLKK!
GRK!
RRRRRMBLLL
BLLLLRP!

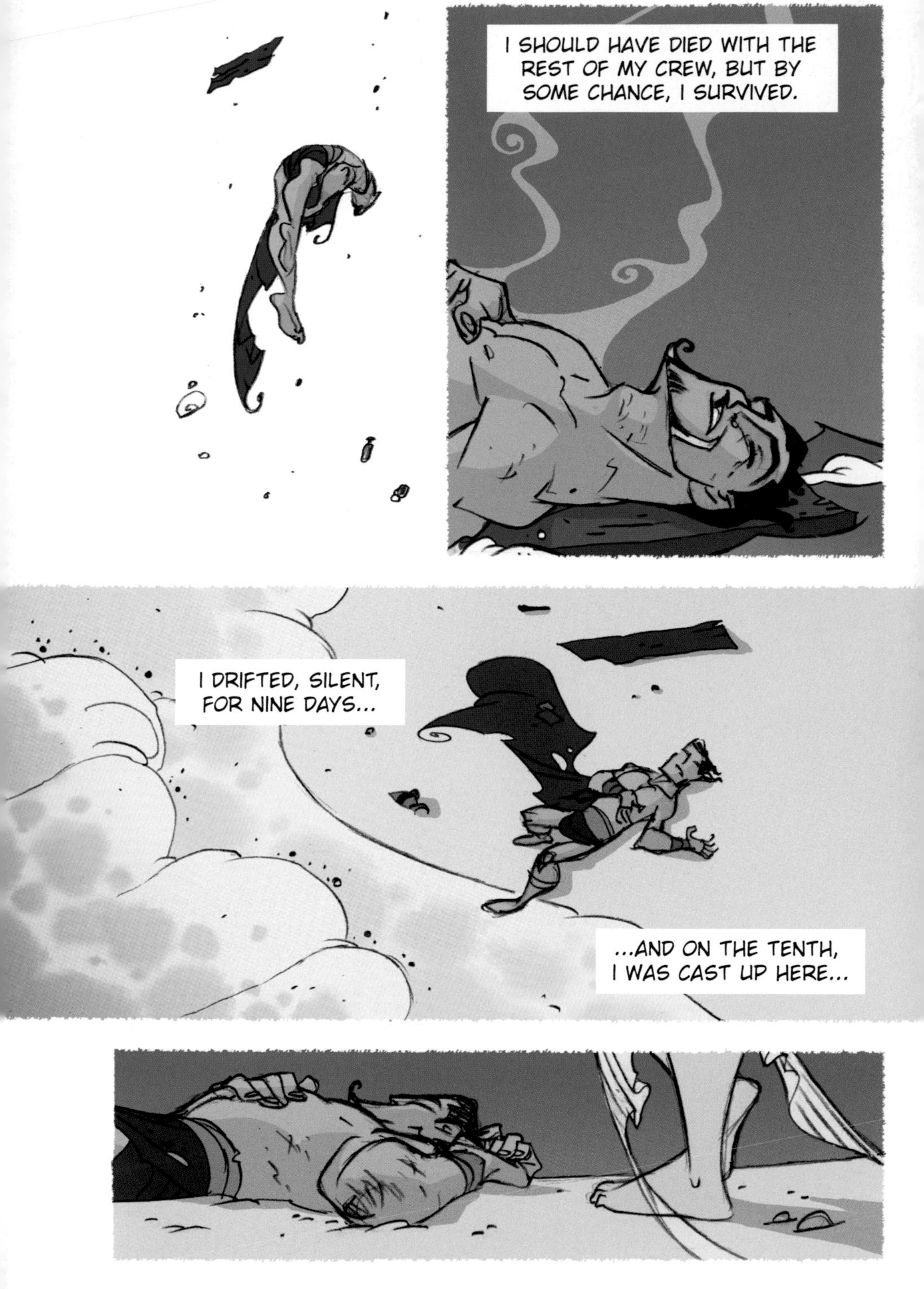
I SHOULD HAVE DIED WITH THE REST OF MY CREW, BUT BY SOME CHANCE, I SURVIVED.
I DRIFTED, SILENT, FOR NINE DAYS...
...AND ON THE TENTH, I WAS CAST UP HERE...

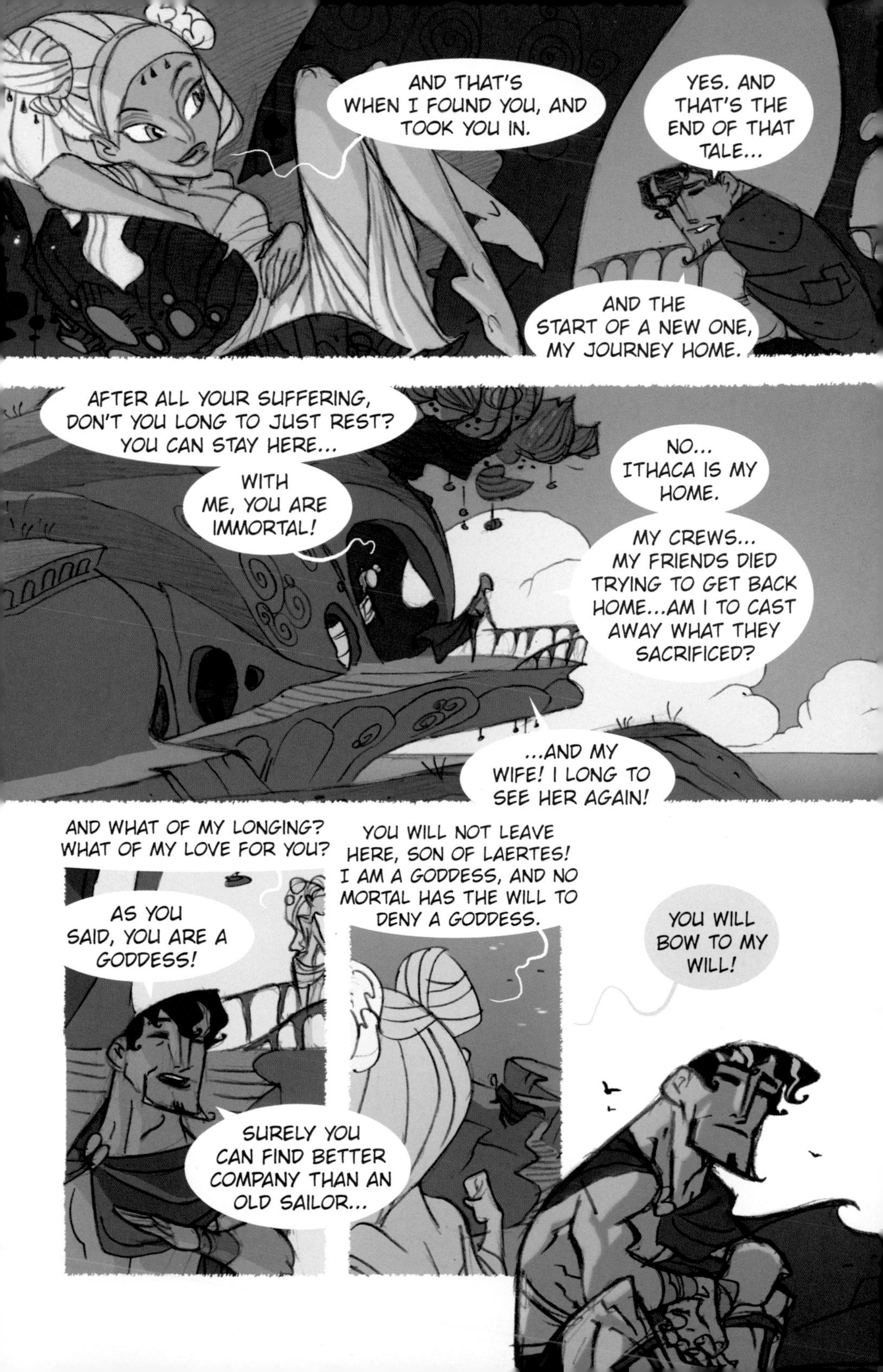
AND THAT'S WHEN I FOUND YOU, AND TOOK YOU IN.
YES. AND THAT'S THE END OF THAT TALE...
AND THE START OF A NEW ONE, MY JOURNEY HOME.
AFTER ALL YOUR SUFFERING, DON'T YOU LONG TO JUST REST? YOU CAN STAY HERE...
WITH ME, YOU ARE IMMORTAL!
NO... ITHACA IS MY HOME.
MY CREWS... MY FRIENDS DIED TRYING TO GET BACK HOME...AM I TO CAST AWAY WHAT THEY SACRIFICED?
...AND MY WIFE! I LONG TO SEE HER AGAIN!
AND WHAT OF MY LONGING? WHAT OF MY LOVE FOR YOU?
AS YOU SAID, YOU ARE A GODDESS!
SURELY YOU CAN FIND BETTER COMPANY THAN AN OLD SAILOR...
YOU WILL NOT LEAVE HERE, SON OF LAERTES! I AM A GODDESS, AND NO MORTAL HAS THE WILL TO DENY A GODDESS.
YOU WILL BOW TO MY WILL!

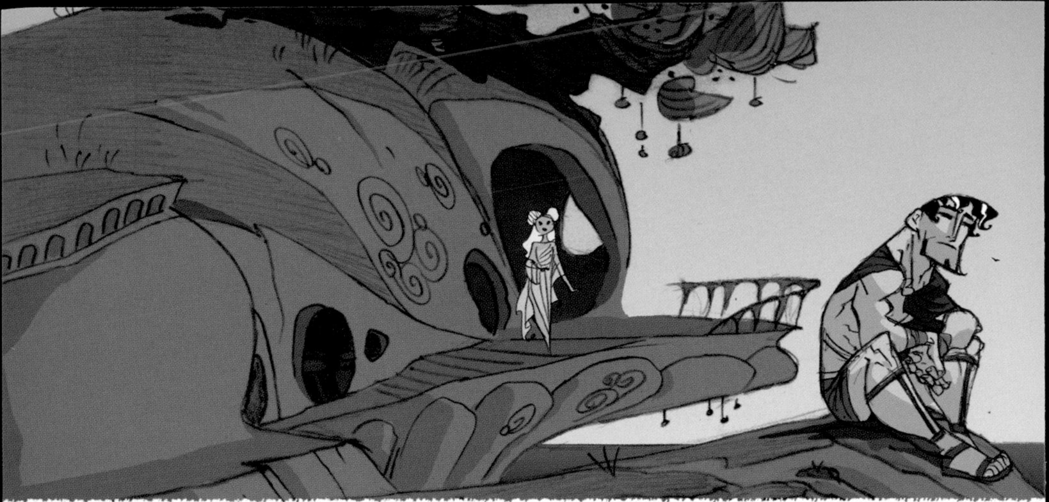

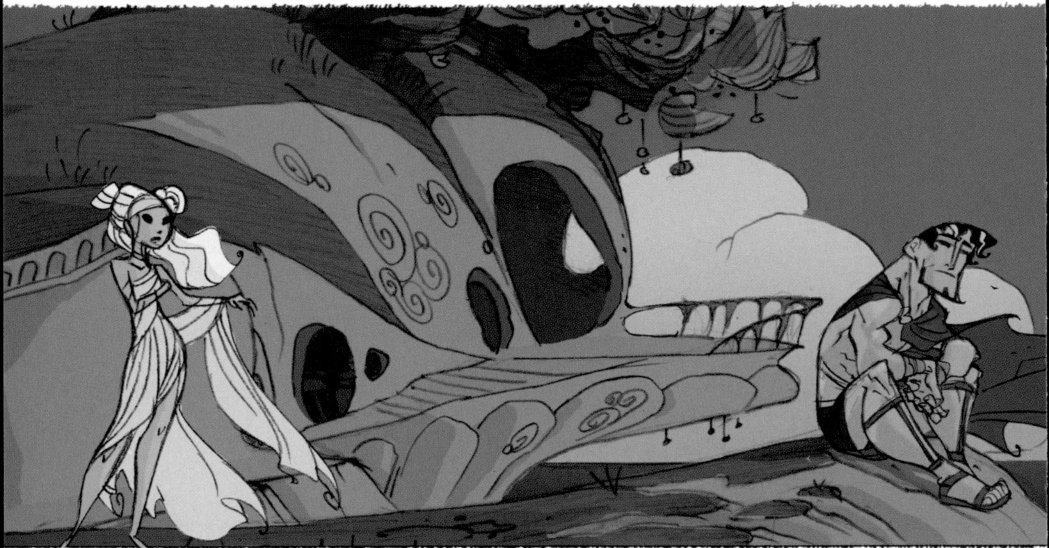

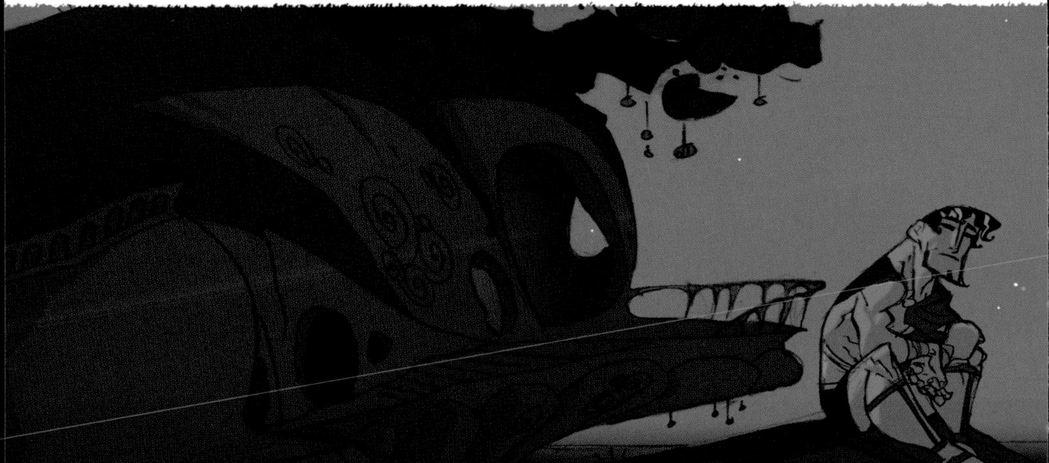

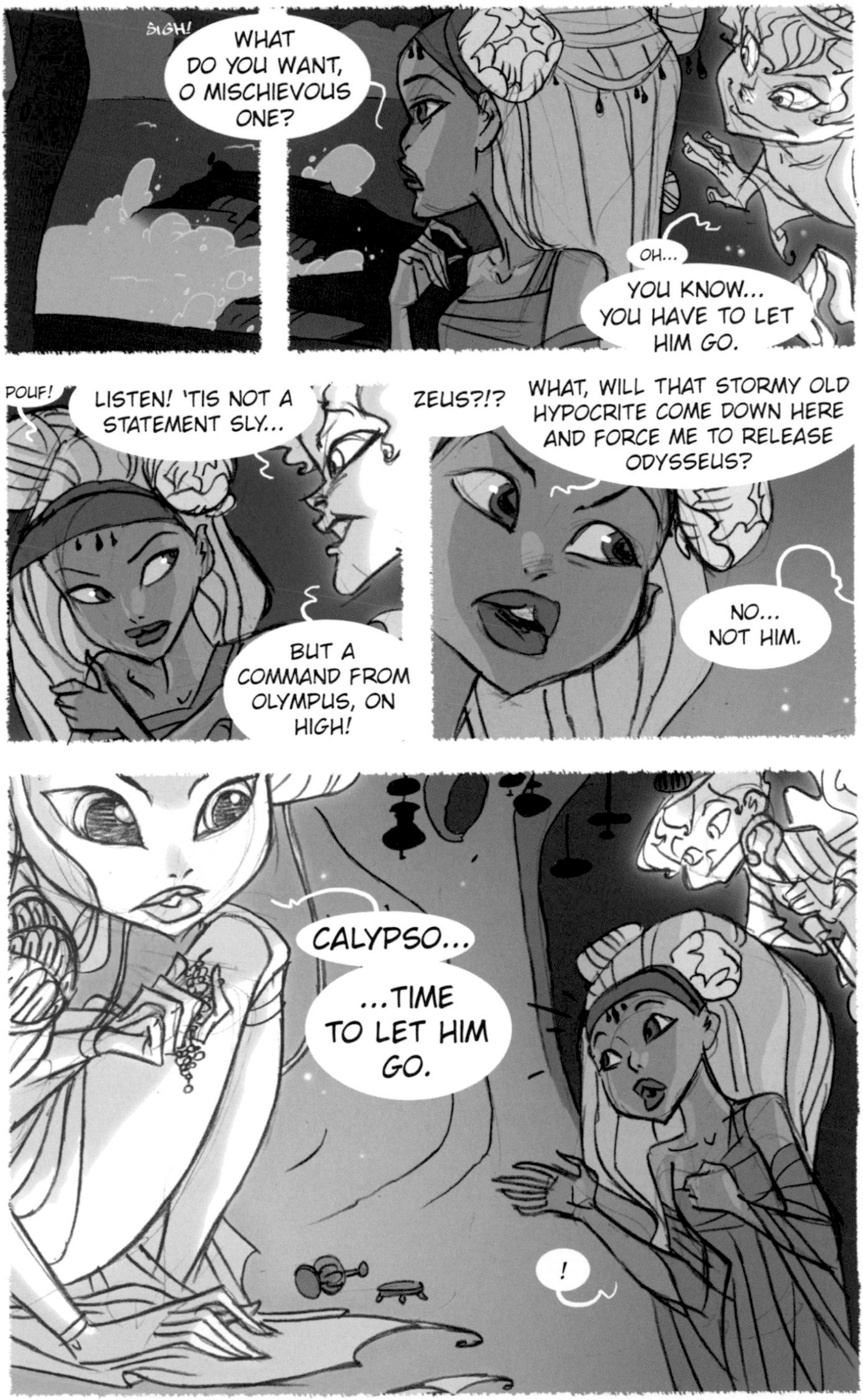
SIGH!
WHAT DO YOU WANT, O MISCHIEVOUS ONE?
OH...
YOU KNOW... YOU HAVE TO LET HIM GO.
POUF!
LISTEN! 'TIS NOT A STATEMENT SLY...
BUT A COMMAND FROM OLYMPUS, ON HIGH!
ZEUS?!?
WHAT, WILL THAT STORMY OLD HYPOCRITE COME DOWN HERE AND FORCE ME TO RELEASE ODYSSEUS?
NO... NOT HIM.
CALYPSO...
...TIME TO LET HIM GO.
!

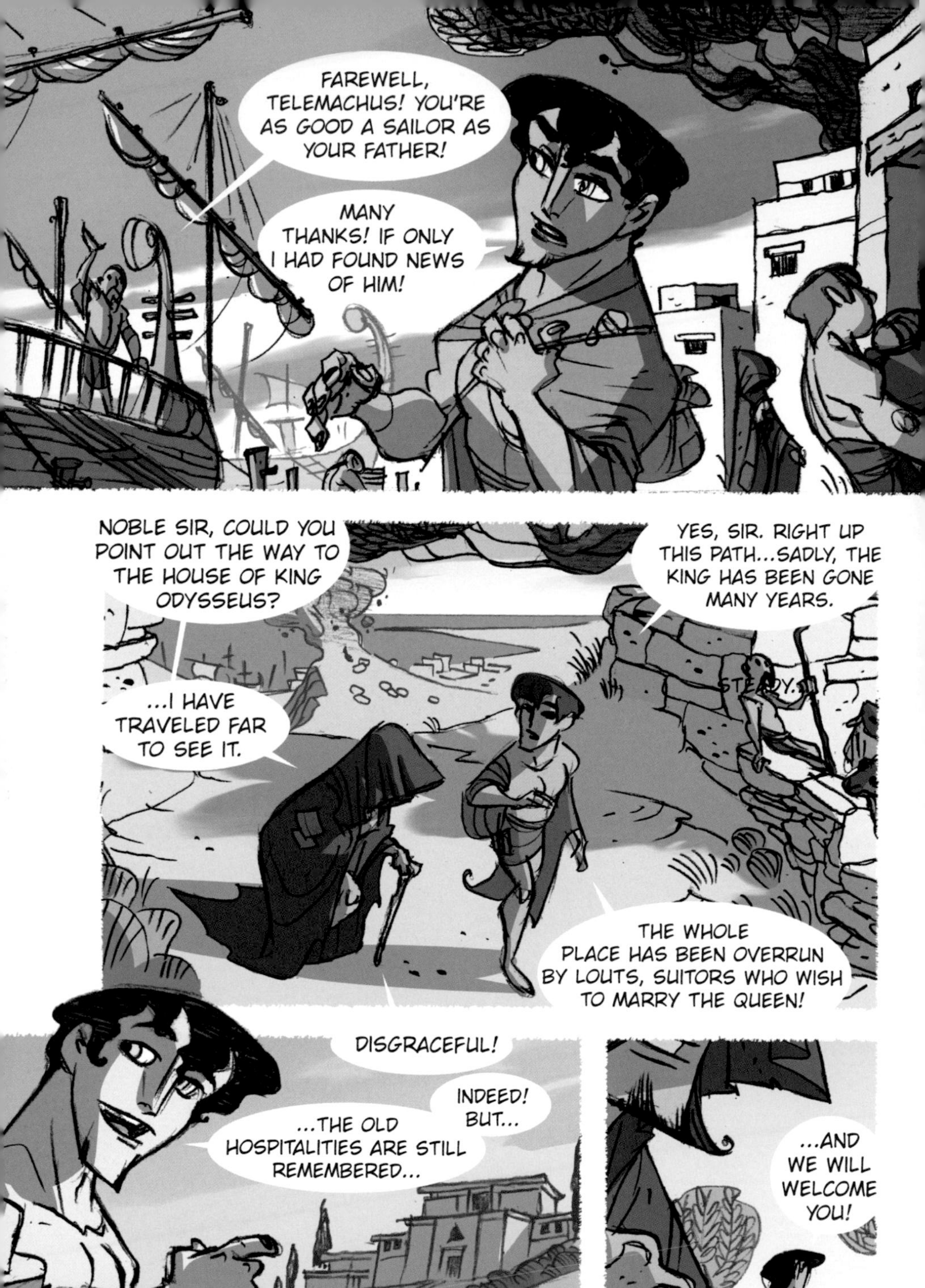

FAREWELL, TELEMACHUS! YOU'RE AS GOOD A SAILOR AS YOUR FATHER!
MANY THANKS! IF ONLY I HAD FOUND NEWS OF HIM!
NOBLE SIR, COULD YOU POINT OUT THE WAY TO THE HOUSE OF KING ODYSSEUS?
...I HAVE TRAVELED FAR TO SEE IT.
YES, SIR. RIGHT UP THIS PATH...SADLY, THE KING HAS BEEN GONE MANY YEARS.
THE WHOLE PLACE HAS BEEN OVERRUN BY LOUTS, SUITORS WHO WISH TO MARRY THE QUEEN!
DISGRACEFUL!
INDEED! BUT...
...THE OLD HOSPITALITIES ARE STILL REMEMBERED...
...AND WE WILL WELCOME YOU!

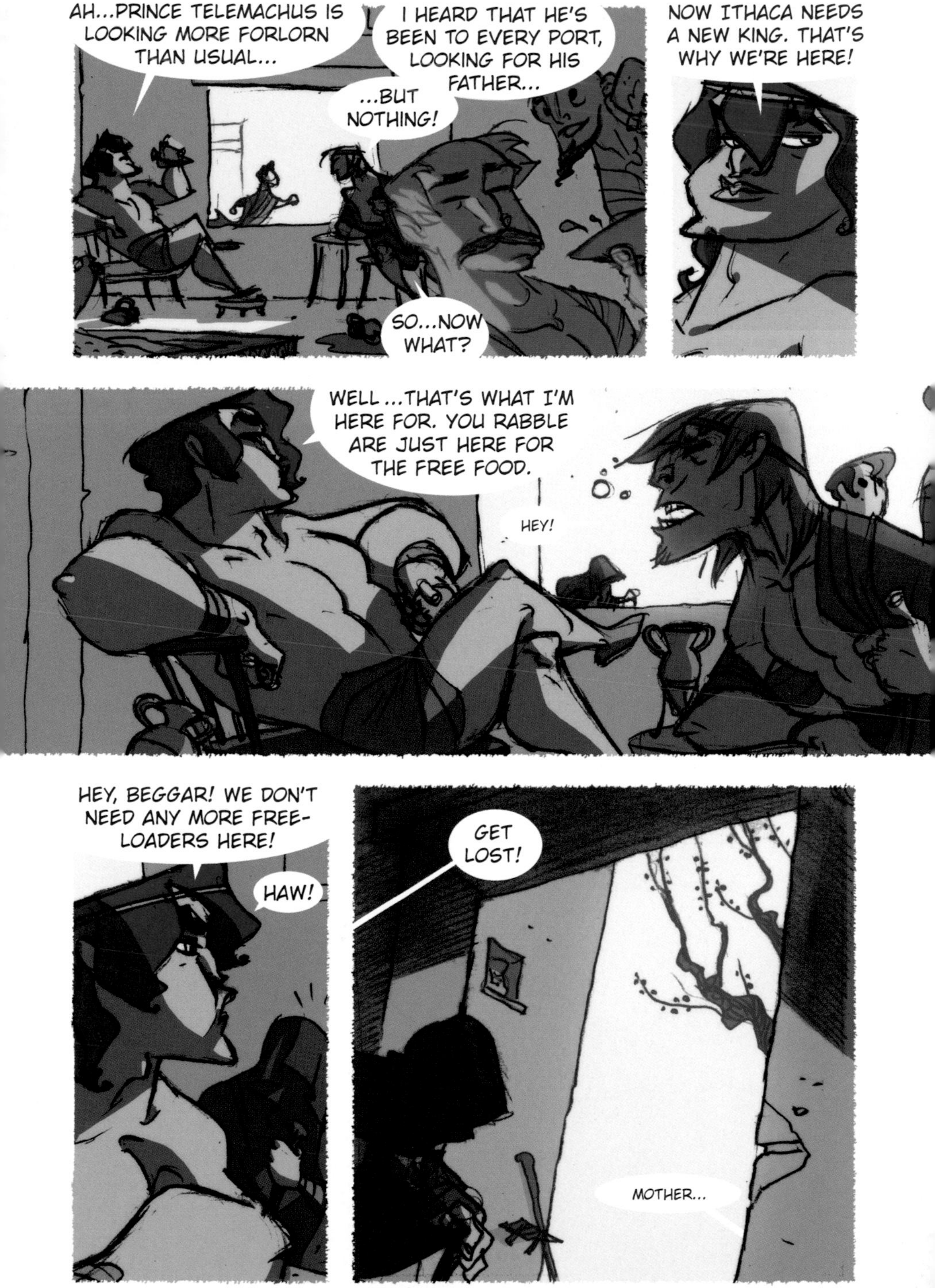
AH...PRINCE TELEMACHUS IS LOOKING MORE FORLORN THAN USUAL...
I HEARD THAT HE'S BEEN TO EVERY PORT, LOOKING FOR HIS FATHER...
...BUT NOTHING!
SO...NOW WHAT?
NOW ITHACA NEEDS A NEW KING. THAT'S WHY WE'RE HERE!
WELL ...THAT'S WHAT I'M HERE FOR. YOU RABBLE ARE JUST HERE FOR THE FREE FOOD.
HEY!
HEY, BEGGAR! WE DON'T NEED ANY MORE FREE-LOADERS HERE!
HAW!
GET LOST!
MOTHER...

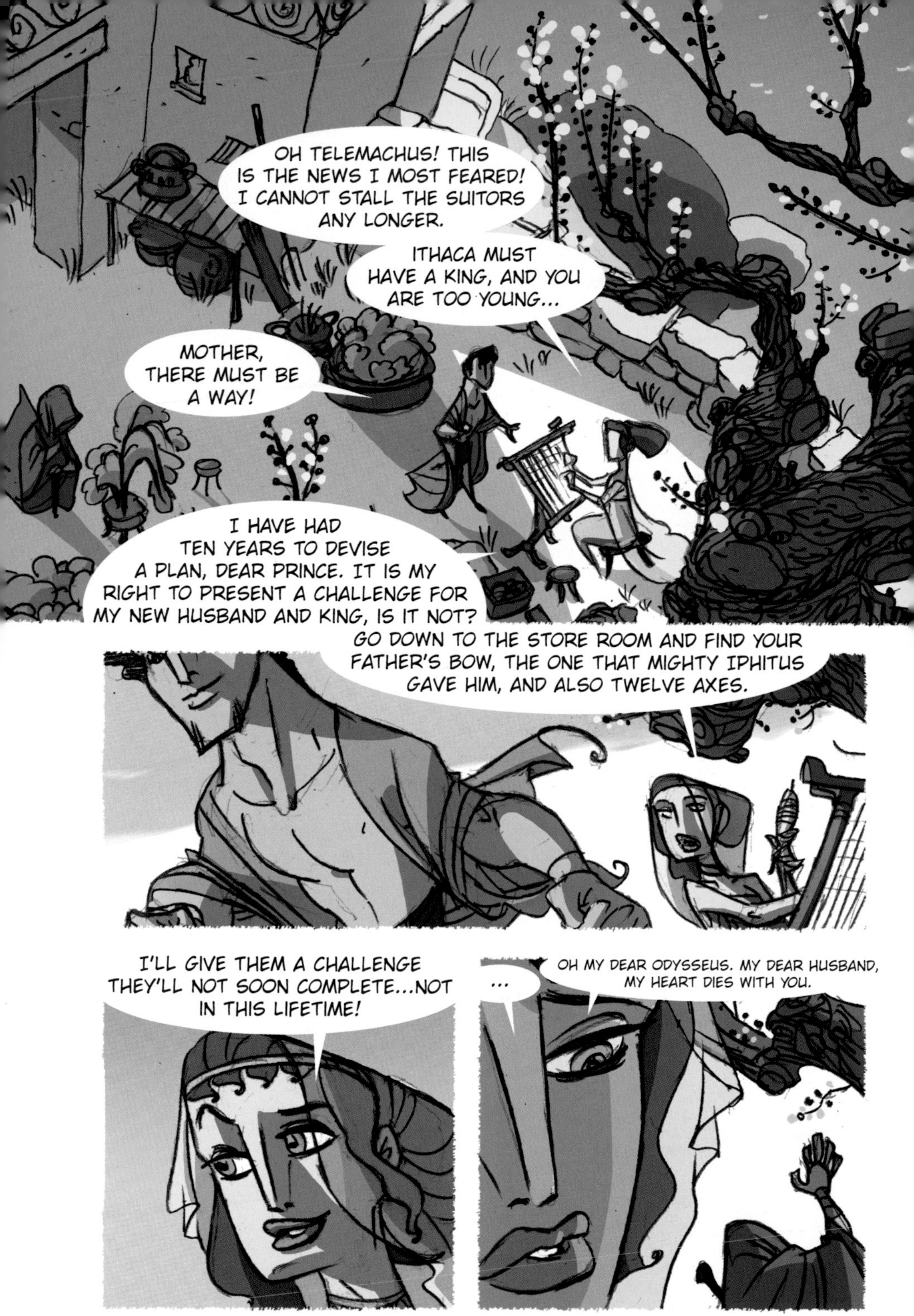
OH TELEMACHUS! THIS IS THE NEWS I MOST FEARED! I CANNOT STALL THE SUITORS ANY LONGER.
ITHACA MUST HAVE A KING, AND YOU ARE TOO YOUNG...
MOTHER, THERE MUST BE A WAY!
I HAVE HAD TEN YEARS TO DEVISE A PLAN, DEAR PRINCE. IT IS MY RIGHT TO PRESENT A CHALLENGE FOR MY NEW HUSBAND AND KING, IS IT NOT?
GO DOWN TO THE STORE ROOM AND FIND YOUR FATHER'S BOW, THE ONE THAT MIGHTY IPHITUS GAVE HIM, AND ALSO TWELVE AXES.
I'LL GIVE THEM A CHALLENGE THEY'LL NOT SOON COMPLETE...NOT IN THIS LIFETIME!
...
OH MY DEAR ODYSSEUS. MY DEAR HUSBAND, MY HEART DIES WITH YOU.

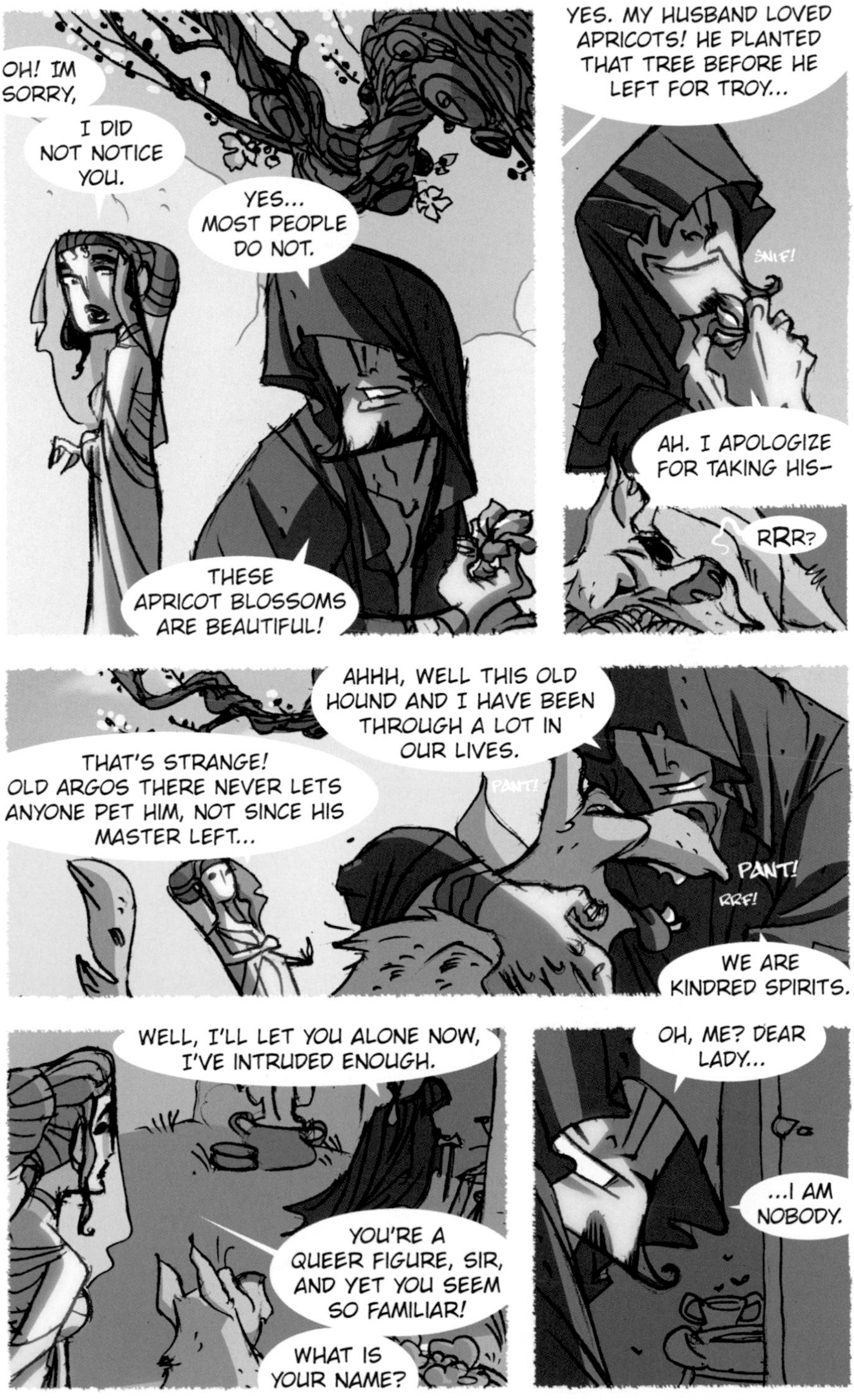
OH! IM SORRY,
I DID NOT NOTICE YOU.
YES... MOST PEOPLE DO NOT.
THESE APRICOT BLOSSOMS ARE BEAUTIFUL!
YES. MY HUSBAND LOVED APRICOTS! HE PLANTED THAT TREE BEFORE HE LEFT FOR TROY...
SNIF!
AH. I APOLOGIZE FOR TAKING HIS-
RRR?
THAT'S STRANGE! OLD ARGOS THERE NEVER LETS ANYONE PET HIM, NOT SINCE HIS MASTER LEFT...
AHHH, WELL THIS OLD HOUND AND I HAVE BEEN THROUGH A LOT IN OUR LIVES.
PANT!
PANT!
RRF!
WE ARE KINDRED SPIRITS.
WELL, I'LL LET YOU ALONE NOW, I'VE INTRUDED ENOUGH.
YOU'RE A QUEER FIGURE, SIR, AND YET YOU SEEM SO FAMILIAR!
WHAT IS YOUR NAME?
OH, ME? DEAR LADY...
...I AM NOBODY.

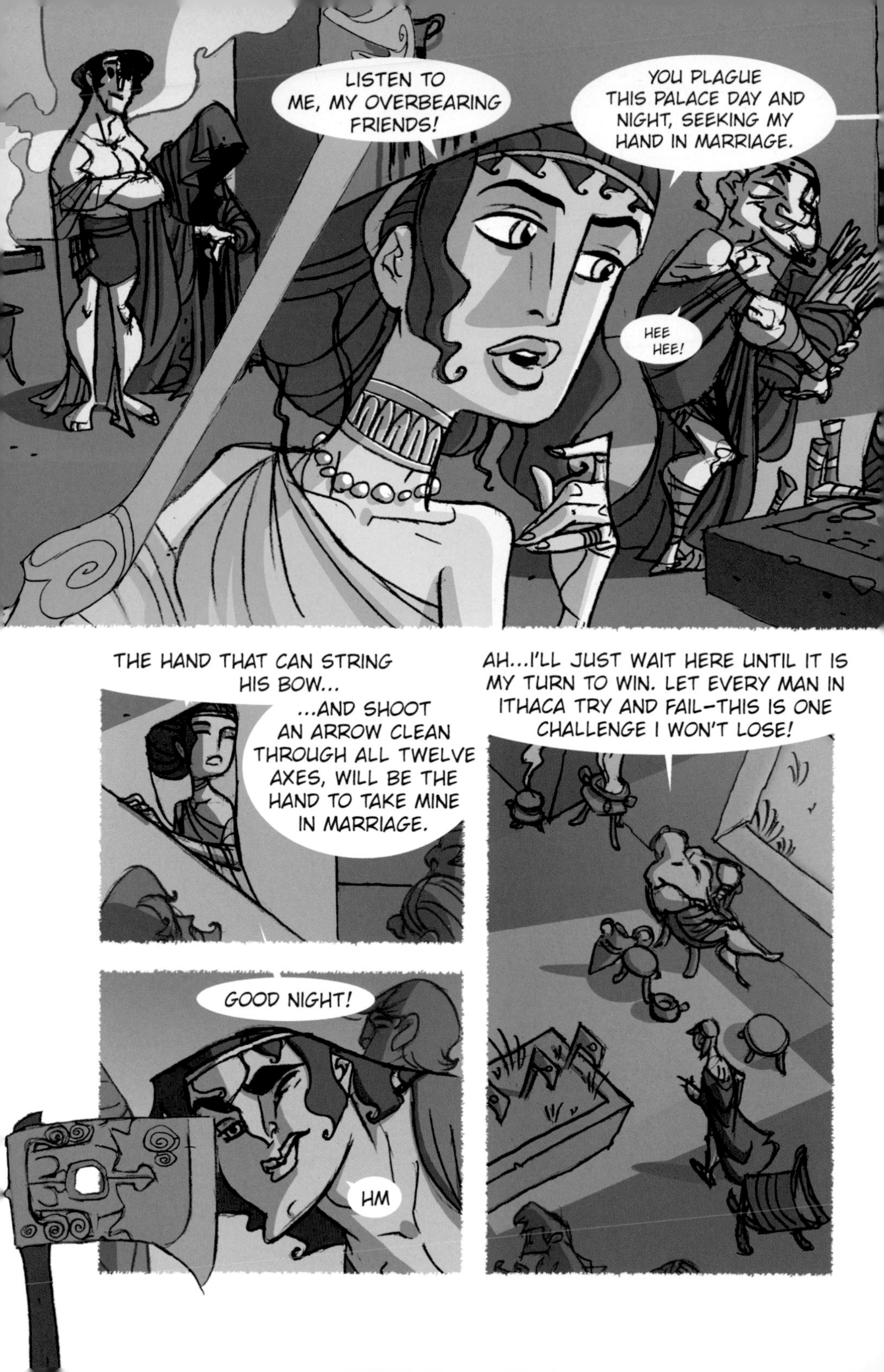
LISTEN TO ME, MY OVERBEARING FRIENDS!
YOU PLAGUE THIS PALACE DAY AND NIGHT, SEEKING MY HAND IN MARRIAGE.
HEE HEE!
THE HAND THAT CAN STRING HIS BOW...
...AND SHOOT AN ARROW CLEAN THROUGH ALL TWELVE AXES, WILL BE THE HAND TO TAKE MINE IN MARRIAGE.
GOOD NIGHT!
HM
AH...I'LL JUST WAIT HERE UNTIL IT IS MY TURN TO WIN. LET EVERY MAN IN ITHACA TRY AND FAIL—THIS IS ONE CHALLENGE I WON'T LOSE!

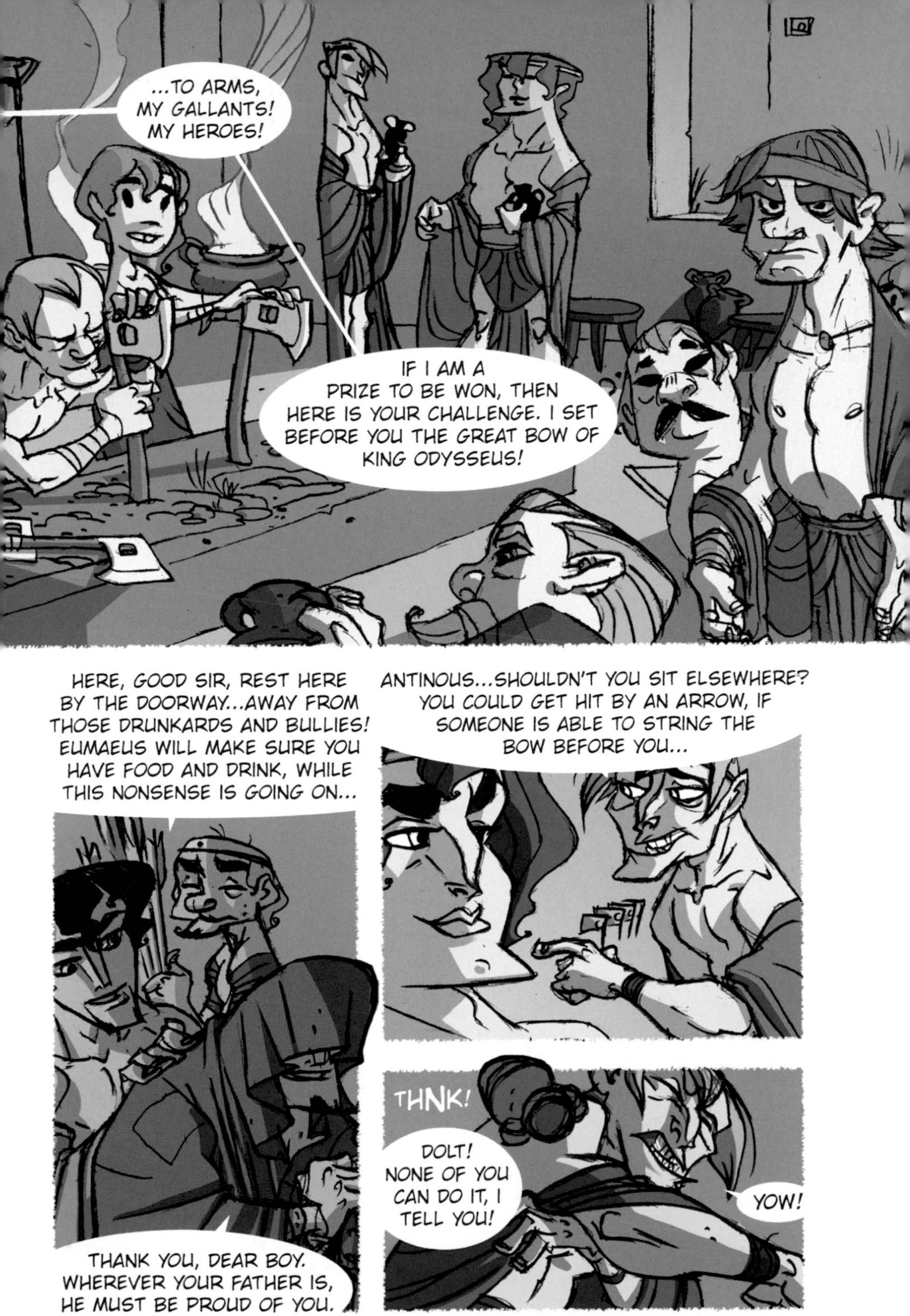
...TO ARMS, MY GALLANTS! MY HEROES!
IF I AM A PRIZE TO BE WON, THEN HERE IS YOUR CHALLENGE. I SET BEFORE YOU THE GREAT BOW OF KING ODYSSEUS!
HERE, GOOD SIR, REST HERE BY THE DOORWAY...AWAY FROM THOSE DRUNKARDS AND BULLIES! EUMAEUS WILL MAKE SURE YOU HAVE FOOD AND DRINK, WHILE THIS NONSENSE IS GOING ON...
THANK YOU, DEAR BOY. WHEREVER YOUR FATHER IS, HE MUST BE PROUD OF YOU.
ANTINOUS...SHOULDN'T YOU SIT ELSEWHERE? YOU COULD GET HIT BY AN ARROW, IF SOMEONE IS ABLE TO STRING THE BOW BEFORE YOU...
THNK!
DOLT! NONE OF YOU CAN DO IT, I TELL YOU!
YOW!

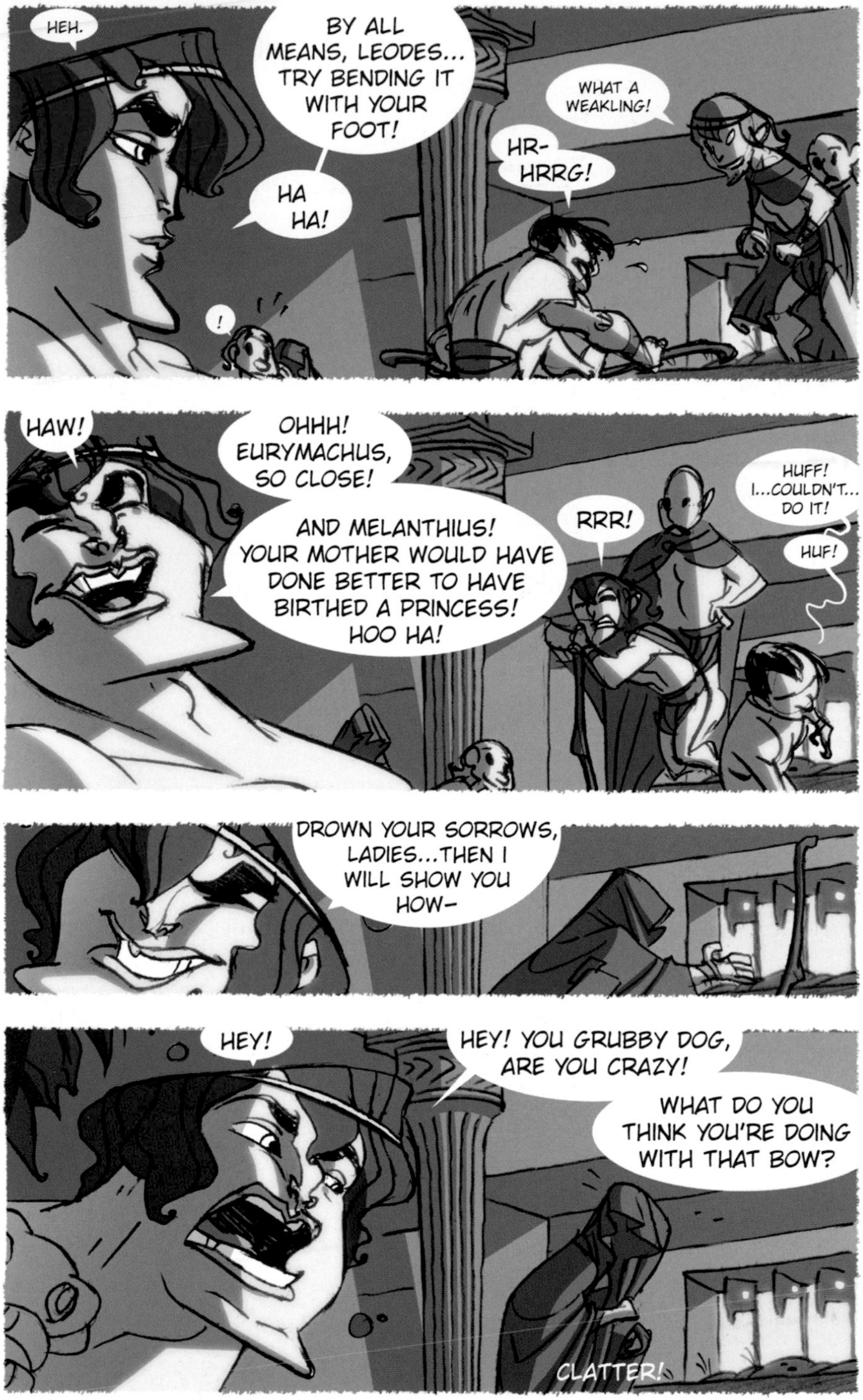
HEH.
BY ALL MEANS, LEODES... TRY BENDING IT WITH YOUR FOOT!
HA HA!
WHAT A WEAKLING!
HR-HRRG!
!
HAW!
OHHH! EURYMACHUS, SO CLOSE!
AND MELANTHIUS! YOUR MOTHER WOULD HAVE DONE BETTER TO HAVE BIRTHED A PRINCESS! HOO HA!
RRR!
HUFF! I...COULDN'T... DO IT!
HUF!
DROWN YOUR SORROWS, LADIES...THEN I WILL SHOW YOU HOW-
HEY!
HEY! YOU GRUBBY DOG, ARE YOU CRAZY!
WHAT DO YOU THINK YOU'RE DOING WITH THAT BOW?
CLATTER!

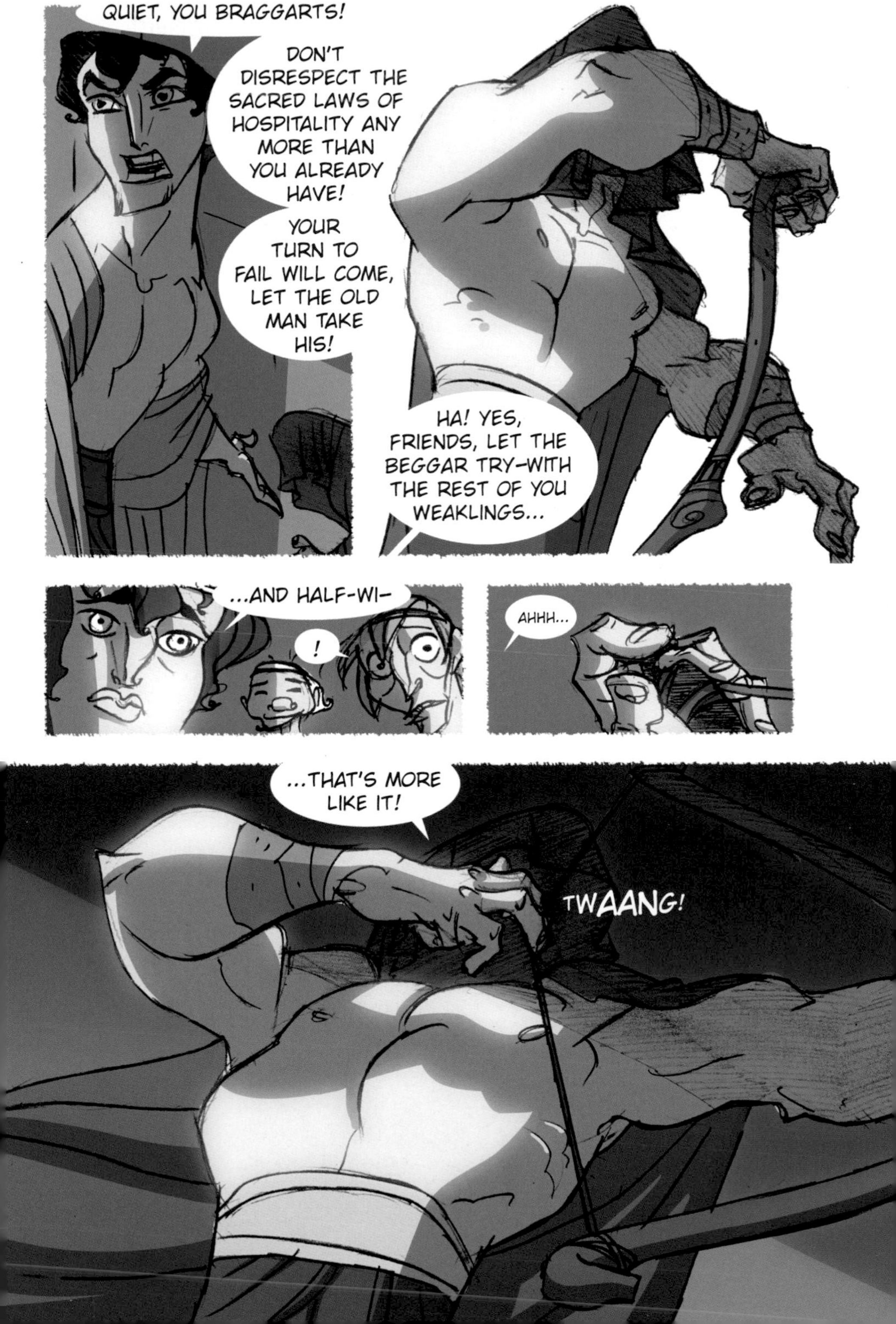
QUIET, YOU BRAGGARTS!
DON'T DISRESPECT THE SACRED LAWS OF HOSPITALITY ANY MORE THAN YOU ALREADY HAVE!
YOUR TURN TO FAIL WILL COME, LET THE OLD MAN TAKE HIS!
HA! YES, FRIENDS, LET THE BEGGAR TRY–WITH THE REST OF YOU WEAKLINGS...
...AND HALF-WI–
!
AHHH...
...THAT'S MORE LIKE IT!
TWAANG!

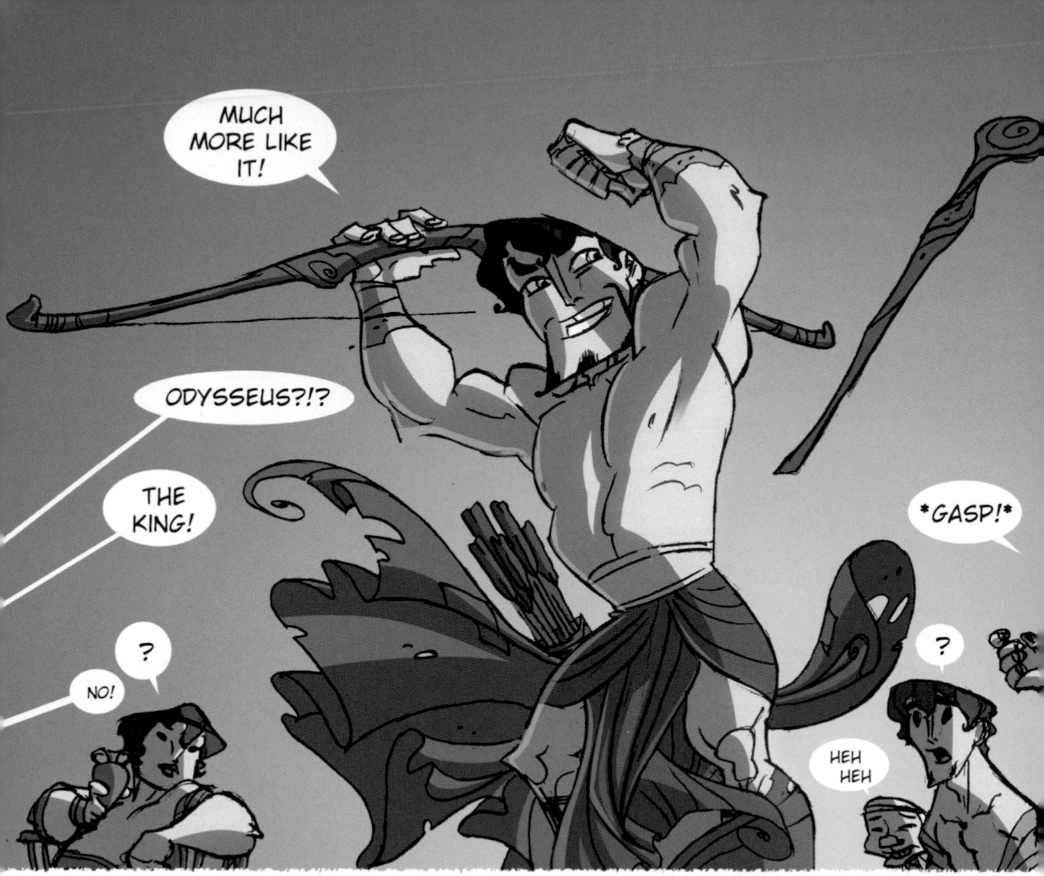
MUCH MORE LIKE IT!
ODYSSEUS?!?
THE KING!
GASP!
?
NO!
?
HEH HEH

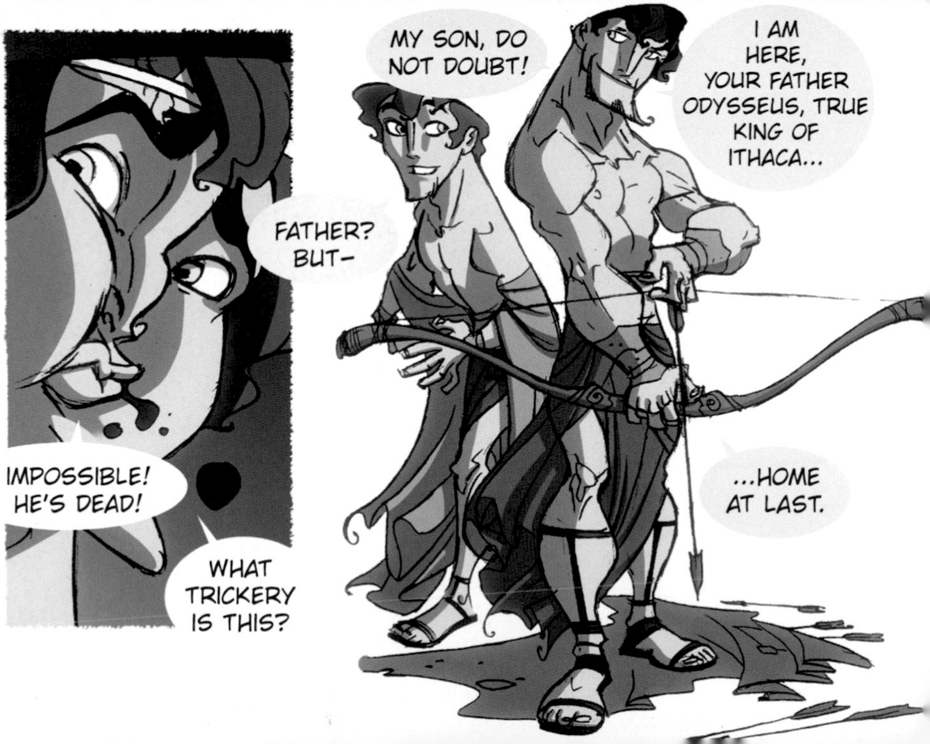
MY SON, DO NOT DOUBT!
I AM HERE, YOUR FATHER ODYSSEUS, TRUE KING OF ITHACA...
FATHER? BUT-
IMPOSSIBLE! HE'S DEAD!
WHAT TRICKERY IS THIS?
...HOME AT LAST.

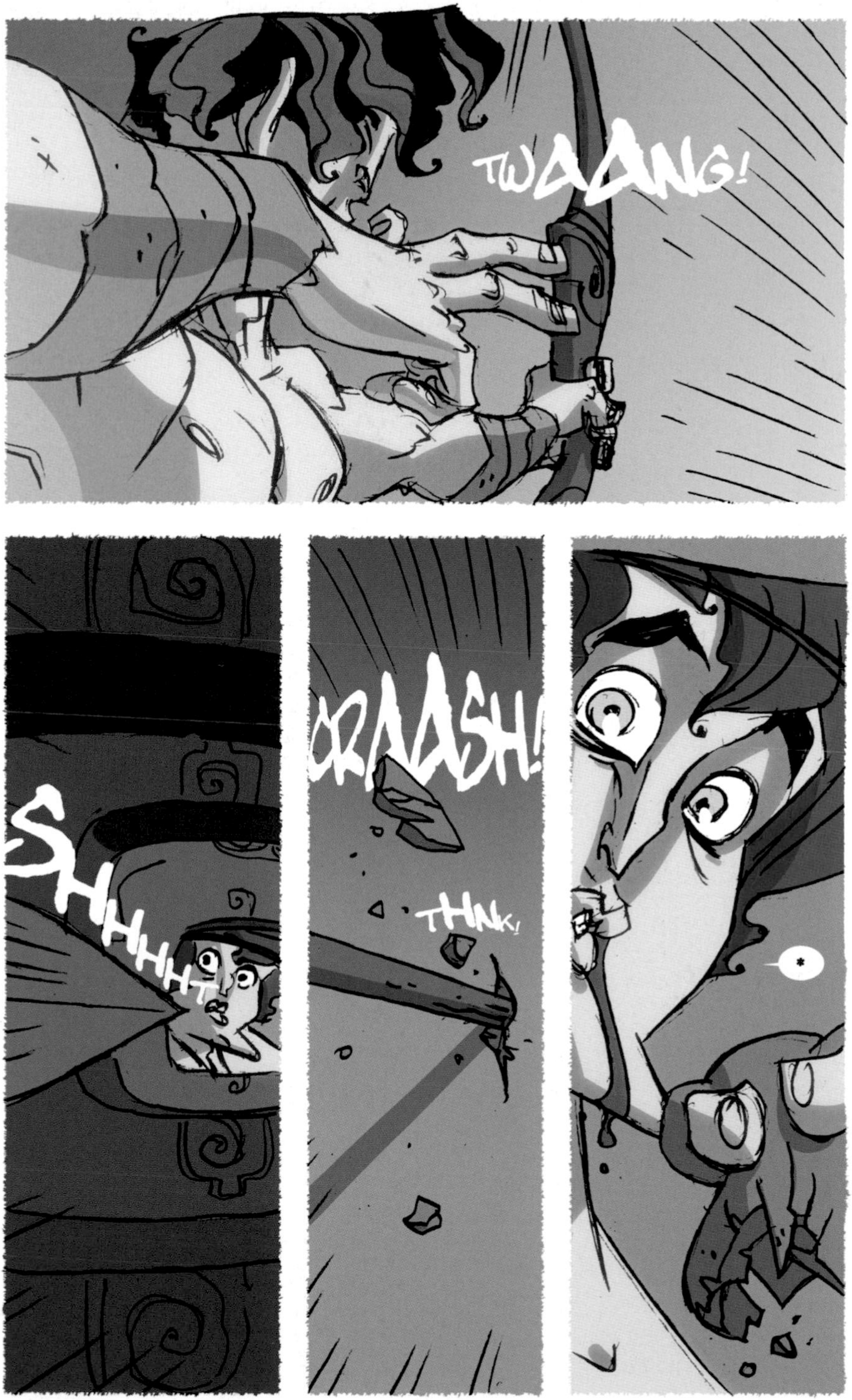
TWAANG!
SHHHHHT
CRAASH!
THNK!
*

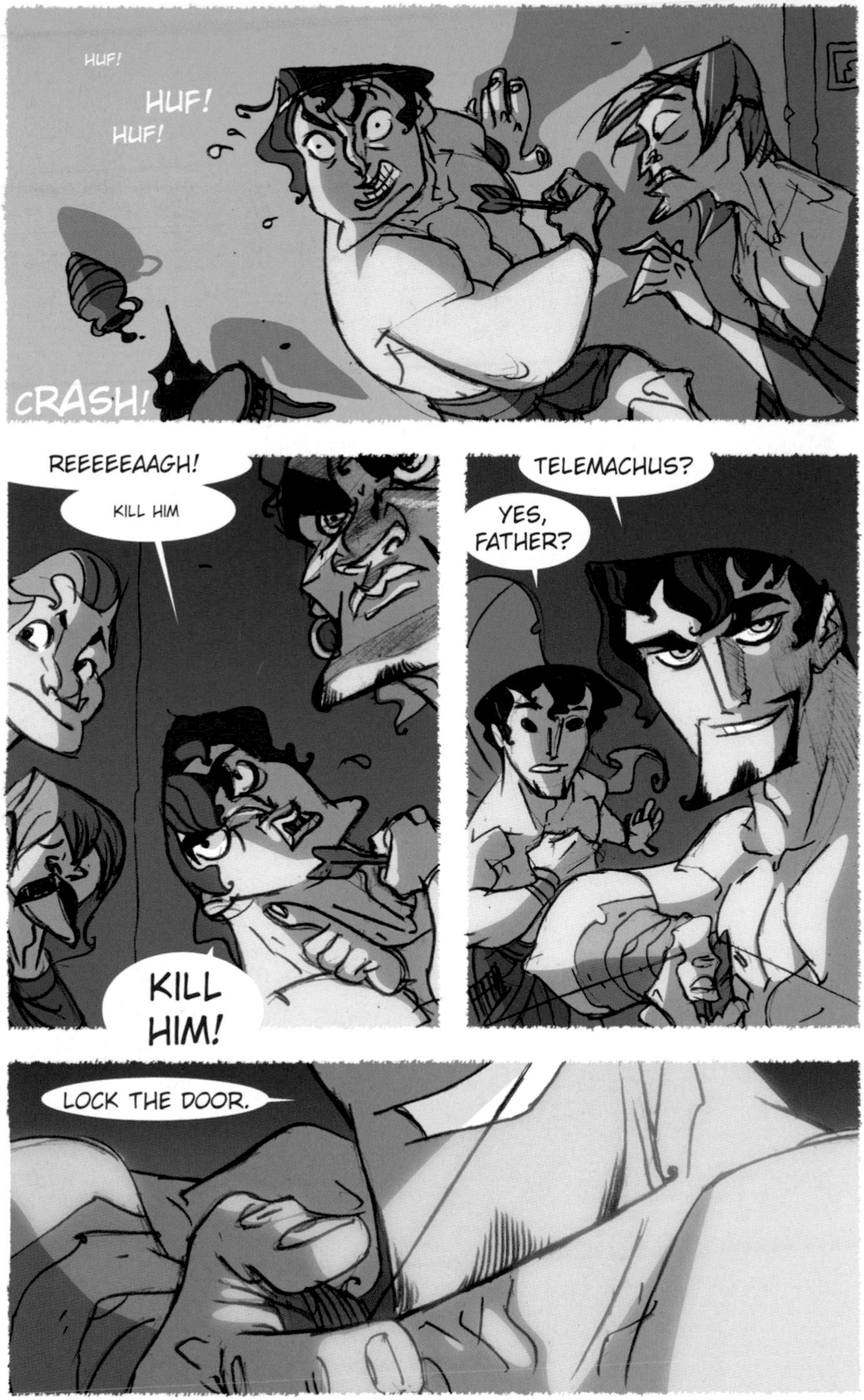
HUF!
HUF!
HUF!
CRASH!
REEEEEAAGH!
KILL HIM
KILL HIM!
TELEMACHUS?
YES, FATHER?
LOCK THE DOOR.

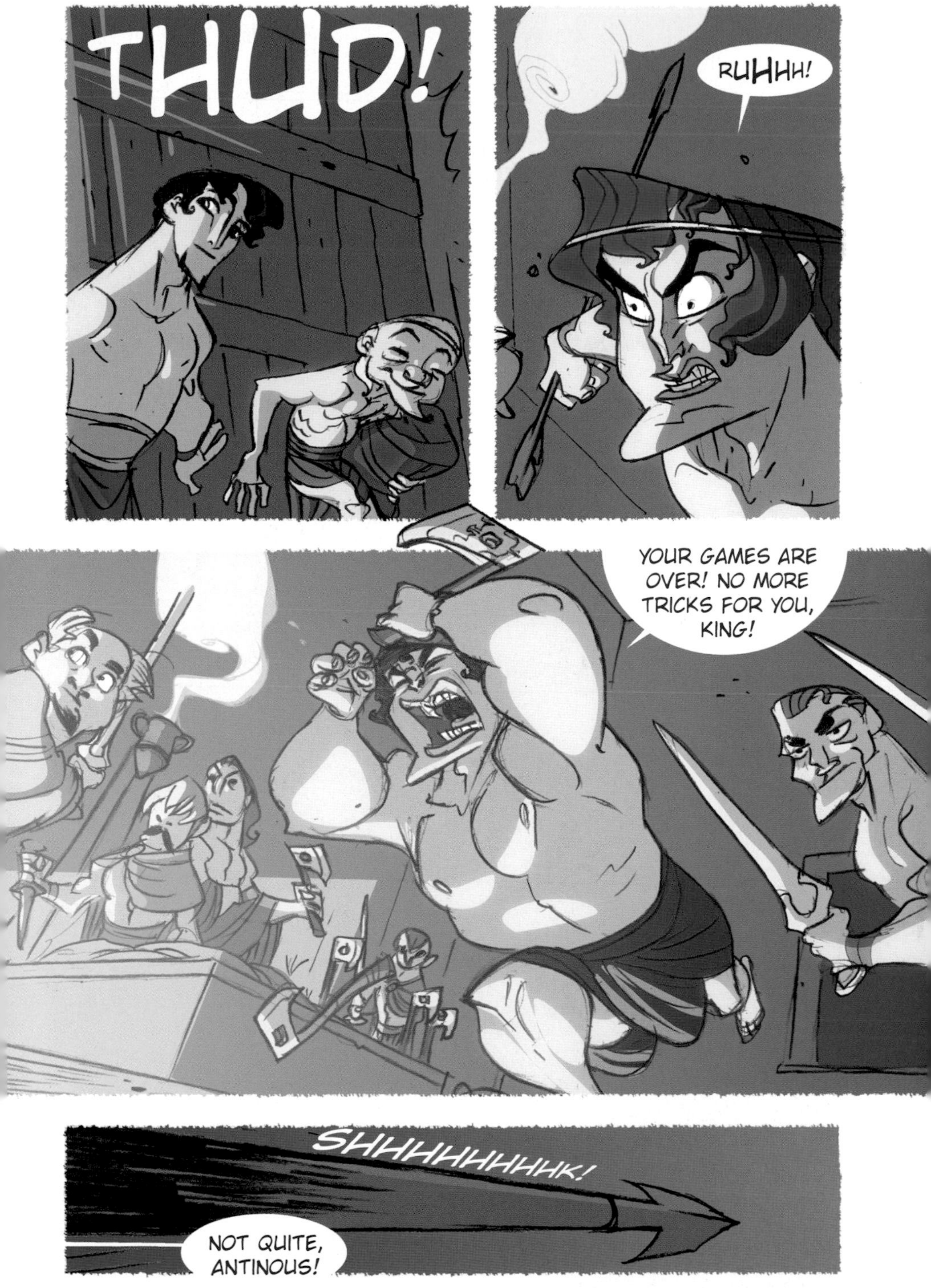
THUD!
RUHHH!
YOUR GAMES ARE OVER! NO MORE TRICKS FOR YOU, KING!
SHHHHHHHHK!
NOT QUITE, ANTINOUS!

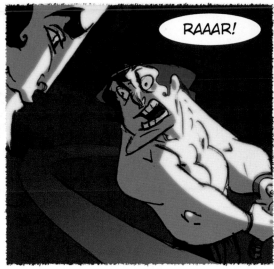

RAAAR!

YOU FOOLS! YOU NEVER IMAGINED I'D RETURN! YOU THOUGHT YOU COULD GO ON BLEEDING MY HOUSE TO DEATH, ABUSING MY SERVANTS, AND WOOING MY WIFE, WITH NO FEAR OF RECKONING! BUT NOW...

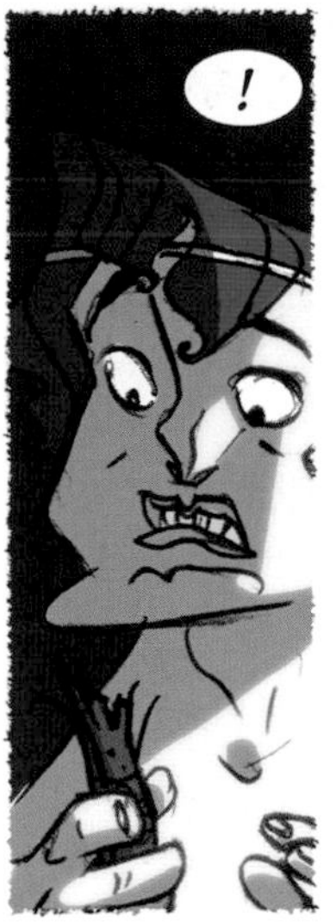
!

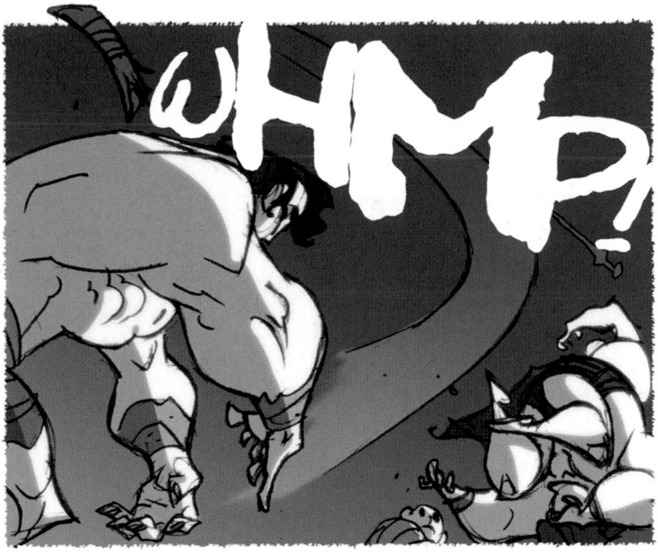
WHMP!

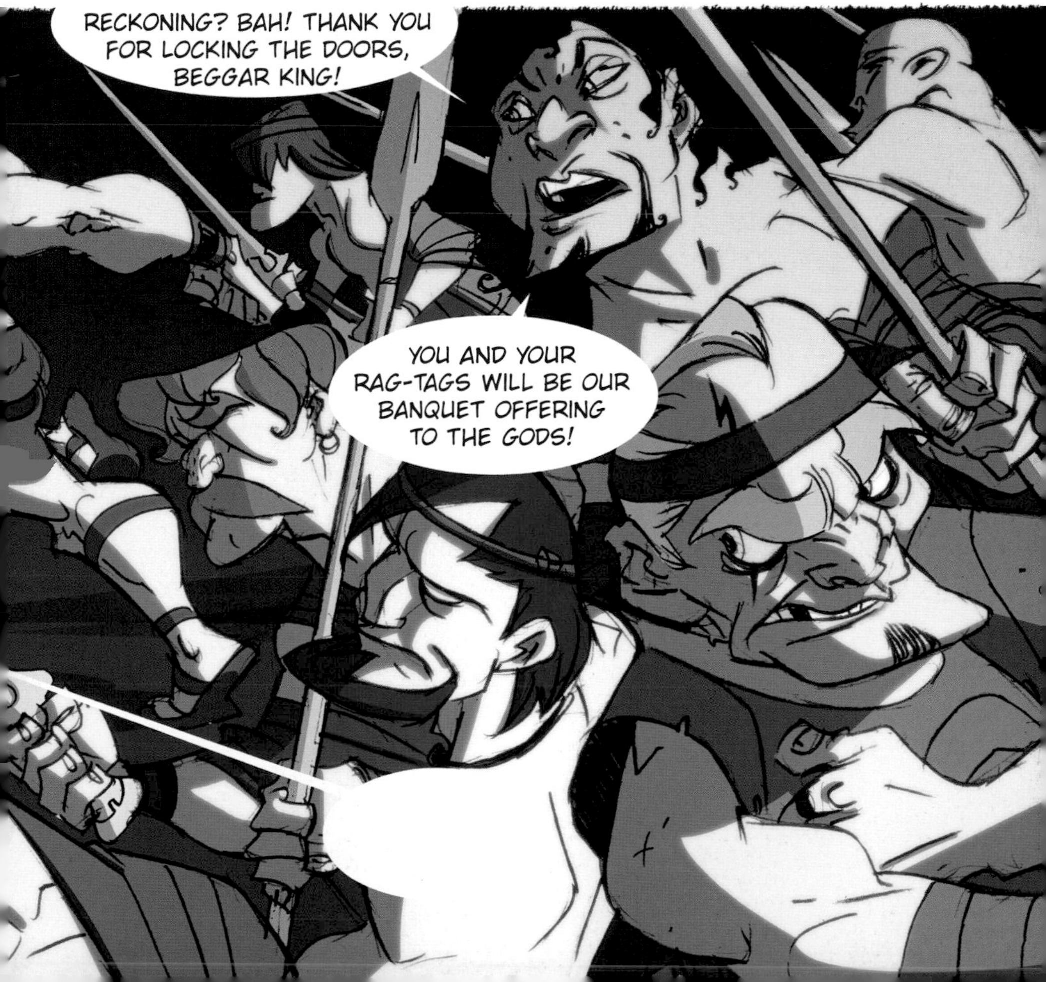
RECKONING? BAH! THANK YOU FOR LOCKING THE DOORS, BEGGAR KING!
YOU AND YOUR RAG-TAGS WILL BE OUR BANQUET OFFERING TO THE GODS!

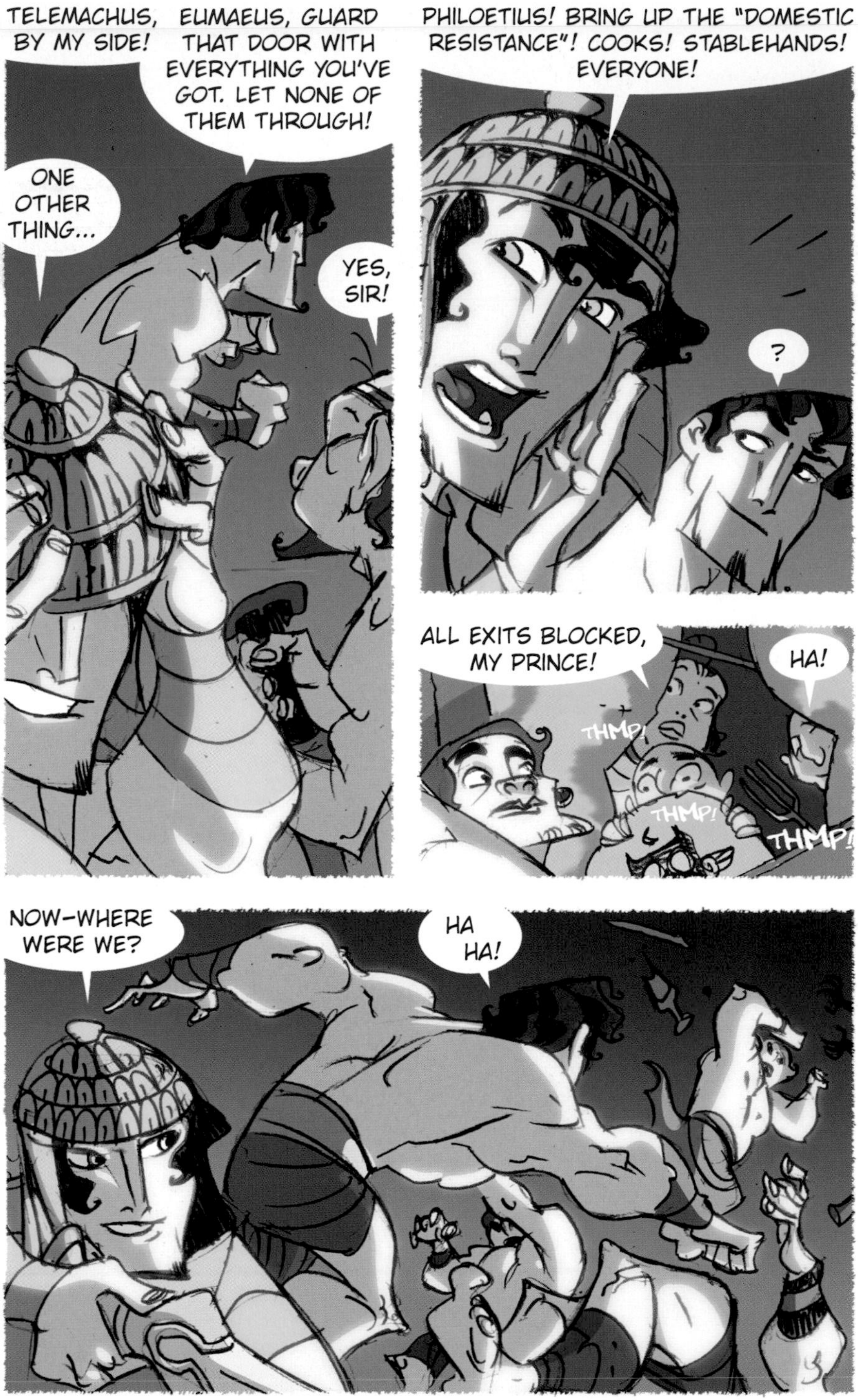
TELEMACHUS, BY MY SIDE!
EUMAEUS, GUARD THAT DOOR WITH EVERYTHING YOU'VE GOT. LET NONE OF THEM THROUGH!
ONE OTHER THING...
YES, SIR!
PHILOETIUS! BRING UP THE "DOMESTIC RESISTANCE"! COOKS! STABLEHANDS! EVERYONE!
?
ALL EXITS BLOCKED, MY PRINCE!
HA!
THMP!
THMP!
THMP!
NOW—WHERE WERE WE?
HA HA!

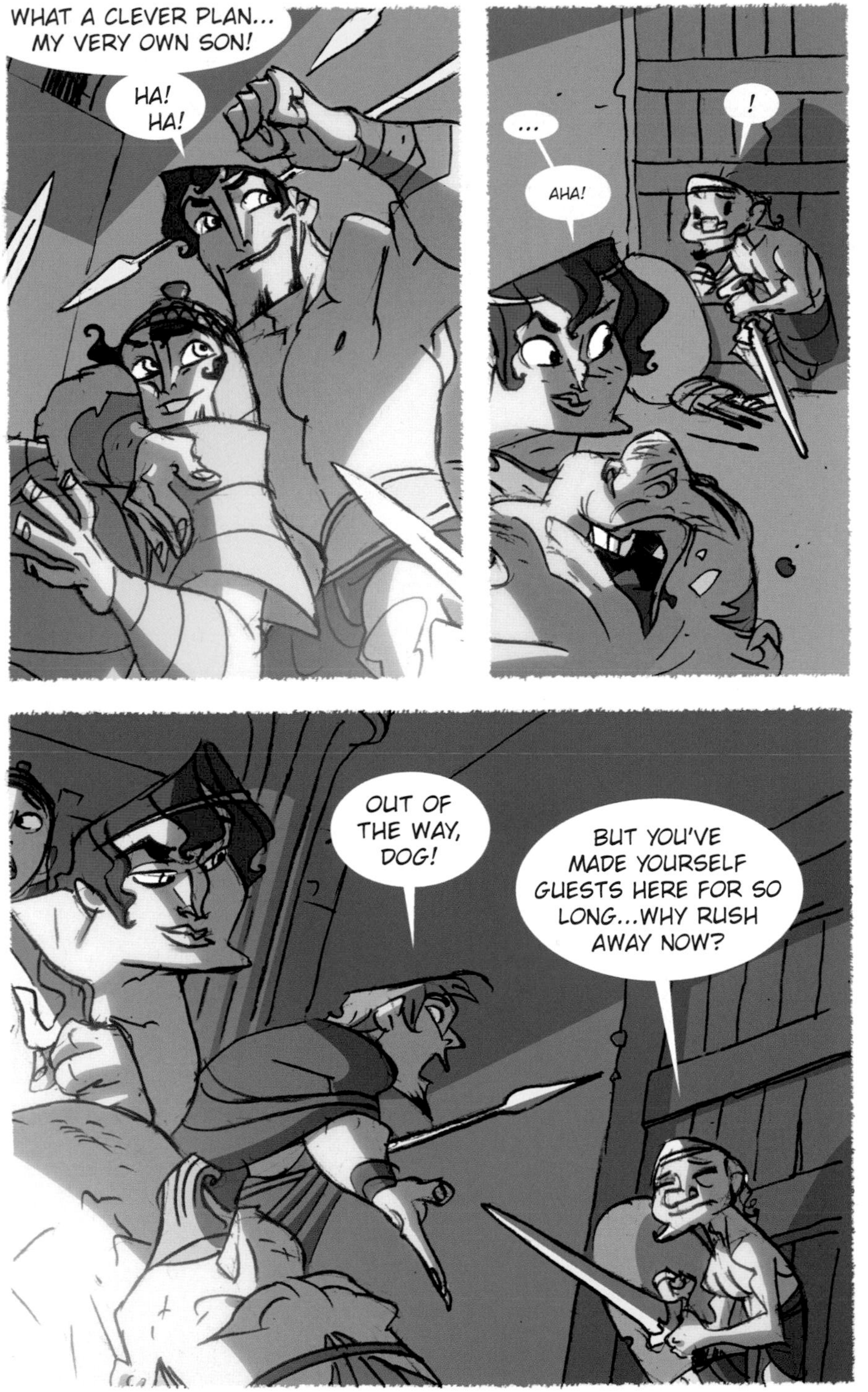
WHAT A CLEVER PLAN...
MY VERY OWN SON!
HA!
HA!
...
AHA!
!
OUT OF THE WAY, DOG!
BUT YOU'VE MADE YOURSELF GUESTS HERE FOR SO LONG...WHY RUSH AWAY NOW?

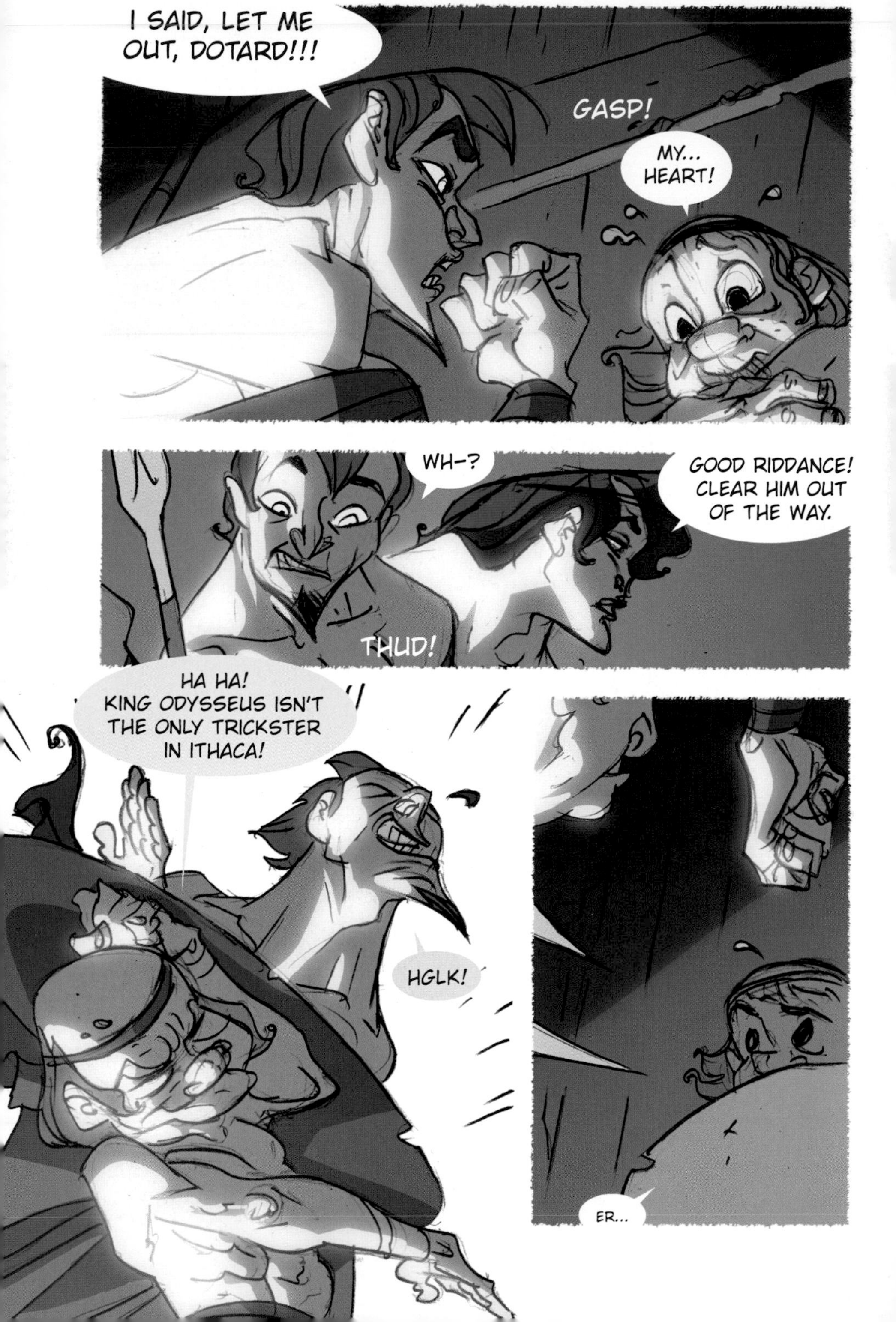
I SAID, LET ME OUT, DOTARD!!!
GASP!
MY... HEART!
WH-?
GOOD RIDDANCE! CLEAR HIM OUT OF THE WAY.
THUD!
HA HA! KING ODYSSEUS ISN'T THE ONLY TRICKSTER IN ITHACA!
HGLK!
ER...

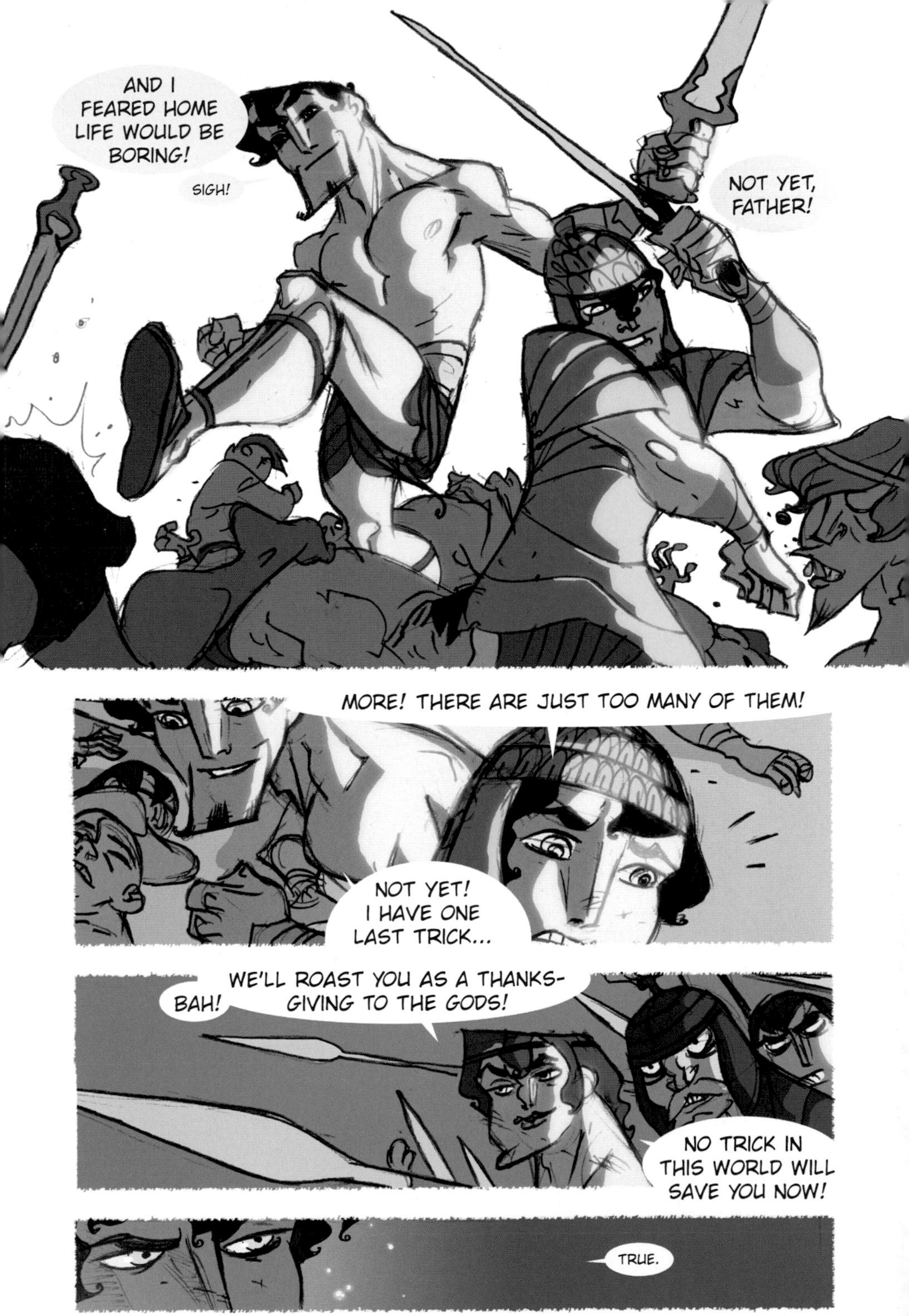
AND I FEARED HOME LIFE WOULD BE BORING!
SIGH!
NOT YET, FATHER!
MORE! THERE ARE JUST TOO MANY OF THEM!
NOT YET! I HAVE ONE LAST TRICK...
BAH!
WE'LL ROAST YOU AS A THANKS-GIVING TO THE GODS!
NO TRICK IN THIS WORLD WILL SAVE YOU NOW!
TRUE.

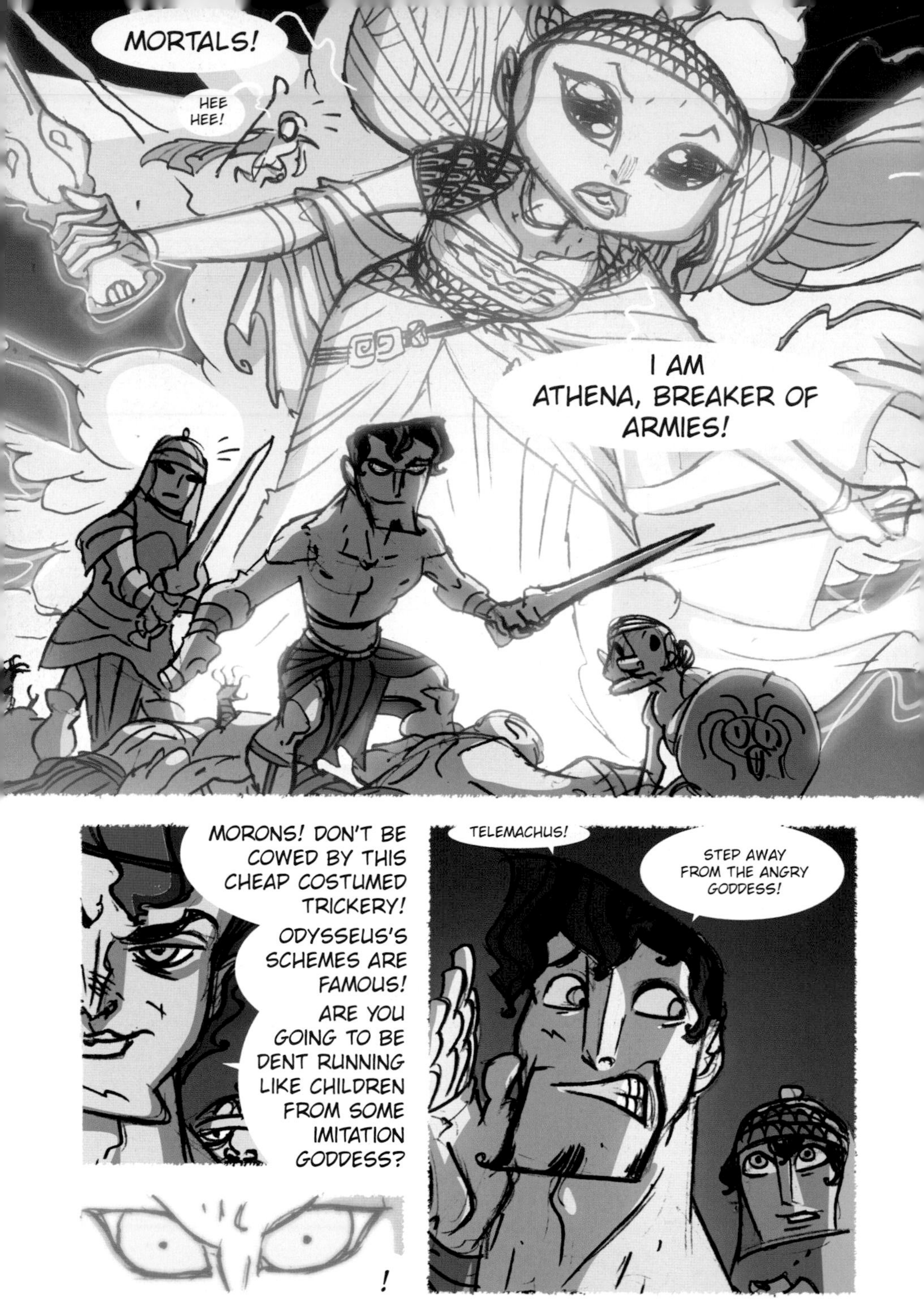
MORTALS!
HEE HEE!
I AM ATHENA, BREAKER OF ARMIES!
MORONS! DON'T BE COWED BY THIS CHEAP COSTUMED TRICKERY!
ODYSSEUS'S SCHEMES ARE FAMOUS!
ARE YOU GOING TO BE DENT RUNNING LIKE CHILDREN FROM SOME IMITATION GODDESS?
!
TELEMACHUS!
STEP AWAY FROM THE ANGRY GODDESS!

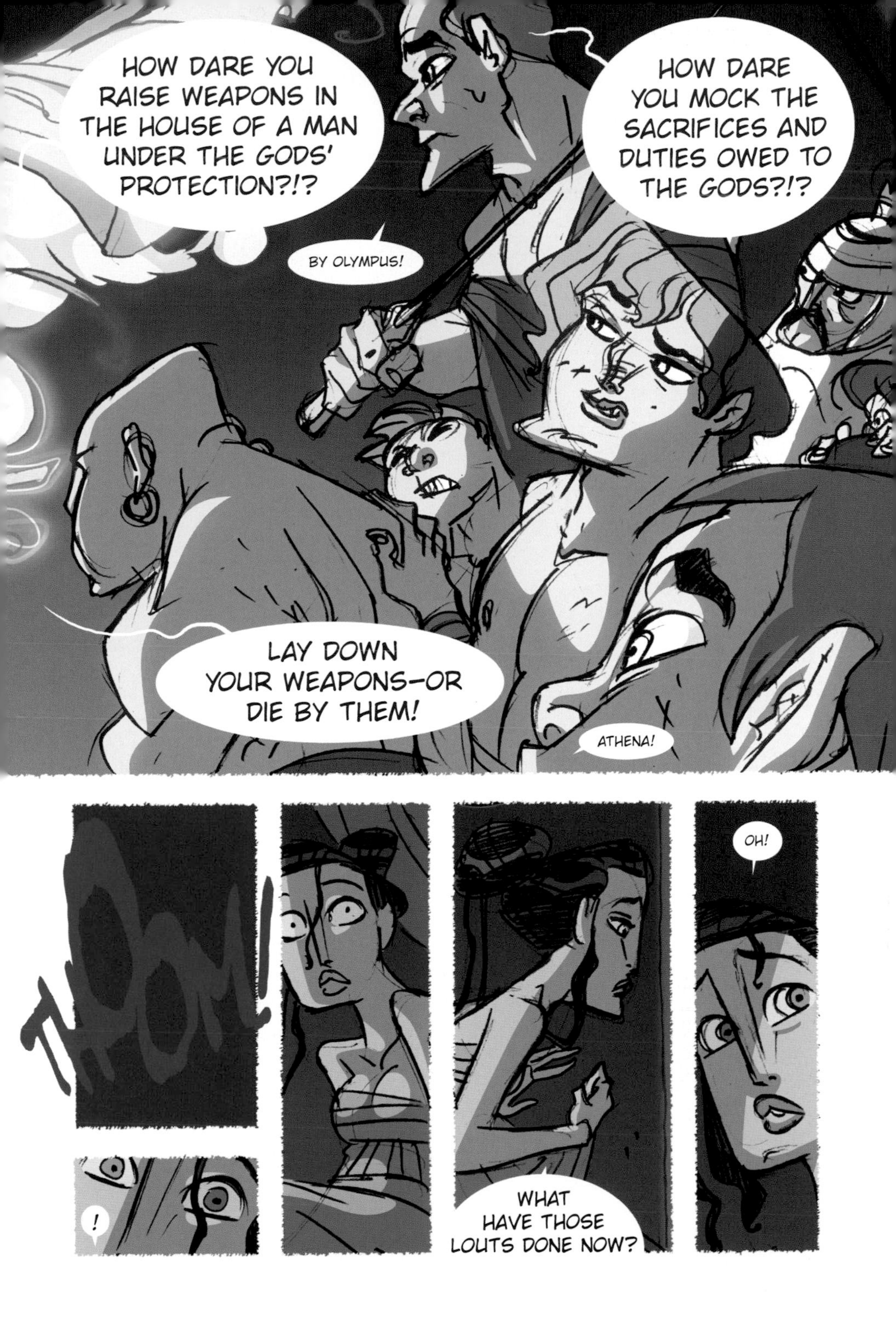
HOW DARE YOU RAISE WEAPONS IN THE HOUSE OF A MAN UNDER THE GODS' PROTECTION?!?
HOW DARE YOU MOCK THE SACRIFICES AND DUTIES OWED TO THE GODS?!?
BY OLYMPUS!
LAY DOWN YOUR WEAPONS—OR DIE BY THEM!
ATHENA!
THOOM!
!
WHAT HAVE THOSE LOUTS DONE NOW?
OH!

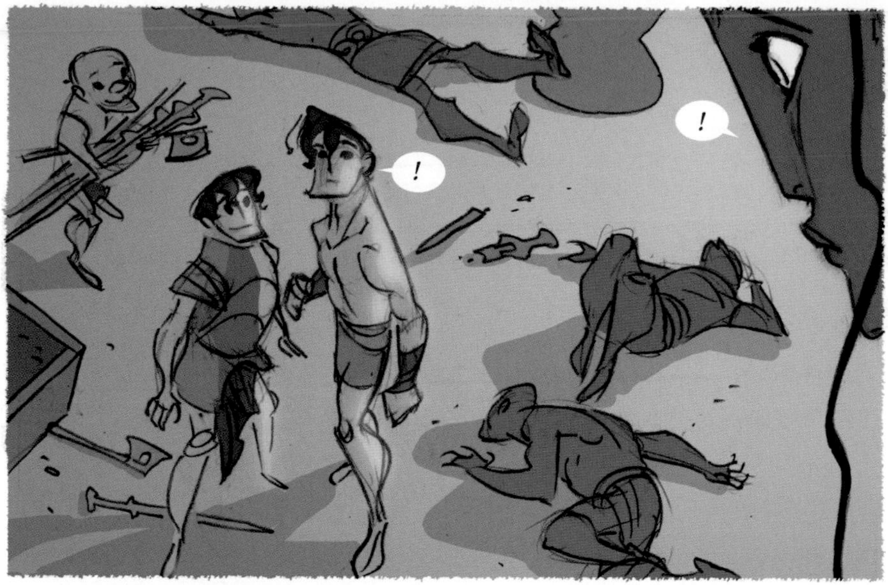
!
!

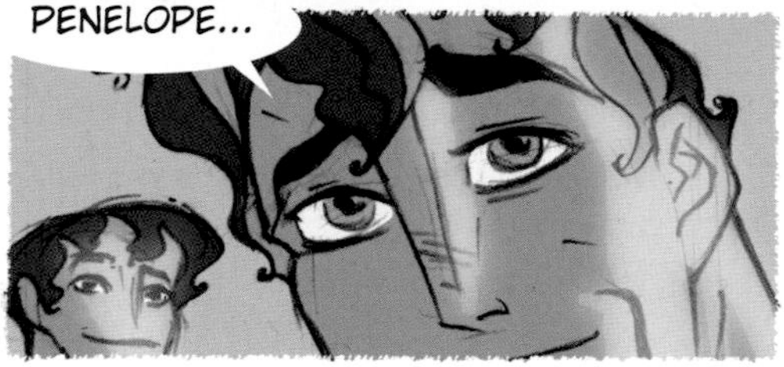
PENELOPE...

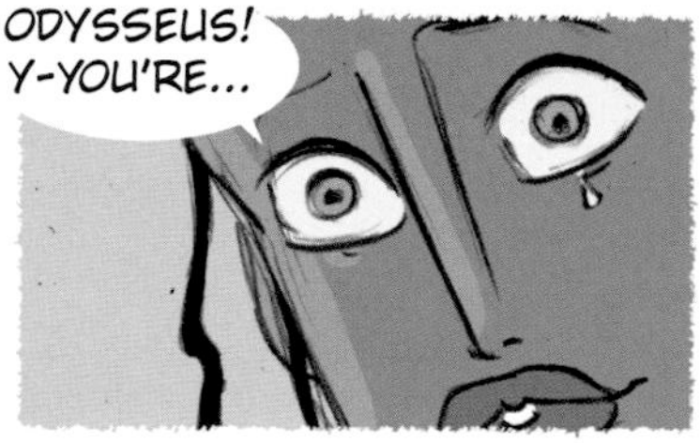
ODYSSEUS!
Y-YOU'RE...

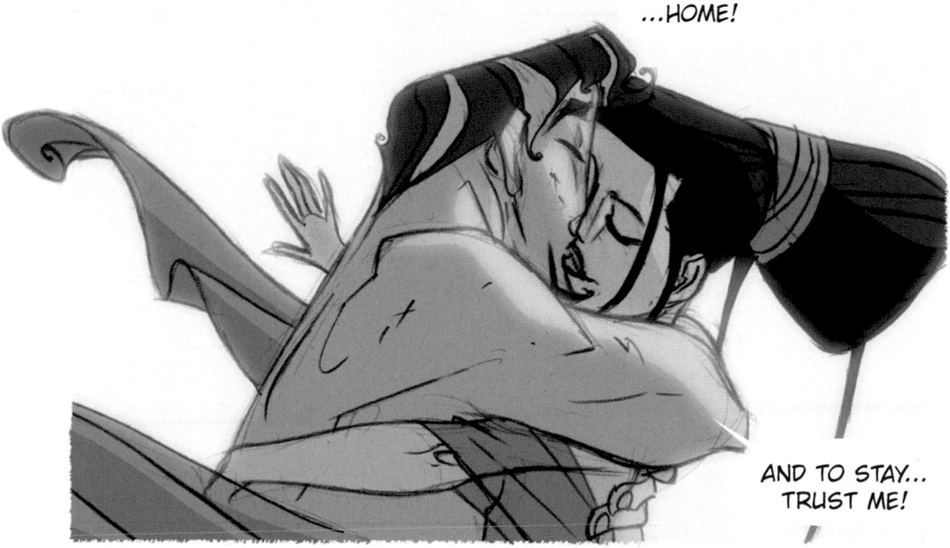
...HOME!
AND TO STAY... TRUST ME!

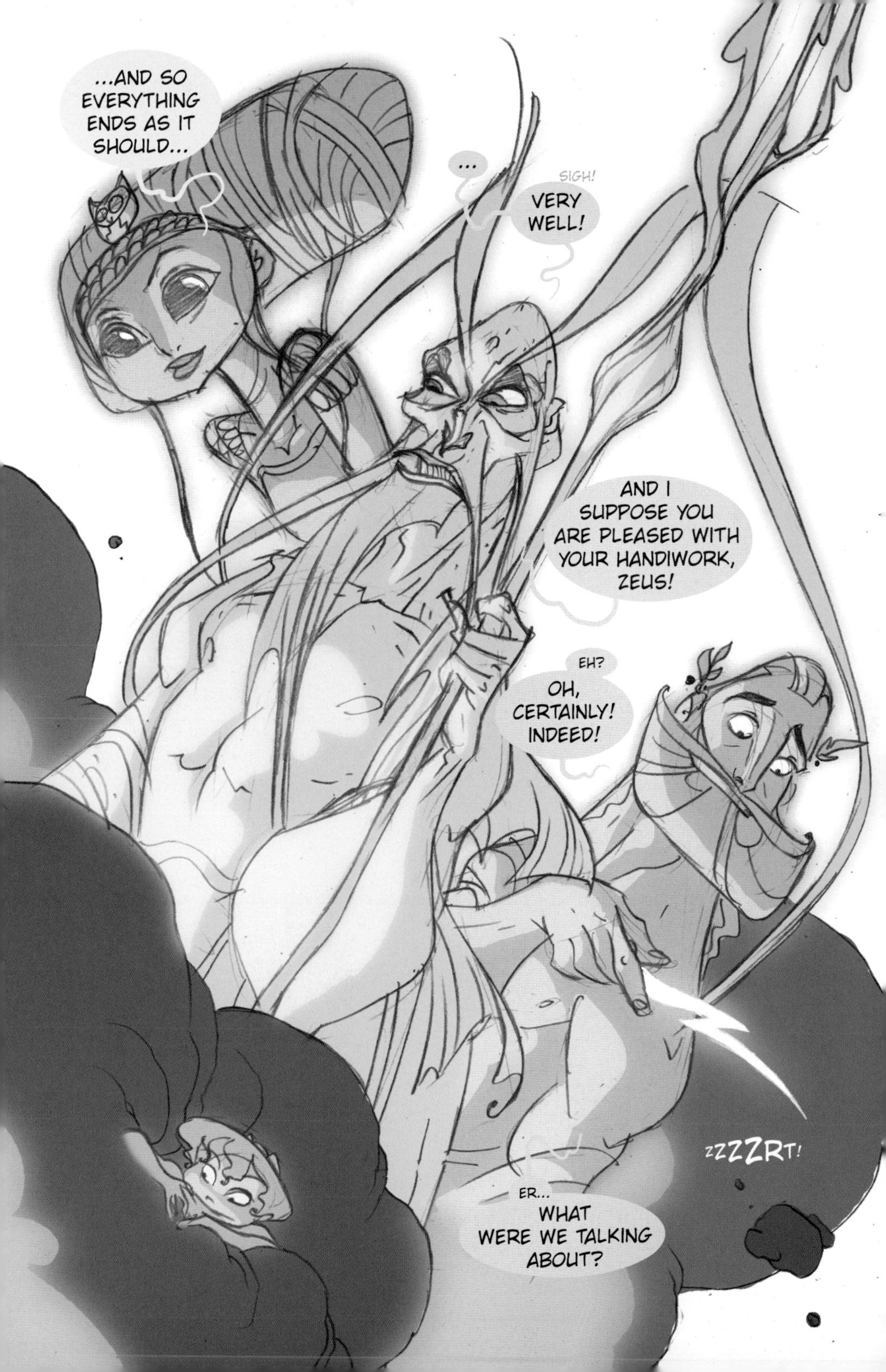
...AND SO EVERYTHING ENDS AS IT SHOULD...
...
SIGH!
VERY WELL!
AND I SUPPOSE YOU ARE PLEASED WITH YOUR HANDIWORK, ZEUS!
EH?
OH, CERTAINLY! INDEED!
ZZZZRT!
ER...
WHAT WERE WE TALKING ABOUT?

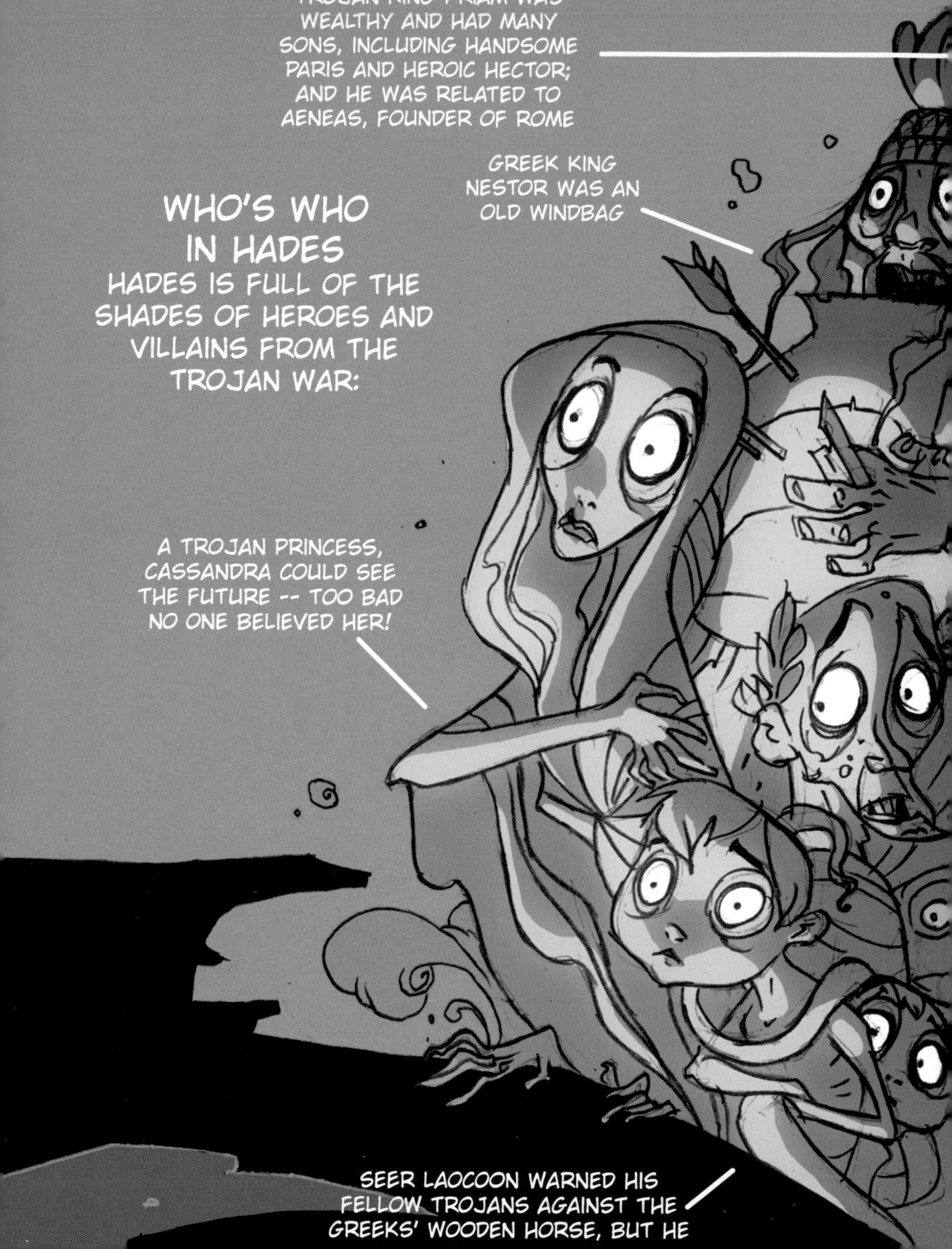
WHO'S WHO IN HADES
HADES IS FULL OF THE SHADES OF HEROES AND VILLAINS FROM THE TROJAN WAR:
TROJAN KING PRIAM WAS WEALTHY AND HAD MANY SONS, INCLUDING HANDSOME PARIS AND HEROIC HECTOR; AND HE WAS RELATED TO AENEAS, FOUNDER OF ROME
GREEK KING NESTOR WAS AN OLD WINDBAG
A TROJAN PRINCESS, CASSANDRA COULD SEE THE FUTURE -- TOO BAD NO ONE BELIEVED HER!
SEER LAOCOON WARNED HIS FELLOW TROJANS AGAINST THE GREEKS' WOODEN HORSE, BUT HE

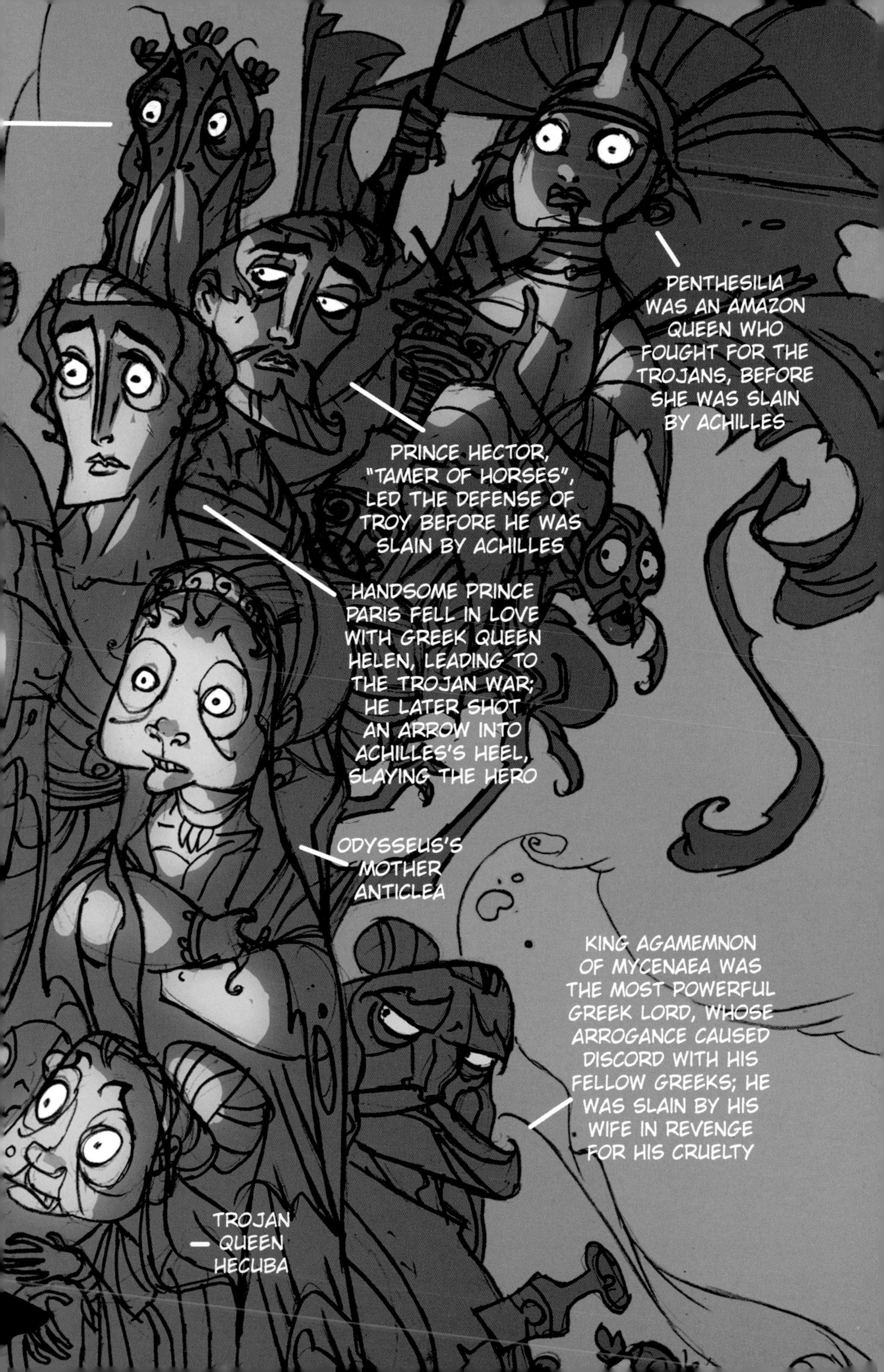
PENTHESILIA WAS AN AMAZON QUEEN WHO FOUGHT FOR THE TROJANS, BEFORE SHE WAS SLAIN BY ACHILLES
PRINCE HECTOR, "TAMER OF HORSES", LED THE DEFENSE OF TROY BEFORE HE WAS SLAIN BY ACHILLES
HANDSOME PRINCE PARIS FELL IN LOVE WITH GREEK QUEEN HELEN, LEADING TO THE TROJAN WAR; HE LATER SHOT AN ARROW INTO ACHILLES'S HEEL, SLAYING THE HERO
ODYSSEUS'S MOTHER ANTICLEA
KING AGAMEMNON OF MYCENAEA WAS THE MOST POWERFUL GREEK LORD, WHOSE ARROGANCE CAUSED DISCORD WITH HIS FELLOW GREEKS; HE WAS SLAIN BY HIS WIFE IN REVENGE FOR HIS CRUELTY
TROJAN QUEEN HECUBA

HOME SWEET HOMER

"THE ODYSSEY" IS THE SEQUEL TO THE EPIC "THE ILIAD," WHICH CHRONICLED THE MASSIVE WAR BETWEEN GREEK KINGS AND THE MIGHTY CITY OF TROY. BOTH POEMS (AMOUNTING TO OVER 25,000 LINES OF ACTION-PACKED POETRY) ARE BELIEVED TO BE THE WORK OF A BLIND BARD FROM THE GREEK ISLANDS, NAMED HOMER. IF SO, HE LIVED LONG BEFORE THE GREEKS HAD A WRITTEN LANGUAGE, AND COMPOSED, MEMORIZED AND RECITED THIS VAST WORK ENTIRELY FROM HIS HEAD!

MODERN HISTORIANS DISMISSED THESE STORIES UNTIL ARCHAEOLOGIST HEINRICH SCHLIEMANN UNCOVERED THE ENORMOUSLY STRONG AND WEALTHY RUINS OF TROY, ON THE TURKISH COAST. ALTHOUGH WE WILL NEVER KNOW ALL THE ANSWERS, THE TROJAN WAR WAS PROBABLY FOUGHT AROUND 1,200 BC, WHEN THE CITY WAS CONSUMED BY FLAMES. HOMER HIMSELF LIVED HUNDREDS OF YEARS LATER, AND WHILE HE NOTED MANY ACCURATE DETAILS OF LIFE IN THE TROJAN AGE, HE ALSO ADDED MATERIAL FROM HIS OWN DAY— MUCH TO THE CONFUSION OF LATER HISTORIANS!

WHILE THEY BELIEVED IN THE SHADOWY AFTERWORLD OF HADES, THE GREEKS WERE MUCH MORE CONCERNED WITH THIS LIFE. HEROES WERE EXPECTED TO SHOW "TIME" (HONOR, OR RESPECT FOR THEIR FRIENDS AND FOES) AND "ARETÉ" (GREATNESS, OR ACHIEVING THIER FULL POTENTIAL).

IN A WORLD WITH FEW LAWS AND LITTLE PROTECTION FOR THE WEAK OR VULNERABLE, GREEKS CHERISHED THE DIVINELY ORDAINED LAWS OF HOSPITALITY AND SANCTUARY. ZEUS WAS SOMETIMES CALLED "ZEUS XENIOS," THE PATRON OF GUESTS. HIS PROTECTION EXTENDED TO TEMPLES AND SHRINES—VIOLENCE INSIDE A HOME OR TEMPLE WAS CONSIDERED A CRIME AGAINST THE GODS!

ODYSSEUS HIMSELF WAS NEVER WORSHIPPED IN GLORY LIKE ACHILLES OR HERACLES—HE WAS TOO TRICKY TO BE A ROLE-MODEL. EVEN HIS FELLOW GREEK KINGS WERE SUSPICIOUS OF HIS WILES, ALTHOUGH THEY WERE HAPPY TO TAKE HIS ADVICE! BUT HE PERSONIFIED THE GREEK IDEAL OF THE "VERSATILE MAN" WHO WAS READY FOR ANY CHALLENGE.

BAH!